> *"We've only just begun. As yet, we do not know the dramatic extent or the great uses we can expect to find. We are standing on the beach studying footprints in the sand we have never seen before."*
>
> Dr. Gregory Palmer,
> Head of stem cell research at Changing Biology

Santa Monica is a place of amazing sunsets, spectacular scenery, great hotels, five star restaurants, perfect weather, great shopping, theaters and coffee shops. The rich live in million dollar mansions, and the cops wear plain clothes to blend into the scenery, a car worth less than a million is likely to be reported to them. Detective Maddie Martin lives in Mira Vista where a house is available for less than three million.

Rain hammered the roof of the car. She inched along the narrow road with nothing but darkness on both sides. She hadn't seen her ex-husband in over three years. Why would he suddenly need her? To report a crime? He was a suspect in a crime and needed her help to prove his innocence?

Greg? Nonsense.

Inching along in the dark, she thought she was totally lost. A few more turns and she saw a large, sprawling, two-story house tucked beneath huge trees. A completely dark house. No lights. Not one inside, not one outside. A little worm of worry wiggled through her mind.

She pulled up into the driveway and cut the headlights and the motor. The only sound was the splatter and splash of rain. People expecting a visitor turned on lights. At least an outside light. Why no lights? An oversight?

Or a trap.

Set up by her ex-husband? Come now. She grabbed the flash-light from the glove box, flicked it on and slid from the car. Rain pelted her as she sprinted up the brick path toward the house. It was a dark and stormy night—

D1446640

Other Books by Charlene Weir

Unknown
FOOTPRINTS

CHARLENE WEIR

UNKNOWN FOOTPRINTS

Acknowledgements

With much thanks to my daughter Leslie who brought order out of chaos, and to Pat who chased commas, and to Allison who made it happen.

CHAPTER ONE

The nightmare began three seconds after Francine opened her eyes.

Her head ached, nausea roiled in her stomach. She had no idea where she was. Nor how she got there.

A plastic tube ran around her head with two small prongs that fit into her nose. Oxygen? She removed the tube and held the prongs against her cheek. Cool air blew against her face.

The bed, narrow and hard, was raised a few inches at the head, bent at the knees, rails on both sides. White sheet covered her to the waist. She shivered, suddenly cold. Something was very wrong. Maybe she was dreaming. What a very strange dream. Scary. She wanted to wake up in her very own room at home.

Monitors next to the bed beeped jagged lines across the screen. Recessed ceiling light. Very bright. Made her blink. No windows. White walls, large rectangular mirror opposite the foot of the bed. Door next to it. The door was closed.

Small bits of memory floated up that sent little squiggles of worry through her mind. This wasn't a dream. It was real. This place. Wherever she was. Whatever the place was.

Flashes of scenes, like a mostly forgotten movie. The hiss of tires on rain dampened streets. The swish swish of windshield wipers. Begging him to stop so she could use a bathroom. He was reluctant, but she kept saying she really needed a bathroom. She couldn't wait until they got where they were going. Where were they going?

When he stopped, she'd tried to make a phone call. Why? Who was she calling? Had she reached that person? She didn't know.

She remembered a growing sense of dread. She struggled to catch wispy images. She almost managed one or two, then they melted away in fog. It was all so eerie. There was something important about this day, but she couldn't remember what it was.

A queasy thought brought a mouth full of saliva. She swallowed, swallowed again. Was someone in the room earlier? Or had she imagined it? Had she dreamed that someone put a stethoscope against her chest, listened to her heart. A doctor? Must have been. He put a blood pressure cuff around her arm and pumped it up tight.

Hospital?

Something happened.

She plucked at the flimsy green gown. Hospital gown. The ties had come undone and it kept falling off her shoulders. She slipped a hand under it and felt her stomach. No underwear. No bra. Someone had undressed her. The doctor? Was there a nurse?

The bedside table held a pink plastic pitcher, a pink plastic cup with a straw. No phone. No call button to summon a nurse. No television set. No clock either. Didn't hospital rooms always have a clock?

Maybe she'd been in an accident. That must be it. Except for a headache and the nausea, she felt okay. Sort of. She'd been in a car with—a man. He must have hit something, or maybe someone hit him. Had he told her his name? She thought so, but no matter how hard she tried, she couldn't dredge it up. Nor could she recall what he looked like. He said he was a friend of—Paul!

The man—the one who came to get her—said he was a good friend of Paul's. She didn't remember Paul ever mentioning him. She thought she knew all of Paul's friends. Obviously not. She was a little upset. It wasn't that she felt she had to know every detail of Paul's life, but this felt so odd, surely he would have mentioned— Oh God, something happened to Paul? He was hurt. Bad. In a bed somewhere else in this hospital? Yes, that was it. Paul was in an accident and he had sent this friend to pick her up and bring her to him. Oh my God, how was he?

At least, he was able to talk. Since he told this friend to come and get her. At least, he was able to think. Oh God, she prayed, please let him not be seriously injured. Not serious, only a slight injury.

She had to see him for herself.

"Nurse! Nurse!" She waited. "*Nurse!*"

No one came.

Why wasn't there a call button? She was going to complain to somebody. What if she needed help? How could she make anybody aware of it?

How long had she been here? Her wristwatch was missing. No windows meant she couldn't guess whether it was night or day.

After struggling to lower the bed rails with no success, she flung aside the sheets and slithered down over the foot of the bed. She stood up. Swayed. *Dizzy. Oh boy, dizzy.* She grabbed a rail.

Seconds passed before her head stopped swimming. With unsteady steps, she got to the door. It wasn't that far. Only eleven steps and she could barely make it. There must have been an accident to make her feel so yucky. She twisted the door knob. Locked. How could that be?

Was she in the loony bin? She tried again. Definitely locked.

Hospitals didn't lock doors. Only in psych wards. She didn't feel crazy. Loonies probably didn't either.

She didn't like this place. It was too weird. Let her out of here.

She rattled the knob, knocked. "Hello? Anyone there? I can't get the door open."

No answer.

She pounded. "Hey! Help! Somebody! I can't get out!"

No response.

Suddenly, she was afraid. Heavy sense of evil settled like a malevolent ghost in the shadowy corners. Panicky breathing and rapid heartbeat mixed with the beeping of monitors.

Wait. She heard— footsteps?

Someone was coming. Something?

Who? Doctor?

It must be. She was relieved. First, she'd demand to know about Paul, then find out why she was here. But most of all, she wanted to be released immediately.

The door slowly began to inch inward.

In the distance, a generator hummed. It seemed to say, danger. Danger.

Fear skittered along the back of her neck.

CHAPTER TWO

The cluster of oocytes floated in a drop of fluid under a thin layer of mineral oil. Using microscopic magnification, he guided the blunt end of the pipette toward the cluster. With careful suction, he selected one oocyte from the group of sixty or so that were all exactly the same. The one he chose was simply closest to the end of the glass rod. Like the rest, it looked healthy. Each one had been removed prematurely from an ovary and nurtured to maturity in vitro. They had reached the stage ready for spermatic penetration, but that would not occur. These female gametes had a special purpose.

He took another pipette, and edged the needle-sharp tip ever closer to an immobile gamete. With expert skill, he tapped the end of the pipette and the tip penetrated the cell. Slight suction snagged the nucleus and slickly extracted it.

The phone rang. His hand jerked. Damn it! He'd forgotten to turn the fool thing off. He hated phone calls. Even routine procedures were delicate, but beyond that, he intensely hated being interrupted when he was working.

On the second ring, he grabbed the receiver. "What!"

"Do you have anything for me?"

"I'm not baking cookies!"

A crisp voice pushed words through heavy impatience. "When can you deliver?"

"I told you—" And he was getting heartily sick of repeating himself.

"Yes, yes, many factors involved. You told me. I'm telling you, you'd better get these *factors* under control or changes will be made."

"Changes?" The fool was threatening him.

"That is exactly right."

He wanted to point out the stupidity of threats, to explain that not every jerk who'd ever been in a lab could do what he was doing, to stress that even if someone could be found who was capable of performing the task, how many would agree to the demands. "It's not a matter of—"

A click and a dial tone.

"God damn fools who don't understand." He yanked open a metal cabinet door and pulled out the blood pressure machine, jammed the plug in an outlet and slapped the cuff around his right arm. He pressed the button and the cuff inflated.

When the reading showed a hundred and ninety over ninety-five, he ripped off the cuff and wrapped it around his left arm. He got the same numbers. The idiot was heading him toward a stroke. He huffed, pulled air in and out. This would never do.

He skipped his fingers through the CDs in the cabinet until he found the relaxation exercises and slid it into the player. He dropped into the wooden rocker and propped his feet on a foot stool. Concentrate! *Take a slow deep breath in through your nose. Slowly release it through your mouth. Relax your toes. Take a slow deep breath in through your nose. Slowly release it through your mouth. Relax your—*

Twice he got as far as his thighs and lost it when irritation took over. He turned off the machine and tossed the CD back in the drawer. It was nonsense anyway.

Later he checked the gamete to make sure it had come through the nuclear removal in good condition. Once more a pipette was used for penetration. This time a tiny drop of fluid was injected. This fluid contained a single adult cell that came from the scraping of a human mouth.

When he was finished, he noted the time and recorded each process in his journal.

CHAPTER THREE

Detective Maddie Martin was dreaming, always the same dream. Alone and uneasy, she stumbled over uneven ground. Clouds scudded across the moon. Wind howled and the tree limbs thrashed. Her flashlight beam flickered over shallow mounds of leaves that stirred and shifted. And then fingertips arose—

Thunder woke her. Momentarily disoriented, she pushed through the cobwebs of nightmare. Darkened room, blankets tangled, pajamas twisted and sweaty, rain splattering against the window. Thunder? Hampstead, Kansas had thunderstorms. She wasn't in Kansas, she was in California. There was a wide-spread rumor that Southern California didn't have rain in the summertime, and never thunderstorms.

The clock on the bedside table showed two minutes to eight. Two paperback books, a bottle of water, a flashlight in case of earthquake, a pad and pencil, and a small framed picture of her sister and niece were cluttered around it. Easy chair in the corner had her fleece robe over the arm. The closet door was ajar.

"I'm fine," she told herself. She'd been telling herself that a lot lately, like whistling in the dark, trying to calm the panic sneaking around in the bottom of her mind.

"You won't get better in a day," the doctor said when he

released her from the hospital. "Gunshot wounds heal in their own time. Take the meds for pain and be patient."

The drugs turned her mind to mush and left her too fuzzy-headed to think. With one hand, she scraped her hair back and rubbed her face with the other. She needed to get back on the job. The job defined who she was. She loved her job, without it she had no life. From the time she was ten years old, all she ever wanted to be was a cop.

With unnecessary force, she beat up a pillow, flopped onto her back and stared at the light skittering across the ceiling. What was causing that? The storm, probably. She listened for thunder but didn't hear any. The bedside clock now read eight-ten. Twelve whole minutes used out of the day. How long would it take to figure the number of twelve minute units remaining in this day? She decided it wasn't worth the effort. Math had never been her strong point.

By this time, she should be at her desk, drinking coffee, grumbling about poor pay and overwork, discussing the latest cases, getting ready to go out and fight for truth and justice. Nothing compared with the high of closing in on a case—not sex, not chocolate, not cherry pie with whipped cream. She turned on her side, bashed the pillow and shoved it under her head. The scary thing was, the highs were gone. The ones she felt after plodding along putting pieces together until she got something, then shifting from excitement to all systems alert.

And suddenly it was gone, the excitement, the satisfaction. How long, she wondered, had it been gone? How could she lose something that she depended on? Drowsiness took over, and she drifted into sleep. The ringing phone yanked her awake.

Her answering machine kicked in. "Maddie, it's Elena. Are you all right?"

She picked up the phone. "I'm fine." She cleared her throat. "Yeah. Why?" She wasn't all right. She was worried that she'd lost something important that she'd always counted on. Burnout? Maybe she was getting the flu.

"According to my schedule," Elena said. "We were supposed to be having lunch today."

Lunch! With Elena. Oh my God! Maddie looked at the clock. It said six. Six pm? She had slept ten hours? Damn those pain pills.

"Oh Elena, I'm so sorry. I've been taking *drugs*." Maddie tried to sound lighthearted. "I sleep through everything. Will next week work?"

"Okay. Next week then. How about Thursday? And just for the record, you don't sound fine."

Good thing she forgot their lunch date. Maddie thought Elena was too sharp. When the phone rang again, Maddie ignored it.

"God damn it, Maddie, where are you! Pick up!" The voice of her boss.

She reached out, fumbled the phone and dropped it, jumped out of bed and got one foot tangled in the blankets.

"You're supposed to be home, damn it! Oh hell, call me!"

She hopped on her right foot as she unwound her left.

Volume diminished as he muttered. "...don't know why I even bother..."

She snatched the phone.

"... never do as you're told..." A click sounded in her ear.

She punched in the number for the Sheriff's Department. The green light on her answering machine blinked six times. Six messages and she never heard the phone ring? The pain meds obviously worked.

"Maddie!" The dispatcher said. "I heard you were out of the hospital. How you doing, baby girl?"

"Doing good. Trying to catch up. You know how it is. Can you put me through to the Sheriff?"

"Sure can. He's been tryin' to reach you. And you listen now. As soon as you're feelin' better we have to get together, you hear?"

"Absolutely."

A click and a ring. "Dirks."

"It's Detective Martin, sir. You called me?"

"Yeah. Twice. How's your shoulder?"

"Good, sir."

He grunted. "Uh-huh. You feel okay enough to do some checking?"

"Yes, sir. What checking?"

"Ramsey's. They work a ranch out east of you. Got a kid named Francine."

Maddie didn't know them, but said, "Yes."

"The daughter's overdue. Drive out and look into it."

"Overdue?" It sounded like the daughter needed a midwife, not a detective.

"Probably nothing. Didn't come home when expected. Like as not, hooked up with a friend and neglected to call. Only child. Lives at home. Parents might be a bit over-protective. Maybe the kid will have turned up before you get there. Go earn your keep." He paused, then added with a growl, "Unless you're not up to it."

If she told him her head pounded because some maniac inside her skull was swinging a hammer, Dirks would want to know why she'd agreed to return to work if she couldn't do the job. Then, like as not, he'd shove her right back to sick leave. And then she might have more of these ridiculous thoughts that she no longer loved her work.

"I'm fine, sir." Just what she needed, to get back to work. Give her a little time and a case to work and she'd be her old self.

She didn't like the sound of another young woman missing. Six months ago a young woman, a kindergarten teacher, had disappeared after a fight with her mother. A situation which escalated to the point where the mother had said, "My house and my rules. You don't like it, you can leave." And the girl had said, "Okay, I'm leaving."

No matter how hard the cops tried, and they had tried hard, they never found a trace of her. Maddie's partner was convinced the girl had run off with her boyfriend. Maddie didn't think so, but couldn't come up with even a hint of a lead to explore.

Four months later, another young woman went missing. A paralegal, who'd stayed late to finish some work for her boss, left the office at nine, stopped to pick up a few items from the supermarket and never made it home. Her car was still in the parking lot the next day with a loaf of bread and a carton of milk on the passenger's seat but she had vanished.

Now a third girl was missing.

Maddie pressed a button on the answering machine. The first message was from her partner. Jesse wanted to know how she was, and if she needed anything. The second was from Shapely, a neighbor, who wanted to know the same, then a hang-up. The next two were the Sheriff with swear words and mutterings about damn machines.

The last one was her sister Pamela. "Maddie, aren't you ever home. Call me!"

She called Jesse's cell. He was a ten-year veteran of the Mira Vista Sheriff's Department. She was a newcomer with two years as his partner, long enough to forge a solid partnership, the kind that brought unconditional loyalty and unwavering trust. Nobody knew him like she did, not his wife, not his family, not his friends.

Not only did he trust her with his life, he trusted her with his deepest secret, that his actual name was Jesimiel. As far as Maddie was aware, she was one of only two people privy to this knowledge. The other was his wife.

Maddie found this condition of trust tricky. It wasn't that she couldn't trust—not exactly—but she had to have damn good evidence that her trust was warranted. Because he had an investment in her, she felt pressure to trust in return. And trust him she did. At least with her life. Not, however, with her deepest secrets.

Her call went straight to his voice mail. She left a message that she was on the job and would call again later. A quick call to her sister was not possible. A quick call to Pam was never possible. She'd deal with Pam later.

The shower helped clear her mind of drug remnants. She slipped into black pants, yanked a gray sweater over her head and wriggled her arms into the sleeves. Her black ankle boots sat in the corner where she'd tossed them. She pulled them on and took her raincoat from the closet. With no time to make coffee, she fished a Dr. Pepper from the fridge for a little caffeine, retrieved her gun from the lockbox, and eased the strap of her purse over her shoulder.

Heigh-ho, heigh-ho, it's back to work we go. Already breathless, but not from that feeling of excitement she always got. Never mind, she'd improve with a case to focus on. Just as she opened the door from the kitchen into the garage, the phone rang again. Thinking it might be Dirks with more instructions, she dashed back and grabbed the receiver.

"Fay Palmer?"

She stiffened. That name had been boxed up after her divorce and left behind in Kansas with all the other stuff she didn't want to cart out to California. Palmer was dropped and her maiden name, Martin, was picked up again. Fay, her middle name, had been used from first grade on after the little girl at the next desk made fun of Madeleine, calling it a stupid name and anybody with such a stupid name must be really stupid. "Stupid Mad Lane. Stupid Mad Lane."

"It's Greg," the caller said. "Greg Palmer."

She knew who he was.

"Fay, I need to talk to you."

The last time he'd said those words was three years ago. "Fay, I need to talk to you." He'd told her he was leaving, he wanted a divorce, the marriage wasn't working. He was sorry, but he wanted out. While she'd built up this huge fantasy of till death us do part, he had found someone else.

"What about?" Her voice was as cool as though his call didn't throw tacks in her life.

"I need your help," he said.

"With what?"

"I can't talk about it over the phone," he said.

The marriage, the one she thought was so firm, was in the end nothing but an embarrassing cliché. Stupid Fay Palmer. She had placed her trust in a man who was ultimately untrustworthy.

"Please, Fay. Just meet me. Dinner. Have dinner with me. I'll explain."

"Dinner? You're in California?"

"Yeah."

"When did that happen?"

"What? Oh, moving here? Not very long ago. About dinner—"

"Sorry, can't make it. I have to work." If there was one thing Dr. Gregory Palmer would understand it was dedication to work.

"Look. Fay, I'll explain. Give me a chance. Dinner. After your shift."

"Greg, I—"

"Please."

Two needs and a please. What could he possibly need from her? "I don't know how late that'll be."

"It doesn't matter. As long—Oh hell, I just remembered. Can you come here?"

Here? "What do you mean here?"

"My house. It isn't far actually from where you live."

His house. Oh, this day just kept getting better and better. "I don't think so."

"If there were any other way—Look, I know this is awkward, it's just that I can't leave. I'm waiting for a package. Please. I wouldn't ask if it wasn't vitally important."

Vitally? Now there was a word he hadn't used before. She hesitated. Vitally. Such a magnetic word. It pulled at her.

She'd moved to a new place, got a new job, was happy here. A few bumps arose in her new life, like a perplexing boss she couldn't understand, and an unexplainable twinge of paranoia that a fellow officer harbored harmful intent toward her. But hey, no life was perfect.

"Fay. I know I have no right to ask. I know it's awkward. Just please—please do this for me."

Awkward? He thought coming to his house where he had a new wife was simply awkward? She meant to say, sorry, can't do it, but her eyebrows rose when he gave her his address with a long set of directions. Everybody knew that whoever lived in Malibu was rich. In LA beautiful men and women arrived in droves hoping for stardom. The handful who succeeded lived in Malibu. The rest go to Mira Vista and get jobs waitressing. The really unfortunate go to work at MacDonalds. Maddie lived in Mira Vista, not working at MacDonalds, but with the Sheriff's Department.

At six-forty-five, she backed her car out of the garage and headed for the Ramsey's to ask about the missing daughter. The only good thought she could dredge up was at least the rain had stopped. She nosed onto Pacific Coast Highway where traffic was always bumper to bumper. Nothing of Kansas was missed except long stretches of open roads.

She rolled down the off-ramp, drove the correct number of miles, made the correct number of turns, and ended up on a two lane road. Fierce wind slammed against the side of the car. Leaves blew along in front of her. Alert for the correct crossroad so long in coming, she feared she was already lost. Finally, it appeared and she took the left fork.

Two miles later she turned left again onto a dirt road and traveled past field after field of bare grape vines. A small tree branch whacked the windshield, startling her. A dreary gray sky sat just above the canyon.

At two-point-five miles, she slowed, eying the mailboxes lined on the side of the road. When she spotted Ramsey, she made a right into a gravel driveway that sloped down. A white barn with a red roof sat back from the road. A mile further, the house popped up, an old Victorian with a wrap-around porch. The weathervane rooster on the roof was whipped by the wind in frenzied half-circles.

She pulled up in front of the house, cut the engine, hit the lights and slid from the car. Wind threatened to blow her backward. Before she reached the porch steps, the front door banged open and a woman dashed out. She stumbled down the steps and ran toward Maddie. Early forties, five two, plump, a soft round face with gentle wrinkles, short blond hair, wild look in her blue eyes. Her jeans were stretched over wide hips and the untucked tails of her white shirt flapped in the wind.

"Something's happened to her." Half crying, sounding

near hysteria. "Something terrible's happened to my baby."

"Mrs. Ramsey?"

"She could be lying in a ditch."

"Mrs. Ramsey, please calm down."

"Calm down? *Calm down!* How can I calm down? My baby's gone. Maybe in the hands of a madman. Being tortured. She could disappear like the little Danforth girl. Oh my God!" She rubbed at her face.

"I need to ask some questions, Mrs. Ramsey. To help me find her."

A man close in age to Mrs. Ramsey came from the house, trotted down the steps and put an arm around her shoulders. He was nearly a foot taller, with dark hair combed straight back, a face all planes and angles, dark hooded eyes, a hawk nose and a mouth pressed in a tight line. He looked angry. Maddie's antenna quivered. He wore loose-fitting jeans that were so baggy as to suggest he'd recently lost weight.

"Robert Ramsey." He stuck out his hand.

"Detective Martin." Maddie shook the offered hand and displayed her ID.

"Let's go in out of the weather," he said. "Come on, Evie." With a nod of invitation to Maddie, he nudged his wife toward the porch steps.

In the living room, he eased Evie onto a sofa upholstered in wine-colored brocade. He snatched the afghan draped over the curved back and spread crocheted rows of green, wine and white across her knees. After Maddie seated herself in an overstuffed chair of the same wine-colored brocade, he slid his bony rear onto the sofa next to his wife.

Words spilled from Evie before Maddie could ask a question. "Francine didn't come home yesterday. Nobody's seen her since she left work. Something's happened to her."

"How old is Francine?"

"Twenty-two. Yesterday was her birthday. Oh my God, you have to find her."

Maddie pulled out her notebook. "You expected her home last night?"

"That's what I've been telling you."

"Okay, Evie." Robert patted her hand. "We'll get to the bottom of this." He sounded more annoyed than worried.

Evie burst into tears.

Maddie wondered why Robert Ramsey wasn't as concerned as his wife. Because he knew something she didn't? Maddie made a mental note to speak with him away from Mrs. Ramsey.

"She gets off work at six." He pulled a square of white handkerchief from his back pocket and offered it to Evie. "We didn't know she hadn't come home. Not till this morning."

"Something's happened to her." Evie took the handkerchief and rubbed her face, then blew her nose. "She had a date last night. To celebrate her birthday. She was so excited. Bought new clothes and everything. We didn't expect her 'til way late. We went on to bed at our usual time. Eleven-thirty, just like always. Right after the news. This morning she wasn't here. We didn't think too much of it. Just assumed she'd gotten up without waking us and went on to work." Evie's bottom lip trembled. She pressed the handkerchief against it.

"Where does she work?" Maddie asked.

"Home Style Cookin'. The restaurant, you know? For over a year now."

"What hours did she work yesterday?"

"Ten to six. Just like always. Paul was picking her up at six."

"And Paul is—?"

"Her boyfriend. Stella called at eleven. Wanted to know where Francine was. She didn't show up for work. Oh my God, what could have happened to her?" Evie dabbed at her nose with the soggy handkerchief.

"Stella is her boss." Maddie said.

"Yes. She loves Francine. Happy to have her working for her. She told me that. Said how great that she could count on her. She could always count on Francine. That's why she was so concerned when Francine didn't show up this morning."

"And Paul's last name is—?"

"Gilford. Paul Gilford. High school sweethearts. Went together all through high school. Real cute with each other."

"Have you spoken with Paul?"

Evie shook her head. "I called his mother. He's not home either. She doesn't know where he is."

"Is it possible they went off somewhere?"

Mrs. Ramsey's face got stiff. "Not without telling us."

"Maybe in a romantic moment, they decided to take a long weekend."

"She wouldn't."

Maddie asked about friends. Mrs. Ramsey had to think. Jill Meisner was Francine's closest friend, then there was Stacy Gruder and Violet Hazel. Maddie jotted down names along with phone numbers and addresses. She asked if Francine seemed bothered by anything lately.

"Like what?"

"An ex-boyfriend. Someone who felt a grudge. Someone who wanted Francine's job."

Evie shook her head. "She never said anything like that and she always told me everything. And she never had an ex-boyfriend. Like I mentioned, it's always been Paul."

"Troubled by a customer?"

"Oh no. Never. In all the time she's worked there, she never had any trouble from customers. They all love her."

Mr. Ramsey looked out the window at the gray clouds that had collected and got up to turn on the two table lamps by the sofa and the floor lamp near the fireplace.

"Has Francine mentioned anything that worried her, or anything that seemed odd?"

"No, nothing like that."

"Was there anyone who was attracted to her, wanted her to go out with him, asked for a date and was turned down?" Maddie wondered about a stalker. Working at a restaurant, maybe she'd caught someone's attention.

"No, no. The only boyfriend she ever had was Paul. They've been together for near onto forever. We were neighbors, you see, when they were little. No, the only thing on her mind was the wedding. Making all the decisions, you know. So much to take care of. Flowers and food for the reception and there's the rehearsal dinner and—"

Mr. Ramsey patted her arm. To shut her up? When Maddie asked Mr. Ramsey if he had anything to add, he shook his head. She tucked away her notebook and rose to her feet.

"You'll look for her," Evie pleaded.

"Yes," Maddie said. "A lot of people will look." She asked Mr. Ramsey if he could tell her the quickest way back to the freeway.

"Sure. Just follow the road in front and at the next road, you turn that way." He pointed.

"Maybe you could show me outside. I have a little trouble with directions." That much was true.

He switched on the porch light and opened the door for her. When they were standing beside her car, she said, "Do you know something about your daughter's whereabouts?"

He shot her a look, then shook his head. "No."

Maddie had a good ear for lies and she'd just heard one. "Mr. Ramsey, your wife is worried sick. Since I haven't yet looked into this, I don't know if Francine is in trouble or not, but I believe you do know something." Maddie paused, then added softly, "And that has me wondering if you're involved in her disappearance somehow."

"My God, no."

"What is it you're not telling me?"

He hesitated. "Oh hell. Nothing. I have no idea where Francine is. I'm just as worried as Evie."

"But?"

He kicked at the gravel on the driveway. "I don't want to give you the wrong idea."

"I won't have any idea at all until you tell me what you know."

He took in a breath. "They had a fight."

"Your wife and daughter?"

"Yes. I don't know what all it was about. Except the wedding, for sure. *The damn wedding!* They've been going at it back and forth about this thing and that thing. Evie has just—she's taken over, planning every last bit without consulting Francine and Francine—she feels it's her wedding and she should have it how she wants. And—oh hell, the two of them go at it till I'm sick to death of the whole wedding thing."

"You think Francine just took off?"

He stuck his hands in his pockets. "I kinda did, yeah."

"Would she worry her mother like that?"

"I wouldn't expect it of her. But she'd just been so upset that I didn't know what to think. But I figured her to call this morning."

"And she didn't," Maddie said.

He drew in another deep breath and let it out on a sigh. "No."

"So now you think something's happened to her."

Again a breath, again a sigh. "I don't know what to think. I keep hoping the phone will ring and Francine'll say they just decided they didn't need all the fuss and went off to get married."

Maddie herself wondered if that was the case. She told him to call her if he thought of anything else, or if they heard from Francine. She got in her car, started the motor and turned on the headlights. A glance in the rear-view mirror as she drove off showed her Mr. Ramsey standing in the driveway watching her leave.

Her watch read nearly eight. Francine got off work at six yesterday evening. She'd now been missing over twenty-four hours. Most victims who were abducted were killed within the first thirty-six hours. If a predator had her, and if she was still alive, she had something like nine hours to live. Maddie sent up a request to a God she hadn't talked with in a long while to please let Francine be someplace perfectly happy with her boyfriend.

Though Maddie was no longer sure she believed in God, she'd never mentioned it to her mother who, when she wasn't convinced she was on an FBI hit list, worried about her immortal soul. Everybody knew about California. All you had to do was watch the news. But then everybody also knew her mother was crazy.

Greg's directions lay on the passenger seat. As the miles went by, she hoped she'd gotten them right. Malibu was the kind of place where a car like hers, worth less than the national debt, was apt to be reported to the police. She went by and around huge mansions that were so secluded many were mostly invisible behind gated driveways. If Greg could afford to live here, he was doing well for himself.

She turned onto a narrow road and a sudden downpour obscured her vision. She switched on the windshield wipers. What could Greg possibly want from her? He needed her. For what? She hadn't seen him in over three years. She hadn't even known he was in California. What could he possibly need her for? To report a crime? Could he be a suspect in some crime? He needed her help to extricate himself?

Greg? And crime? Straight-arrow Gregory?

Rain hammered the roof of the car. She gripped the wheel and leaned forward, straining to see. Normally she loved rain, but in the dark, trying to find an unfamiliar place, she'd just as soon do without it. She searched for the landmarks Greg had mentioned. At a fork in the road, she squinted, turned right and thought of the poem about the road not taken.

Rolling along in the dark, she began to suspect, once again, that she was totally lost. Finally, she saw a large, sprawling, two-story house tucked beneath huge trees. A completely dark house. No lights. Not one inside, not one outside. A little worm of worry wiggled through her mind.

She pulled up into the driveway and cut the headlights and the motor. The only sound was the splattering of rain. People expecting a visitor turned on lights. At least an outside light. Why no lights? An oversight?

Or a trap.

Set up by her ex-husband? Come now. She grabbed the flashlight from the glove box, flicked it on and slid from the car. Rain pelted her as she sprinted up the brick path toward the house. *It was a dark and stormy night—*

An owl hooted. The haunting sound sent her nearly three

feet in the air. Did owls hunt in the rain? Halfway up the porch steps, she felt a prickling high on her spine. *Someone was watching.*

She turned around. Nothing but rain and dark of night. Get a grip. Like anyone could possibly be watching. From where? A tree? With night goggles? Only an idiot wandered around in a downpour, like some ditzy damsel about to enter the dark house of her ex-husband.

She eyed the house. Something had happened to three young women. First the Danforth girl, then Tiffany Kipson and now Francine. Standing on the porch of this large dark house with rain splattering on the roof , Maddie rubbed the back of her neck. The front door had an inset frosted glass oval with fancy gold filigree. She pressed her thumb against the bell and heard chimes peal inside. She waited.

No answer.

Could she be at the wrong house? She aimed the flashlight beam over the brass numbers above the door. The same as the ones she'd written down. She moved the flash over the wooden swing on her right, the kind that rested on a platform. On her left large pots with some kind of plants sat on each side of a wide window. Shading her eyes with cupped hands, she peered inside. A faint light glowed beyond the entryway, in what she guessed was the living room.

Greg got tired of waiting and left?

After all his insistence that he needed to talk with her? Not likely. Something happened that took him away? Like what? She tried the door knob. It twisted under her hand.

On a quick breath with her heart beating fast, she pulled the gun from the pancake holster at her waist. With the toe of one boot, she inched the door inward, eased into the entryway, took a breath and darted into the living room. She shined the light around.

Oh God, she whispered.

Chapter Four

Dark puddles on the floor, swirls and smears on the white walls. She knew from the slaughterhouse smell what it was. Blood. Everywhere. So much blood. She dug out her cell phone and called for backup.

"On the way, wait for it."

"Right." Maddie stowed away her phone.

A voice in her head told her to get the hell out of here and wait for backup like Marla said, but what if Greg was still alive? With this much blood loss, waiting would be fatal.

Gun in hand, she took a further step into the living room. Rivulets of rain ran down the large window. Embers glowed in the fieldstone fireplace. Clock ticked on the mantle. Time eight-twenty-three. A fat tall yellow candle sat on either side of it. Large impressionist painting above of yellow eyes watching from a thick forest.

Against one wall sat a cabinet with television set and CD player. Small green light indicated the CD player was on. Books and ruled note paper were strewn across the black leather couch. Greg, or someone, had been jotting notes in a spiral notebook. More books were lying on the floor.

Maddie ran the flash over their titles. Stem cell research, bioethics, chemistry, invitro fertilization. An open package of chocolate chip cookies lay on the coffee table. Greg's favorite when he was struggling with a problem.

She inched across to a hallway and elbowed the switch for the chandelier in the ceiling. Tear drop crystals burst into light. More blood. Splotches and smears on the floor and the wall. Someone, bleeding heavily, was dragged along the hall toward the stairs. Greg?

On her right, an archway led to the dining room. Oblong table, polished wood, five chairs and a highchair. Stuffed pink rabbit in the tray. Buffet with china inside glass doors. Chandelier with a spray of tear drop bulbs.

Kitchen beyond. She hit the ceiling light. Honey-colored wood floor. Splotches of blood. Table with a blue and white flowered cloth, cobalt blue pottery bowl in the center. Room empty. No dirty dishes in the sink, or food on the stove. Blood spatters on a cabinet door. Someone was hurt in this kitchen, Maddie thought, then the bleeding person was in the living room and then dragged to the hallway. Smears went down the hall to the foot of the stairs. Maddie looked up. Listened. The only sound was rain as it pattered against the window on the landing.

Smears and puddles of blood on the carpet. Greg's blood? The mantle clock struck once. Maddie whirled, finger tight on the trigger. Heart banging like a drum, she took a deep breath. Only the clock marking the time. Eight-thirty. She eased her finger back. Keeping to one side on the stairs to avoid creaks, and stay away from the blood, she went up slowly.

At the landing, she stopped. Listened. Did she hear something besides rain? She moved up a step. Another. Another. Stopped to listen. Low strains of jazz came from hidden speakers. Second floor. Two doors on one side of the hall, both closed. *Oh God, who was inside the two closed doors?*

She stood beside the first one. Listened. No sound. Open the door? Would it be the last thing she ever did? Was whoever created this carnage standing inside with a knife in his hand? Was he listening, just as she was? With her pulse beating in her ears, she swallowed, took a breath, opened the door. Dark. She shined the flash inside.

Bed neatly made. Top of chest bare. Empty hangers in the closet. Guest bedroom she thought. Cashmere sweaters in one drawer. Nothing under the bed. Two framed pictures on the dresser. Both of Greg and the beautiful blond woman he married as soon as his divorce was final.

At the second closed door, she waited. Listened again. Was a killer on the other side of this one? She put her hand on the knob, turned, sucked in air, and opened the door. Dark also.

The flash picked out a tiny girl wearing white pajamas with pink kittens, lying on her stomach, crossways in the crib, face turned to the wall, rump in the air. One foot, in a lacy pink sock, stuck through the bed rails.

No no no! Not a baby!

Motionless. No blood on the clothing, no visible sign of injury. Maddie stood very still and watched. Did the tiny back rise with a breath? Just to make sure the baby was breathing, she put two fingers, very easy, on the baby's back. It rose and fell, with occasionally a shudder.

Alive. Maddie took in a breath and blew it out. The baby was alive. Maddie wanted to give the padded rump a cele-bratory pat.

Suddenly, realization hit. *This is Greg's baby!* Maddie had known the child existed. Acquaintances, even friends, had been quick to spread the news, but Maddie had never seen her. How old was this baby? Maddie tried to remember. She thought the child was about two. No longer a baby really, she supposed.

What kind of father was Greg? Doting? Ambivalent? Preoccupied? Busy? Working on answers to questions in his head and ignoring her? Playing tag with her? Reading her stories?

Maddie's eyes blurred with tears. Even with the light dim, she could see this was a beautiful little girl. Sweet oval face, wispy blond curls damp with perspiration. As though she'd cried herself to exhaustion. Pale eyebrows that suddenly shot up and then drew together. Dreaming? Her name? What was her name? It wouldn't come.

The door across the hallway was open. Her flashlight beam angled in, showed a bathroom. Empty. No towels on the towel bars. Used by the killer to clean away blood? Taken with him when he left?

She shined the light down the hallway. She didn't want to go there. She was afraid of what she would find. It would be bad. Somebody in that room was either seriously hurt or no longer needed help. The person responsible for all this carnage? Was he still around? Waiting for her in that room? She pulled in air. She didn't want to go in that room. She didn't want to do it. Slowly, she walked toward the end of the hallway. Oh Lord, she should really wait for backup. She really should.

With a breath, she grasped the knob and eased the door open. Master bedroom. It had been tossed. She played the light across drawers that were pulled out, contents scattered, closet doors open and clothes spilled on the floor.

A gasp caught in her throat. Silent, motionless, Greg stared with sightless eyes on the king-sized bed. All of a sudden, she couldn't breathe. His wrists were cuffed to the arms of the chair, his ankles tied to the legs. Hair mussed, clothing twisted. Deep wounds in his wrists and ankles showed how hard he'd struggled. Gaping cut across his throat, white shirt saturated dark red.

Jagged grief bit at Maddie's throat. Tears filled her eyes. She wanted to scream, no. He couldn't be dead. Not Greg. Strong, confident, always in charge, he'd been made helpless, forced to sit where he would see his new wife.

She lay on the bed, her wrists tied to the bedposts. Her skin was pale gray, the same color as the long-sleeved silk shirt she wore. Her legs, in dark gray pants, knees bent, had fallen to one side. Her eyes stared at the window where rain rippled down the glass. Bloody nicks and cuts marred her beautiful face. Her shirt was ripped in three or four places. Unbuttoned pants exposed an abdomen with several deep stab wounds.

Thoughts jammed up in Maddie's brain until she felt paralyzed. She closed her eyes and concentrated on breathing.

At that moment, all her bitterness and resentment, all her anger and pain, everything negative was erased. She felt only sad. *What was it you wanted to tell me? I'm so sorry, so sorry, I didn't get here sooner.*

She stood close enough to evil to feel it linger in the air, like the smell of brimstone after a lightning stick. Her chest caught fire. Her heart pounded in her ears. I am going to find you, track you down like the vermin you are. You can run and you can hide, but I'm going to win. I'll find you. She dug out her cell phone and punched the number for the Sheriff's Department.

"What's your emergency?"

"It's Maddie again. Two DBs upstairs at—"

"You were supposed to wait. Didn't I tell you backup was on the way?"

"There's a toddler—"

"Injured?"

"I think just asleep. I don't know. Notify CPS."

"Will do."

"Send crime scene techs and—"

"I know," Marla said. "And notify Sheriff Dirks. He won't like it."

Neither will Jesse. He had something important on deck tonight with his wife and daughter. She disconnected and shoved the phone in her pocket.

She rubbed at the tears on her face, swiped a hand under her nose. An urge came over her to cut away the rope, brush the hair from his forehead, straighten his shirt. *Oh Greg, what have you done, that it's come to this?*

One last glance at the mess of scattered clothes and emptied drawers and she backed out. Whoever killed them was obviously looking for something. She wondered what it was and if he'd found it. Head down, she concentrated on avoiding bloody smears on the carpet. As she passed the child's bedroom, she heard a noise. She stopped. Had the child wakened? She shined the light inside. The little girl hadn't moved. Probably just the rain, she decided.

Suddenly spooked, she headed for the stairs. Near the

closed door of the guest room, she sensed someone was inside. Had she heard movement? Impossible. She'd checked that room. It was empty. Then why did she have raised bumps on her arm? Could someone have slipped in while she'd been in the master bedroom? No. She would have noticed.

Would she? She'd been focused on Greg and his new wife. Oh come on. Not so focused that she wouldn't have noticed a homicidal maniac with a bloody knife skulking into the guest room. She was letting this place get to her, the smell, the horror of it, the torture, the blood, the terrible death of her former husband, the man she had loved. Stop it, she told herself. Take yourself in hand and get yourself out of here before you start believing in ghosts.

Before she could follow her advice, she heard a soft creak. She heard it again. This time she recognized it. A step on a stair. Someone was coming up the stairway! She melted back into the child's bedroom. With the door open about an inch and her nose in the crack, she waited.

Seconds later, a tall skinny man in a long black raincoat, appeared on the top step. Gun gripped in his right hand, he approached, halted at the guest room door. She held her breath. He turned his head as though listening. She raised her hand, tightened it on her gun, took a breath, ready to step out, and identify herself.

He went past her door, headed for the master bedroom.

She darted out behind him. "Police! Drop the gun!"

He started to turn.

"Freeze!" Jazzed up on fear and rage, she wanted an excuse to pull the trigger.

"Take is easy," he said.

"Drop the gun! Now!"

"Yes, all right, just be calm."

"Gun! On the floor!"

"Look—"

"Now!"

"All right. Just be cool." He bent, placed the gun at his feet, and straightened.

"Kick it this way!"

He nudged it her direction with his black shiny lace-up shoe.

"Hands on your head!"

He laced his fingers over the top of his head. "I'm going to reach with my right hand into my jacket— Slowly," he added, "for my ID. Okay? Slowly."

He held up his left hand and slid the right into the inside pocket of his suit coat.

She tensed, finger around the trigger.

Jesse checked his watch as he trotted to his car, happy to see he'd be home in plenty of time to see his four-year-old daughter make her acting debut. The story line was unclear, but Cindy played a frog on a lily pad. She'd been higher than a helium balloon from the time she'd bounced out of bed that morning. She'd insisted he listen to her part in the play, which she proceeded to perform as she ate a bowl of Chee-rios.

He nearly drove past a street corner before the flower stall registered. He pulled over and cut the motor. With one eye on traffic, he trotted across the street to the vendor and grabbed the biggest bunch of flowers available. In digging change from his pocket, he bumped the man behind and turned to apologize. A kindly grandfatherly type gave him a sweet smile. Bald except for a wispy white fringe of hair above his ears, round face, wearing a blue suit, blue shirt and a yellow tie with blue sail boats.

He nodded at Jesse. "Been a long time," he said in a soft voice.

Seemed like a message rested on those words, but Jesse was in a hurry and counting out quarters. Two seconds later, one brain cell rubbed another. Clayton Thorne. Jesse had nailed the scumbag for kidnapping and child molestation.

"Twelve years actually," Thorne said.

Not long enough in Jesse's opinion. He threw bills and coins on the counter.

"I've been paroled."

Paroled? Jesse wondered how he'd missed it. Thorne had changed some in the past twelve years. Prison will do that. Thorne must be approaching fifty by now, and looked at least ten years older. The thick brown hair Jesse remembered was now white, his skin was pale and unhealthy looking. The expensive suits of the past had given way to cheap wool, the fancy shoes were replaced by a Target special.

Thorne bestowed another smile. The smile hadn't changed, nor had the eyes. They were kind, interested, and projected a sweet old man. He looked like Santa Claus. He appeared so nice, so kind that even those who should know better couldn't believe he'd done the horrible things he was accused of.

"I hear you made detective."

A little trickle of concern slid through Jesse's mind. Thorne had been asking questions about him?

"Must be exciting, walking these mean streets," Thorne said. "I understand LA has gotten meaner."

Thorne's source of information, whoever it was, wasn't up to date. Jesse'd left the LA force six years ago, given up life in the fast lane for the Sheriff's Department in Mira Vista County. Gone from LA with a homicide every three days to Mira Vista with three a year. If that.

The flower vendor collected Jesse's money, dropped it in a tray and ripped off a receipt. Jesse shoved it in his pocket and grabbed his bouquet.

Thorne smiled, an I-know-something-you-don't-know smile. "Got time off for good behavior. I've been cured."

Cured. Sometimes Jesse wondered about the stupidity of people in charge of sick creeps like Thorne. Pedophiles didn't get cured. They just hid in the weeds until another victim skipped by.

"It's a pleasure to see you and hear how successful you've become." Thorne brought two fingers to his temple in a mock salute. "We'll be seeing more of each other."

What the hell did he mean by that? Jesse threw the bouquet in the passenger's seat and took off for home.

Right away when he walked in the door, he could tell

Lara was hopping mad. He couldn't figure out why. A glance at his watch told him they had plenty of time for dinner and getting to the school.

Lara stood in the doorway between the kitchen and dining room, arms crossed. She wore tailored brown pants, brown sweater, and small gold cross at her neck that didn't go with the pissed expression on her face. Her hair, shoulder length and curled up at the ends, was just a shade lighter than the sweater and her eyes were hazel when she wasn't mad.

"Did you forget something?" she said.

Obviously, he had. What? Anniversary? Birthday? Dinner with friends? Pick up item from super market?

"Daddy Daddy!" Cindy raced down the hallway like a rocket and launched herself at him. He caught her in one arm and swung her off the floor. Then he remembered. Oh shit. He was supposed to pick Cindy up at the baby sitter's. He wondered whether it would help if he gave the bouquet, which he'd forgotten and left in the car, to Lara.

"Want to see what I did in school today, Daddy?" Cindy wriggled free. "Do you? You'll never guess. Come on. I'll show you. Come *on*." Cindy tugged on his arm.

"Go ahead." Lara's tone had little barbed hooks. "Dinner isn't for another ten minutes. Spend some time with your daughter."

Another little dig. Too often, he didn't get home to read Cindy a story and give her a kiss before she was tucked in bed. All he could do was tiptoe into her room and lightly kiss her forehead.

"Come on." Cindy pulled him to her room. He removed the skateboard and a dozen stuffed animals so he could sit on the edge of the bed while she retrieved things from a pink backpack with a fluffy white kitten on the front.

"…and this is my arithmetic." She pressed a wrinkled slip of paper into his hand.

"And this is my spelling." Another grimy crumpled page. "…and this is my story…and this is my letters…see the whole page…and this is my…"

"Wait, wait. You wrote a story?"

"Uh-huh." She snatched it back.

"Wait a minute. What's your story about?"

"Well—" She looked like her mother except Cindy's hair was a lighter brown, but her eyes were the same hazel color. With a faraway look, she twisted her mouth to one side. A sure sign she'd forgotten the plot line.

Five seconds of silence slid by, then her face brightened. "About Peter the Puppy, of course." She launched into a long description of a black-and-white puppy that was smarter than every human around. She'd been campaigning for a puppy ever since her friend Lucy acquired one.

Lara had laid down a swift and firm NO. Since then Cindy had been softening him up. So far he'd managed to remain steadfast behind Lara's decision.

"And then they lived happily ever after," Cindy said and rummaged in her backpack for more tattered slips of paper.

Jesse applauded. "Great story."

Crafty smile on her face, she tossed the backpack aside and made little hopping jumps over to him. Leaning against his knee, she looked up and whispered, "When can we get a puppy?"

"Okay, guys," Lara called, "dinner."

He grabbed Cindy and planted a loud kiss on her neck. "Not before dinner. You know how your Mom feels about anybody late for dinner." He set his daughter on her feet and smacked her butt.

"I'm faster than you are." Giggling, Cindy raced for the dining room. "Daddy says when I'm older we can get a puppy just like Lucy's." She scooted onto a chair. "How old is older, Mommy?"

Lara sent him a glance like rifle barrels. "Daddy said that, did he?"

"… and I'm going to be five," Cindy held up five fingers, "and then I'll be older and then can I get a puppy?"

"And did Daddy say he was going to take care of this puppy? Puppies take a lot of care. And a lot of time. Since

Daddy is so busy, when would he have time to take care of the puppy?"

"I'll do it. I'll take care of him." Cindy's great big smile bespoke a solution to the problem.

"See what you started?" Lara shoved her chair back and got up. He could almost see an icy vapor trail floating from the kitchen.

"Am I older enough now?" Cindy said when Lara returned.

"Not quite." From the tone of Lara's voice, Cindy knew not to push it. The upcoming performance at school was enough excitement to smooth over her disappointment.

"I'm a frog," Cindy told Jesse.

"So I heard."

"Are you coming to see me be a frog?"

"I can't wait."

Neither could Cindy, who wiggled with anticipation. "And I wear a frog costume."

"You," Jesse said, "will be the best frog. Ever. No better frog in the whole world."

"Daddy." She giggled.

The kitchen phone rang. Lara threw him the I-knew-it look as she got up to get the salad from the kitchen. She'd been using that look a lot lately. The anticipated joy of this evening had started to go down hill from the moment he left work, and now the slope had likely just gotten steeper.

He hoped against hope that the call wasn't for him. When Lara brought the cordless phone to the dining room, his heart sank. She handed him the phone. He spoke with the dispatcher and scribbled down the address she rattled off. Damn it. Not only would he miss his daughter's interpretation of a frog, but Lara was nearly livid.

"Sorry," he said.

"What is it this time?"

Hearing the edge in her mother's voice, Cindy slid from her chair and scampered off.

"Maddie just reported a crime." Two dead. Gruesome scene. He didn't mention that to Lara.

"You spend more time with that woman than you do with me."

"*That woman* is my partner." There was never any doubt that Lara didn't care for Maddie. If they were in the same place at the same time, they were civil but the brittle politeness couldn't be mistaken for friendship. In the last two years, he and Lara argued more than they had in all the years of their marriage, and a large proportion of those arguments was about Maddie. Lara saw her as arrogant, stubborn, and reckless, someone who leaped into action without considering the consequences, consequences that might get Jesse hurt. Or worse.

Jesse's take was different. He saw the arrogance, the recklessness and the rest of it as cover for insecurity. Maddie had this burning need to prove herself, show she was competent, able to handle any situation no matter how tough. And it got her shot awhile back.

"Oh, well, if she's your partner," Lara said.

Christ, now Lara was jealous? He almost snapped at her, but thought better of it. Probably he was partly responsible for her animosity toward Maddie. How many times had he stomped home, locked up his gun, thrown his keys on the dresser and gone into a tirade about Maddie's fuck-ups?

Had he ever mentioned the things she did well? And there were many. Her stubbornness kept her digging for answers. A case that went nowhere but cold, with all leads followed, had her going back to the beginning. She re-read the files, re-interviewed witnesses, sometimes over and over. She re-searched data-bases. And by God if she didn't, many times, come up with something. Maybe only a little something, but she kept teasing at it until it went somewhere. She was intuitive, expert at reading body language and could spot a lie better than anybody. Also she was getting pretty good at interrogation.

"I have to go," he said.

"Like always."

"It's my job. What do you want me to do?"

"Go. Just go."

He sighed.

She waved him off. "Go tell your daughter."

He went to tell Cindy he had to miss her performance.

Cindy's eyes, so like Lara's, looked at him accusingly. "But Daddy, you promised!"

"I know, sweetheart." He picked her up. She stiffened and slithered from his arms.

"I'm really sorry."

"You're supposed to keep promises. That's what promises are for."

"That's true. But I have to work."

"You won't see me be a frog."

"More than anything, I wanted to see you be a frog."

"Then why don't you come?"

"I can't. I have to work."

"You always have to work." She crawled up onto the bed and picked up the pillow.

"Not always."

She shrugged, that comment not worth a response.

"Can I have a kiss before I go?"

She stuck out her bottom lip. "No."

He wasn't any more successful with Lara. When he attempted to land a kiss on her mouth, she turned her head. Okay, be childish.

He stormed out, got in his car and peeled off. He hadn't gone far when he thought, now who was being childish and slowed down. Both the females in his life were mad at him. He had some serious bridges to mend.

At the moment there was nothing he could do about the problem at home. What kind of trouble had his partner gotten herself into? He'd been thinking she was starting to listen, learn from her mistakes. With very little effort, he could remember a time when he'd been slow at both those things.

Across the street, Clayton Thorne tilted his umbrella against the rain. When the car turned the corner, Clayton lowered his umbrella. The little girl stood at the window watching her father leave. Pretty little thing. Clayton waved, she waved back.

He smiled.

CHAPTER FIVE

Jesse arrived at the scene behind two squad cars. He sent one uniformed officer to check the rear of the house and the other to secure the premises. Gun in hand, he took the porch steps two at a time, and slid in through the front door. Large splotches of blood on the walls, puddles of it on the floor, stopped him in his tracks. Jesus, what had happened here? That explained the two dead people. Whoever lost this much blood was no longer among the living. Where the hell was his partner? She was told to wait for backup. Didn't listen. Probably get her killed one day. He hoped it wasn't today.

Using care to avoid stepping in blood, he went through the dining room and sent a quick glance into the kitchen. No sign of Maddie. He didn't touch anything. Crime scene techs were more territorial than junk yard dogs, and about as friendly, when it came to protecting evidence.

"Up here," Maddie called.

He took a breath with relief riding on it. "Where's here?"

"Upstairs hallway."

He went up slowly, a step at a time, watching where he put his feet. "Maddie?"

She stood a short distance down the hall, gun aimed at some guy. Dispatch hadn't mentioned a suspect. This one seemed familiar. Tall, skinny guy with dark hair. Black pants, white shirt and tie. Shiny black shoes. When he turned, Jesse recognized him.

"Cutter." Jesse shoved his gun back in the shoulder holster. "What the hell are you doing here?"

"I was about to ask your detective that same thing." Cutter slid his ID in his pocket and looked at Maddie. "You mind if I get my gun back?" Without waiting for an answer, he retrieved his weapon from the floor and slipped it in the holster on his hip. "The Bureau considers giving up one's weapon a big no-no."

Jesse knew this guy, Maddie thought.

"Detective Maddie Martin," Jesse said, "meet Special Agent Mike Cutter."

"You need to keep an eye on your detective," Cutter told Jesse. "She's a little on the ragged edge."

"Yeah, well, she's young. You didn't answer my question." Jesse said.

"What question was that?"

"Don't be cute. What is the FBI doing here?"

"I'm afraid I can't tell you that."

"Come on, don't give me that nonsense."

"I really can't say."

"Can't," Jesse repeated dryly.

"Sorry."

"Mind telling me why you *can't*?"

A banshee started wailing. Startled, Jesse looked at Maddie.

"Baby," she said.

"Take care of it," Jesse snapped, then looked at Cutter. "You still didn't answer my question."

"I'm not at liberty to say." Smarmy smile.

Maddie looked from one to the other. The pissing contest going on suggested these two had some background.

Cutter smiled wider. Jesse got mad. She could see he itched to wipe the smile from the agent's face. To her relief, Jesse stuck his hands in his back pockets. She went to get the screaming baby.

"Come on, Cutter, you've gone from cute to irritating.

The FBI doesn't get involved in a local homicide. What got you here?"

Maddie returned with a shrieking child who shoved tiny fists against her chest. The child arched her back and squirmed to get away.

"I can tell you we had a tip." Cutter raised his voice to be heard.

"From who?"

"Whom," Cutter corrected.

"Oh, for God's sake."

Cutter was pushing it. Maddie could tell Jesse was running out of patience.

"Concerned citizen called," Cutter said.

"What concerned citizen? What are you talking about?"

"A concerned citizen," Cutter repeated. "Called and reported a burglary in progress."

"A concerned citizen called the FBI to report a burglary? Not the local police? This is not making sense, Cutter."

Maddie jiggled, patted and cooed at the baby, who screamed louder.

Cutter shrugged. "When I got here I found your detective. That's all I know."

Jesse glared at Maddie. "I did not break in," she said.

"Right," Jesse said and asked Cutter, "Who was this concerned citizen?"

"Didn't care to leave a name."

A siren sounded in the distance, and grew louder as it approached. Revolving lights flickered blue and red across the ceiling. Doors slammed, footsteps tromped on the porch.

"And the FBI always sends an agent to follow up on an anonymous tip," Jesse said with a pile of sarcasm.

"We try out best." The smile again.

"Come on, Cutter, stop bullshitting. The FBI does not respond to a diddly break-in. What's going on here?"

"Double homicide," Maddie said.

Jesse shot her a shut-up look.

Cutter didn't seem surprised at her comment. Did he

already know? He had been coming up the stairs when she stopped him. Had he previously been inside the house and seen what was in the master bedroom? Or maybe he knew they were there because he killed them.

"Give me some help here, Cutter. I've got a double homicide on my hands. With no visible leads to follow."

"Sorry. I can't tell you more."

"God damn it, Cutter."

"I'm not privy to any information."

Jesse snorted with disgust. "Just following orders."

"Actually, yes."

"Right. Good seeing you again, Cutter. You can run along now. We'll take over. Anything else you'd like to add?"

"Nothing comes to mind."

"Then I guess you might want to leave now."

Cutter gave Jesse a quick nod and said to Maddie, "Interesting meeting you, Detective Martin. Let me give you a little tip." He lowered his voice. "You might want to watch that urge to pull the trigger. It leads to paperwork and other undesirables." He did that smile thing again at Jesse and headed for the stairs.

Maddie, still trying to quiet the baby with jiggling and murmuring, was having no luck. "What's your quarrel with this guy?" she asked Jesse.

"Forget it. Why are you here?"

"Two bodies." She pointed to the end room.

"You knew there were two dead people here?"

"Of course not. How could I?"

"That's what I'm, trying to find out. You didn't answer my question. He gave her a look that said he had more questions, then walked carefully down to the end room and stuck his head in the door.

Two young males in blue jumpsuits burst up the stairs. One started unloading equipment, the other came toward Maddie, slapping a stethoscope around his neck. The baby shrieked in Maddie's ear. Poor thing was terrified, Maggie thought, and wished she knew how to calm her.

"Keep her quiet." The EMT laid a stethoscope against the

child's heaving chest.

"If I could do that—" Maddie snapped..

"Hold her still." He tried to listen. "You have to keep her quiet. I can't hear anything."

"I certainly would, if I could."

The paramedic looked up. "Can't you do anything?"

Maddie just stared at him.

"It will only take a minute." He tried again to listen past ear-splitting shrieks.

"You're scaring her," Maddie said.

"Look, if you'd just make her shut up—"

"What is it about would *if I could* that you don't understand?" Maddie was getting irritated.

"Down there." Jesse aimed a thumb at the paramedics, then pointed at the other end of the hallway.

When they headed off, he got in Maddie's face and demanded, "What are you doing here?"

The look of fury that crossed her face shocked him. What the hell? He'd never seen her in a rage. "This one personal to you some way, Maddie?"

"Let it go."

"I will not let it go." He yanked back on his temper and spoke evenly, "You will tell me what has happened here and what you know about it. And you will tell me now."

"Take this baby. You know more about babies than I do." Hands under the child's armpits, Maddie thrust her, kicking and screaming, into the air.

Suddenly, the shrieking stopped. Blessed silence. The baby looked at Maddie and cooed and gurgled, twisted Maddie's hair with slobbery fists. After a startled second, Maddie gurgled and cooed back.

Jesse'd had it. He would not continue to stand here while Maddie grinned like a Halloween pumpkin at the kid. "Downstairs." He took her elbow and urged her along to the stairway.

She went down carefully. CSIs were coming into the house with all their gear. The kid started whimpering. Jesse herded both Maddie and baby through the living room to the entryway and out onto the porch. Rain pattered against the roof and spilled over the eaves.

"Who are the victims?" This day had been a bitch and he had just run out of patience. "Why was the FBI here? Start talking."

"I don't know."

"Don't know what?" He wished the light were better, he wanted a better look at her eyes. "Are you on something?"

"What! Of course not! You accusing me of taking drugs now?" She obviously didn't have a great supply of patience either.

"Maddie—"

The baby squirmed, stiffened and started to cry. Maddie shushed her and jiggled her. "I really don't know anything. Not about the FBI. I didn't even know he was an agent."

"Okay. Then what are you doing here?"

She stared at the curtain of rain spilling over the edge of the roof. "Thirteen years—" The words seemed to stick in her throat.

Maybe he should have asked the paramedics to take a look at her. She was acting weird, not at all like herself.

"A long time ago." She cuddled the kid and made cooing noises. Blue eyes, big and round and inquisitive, stared at her. "College," she said, "Pre-med."

"You wanted to be a doctor?" That surprised him.

She shook her head. "There was this boy. I was young and in love."

Ah shit, Jesse thought. This was just the kind of stuff he didn't need to hear. "Tell me about it." He was proud that he didn't even sound resigned.

"This boy wanted to be a doctor. I wanted to be with him."

Jesse didn't like where this was going. "You knew the people that got sliced."

"No."

"You just said—"

"Only Greg."

"And Greg is—?"

"Master bedroom," she said. "Tied to a chair."

"And the woman? You knew her too?"

Maddie stared at the rain and saw memories. Long lazy Sundays with the newspaper. Reading interesting bits to each other. Hot sweet nights of making love. Going for a long walk under a full moon. Bringing home Chinese food and laughing at the fortunes.

"Maddie! Wake up here! You knew them."

"Only him. Greg. Gregory Palmer. I have to call his family. Oh my God, what am I going to say? His father is retired. A mechanic, automobile mechanic. He just retired a couple years ago. They were planning to travel. See the country, you know?"

"Maddie?"

"His mother's not been well. She has a heart condition. What will this do to her? His older brother. Maybe I should call him first. I think I have his number somewhere."

"Maddie! What do you know about those two victims?"

"We were married." A thin note approaching hysteria ran through her voice.

"What?" Jesse felt a wave of irritation. Maddie was married and he never knew about it?

Tears brimmed in her eyes, spilled over and rolled down her face. "I haven't heard from Greg in more than five years. I didn't even know he was in California."

"What were you doing in this house? And if you space out again, I'm going to smack you."

"He called."

"This Greg guy? When?"

"Just after the sheriff told me to go talk with the Ramseys about their missing daughter."

"Just like that. Out of the blue. This guy—this ex-husband—gives you a call."

"He said he needed my help."

"With what?"

"He couldn't talk about it over the phone. If I'd come sooner—" Her voice faded away somewhere in the memories she found on the other side of the rain.

Jesse pinched her chin and turned her face directly toward him. "Couldn't talk about it over the phone? Yeah, right. Good way to get you here. Was he setting you up?"

"For what?"

"That's what I'm asking. You came running. Think about it."

"No. Of course not. Why would he? We weren't enemies. We got divorced. It happens."

During the hours the crime scene guys were taking pictures, tweezering up hairs and fibers and collecting fingerprints, Jesse picked at her. Question after question after question. She didn't have time to think. Each question got progressively sharper and more invasive until he reached her hidden soul, then he proceeded to chip away pieces of it. He wouldn't stop. The questions went on and on until she felt riddled with holes, like a thin piece of lacy glass that a flick of a fingernail would shatter.

Then it got worse.

"Why are you hands bloody?" he said.

Maddie looked at her hands as though she couldn't remember how blood had gotten on them. "I touched him. Greg and—then his wife."

"Why?"

"To check for a pulse."

Eyes dark with suspicion, he said, "A pulse? When it was obvious they were dead?"

She knew that look. It was the look that listed her under Suspect.

When Cutter walked into the office, he knew his boss had been waiting. Roy leaned back in his desk chair and right away Cutter was nervous. Roy Lindstrom's office always made Cutter uncomfortable. Too hushed, too opulent, too much of a good thing. Cutter always felt he'd been dropped in the middle of a movie set, office of powerful man. Roy leaned back in his desk chair. He looked impatient.

Dim lighting. Floor to ceiling bookcases on two walls, expensive art work, thick burgundy carpet, couch and two chairs of black leather, an acre of mahogany desk polished to a high shine, cabinet with bar on one wall, expensive liquor and fancy glasses inside. Nothing in the boss's office was standard Bureau furniture. All the expensive stuff came from the boss's wife, a Texan with a strong accent.

The first time Cutter met her was at a Christmas party some years back. Everybody got tipsy at those things, but Chrystal got drunk. Cutter didn't recall that she did anything exceptionally embarrassing. In fact, he found her funny. She had a sharp ability to mimic. Some of the more buttoned-down agents were not amused. From then on Roy strictly monitored her alcohol content.

"Did you talk with Palmer?" Roy's deep baritone voice, skated near displeased.

"No." Cutter made his way to one of the chairs, and sat. The cushion released a soft sigh. My sentiments exactly, he thought. He hoped this wouldn't take long.

"Why not?"

"Somebody got to him first."

"What do you mean?"

"His throat was cut. Wife's also."

"Gregory Palmer is dead?"

"Yes, sir."

"Who killed him?"

"I don't know."

The silence fairly bristled with impatience. And Cutter, being the only one at hand, knew anger would come raining down on his head. Soon.

"Find out!"

"Local cops are handling the investigation."

"I don't care if God himself is handling the investigation. Find out who killed Palmer."

"That's going to be awkward, sir. Unless they request our help, there's not much we can do."

A pause. Roy drummed his fingers on the desk. "Not a problem."

Cutter hadn't been simply pushing Jesse's buttons. He didn't know why the FBI was taking an interest in Gregory Palmer. He only knew the boss had a burr up his ass.

"Why didn't you get there before Palmer was killed? I told you it was of the utmost importance. When was he killed?"

"Two or three hours before I arrived."

"God damn it! Do you think he was killed because of what he was working on?"

"Hard to say, sir, but I assume so."

"Why? Somebody iced him for his notes? Copies of his research?"

"Maybe. If that's what they were after, he probably gave it to them."

"They? More than one?"

Cutter shrugged. "I didn't have an opportunity to look around long enough to answer that, but I would guess two people."

"Why do you think he gave them what they were after?"

"He was threatened— the killer or killers— made him watch while they tied his wife to the bed and threatened to hurt her. My guess is at that time he gave them everything."

"You believe he simply handed over his work."

"Yes, sir, that's what I think. That he would have given the bastards anything to save his wife. Then, my guess would be, they killed her anyway."

"Maybe it was just a random robbery gone wrong."

"No, sir."

"Right. Did you notice anything at all when you were there?"

"The bedroom was tossed."

"Why? If he gave them everything?"

"Maybe they searched before killing him. Or maybe they killed him before they got everything."

A grunt. "Find out who killed him. Don't worry about the locals."

"Yes, sir." Dismissed. Cutter walked out, very uneasy. One thing he knew. This whole mess was going to get a lot messier.

Jesse stomped around muttering to himself and then called Children's Protection Services.

It was after midnight before someone from CPS finally came to pick up the baby and Jesse told Maddie to go home. Since her car was in the driveway with a trail of squad cars, coroner's van, lab van, and unmarked vehicles behind, she had to wait until the whole mess was sorted out before she backed her car free. Then she had to make her way through the chaos of reporters and news vans clustered on the street. She rolled her car slowly, avoiding eye contact, ignoring cameras and boom mikes pecking at the window and questions tossed at her from all sides.

Fatigue settled over her, so heavy that familiar objects morphed into weird shapes. A low shrub became a dog about to dash in front of the car, a stop sign threw a shadow of an elderly man tottering across the street. A wind-blown page of newspaper was a child turning summersaults.

When she pulled into her garage, she turned off the motor and simply sat without moving. Minutes later she slid from the car on trembly legs that she wasn't sure would support her. Shoulder bag in hand, she stumbled into the kitchen, flicked on the ceiling light and blinked in the glare.

The kitchen, like the rest of the house, had no frills, no personal touches, no pictures tacked by magnets to the refrigerator. She sometimes wondered if she'd ever get around to making where she lived into a home.

Every place looked just like the one before. When she moved, she settled in and invested her energies in her job.

When her few belongings were taken care of, she went about locating the usual necessary businesses, grocery stores, dry cleaners, pharmacies, library, etc. and learned the streets to get to them. She hung the same two paintings in every living room, and placed the same three pieces of furniture around: sofa, matching chair, wooden rocker that had belonged to her grandmother.

She didn't cart around extraneous items, no plants that needed watering, no pets that needed care and feeding, no significant other who needed the same. The only things of importance, packed carefully and brought with her at every move, were her piano, her books, and her music.

She plodded to the bathroom and hit the light switch. Her bloody hands that made Jesse list her under Suspect had her feeling like Lady Macbeth. She washed them thoroughly, brushed her teeth even though an evil fairy said she could miss one day. It really wouldn't matter. She put one foot in front of the other until she reached the bedroom and kicked off her shoes. Make the phone calls, she told herself. Even though Jesse had said he'd take care of it, letting the family know was her responsibility. Her watch read two-ten which made it after four in Kansas. Should she wait? Let them sleep for two more hours before she dropped tragedy on them?

She tumbled into bed. Memories like old movies played across her mind.

They'd met waiting at the checkstand in a drug store. Both were running late. She was a sophomore majoring in psychology, and had dashed in to pick up a spiral notebook. Greg, a senior in pre-med, had just broken up with his lab partner and had come in for aspirin to ease his headache. After only two minutes, she knew she was in love. That he felt the same about her was a miracle. He was six feet one, tightly muscled, blond hair and vivid blue eyes, a square jaw like the hero in old westerns who came into the saloon and everybody stopped talking to stare.

Deliriously happy, she felt she was floating two inches above the ground. His family, however, wasn't so happy. They didn't feel, especially his mother, that she was a suitable wife for their son. His mother even went so far as to try to convince Maddie to walk away. She explained that Maddie was inappropriate for Greg and would only be a hindrance. "That young woman is simply not polished," she told Greg. "She wouldn't fit in. Think of her welfare. She would feel totally inferior to your contempories."

His mother was so sure that Maddie would ruin his life,

if not worse, that Maddie wondered if maybe she was right. Greg ignored his mother's worries, laughed at her predictions of future disaster. When she wouldn't desist, he told her they were going away somewhere and would have a simple marriage by a justice of the peace.

Greg's mother was horrified. If her son persisted in marrying *this girl,* they must, at least, have a wedding that wouldn't embarrass them. She threw herself into the breach, and Maddie had a story-book wedding in church. Organ music, long white dress, bridesmaids, niece Dany as a flower girl, sister Pamela as maid of honor, champagne and everything. Despite worry about what her crazy mother might do, Maddie positively glowed with happiness.

He had years of schooling ahead and very little time or money for anything else. He studied, she stood by. He recited all the nerves in the cranium, she checked to make sure he was correct. Internship. Days without sleep for him. Police academy for her. Occasionally, she met him at the hospital and they shared a bowl of soup in the cafeteria.

"And what is it that you do?" his friends would ask. The answer would send their eyebrows shooting up, then would come, "Oh. That sounds very interesting." As in, what in the world is Greg doing with you?

She ripped tissues from the box, blew her nose and hunted down her address book. Brian, older brother, lived in New York. He'd never sent any negative vibes Maddie's way. She thought he liked her, in a mild sort of way. He answered after three rings.

"Maddie? What is it?"

There was no easy way of delivering bad news, but she'd learned that coming right out with it was better than the hemming and hawing and trying to sneak up with it. "Brian, I'm so sorry. Greg was killed tonight."

There was an intake of breath, then silence. A long moment passed. "Killed?" Disbelief and confusion. "What happened?"

"Apparently, the house was broken into."

"Was he shot?"

She did not want to tell him that Greg's throat had been cut. "Stabbed apparently. And—"

"Clarissa?"

Yes, that was her name. "She was killed also."

"Who did it?"

"I don't know, Brian. It's very early yet. The investigation has barely started." But I'm going to see to it that whoever did it is found."

"Mom and Dad?" Brian said.

"I'm going to call them right now," she said.

"Don't call," he said. "I'll tell them."

"Jesse, my partner, will talk with the local police department and ask for an officer to go and tell them in person."

"I'm leaving for their place right now."

"Brian, I am so sorry. You can be sure everything will be done to learn who did this and why."

"You'll keep me informed?'

"Yes, of course." She hesitated. "And I will call them, your parents." It would be a painful call to make, but an obligation. "If there is anything I can do, just tell me."

"Sure, Maddie."

She hung up, stretched out on the bed and watched the time go by. Sleep finally came and then the dream.

Wind howled and whipped through the trees bending branches nearly double. She stumbled over uneven ground as she swung her flashlight back and forth. Tree limbs reached out and clawed at her hair and tore at her clothes.

The body lay in a shallow grave, curled in a fetal position, face turned toward her. One cheek resting on loose dirt. Slowly Maddie circled the corpse. No evidence of gunshot or stabbing. No trauma at all that she could see. She squatted to shine the light into the bloodless face.

The wind rose in pitch, hummed like high tension wires stretched too tight. Suddenly, the dead eyes opened. Black and accusing. The mouth moved. Lips formed a word.

Maddie couldn't understand. She leaned closer to hear

better. The dead woman licked her lips, opened her mouth, closed it.

"What?" Maddie said. "What is it?"

The corpse opened her mouth, licked her lips again, and said—

Maddie woke gasping for air. Damn it! Just as she was about to hear what the dead woman was trying to say. Of course, her shrink would point out that Maddie knew the answer. Something in her psyche. Well, why didn't her damn psyche just come right out and tell her, so she could stop having this dream?

She was mightily tired of it. If it was coming from her psyche, her psyche was shit-ass scary.

Just as the darkness outside the window faded to gray, she dozed again, following a silent stream until she hit a large rock. Her partner sat on top, his eyes hard with suspicion.

Why are your hands bloody?

Chapter Six

The unfertilized gametes floated in a drop of fluid under the oil that prevented their drying out and kept them alive. Yes, he thought. Alive and healthy, all of them.

Using magnification, he guided the tip of a pipette over one gamete and, experienced as he was, gently tapped the pipette. A tiny drop got injected into the zona pellucida. That drop contained one cell scraped from the interior of a human mouth.

He watched, satisfied that all was well and made some notes. Then though it irritated him, he made a phone call to report progress.

The grunt on the other end of the line might have been pleasure at the good news or impatience at the paltry results.

He paid no attention. He had much to do.

As usual, whenever Jesse tried to be quiet so he wouldn't wake Lara, he banged into things, knocked over things or couldn't find things he needed. He'd gotten home late last night and Lara was already in bed pretending to be asleep. He had no chance to make apologies with appreciative words or even say good night. This morning he had no time. He was showered, shaved and looking for a tie when Lara murmured and sat up.

"Go back to sleep," he said.

"I'll get your breakfast." She stretched her arms out, swung her legs over the side of the bed and planted her feet on the floor.

"Don't get up. I'll pick up coffee on the way."

"Fine with me."

She lay back down, turned away from him, and pulled the covers over her shoulder.

Obviously, a night's sleep hadn't brought any improvement in the state of his marriage. He didn't know if she was still mad about his missing Cindy's play, or because he got home so late, or something else entirely. He figured whatever he said would only make things worse so he kept his mouth shut.

Lara didn't go back to sleep.

She worried that he had left without kissing her goodbye. What if something terrible happened to him today? She shouldn't have said what she did about Maddie. Coming off like the jealous wife. According to Jesse, Lara was the one with a problem.

But, damn it, he did spend more time with Maddie than he did with her. Okay, maybe she was just imaging things like he said, but Maddie was attractive, and had a zillion more things in common with him than she did.

When Lara complained he was always working, he said they all were. With another young woman abducted and now two people murdered—one of them some big important science geek with degrees after his name and friends in high places—it would only get worse. They'd all be working their asses off. Be prepared to see him when she saw him. The first chance she got, she'd tell him she was sorry.

Cindy bounced in, climbed on the bed, and scooted herself under the covers. She only lay still for about thirty seconds, then she sat up, grabbed Lara's arm and gave it a good shake.

"Mommy? Are you awake?"

"No. I'm sleeping."

Cindy giggled. "You're not sleeping, you're talking."

"Not any more." She grabbed her daughter, tickled her to flat-out surrender, and kissed her forehead. She rolled out of bed and slipped on her robe.

Cindy took her hand and tugged her to the kitchen. "What are we having for breakfast?"

"Oatmeal," Lara said firmly.

Cindy put a finger on her cheek and tipped her head. "I think it's time we had scrambled eggs."

"You do, do you?"

"Uh-huh, uh-huh? Can we? Please? Please?"

Lara pretended to think. "Well, maybe, if—"

"What if?"

"If after we eat, you entertain yourself while I take a shower."

Cindy twirled around saying, "I will. I will. I promise."

Lara scrambled eggs and Cindy, who never let food interfere with conversation, chatted as she scarfed up her breakfast and drank her milk.

"Remember your promise," Lara said when Cindy finished.

Cindy nodded solemnly and scampered off to her room.

Not wanting to stretch the promise too tight, Lara left the dishes and headed to the bathroom.

From the bookshelf, Cindy pulled out a coloring book and found her crayons. First a dwarf. After careful consideration, she colored Dopey red. Sleepy? What should she use for him? Maybe she'd do Snow White instead. The prettiest pink for her. Halfway through the dress, she needed to hear a story. She knelt and pulled out her box of CDs from under the bed.

It was an important decision. She consulted her lion, and her white cat, and her teddy bear, then selected Winnie the Pooh. She stuck it in the player, hit the button and sat on her skateboard while she listened to how the wind was blowing leaves. She looked out her window to see whether the wind was blowing there.

It was raining. She liked rain.

She got her red rain boots from the closet, sat down and tugged them on. Her rain coat was yellow and she put it on too, then went outside.

A huge great big gigantic puddle was by the gate next to the driveway. She crouched, sprang up, and leaped into the puddle. It made a wonderful splash.

She crouched, ready to jump again, higher this time, for an even better splash when she heard someone call her name. She looked up.

A man stood on the other side of the gate by the driveway. He had white hair and a happy smile. He looked really nice. The box he held, kind of like a shoe box, had a big pink bow. He shifted it to his other hand and turned up the collar of his coat. It was long and black and must keep him really warm and dry.

"Hello, Cindy." He smiled.

"Hello."

"Are you by yourself? Where's your Mommy?"

"Taking a shower."

Wrapped in a towel, Lara left the steamy bathroom, and heard Winnie the Pooh as she passed Cindy's bedroom door. Good. That should keep her busy for another few minutes. Lara pulled on jeans and a sweatshirt and went to clean up the kitchen. She gathered the breakfast dishes and stacked them in the dishwasher, wiped down the table, and cleaned the skillet. She swept the floor, and put the broom away, got down a mug and filled it with coffee. Black was not the way she liked her coffee, but Cindy needed the milk for her breakfast. A trip to the grocery store was due this afternoon.

"I'm not supposed to talk to strangers." Cindy curled her fingers through the wire on the gate.

"I'm not a stranger. Your Daddy told me to come. I'm looking for a little girl who has a birthday in three days. Do you know who that might be?"

"Me!"

He looked surprised. "Are you sure?"

"That's me! I'll be five!"

"Really? Five is way grown up."

She nodded. "What's in the box?"

He held it out between both hands like he was being very careful. "This box?"

"Uh-huh."

"This box has something in it for Cindy who has a birthday in three days. Is your name Cindy?"

"It is! It is! My birthday's in three days! Is it a birthday present?"

"That's exactly what it is."

"For me?" Cindy clung to the gate.

"It must be." He looked up. "Hmmm."

"What?" She hoped he wasn't thinking of some other girl named Cindy who had a birthday in three days.

"I was wondering. Do you like Halloween?"

"I love Halloween. You get to dress up as whoever you want and you get gobs and gobs and gobs of candy."

"That's right. This is a Halloween present and a birthday present. If I give it to you, can you promise to be very careful with it?"

"Yes." Cindy nodded solemnly.

"You know who this birthday present is from?"

"From you?"

"No. It's from your Daddy." The nice man held the box by both ends. "He told me to bring it to you."

She reached up.

"Be very careful how you hold it. Use two hands. You have to keep it this way. You can't tip it over."

"Why?"

"Because there is something very special inside."

"Is it a birthday cake?"

"You'll see. Remember to keep it level."

"Okay." She held up both hands and he set the box between them. She held on as she lowered her hands. Even though she was very very careful, the box tilted anyway. She hoped he wouldn't take it back. She held tight so it didn't fall. Something shifted around inside. That was scary. What if it jumped out at her? "What is it?"

"A surprise."

She shook it and heard a scratching sound.

"It's not a good idea to shake it. That might upset it."

"There's a hole here. On the top." More than one. Just big enough for her little finger. She poked it inside. Something wet touched it! She jerked her hand back and wiped it on a pants leg. This was kind of a scary present. She wasn't sure she wanted it. "What is it?"

"I can't tell you. That would spoil the surprise."

She forgot she wasn't supposed to and shook the box again.

"Remember, I told you to be careful," he said. "That might hurt it."

"Can I open it now?"

"Not till I leave." He waved goodbye. "I'll be back soon to see how you like it."

"Thank you for the birthday present," she called after him.

While Lara sipped coffee, she made out a list of what she needed from the grocery store. Would Jesse be home in time for dinner? Maybe she'd make some chili. He liked hot chili, and then it wouldn't matter when he got home. It could be heated up any time. She swallowed the last of the coffee and looked out the window as she put the mug in the dishwasher. Raining again, big drops bounced pockmarks in the puddles under the swings. She went to see if Cindy had gotten herself dressed, and if whatever she'd chosen was appropriate for a cold rainy day.

When she reached to open Cindy's bedroom door, she heard her daughter say in a high false voice, "I don't want to pick up my toys."

Switch to a deep voice. "Don't whine. You know what I told you about whining."

Lara recognized her own words coming back to her. She opened the door and Cindy came barreling out.

"Mommy!"

"Who are you talking to?"

"My new friend, of course."

"Your new friend sounds a lot like you."

"That's cause he can't talk and I have to talk for him. I'm hungry. I need a snack."

"You just had breakfast."

"But I'm hungry."

Lara almost said "Don't whine", but kissed the top of her daughter's head instead. Cindy had put on blue denim pants and a red sweater. Good enough.

"Can I have a snack?"

Lara brushed Cindy's light brown hair, gathered it into a pony tail and stretched on a blue scrunnchy. "What would you like for a snack?"

"Chocolate chip cookie, and Haley would like one too."

"Who's Haley?"

"My new friend."

"Ah. Does that mean two cookies?"

Cindy gave her mother the look saved for adults being stupid. Lara gave her a little swat on the bottom. Cindy ran, giggling, to the kitchen. Lara took two cookies from the box on the refrigerator. Cindy took one in each hand, and crunched a large bite.

"What do you say?"

"Thank you," Cindy mumbled around crumbs.

Lara got another cookie. This, she told herself as she nibbled, is where that extra ten pounds came from.

"When did you meet Haley?" Who was this Haley? A kid at the preschool she went to? Lara couldn't recall a Haley. Maybe a character in one of her books?

"Hours and hours and hours ago."

"When will I meet him?"

Cindy thought, then shook her head. "You wouldn't like him."

"Why wouldn't I?" Cindy usually bubbled over with eagerness to introduce a new friend. She'd give a long run-down on their backgrounds, likes and dislikes and point out things that she herself did better.

"Cause you just wouldn't."

"Why not?"

"He's kind of little and funny looking."

"You're kind of little and funny looking and I like you."

"Mom-my."

"Okay. You're my beautiful daughter. How is Haley funny looking?"

Cindy shrugged. "He doesn't really know anything."

Ah, just the way Lara felt some days. Cindy finished one cookie and started on the second.

"Hey, isn't that for Haley?"

"Oops." Cindy put a hand over her mouth. "I don't suppose I can have another one."

"You don't suppose right."

Cindy took in a breath with a little huff. "Poor Haley." A mournful look turned down the corners of her mouth, then she brightened. "I'll tell him maybe next time."

Again Lara heard the sound of her own voice. She'd have to watch it. This echo coming back was embarrassing.

"Haley wants to swing now. Can we go out?"

"It's raining."

"I know, but we want to go out anyway."

Lara was about to say no, when Cindy got that pleading look. To avoid hassle, Lara gave in. "Wear your raincoat."

Cindy skipped off to her room and scurried back in boots and raincoat, pink cowboy hat cradled against her chest.

"What's in the hat?"

"Haley, acourse." Cindy danced out the kitchen door.

Lara checked her grocery list, added a few items she had forgotten, and looked over the rest of her errands, the ones that absolutely had to be done today. Pick up the dry cleaning. Stop at the hardware store. Return library books. Get gas. When she glanced at the clock, she was startled to see twenty minutes had gone by. She jumped up and looked out the window. At least the rain had stopped. Her daughter sat in one swing and her pink cowboy hat was in the other.

What on earth did Cindy have under the hat? Lara went outside.

"You can't swing, Mommy. It's Haley's turn."

"Haley's been swinging quite a while. Don't you think he's had enough?"

"Not yet."

"Well, I think Haley's had enough and it's my turn." Lara picked up the cowboy hat.

She shrieked at her daughter. "Cindy? Where did you get this?"

CHAPTER SEVEN

Tuesday morning, the sheriff, detectives, uniforms, Doctor Lanery from the coroner's office, Cutter from the FBI, and Maddie all crowded into the conference room clogged with chairs and abuzz with talk. Maddie edged through and around people and went to stand beside her partner.

"What's going on?" she asked him.

Jesse nodded at Cutter. "The FBI has been invited."

"Why?"

Jesse shot her a look. "You'd know more than I do."

"What?" Obviously, she'd done something to make him mad?

"All right, everybody." Sheriff Dirks, fifties, thick gray hair in a buzz cut, thin face, all-seeing dark eyes. Short-tempered when faced with stupid errors. Lately, he'd been short-tempered in general. Even the dispatcher, who'd been with the department forever and knew him better than anyone, couldn't determine what was bothering him. Dirks placed a hand on each side of the podium, waited until the talk died down.

When quiet prevailed, he said, "You all know about the two homicides that occurred yesterday. Dr. Gregory Palmer, who was the director of Changing Biology, Inc. was killed and his wife also. The FBI has been called in—" Low-level murmurs arose.

"Anybody have anything to say?" Dirks demanded.

Deputy Fenton, otherwise known as Fuckup Fenton, took that instance to try and slip in unnoticed. No luck.

Irritation crossed Dirks's face. He looked pointedly at his watch. "Well, Fenton, glad you could join us. I was just informing everyone that the FBI is giving us some help on this one. You have anything to add?"

"No, sir." Fenton sidled past those in the last row, stepped on someone's foot, murmured an apology, and pasted his back against the wall.

"Anybody else have a comment?"

Somebody said, "Why?"

Dirks shot a look over the room, but whoever spoke wasn't admitting it. "To help with the investigation."

Nobody felt they needed help, her partner included. Maddie was of the same mind. Law enforcement agencies were possessive of cases in their jurisdiction. When circumstances forced togetherness, it often led to hoarding information. Dirks wasn't any different. He was as possessive of his cases as a pit bull with a bone. The FBI being invited in meant he had already gotten pressure from above. The homicides had occurred just yesterday. Investigation had barely begun. Maddie sent a slanted-eyed look at Jesse, wondering if he knew what was going on.

"This one has ramifications," Dirks said. "Some of you know Special Agent Cutter." Dirks gestured toward the FBI agent sitting in the corner on the back wall. "You want to stand up, Mike, so everybody can see you?"

Cutter rose, gave a short nod. Maddie thought he didn't look any happier to be here than Mira Vista Sheriff's Department was to have him.

Dirks leaned forward. For each word, he stabbed a forefinger against the speaker's stand. "These homicides will be cleared immediately!" Obviously, orders from higher-ups. *Make this go away. Now.*

Dirks straightened. "One other thing. And this is imperative. I want every one to listen up!" He raised *The Mira Vista Times,* showed it around. "Today's paper. I don't know how many of you have seen this." He looked at the front page, tapped an article with his finger. "Matthew Lockner did an article on the Palmer murders." Dirks went from face to face with a hard stare, making sure each one in the room knew the extent of his anger. "Somebody gave the—"

Maddie wondered what derogatory term Dirks would use.

"...*reporter*..." Infused with disgust. "...information. I am telling you all here and now that no one, repeat *no one*, is to talk to the media about this case. Understood?" He folded the paper and smacked it against the podium. "Anybody have anything to say?"

He waited. If anybody did, he wisely kept it to himself. "All right, people, let's get to work."

As they were all filing out, Sheriff Dirks said to Maddie, "Detective Martin."

Oh, Lord, he was mad at her for something?

"My office." He jerked his head that direction and strode off. She followed, trying to figure out which of her sins he was going to shout at her about. Was it going into Greg's house? Did someone dig up a stupid motive why she might have done the murders? Had Jesse suggested that she might be guilty?

Dirks closed the door after her and dropped into his chair. "Sit."

She perched on the edge of the straight-backed chair against the wall, heart jumping rapidly. Obviously, she was going to get a reprimand. Dirks didn't say anything, just leaned back in his chair and looked at her. She stiffened against the urge to fidget, and forced herself to wait. This was working up to more than a simple she went inside the house.

After an hour, or maybe twenty seconds, he said, "You're married to Palmer." It was an accusation.

Words jammed up against her teeth. She held them in, knowing if she let them escape, she'd say the wrong thing and make her situation worse. Whatever her situation was.

He leaned forward with a squeak of the chair, planted his elbows on the desk blotter, and demanded, "Well?"

"No, sir. Not really."

"What does that mean? Not really? You're either married to him or you're not."

"Not, sir. Divorced."

Dirks looked at her with impatience.

"Sir," she added.

The interrogation Jesse had put her through was nothing to what Dirks did. He grilled her, thoroughly on one side, then the other. Endless questions about Greg, their life together, his education, his work, the contact after divorce, and why she came to Mira Vista. Who sent her, who did she know here? Questions about Greg's second wife, questions about questions, questions the answers to which, she didn't know.

Her replies were tentative, tangled, her voice tight and shaky. Even to her own ear, she sounded guilty of something. Dirks just sat and waited for her to tangle herself up in words. Did he plan to fire her? She loved her job. She was good at it. She hadn't done anything to deserve getting axed. Okay, so she did agree to meet Greg. There was nothing wrong with that. And she did go out to his house. Nothing wrong with that either. She went inside when she should have waited for backup, but her reason was valid. Get help immediately, if someone were still alive.

"You're off the case."

She was so focused on her excuse for entering the house that she wasn't sure she heard correctly. He picked up his glasses and fitted the ear pieces around his ears.

"Sir—?"

"I'm not having some scumbag defense attorney getting the bastard off by claiming conflict of interest." He reached for the folder on the corner of his desk and held it out to her. "Take care of this."

"We've been divorced three years, sir." No way would she let this go. Greg had been her husband. She loved him. In spite of everything, the divorce, his remarriage, they were still connected. "I haven't seen or spoken to Greg Palmer once during that time. I'd like to stay on it, sir."

"No."

"I need to be in on this investigation."

The sheriff gave her a beady-eyed stare.

"Sir," she added quickly.

"Why?"

Because in some weird way she had to find the killer. She just had to, that was all there was. Maybe because she felt guilty. He'd asked for her help and she was too late. Maybe a little quicker getting to his house she might have prevented the slaughter. Maybe if she'd given him one more minute on the phone when he called maybe he'd have hinted at why he needed her help. If if if. Given a little time, she could come up with a dozen more.

She *would* be involved. She couldn't step aside any more than she could stop breathing. "Let me work it with Jesse. Background stuff only. If something comes up that might tie me to Greg, I'll back off."

Dirks looked at her over the tops of his glasses.

"I will, sir. I absolutely promise. Back immediately away."

He held the look for several seconds. She began to take an easy breath.

"No," he said. "Now, if that's all, get back to work."

She stood and started for the door.

"Maddie," two syllable warning.

She turned, one hand on the doorknob.

"Use your head."

"Information, sir. It's Jesse's case, but if he needs research or to check into medical records on the child or—"

"No. Now, unless you have anything to add, get out."

Maddie got out. She wasn't confrontational, she never felt like she was successful at it. She was a good officer, just like she'd been a good little girl. She kept a low profile, did her job efficiently, didn't make waves. Just like she used to keep her room neat, have her homework done, and clean off the kitchen table. For any other case, if she was told to leave it alone, she would. But not this one. This was Greg. He was hers. And she had promised. She'd stood in his torn-up bedroom with him tied to a chair, his murdered wife in the bed where he could see her, and she had promised she would get the bastard who killed them. She intended to keep that promise.

She ignored the tiny voice in the back of her mind that whispered if she persisted she could very well lose her job.

He didn't need this. Dirks reached for a file from his in-box and flipped it open. He recognized stubborn when he saw it, and Detective Martin had stubborn all over her pretty little face. Maybe he should fire her now. Except he didn't have a valid reason, and were he to fire her he'd have no control over what she did. She'd be right out there in the midst of it. Not only were there politics surrounding the Palmer homicide, but he was forced to acccept the intrusion of the FBI before the investigation even got started. He tried to get his mind elsewhere by reading the report in front of him. The words turned into a jumble of black marks like spiders running across the page.

He rubbed his chest, where pain tingled toward his arm and yanked open the middle desk drawer. Scrabbling fingers shoved aside junk in search of the small vial with the little white pills. He unscrewed the top, shook one into his palm and popped it under his tongue.

Maddie weaved around desks toward her cubicle. Eyes watched her all the way. Probably wondering what Dirks was yelling about. At her desk, Maddie spread open the newspaper she'd bought on her way to work, and quickly scanned the article Dirks had pointed out in the meeting.

"Aren't you supposed to be working instead of frittering away your time reading the paper?" Jesse had two cups of Starbucks coffee. He handed her one, rested a hip on the corner of her desk and took a sip from the other.

"Famous Biologist Murdered." She read aloud. "Dr Gregory Palmer and his wife Clarissa were found in their blood-spattered home sometime yesterday evening. Mira Vista Sheriff's Department officers are investigating."

"That would be me."

" 'A source told this reporter one of the investigators had been close to Dr. Palmer.' " She looked up. "Would that be you?"

"Don't be an ass," Jesse said. "Throw that in the trash and get to work."

Maddie went on as though reading. "The same spokesman also told this reporter that Detective Martin could have prevented the slaughter, if she'd gotten to the victim's home sooner."

"It does not say that."

"Yeah, well maybe it should."

Jesse snatched the newspaper and dropped it in the waste basket. "Snap out of it. That's stupid and you know it. Get off your duff and get to work."

"I was married to him once, Jesimiel."

"Don't call me that."

"Why not? It's your name."

"Would you listen to what I'm telling you? You are *not* responsible for what happened to those two people. I'm sorry they were killed. Thinking about that little kid in the house when all that slaughter was going on, makes me want to grab my trusty six-shooter and blow holes in the dirtbag who did it, then race home and hug my little girl."

"He made Greg watch, Jesse." Just the thought of what Greg was forced to endure made her sick. "While his wife was murdered. While her throat was cut and her blood arced up to splatter over the walls. He had to watch it spill down—"

Jesse crossed his arms and nodded his head wisely. "You don't know that. He might have gotten axed first. But I get what's bothering you. Loose ends. You're trying to tidy up stuff that didn't get tied off during the marriage, or the break-up."

"You can be so sensitive sometimes."

"So my wife tells me."

"Greg is still dead no matter what loose ends dangle around. Along with his wife. The little girl heard what went on. Did she cry? Beg for her parents to come? Realize something terrible was happening?"

Jesse opened his mouth to say something, closed it and

began again. "The sooner I get started, the sooner I can catch this evil fuck. I will arrest him, cuff him, then hold him down while you beat him up." Jesse drained his coffee, dropped the cup in the trash, went to his desk and collected his gun.

She retrieved the newspaper and studied the picture of Dr. Gregory Palmer, the man she had loved with all her heart.

She had to be careful. So she'd be careful. If Jesse thought she was messing with his case, he'd see that she got chained to her desk. If the sheriff knew, he'd likely split a gut having a spectacular yelling fit. And just as likely, throw her out on her ass.

From her bottom desk drawer, she grabbed her gun and her bag, slipped the strap over her shoulder and left the building. Sun blazed down from a cloudless sky. She was already hot as she walked across the parking lot. A creepy feeling prickled a spot high on her spine. Someone was watching. She turned, looked around. Out on the street, beyond the mesh fence, two cars were parked, nobody in either. A woman trotted by with a small dog on a leash. A whole bunch of little bitty black birds pecked away at the grass.

Nobody, not even the birds, paid any attention to her. Reading too many thrillers, too much imagination, turning into a neurotic? All of the above.

He watched Maddie Martin cross the lot. Attractive. Blond, trim, moving with purpose. Everything he knew about her said she was driven, ambitious, got her teeth into something and didn't give up. He believed it. The set of her shoulders and firm step spoke of tenacity and determination.

Had Palmer told her anything? The possibility was too big to ignore. Something had to be done about her. Too bad. He liked her. With one finger, he caressed the knife's handle and pressed the catch. The six inch blade sprang out. He folded it back, pressed the catch again and tested the point with the ball of his thumb. The knife was sharp. He kept it that way. A dull knife wouldn't cut. He pressed the blade shut and popped it open. He did like tools that worked well.

The car was warm inside from sitting in the sun. Maddie clicked in her seat belt, put the car in gear and started to back out when her cell phone rang. Caller ID showed a number she didn't recognize. "Detective Martin."

"Good afternoon, Detective. This is Matt Lockner, reporter for the *Mira Vista Times*."

"Yes, Mr. Lockner, what can I do for you?"

"We've met, haven't we? Didn't I run into you a time or two at the Sheriff's Department?"

"You may have." He'd been trying to get information on the young women who were missing. Maddie recalled acting vaguely muddled, and he'd moved on to Jesse who told him to get lost.

"I'd like to talk with you about the murders that occurred yesterday."

"I'm not part of the investigation, Mr. Lockner. Speak with the Sheriff."

"Right, I'll do that. I'd also like to take you to lunch."

"I'm simply too pushed right now. Thanks anyway."

"Come on. Just a quick lunch. Be nice to reporters. They have to eat too."

"Sorry, Mr. Lockner. I need to hang up and get to work."

"You're investigating the missing women?"

"I haven't anything new to give you. Try Sheriff Dirks."

"I'd much rather talk to you. Reconsider the lunch offer."

"I'm sorry. I really am busy. I have to go."

"Will one o'clock work for you?"

"One thing I can say, you are tenacious. Please excuse me, I have work to do."

"Come on. You might need a favor some day."

"Not today though. Excuse me. Please."

"I know a great Mexican place. I'll pick you up. We can talk about Dr. Palmer. I'll tell you what I know."

Maddie suddenly paid attention. Was he suggesting he

knew something about the murders? Or that he knew Greg? "What can you tell me?"

"I'll tell you at lunch."

She was ninety per-cent certain Lockner was just dangling a carrot. He probably knew nothing. It was that other ten per cent that kept her wondering. Okay, Mexican food. "I don't know exactly where I'll be at one. Maybe I could meet you there?"

"Great. Marietta's." He gave her the address.

Maddie hung up, and wondered just what it was he was after. Any fodder for a news article? Or something specific?

Just remember, she told herself. There's no such thing as a free lunch.

CHAPTER EIGHT

Elbows on the chair arms, fingertips together, he watched Francine through the one-way glass. She grabbed the door-knob, yanked and shook. She kept pulling and twisting, not wanting to give it up. She peered at the lock and examined the hinges. Apparently deciding she couldn't open it, she moved around the room.

No matter how hard she looked, she wouldn't find a way out. It was your basic hospital room, heart monitor, blood pressure machine, oxygen tubing. So far she didn't seem panicky, just confused.

She was young, trusting, pretty, a bit naïve, very friendly. With a little prompting, she'd bubbled over with news. Her face was oval-shaped and sweet, her eyes hazel. Her chestnut brown hair curled in the dots of perspiration on her fore-head.

Adequate air conditioning would be nice, but the building didn't come with such luxury. It didn't come with much of anything adequate. The building was old. It sat, neglected for years, in the middle of nowhere. Even Southern California had a middle of nowhere.

He'd been a long time searching for just such a place. This was perfect. At one time it had been a clinic for the mental-ly ill. Long since closed. The realty company that held the listing had nearly forgotten it. Extensive work was needed before it was habitable, and nobody was interested. The owners—distant cousins of the original owner—couldn't agree on anything, and had an inflated idea of its worth. They'd left it empty and when he found it, the building was in sad shape.

Timing is all. He came along when the squabbling cousins finally realized that the longer they let it deteriorate, the more it lost in value. At long last, they put aside their squabbles and agreed to sell. He was ready with his checkbook.

Brick, four stories, built on top a hill, forty rooms. Many bathrooms, all needing extensive remodeling, a kitchen that had to be gutted. And then there was the basement, a warren of rooms extending far down into the hillside, and also the sub-basement. He paid the asking price without a quibble, and equipped it for his needs. When he was finished, he had a small hospital with a well-appointed lab, storage rooms, and offices with the latest in electronics.

And, oh yes, the room Francine was in. It was actually a holding cell, used as a place to keep subjects until he was ready for them. They couldn't get away, they were available when needed, and there was the added benefit of a room so empty, so cold, so quiet and dark, they were not only glad to see him when he came, but jumping at the chance to break the boredom.

How many subjects he'd use depended on the circumstances and how his research was progressing.

"Hey!" Francine grabbed the sheet from the bed and swirled it around her shoulders. "Let me go! Let me out of here!" She aimed a series of kicks at the door.

He banged a metal pipe against it.

She froze.

He flipped a switch so she could hear him. "Make all the noise you want. Not only is the place soundproofed, but it's isolated. Nobody can hear you. Scream some more if you like."

She gulped like she couldn't get enough air, then searched the ceiling for the source of his voice.

"More screaming? No? All finished? Okay then, I'll tell

you how this is going to work."

He shelved the pipe, picked up his camera, unlocked the door and entered the room. Her eyes went wide, wary as a wild animal. He thought she might try to attack him, and was prepared for it, but she took a step toward the bed.

"Now, here's what you have to do."

She started inching away.

"Stay where you are!" He snapped pictures of her, moved around to get her from all angles. "The first thing is cooperate, do what I say, willingly and without being troublesome."

A stubborn look crossed her face and he wondered if she had more spunk than he gave her credit for.

"If you do everything exactly as I tell you, then in two months, maybe a little more, but no more than ten weeks, I'll drug you again and you can sleep all the way back to Mira Vista. I'll let you out near the spot where I picked you up. Since you don't know where you are and you don't know my name, I'm not worried about what you do after that."

He waited a moment. "Understand?"

She stared at him.

"If you don't cooperate," his voice softened. "And agree to do whatever I want, the consequences are serious. I might have to bury you next to your beloved."

A pulse fluttered in her throat.

"You're not saying anything. Are you listening? I know it takes a bit to digest, so just nod if you're with me so far. Okay? Okay!"

She nodded.

"Good. Now, this is how it'll go. While you're here—and like I said, it'll probably be two months, maybe ten weeks— you'll be a subject in my research."

Her lips felt numb, unable to form clear words. "Paul?"

"Yes, I've given some thought to that and what I've come up with is you're going to write letters. You know, to his mother and his boss and whoever else and tell them he went off to—oh, pick a place. Tahiti, for all I care. He got a job and decided to relocate."

"No—"

He shook his head. "Uh uh uh. Be careful. Maybe I didn't make myself clear. You have two choices. Go along with the program for ten weeks, or—"

A whimper slipped out.

"Maybe all this doesn't sound fair, but fair doesn't play into it. I'm a scientist and my only interest is my research."

He slipped the camera in his jacket pocket. "It's mainly a matter of blood tests, and a few other minor procedures. Nothing to worry about. You won't experience any pain."

Then his voice changed. It got all weird and eerie, like all this heat and madness slipped in. "It'll make my name. Journal articles. A book."

Oh God, he's crazy. Her mind kept skittering away from the horror of her situation. She couldn't seem to get enough saliva in her mouth to make words.

Hands on his hips, he looked at her with exasperation. "I'm beginning to think you're a little slow. Should I throw you back?"

"Yes! Let me go! Please!"

"Well—"

"Please."

"Naw." He shook his head. "I've gone to all this trouble, the planning and labor, laying in supplies. I've worked like a dog. I'm tired, edgy, strung out on nerves and just about dead on my feet. Now, you decide. However, I think it's fair to tell you, if you don't agree to my proposal, I'll just tie you to the bed, use you and put a bullet in your brain. What's your decision?"

All she could manage was a croak. "I—I—"

"Is that a yes? You agree to do whatever I want?"

Oh God, she couldn't—

"A yes?"

Reluctantly, she nodded.

"I can't hear you."

"Yes," she whispered.

"Yes, what?"

"Yes. Whatever you want. I'll do it."

He clapped his hands, big smile. "Good."

"Paul—?"

"Don't worry about him. He was getting ready to dump you anyway. He just didn't know how to tell you. He was tired of your whining about the wedding and he found somebody else."

Not true! Was it? Dump her on her birthday? He didn't want to marry her? He'd found somebody else? No.

"Take off the gown."

"What?" Terror had her trembling so she could barely stand.

"I need to take more pictures."

With awkward hands, she fingered the ties on the hospital gown.

"You need some help?"

She managed to free the ties and slip the gown off her shoulders.

"All the way."

She just stood there.

"Get over it. It's part of my research."

She didn't move.

"Francine!" He hit the wall with the flat of his hand. The sharp bang made her jump. "Do I have to show you what I'll do if you don't cooperate? Take it off!"

She let the gown fall to the floor. She shivered, so terrified she couldn't draw a breath. Tears ran down her face.

"Please—" She kept trying to cover herself, moving her arms here and there over her naked body. "Please, let me go."

"Be a good girl, and I'll think about it."

What happened? If only her head wouldn't hurt so much. Francine closed her eyes. *Think, think.* Sunday was her birthday. Half the day she'd silently sung Happy Birthday to herself. A magical, wonderful evening was planned. First dinner and then dancing. Then late late late, or early early early, they'd go someplace and watch the sun come up. Paul was taking her some place special—he wouldn't tell her where—to celebrate. When the world was just turning light, he planned to give her a ring. She knew it, she just knew it.

All day long she'd been a klutz. One tray with dinner orders meant for the customer in the rear booth slipped through her hands and a plate of spaghetti slid off. Fortunately, tomato sauce, meatballs, and pasta landed on the floor and not on the customer. She apologized profusely.

And that wasn't the only thing. Think, think! Racing into the kitchen to pick up something, she bumped into another waitress who had a tray of water glasses. Water and ice and glasses went flying.

Francine carefully touched her temples with her fingertips. If only she didn't feel so fuzzy, she could think better. *There was the call.*

Stella, her boss, told her. From Stella's face Francine knew something was wrong. "What? What is it?"

"You had a phone call."

Francine's heart banged against her ribs. Her father? Heart attack? Mother? A fall?

"...accident...critical..."

"My father in an accident?"

"No, not your father," Stella said. "Paul. Hit by a car. Crossing the street. Apparently, it's bad."

"Where? I need to go."

"He's in surgery."

"Oh my God. Where? Tell me where he is."

"Someone's coming to get you. He'll take you there. A friend.

"What friend?"

"He didn't say."

"When? When is he coming?"

"As soon as he can get here."

Oh my God, oh my God. Surgery? "That sounds serious, doesn't it?" She clasped her hands together to keep from shaking.

Stella took both hands in hers and held them still. "It's going to be all right." Stella gave her hands a little shake. "His friend will be here soon."

Oh God, please let Paul be all right?

The black car rumbled up to the back door, Stella gave her a hug. "He's going to be fine." She opened the door to let Francine out.

The night air was cold. Francine shivered and held her coat closed at the throat as she ran to the car. The dome light didn't come on, but light from the dash smeared greenish tinge over one side of his face.

Short dark hair, square jaw, straight nose. He gave her a nod when she got in. *A kid. Maybe sixteen. She'd never seen him before. Something was not right.* Who was this kid? How did Paul know him?

"How is he?" She reached for the seatbelt and clicked it snug. "Is he badly hurt?"

The kid shrugged. "I don't know."

Oh God oh God oh God. Please let him be all right. Please please. For a moment she was so scared she couldn't take a breath. "Where is he? What happened?"

"I can't tell you."

"What do you mean, you can't tell me! I have a right to know!"

"I wasn't told."

Francine sputtered when she asked why he wasn't told. The kid shrugged again. She wanted to kick him. "How do you know Paul?"

"There's some coffee in the thermos, if you want." He aimed a thumb over his shoulder. "It's just behind the seat."

Her unease grew. She was in a car with a total stranger and didn't know where they were going. All the books and articles about self-defense said not to get in an automobile with him. Was the coffee drugged? She unclipped the seat belt and squirmed around to reach back for the thermos. "You want some?"

He nodded. "There should be an extra cup in the glove box."

She found the cup, filled it with coffee, and handed it to him.. "What's your name?"

"You don't know me."

"You'd be surprised. I know just about everybody in town." She poured coffee for herself and took a sip.

"I'm just visiting."

The dark, and the quiet and the hum of tires on the road seemed hypnotic. She started to feel sleepy. Was the coffee drugged? Her eyelids drooped, she let her head tilt against the seatback. *Please Paul, please hang on. I'm coming. I'm coming.*

She came awake with a jerk and stared out the window. There was nothing out there. No street lights, no street signs, no houses. Only black empty fields. She didn't know where he was taking her, but she had to get away from him. "I need a bathroom."

"There's bathrooms in the hospital."

"Now. I need one now."

He glanced at her briefly, then shifted his eyes back to the road. He sighed. "Calm down. Just ahead I'll stop for gas."

"Good. Okay."

At the city limits, he lowered his speed.

"There!" She pointed at a service station.

He drove on.

"Why didn't you stop?"

"Wrong side of the street."

Maybe so, but he could have gone around the block. Just when she thought he wouldn't stop he pulled in at a café in some little town she'd never been to.

The ladies room was way in the back. At the shiny sink, she stared at herself in the mirror. She'd gotten in a car with a stranger. Nobody knew where she was. How could she have been so stupid?

CHAPTER NINE

Pamela thought the day would never end. Work went slow because the fight she'd had with her daughter kept edging its way into her mind. With the certainty of a sixteen-year-old, Idana felt entitled to make her own decisions, confident she could handle any situation she got into.

When Pam said no to the party, Dany's response was typical adolescent. "Why can't I go? All my friends are going."

If Pam hadn't been in such a hurry, she might have handled it better, but she needed to get to work.

"To a party given by a twenty-two year old college boy? I find that hard to believe."

"That's because you don't trust me. You think I'm this little kid who can't cross the street by myself."

Okay, so there was some truth to that. Pam did tend to clutch and keep Dany at home where she'd be safe. College boys who invited sixteen-year-olds to their party raised the hackles on the back of her neck. "How many adults are invited?"

"How should I know? I didn't ask for a list."

"You don't know this boy."

"I met him. I know a lot of the kids he invited."

"Where did you meet him?"

"Around."

"Around where?"

"Just around. Why can't I go?"

Pam felt a headache coming on. "Because I said no, and I'm the parent."

"You never want me to have any fun."

Instead of saying she wanted Idana to survive into adulthood, Pam said she had to get to work. "Put the breakfast dishes in the dishwasher, please."

"Aunt Maddie wouldn't say no to everything."

"Yeah, well, your Aunt Maddie has a gun. Twenty-two year old college boys would know better than to ask her sixteen-year-old niece to a party." Pam checked her purse for sunglasses and tissues, pulled out her car keys and drove to the office.

At five-thirty, she eyed the work still not done. It had to be on her boss's desk before she could leave. He needed it in the morning. Her headache returned and she softly rubbed her temples. At twenty past six, she finished and sent it all to the printer. She collected the pages, tapped them easily against her desktop to even up the edges and placed the stack in the center of his desk.

At home, she collected the mail from the box by the door and glanced through it. More bills. Just when she thought she might get a little ahead, more bills. She kicked off her shoes and padded to the bathroom for Tylenol, shook two in her hand and swallowed them with a gulp of water.

Ten-year-old Molly came clattering down from upstairs. "Hi, Mom."

"Hey, baby, how you doing'?"

"Good."

Pamela pulled her close with a one-armed hug and kissed her cheek. "Is Dany in her room?"

"Un-uh. Can we have hotdogs for dinner?"

"Where is she?"

Molly shrugged.

"She was supposed to be here with you."

"She was here, but then she left."

"Where did she go?" Pamela was going to ground that

child until she was thirty. At least.

Molly quickly looked away and shrugged again.

Pam's headache was getting worse. "When was she here?"

"A while ago. When are we having dinner?"

"Let me change my clothes first." Pamela looked at her watch. It was a few minutes after seven. Where was Dany? She knew she was to come straight home from school to watch her little sister. All day Pam felt guilty about the argument and had planned to suggest a DVD of Dany's choice, and all the popcorn she could eat.

She was even going so far as to mention a trip to the mall this weekend for another look at the sweater Dany was so enamored of. But after leaving her sister alone all afternoon the mall was out.

She found her purse on her bed, dug out her phone and hit the first number on speed dial. After four rings the call went to voice mail. "Where are you, Idana? Call me this minute." She pressed end and hung up.

Twenty minutes went by with no call from Dany. Pam called again and left a second message, then went to the kitchen to see about dinner.

Molly slouched in, her face pinched with concern. "Mom?"

"What, sweetheart?"

"Is something wrong?"

"No, baby, of course not."

"Then what did you say to Dany?"

"I just left a message for her to call. She's probably on her way home. You want to see if we have any hotdogs?"

"Yeah!" Molly stuck her head in the refrigerator and searched. She turned to her mother with tears. "We don't have any."

"We can have something else. How about fish sticks?"

"I really wanted hotdogs." Molly wiped her face.

It wasn't like Molly to get so upset about hotdogs. Something wasn't right here. Pam pulled out a chair, sat down, and patted the seat of the chair beside her. "Come over here a minute."

Reluctantly, Molly scooted onto the empty chair.

"Do you know where your sister is?" Pam asked.

"No."

Pam looked at her. "Molly, are you sure? If you know anything, I expect you to tell me."

"I don't really know."

"Did you see her after school?"

Molly nodded.

"What did she say to you?"

"Nothing. She got all dressed up. In her new jeans and the shirt that she only wears for special stuff."

"Where was she going?"

Molly shrugged.

Pam picked up both Molly's hands and bent to look straight into her daughter's eyes. "Did your sister say where she was going?"

"Are you mad at me?"

"No, sweetie."

"You're mad at Dany?"

"Maybe a little. Are you sure you don't you know where she is?"

"No."

Pam waited a moment. "Molly, are you real sure? If you know anything, I expect you to tell me."

"She made me promise not to tell."

"Not to tell what?"

Molly scrunched her face in a frown. "That she was going out."

"Where was she going?"

"I don't know," Molly said unhappily. "She just left."

"Did she say anything before she left?"

"She said she had something to do. No, I think she said she had somewhere to go."

That party? Pam tried to keep the anger from her voice. "Instead of fish sticks, how would you feel about pizza?"

"Yeah!"

When the pizza arrived, Pam let Molly pick out a DVD and they ate watching *The Little Mermaid*. By that time Pam was furious. After being told no, Dany went to that party.

When the film was over, Pam busied herself supervising Molly's bedtime routine, ignoring the buzz of worry just poking around her mind. After Molly got tucked into bed, Pam heated coffee in the microwave and hit speed dial on her cell phone.

"Please call me, Dany. I need to know you're all right." She hesitated, then said, "I'm sorry about the fight. Maybe I do tend to be a little overprotective. Anyway, give me a call and we'll talk about it." She paused, then added, "I love you."

She hung up and waited.

And waited.

After thirty minutes, she couldn't wait any longer and left another message. When she got no response to the second message, she started calling Dany's friends. She asked each one, Do you know where Dany is? When was the last time you saw her? Who had a party tonight? Where was it? Do you have a phone number?

Each one said Dany hadn't been at the party. Nobody had seen her since yesterday. Marie, her closest friend, had texted her after school to find out what time she was going to the party. Dany had texted back that she couldn't go, she had something else she had to do. Marie didn't know what the something else was.

Dany wasn't home by midnight.

She wasn't home by six a.m.

CHAPTER TEN

Maddie inserted her car into the thick of the traffic and set off for west LA and Home Cookin', the restaurant where Francine worked. Stella Foster had been the manager for six years. Her office, about the same size as Maddie's cubicle at the Sheriff's Department, had a window, but it was blocked off by a file cabinet.

"Can I get you anything? Coffee? Tea? Pastry? Sandwich?" Stella was tall and trim with blond hair piled on her head making her seem even taller, oval face and small gold studs in her ears. In an ankle-length black skirt and a white silk blouse with gold buttons and gold cuff links, she was both elegant and business-like. File folders, menus, papers, and scribbled notes were piled on her desk.

Maddie said no thank you to offers of food or drink. She inserted herself between newspapers and menus on the brown tweed couch, careful not to fidget and send items cascading to the floor. A second file cabinet was wedged in at one end that held overflow.

"Is there any news about Francine?" Stella leaned forward with her forearms on her desk and linked her fingers together.

"Not so far. Was she a good employee?"

Stella nodded. "And very sweet."

"Sweet meaning good? Or sweet as a nice way of saying

not good?"

Stella smiled. "Very good. I wish I had more like her."

"Reliable?"

"Absolutely. And let me tell you that's not usual. My biggest problem is finding good help. Young people don't seem to grasp the fact that I'm counting on them and if they don't show up, or amble in an hour late, I have to scurry around and find somebody to cover for them."

"She was good with customers?"

"They liked her. She was friendly."

Maddie saw Stella hesitating, deciding whether to mention something further. Maddie waited in silence.

"Almost too friendly," Stella said.

"Too friendly?"

"She talked. You know, chatted away and mentioned things about her personal life. I told her a time or two that maybe this wasn't a good idea. To let people know things about herself. It could lead to complications. It seemed like she just couldn't help herself. She bubbled over. Happy. Positive."

"You like her," Maddie said.

"I do. You can't help but like her."

"You think somebody may have gotten the wrong idea? About spilling over facts in her life? A customer? Maybe got the idea she might be interested in him?"

Stella sighed. "No, no, not really. She said she only talked personal stuff with people she knew, but *knew* really meant anybody who'd been in before."

"But you were worried about someone in particular."

Stella took in a breath. "Maybe." She stretched the word into two long syllables. "There was this one man." She shook her head. "Oh, I'm sure it's nothing."

"Did someone hassle her? Follow her? Threaten her?"

"Nothing like that. I'm sure I'm wrong about him."

"Tell me about it," Maddie said. "I promise I won't rush right out and arrest him."

Stella gave her a small smile. "He didn't actually do anything. He's probably just lonely. It's just—" She frowned in thought. "It was the way he looked at her. Like she was this shiny new car that he wanted. I could almost see him checking the tires and running a hand over the fenders. He came in several times and he always looked at her the same way. It just kind of worried me."

"What's his name?"

"I don't know."

"Did he pay with credit card?"

"Always cash."

That stirred up suspicions. "What does he look like?"

Stella grimaced. "Oh gosh. Late thirties. Dark hair, dark eyes. Good looking." She picked up a pencil and tapped the eraser end against the desk. "He never caused any trouble or anything. I'd hate for you to think I'm accusing him of anything."

"How tall is he?"

"Six feet. There about."

"Weight?"

"Average, I guess. He certainly isn't overweight, or unusually skinny."

"Anything else about him? Scars? Smell? Accent?"

"Not really. Except—there's this—kind of air of danger."

"Was he in on Sunday?"

Stella thought a moment, then shook her head.

"Give me a call if he comes in again," Maddie said. "Tell me about that day."

"Francine was higher than a kite. It was her birthday and her boyfriend was taking her some place special. She could barely keep her feet on the ground."

"Anything unusual about the shift?"

Stella drew in a breath and blew it out. "Just the phone call."

"For Francine?"

"Yeah. You know, even as I was talking to the guy, I thought there was something kind of not right about the whole thing."

"The caller was a male? Did he give you a name?"

"I don't recall that he did. He started in speaking right

away. I told him to hold on and I'd get Francine so he could talk to her. He said that wasn't necessary and he'd be here soon."

"What time did he call?"

"Just before four. Francine had brought her dress and shoes and everything to work with her so she didn't have to go home to change. She was so excited she could barely keep the orders straight. I told her to get ready early." Stella snatched a tissue from the box on the desk and dabbed at her eyes.

"What else did the caller say?"

"That he was a friend of Paul's—"

"And Paul is?"

"Francine's boyfriend. He said, this caller said, there'd been an accident, and Paul had been hurt. And he—the caller, you know—was coming to get Francine and take her to him. He'd be driving Paul's car."

"Why was he driving Paul's car?"

"Something about she'd recognize the car so she'd realize that he knew Paul. Now that I say that out loud it doesn't make any sense."

"Francine recognized the car, but not the driver?"

"I guess so. She was so worried about Paul, she just dashed right out and got in. The car drove away and that's the last I saw of her."

"What kind of car was it?"

"Black. I can't tell one car from another, but Elsie said it was a Mustang."

Maddie spoke with Elsie, pretty blond, working as a waitress. In LA no one is what they do. Everyone is either an actor or a writer. Elsie was an actress who just happened to be waiting tables at Home Cookin' until her big break came. In the small room where employees stashed their belongings, two couches were pushed against a wall at a right angle.

Elsie sank down on one with a sigh of relief, probably glad to be off her feet. Maddie sat on the other couch and asked about the car that Francine got into. Elsie was certain the car had been a Mustang, new or at least newish, and nearly certain that it belonged to Paul Gilford. She'd seen it several times when Paul either brought Francine to work or picked her up after her shift.

She hadn't seen the driver except for a brief glimpse when Francine opened the passenger door to get in. No dome light came on, but the dash lights lent a slightly green-ish tinge to the driver's profile. "Eerie like, you know? Made me shiver." Elsie produced a replica of the shiver. Maddie thanked her for the information, gave her a card and told her to call if she remembered anything else.

In her car, with a window down to catch any breeze that happened by, Maddie called hospitals, and asked if an accident victim named Paul Gilford was treated or admitted on Sunday evening. No one with that name was seen anywhere. Maddie walked from store to store along the street around Home Cookin' and talked with employees and customers. Did you notice anything, or anyone, unusual on Sunday? Did you see a black Mustang? Did you see anyone acting suspiciously? Anyone loitering? Did you see Francine Ramsey? Notice anyone paying particular attention to Francine? Anyone get hassled? Particularly a woman. Was anyone followed or threatened or frightened for any reason?

Francine had been missing for over a day and a half. Time was running out.

Jesse wondered what his partner was up to. Knowing that streak of stubbornness, he was pretty sure she'd ignore the sheriff's orders to stay clear of the Palmer homicides. His cell phone vibrated and he held the steering wheel in one hand and shifted to get the phone from his pocket. He checked the caller ID. Lara. His heart jumped a notch. First thought, something happened to Cindy.

He flipped the phone open and pushed a button. "What's up?"

"Come home," Lara said. "Now."

"Are you all right?"

"Just come home."

"What's wrong? Are you hurt? Is Cindy all right?"

"Damn it, we talked about this."

"Has something happened to Cindy?" Jesse demanded.

"She's fine."

The big weight on his chest rolled away. "I'll be home later. I'm kind of busy right now."

"I don't care if you're saving mankind from extinction. Come home now. Or you won't find anyone here when you do."

"Lara, what the hell is going on?"

"We agreed."

"About what?"

"Come home!" She hung up.

He started to call back, then shoved the phone back in his pocket and checked with dispatch to let them know he was taking a break for personal business. He made a loop to get on the freeway. Traffic moved smoothly and in ten minutes, he swooped down the off-ramp, made a right turn and took the winding streets home.

This was no time for taking off except for emergency. The Palmer murders were high-profile. The Sheriff was getting pressure from above and Dirks didn't handle pressure gracefully. He was apt to respond like a rattlesnake poked by a stick. Jesse pulled into his driveway, cut the motor and slammed out of the car.

Lara, arms crossed, met him at the door.

"For God's sake, Lara, what's wrong? Where's Cindy."

She gestured toward Cindy's room. He shoved past and strode down the hallway. Cindy, kneeling on the floor, crooned to the pink cowboy hat on the bed. Her expression was a mixture of confusion, guilt and stubbornness. Blood wasn't dripping, she wasn't crying, turning blue, or lying unconscious.

He turned toward Lara who stood in the doorway. "All right, what's going on?"

"As if you didn't know."

"I don't know a fucking thing. You want to explain why you dragged me home?"

Cindy hunched her shoulders, flinching at his tone. "You said a bad word, Daddy."

He yanked back on his temper. "Somebody better say something." While still crisp, he'd lowered the volume.

"Cindy," Lara said. "Show your father what you have under the hat?"

Reluctantly, Cindy lifted the pink hat. Curled on the bed was a little bitty animal. Not stuffed. Alive. It was breathing and shivering, but the size of a rat, which it resembled, except it was beige and had hair on its tail and ears like a bat.

"Tell him where you got that thing," Lara said.

"It's not a thing. It's Haley and he's my friend."

"Cindy—"

"He doesn't like loud noises. Cause they scare him."

"Go ahead," Lara said to Jesse, "ask her where she got that thing."

Jesse crouched. "Cindy." Soft voice, barely above a whisper, he said. "Baby, where did you get this—"

She scooped up the animal, he hardly considered it a dog, and pressed it under her chin. "His name is Haley. He's mine."

"Where did you get him?"

"He's a birthday present."

Lara started to say something and Jesse shot her a glance that shut her up.

"Who gave you this birthday present?" he said.

"You did, Daddy."

Lara, cleared her throat.

"No, Cindy, I'd remember if I gave you this—"

"Haley, his name is Haley."

Giving this dog a name was going to make it more difficult to get rid of. "No, baby, I didn't. And that means you can't keep it."

"When someone gives you a birthday present, you're not supposed to throw it away."

"First, I want to know where you got it."

"The man."

A wiggle of worry crossed his neck. "What man?"

"Your friend. You asked him to give me the puppy."

Again Lara cleared her throat. Jesse ignored her.

"What did he look like, Cindy?"

Brown eyes wide and teary, she said, "Just old."

Jesse could tell she didn't know what she had done wrong, but she was aware that she'd done something. He tried to get a better description, but all he got was the man had a round face and kind of white hair.

"Don't hurt Haley," Cindy clutched the dog tighter, causing it to squeak.

"No, baby, I wont hurt Haley."

"You know you're not supposed to talk to strangers," Lara said.

"He wasn't. He was Daddy's friend."

"Did he look like me?" Jesse twisted his mouth to one side and crossed his eyes.

Cindy giggled through her tears. "Nobody looks like that."

"Were his eyes brown? Like mine?"

"Kinda. Just not so dark."

"Was he as old as you?"

She giggled again. "Daddy, you're silly."

From the look on Lara's face she agreed, and she was not amused.

"Was he as old as me?"

Cindy thought, then shook her head. "More like as old as Santa Claus.

Thorne? On my God. The dirtbag gave my little girl a dog? "I didn't tell him to bring you—uh, Haley. There's some kind of mix-up. That means you can't keep him. We have to fine out who he really belongs to."

He would not allow his daughter to keep a gift from that scum. His knees creaked as he stood up.

"Noooo, Daddy. He's mine. My present. I want him. I love him." Cindy clutched the dog tighter.

Oh shit. Getting rid of it wouldn't be easy. "We'll talk about it later. I need to talk to your Mom for just a minute."

In the kitchen he turned on Lara. "What happened? How

did she get that dog?"

"I don't know."

"What did you see?"

"Nothing."

"Come on, Lara. Cut the nonsense."

"Cindy wanted to go out and swing. So I said she could."

"Weren't you watching her?"

"Of course, I was watching her."

"Then how could some *man* give her a dog?"

"One minute. I took my eyes off her for one minute to take a shower."

"That couldn't have waited? A shower was more important than your daughter?"

Lara glared at him. "The shower is not the point here. We agreed to wait before getting a puppy. Now, you can get rid of it."

His cell phone rang. Caller ID showed the Sheriff's Department. He answered, listened, then hung up.

"I have to go," he said.

"Of course, you do."

He snapped the phone off and trotted to his car. Dispatch had received a call from Maddie. But he hadn't mentioned that to Lara.

He turned the ignition, punched a number in his phone and talked to his friend in sex crimes. "What do you know about Clayton Thorne?"

"Why are you interested in him?"

"I need the name of his parole officer. No time for explanations right now."

CHAPTER ELEVEN

By the time Maddie was free, it was already three o'clock. She was hot, tired, sweaty and all she wanted to do was go home and take a shower. She called Lockner and left apologies, due to her work load, she was unable to meet him for lunch. The reporter immediately called back and insisted it wasn't too late.

"Just come," he said.

"No. I—"

"You need to eat."

Maybe she did. By this time she was hungry, and also curious. Why did he push so hard? He wanted something. Finding out what he wanted might be to her benefit. She told him she'd be there in about fifteen minutes.

By middle of the afternoon, only a few late lunch customers lingered. Lockner, seated at a table in the rear, rose when she entered. He wore a tan cashmere jacket, over a light brown shirt with dark brown pants. No rings or neck chains, his only ornament of Southern California fashion was an expensive-looking watch.

He smiled as she joined him and indicated the plate of guacamole and chips. "Something to do while I waited."

The waitress brought her a glass of water and asked if they were ready to order. Without asking Maddie what she would like, he rattled off an order in Spanish, then turned to her. "Would you like a glass of wine or a beer?"

"Just coffee. I'm working."

"And I'll go with iced tea." Lockner closed the menu and handed it back to the waitress with a practiced smile. She smiled back. Hers was real.

"What are we having?" Maddie said.

"Quesadillas with carnitas, chicken chalupas, and black beans." He was a handsome man with thick wavy brown hair, and brown eyes, slightly over six feet tall, prominent cheek bones, a straight nose, and a full mouth that smiled easily.

The waitress brought her a mug, filled it with coffee, and set down a little pitcher of cream. Maddie added a dollop to the coffee.

"So Maddie." Lockner used his smile. "Short for Madeleine?"

"Yes." What else? "How did you know Gregory Palmer?"

"Ah. 'The face that drove me mad. The lovely Madeleine upon the bar room floor.'"

She managed to tighten her mouth, but it wasn't a smile. At least he didn't go with the one about *warm gules on Madeleine's fair breast*. "Did you even meet him?"

"I'll answer yours, if you'll answer mine." His smile appeared again. He used it a lot. "How long have you been in Mira Vista?"

She was aware he hadn't answered her question. "A little over two years."

"I met Palmer, when he first came here," Lockner said. "I interviewed him for the paper. You moved from some place in Kansas?"

"I did." Maddie saw no reason to tell him from where. He'd probably found it on the internet anyway. She picked up a chip and scooped up a dab of guacamole. Good. She tried another. Just as good.

"What made you leave Kansas for California?"

"I was looking for something new."

"After your divorce."

So she was right on about why he'd wanted her to join him for lunch. He was looking for information. Something specific, or information in general?

"And now here you are working on your ex-husband's murder."

"I feel like I'm being interviewed for your newspaper."

"Sorry. It's habit."

Before she could say I'll bet it is, the waitress returned and set large plates of food in front of them. When she left, he said, "I always do my homework. You were married to him for ten years."

Maddie let that go by without response. Lockner was fishing, hoping she'd be stupid enough to spill a fact or two that he could spin into a news article. "I'm not working that homicide. You need to talk with Detective Jones."

"Strictly off the record," Lockner said. "What was it like being married to a genius?"

"Strictly off the record, it's none of your business." So Lockner did some research on Greg and found out she was married to him. The internet, maybe. It was no big secret that she'd been married and divorced. She just never talked about it.

"Off the record," he said again.

"Off the record." She repeated. "Not a phrase I have much faith in."

"Maddie," he said with mock reproach and his spectacular smile. "I assure you. Whatever you tell me, I will respect your confidentiality."

"Really? Isn't that something like the judge telling the jury to ignore that last testimony?"

"I could hold back information, only print your side of the story when you agreed the time was right."

"What story?"

"The story of your marriage to Gregory Palmer."

"There is no story."

"It's quite a coincidence." He sipped at his iced tea. "Palmer is murdered, and his ex-wife who just happens to be a cop, just happens to find the body. Don't you think there's a fascinating story there? Readers will think so."

The waitress asked if they wanted anything else. When she left, Lockner said, "Why aren't you making an arrest?"

"Detective Jones is investigating."

Lockner nodded. "But you know who killed him."

She just stared at him, then shook her head. If this was his way of extracting information, it wasn't working. "I really need to get going. I have an appointment. Thank you for lunch." She started to slide from the booth.

"He told me."

"Who told you what?"

"Dr. Palmer." Lockner broke crumbled tiny pieces from a tortilla chip. "We talked about the research going on with stem cells. I asked if he got a lot of noise from people who were against it. And he said—" Lockner held out his hand palm up as though presenting her, ta-da. "You. He told me if anything happened to him, you would know who was behind it."

"Really," she said. "Isn't it too bad that he didn't share that information with me?"

"Off the record. I promise you. Why hasn't an arrest been made?"

"You keep asking that. What is your plan here? Creating a news article out of denial?" She stood up. "Thank you for lunch." She dropped her napkin on the table and walked out.

"He told you," Lockner said. "Stop pretending that he didn't."

Not only had she wasted her time, but she didn't even get to eat the lunch. Maddie retrieved her car, stuck the key in the ignition, and then let her hand drop. Why did Lockner believe that she knew who killed Greg? Did he actually believe it, or was he simply goading her, trying to get her to say something?

She turned the ignition. Lockner was lying. That's what newspeople did. They lied to get a story. She put the gear in reverse, backed out of the parking space and pulled away.

Paul Gilford's mother lived on the edge of Mira Vista,

the house a typical California stucco. Beige, one story, large window in front, flower beds here and there surrounded by white pebbles. A cold breeze tickled Maddie's face when she got out of the car. She slung the strap of her bag over her shoulder and hurried to the door.

Darleen Gilford answered. Forty-plus, wearing baggy gray pants and a gray sweatshirt, sleeves pushed up to her elbows. Faded blue eyes, light brown hair tied loosely in a jaunty yellow ribbon at the nape of her neck. Her eyes looked tired, red-rimmed as though she hadn't gotten much sleep. Lines that might have been considered laugh lines yesterday had deepened and overnight caused her to look older.

"Have you found Paul?" Hope surrounded the words. "Is he all right?"

"We're still looking." Maddie mentioned the phone call Stella had received from a man who claimed to be Francine's friend, who said Paul had been injured.

"Stella told me about that. I just don't understand. It doesn't make any sense. Why would some friend say Paul was in an accident and not say where he was? What friend? Wouldn't he call me and let me know what happened and where Paul was? And if he was okay?"

Suddenly Darleen seemed to realize they were still standing in the doorway. "Oh, I'm so sorry. I'm just so upset I don't know what I'm doing. Please come in."

She led the way to the living room. "It's kind of a mess, I'm afraid."

Books and magazines were stacked everywhere, on the piano bench, on the floor around the old upright piano, on the over-stuffed chair by the fireplace, and on the gray tweed sofa that had a shawl draped across the back with an embroidered angel playing a harp.

"What can I get you?" Darleen said. "Coffee? A cup of tea?"

"Nothing, thank you." Maddie seated herself in the over-stuffed chair.

"Coffee. It won't take but a minute." Darleen started for the kitchen.

"Please don't bother. I just need to ask a few questions."

"Are you sure?"

Maddie said she was sure. Darleen seemed disappointed. With no coffee to make, she didn't quite know what to do. She looked around uncertainly, then sat on the edge of the sofa and clasped her hands together between her knees.

"Excuse the way I look. I've been cleaning things." Darleen nudged a pile of magazines with her toe. "Closets. And then I get distracted and pick up something else. Just to keep busy. Sitting and worrying gets to you, you know?"

Maddie nodded.

"I don't understand what could possibly have happened. Paul's very responsible. Have you learned anything about Francine? I know her parents are frantic. Both kids. Just gone, like they vanished."

Darleen twisted her fingers together. "It's not good, is it?" she said softly.

Not good at all, Maddie thought. "Do you know if they had an argument?"

"Never. They got along like best friends." Darleen tried for a smile. "Maybe because they knew each other all their lives. Grew up together. We were neighbors when they were little."

Her words caught on a sob. "Have you found out anything? Anything at all?" She was pleading for some little fact that would suggest the situation wasn't as grim as she was afraid it was.

"Does your son carry a driver's license?"

"Of course. And he's a very careful driver."

If he had a license, or some other form of ID on him, a hospital would have his name. Did that mean he hadn't been carrying an ID? It had been stolen? Lost? Who was the male who phoned Stella, claiming to be Paul's friend? How did he get Paul's car?

Could Paul and Francine have concocted this story and taken off together? Gone to someplace like Las Vegas and gotten married? Could they have been abducted? The pair of them? Maddie asked questions about Paul, his friends. Had he mentioned any problem, anything troubling him? Was he happy about the upcoming wedding?

"Yes, yes, of course." Darleen was quick to jump in.

Oh oh, Maddie thought. A little bit of trouble about the wedding? "Mrs. Gilford," Maddie leaned forward. "I know you love your son—"

"More than anything." Darleen laced her fingers together.

"That's why it's important you tell me the truth. To find him, I need all the information you can give me. Did he and Francine have a fight?"

Darleen turned her laced fingers straight up.

Maddie could see her getting ready to deny it. "Unless I look in the right direction, I might not find him."

Darleen took in a deep breath and let it out with a little wheeze. "I don't know. It's true," she added quickly, as though Maddie might call her a liar. "I only know something wasn't right. I asked Paul, but he never talks about things. He was like his Daddy that way. Paul always said everything was fine. I knew that wasn't true so I pushed, but all I could get out of him was this girl he was studying with. She was taking some class the same as him."

"Someone he was interested in?"

"I don't think it was like that."

"What class?"

"Oh, gosh, I really don't know. It was just a class he was taking for fun. I think it might have been an art class. Why Paul wanted to take it, I have no idea."

Maddie made a mental note to check Paul's classes and find out who this girl was. Had Paul met someone new and his love for Francine cooled? Had he done something to her?

At six o'clock, Maddie left Darleen's house, tired and discouraged. Time was moving quickly. Maybe it had already run out for Paul and Francine. Maddie intended to get her weary self home, and use what remaining energy she had for a hot bath with Bach on the CD player.

Before she got her car started, Lockner's words played in her mind. Could Greg have written something in one of his notebooks? Scribbled something in a notebook?

That could be. Greg always did scribble in notebooks, the spiral kind with lined paper. Why would he have told Lockner that she would know who did it if something happened to him?

Like what? Could he actually believe that? Greg was always writing in spiral notebooks and leaving them all over the house. Could Greg have written down a motive for the murder? And the cops didn't find it? No that was ridiculous.

But there was that phone call to her. He was worried, said he needed help. He needed *her* help. For what possible reason could he need her help? And why would he tell any such thing to a reporter? Could he have been worried for some time before he called her? Possibly. He was leaving hints, making sure, if anything happened to him, the culprit would be caught.

Forget it. Lockner was blowing smoke. Get back to work. Find the missing Francine and her boyfriend.

Maddie put the car in gear and pulled out into the street. He wouldn't have. Lockner lied. Go home. She started to do that very thing, but there was just that little whisper that tickled her with images of Greg scribbling away. He had so much paper lying around with so much scribbling that unless he wrote something very clear like *if anything happens to me, this is the person who did it,* then it might have been overlooked. She turned on the headlights and set off for Greg's house.

You're wasting your time, Maddie. Headlights flickered on the trees as she drove the endless dark roads. Crime scene investigators and detectives had been all over the place. They didn't miss things.

She was relieved that no squad cars were parked in front of the house, no uniforms were keeping an eye on the place. Nothing moved but the yellow crime scene tape that fluttered in the wind. She retrieved a flashlight from the glove box, and slid from the car. The ocean breeze stung her face. The house was completely dark against a black sky, just like it had been the night of the murders. Hair stirred on the back of her neck. She shivered.

CHAPTER TWELVE

A teenage girl, sixteen or seventeen, with dark hair, dropped her tote bag on the step, shrugged off an over-stuffed backpack and pressed a thumb against the doorbell. She didn't get an answer. He knew she wouldn't. He knew Maddie had left hours ago. He'd watched her leave and planned on letting himself in right about now to check on the electronic equipment.

The girl folded herself down onto the porch step and dug around in the tote bag. Who was this kid? She came up with a cell phone and poked in numbers, spoke a moment and put the phone back. Had she talked to Maddie? He thought about wandering up, introducing himself as a neighbor and finding out her name, but he decided to wait and see if whoever she had called would show up.

About ten minutes later, a taxi pulled up and he heard her tell the driver, "Take me to the nearest shopping mall."

The driver didn't seem to know much English. He muttered something and took off. He got on a freeway and drove and drove and drove. For all she knew, he was taking her miles in the opposite direction. Or delivering her to some scumbag who would sell her into prostitution. Finally, he got off the freeway and turned into a parking lot. She swallowed a big bubble of relief.

"Which store," he said.

She pointed to Macy's and dug out her wallet. After she paid him, she had twenty dollars left. All the money she possessed between her and starvation. She lugged her belongings to the nearest entry.

The tote bag and backpack were a nuisance maneuvering through stores. Forget shopping. Forget looking at anything. Don't even glance at the rows and rows of purses. Okay, maybe, a quick peek at the cosmetics counters. A new lipstick would be fun, except it was too expensive. Her stomach rumbled and reminded her she hadn't eaten in hours and hours. Food. Any food. She wasn't picky. Breakfast had been a granola bar and now she was ready to eat the wrapper she'd stuffed in her pocket.

Her shoulders ached from the backpack. It weighed a ton. Why had she crammed so much in? She hiked it further up and walked around searching for a place that had food. Aha! Finally, she found a map and studied it. A bakery was just three shops down. All right! Not exactly what she most wanted, but food was food. She was famished.

The bakery turned out to be farther than it looked on the map and her feet hurt when she finally got there. A menu printed on the wall behind the counter listed all kinds of stuff. They had real food in addition to doughnuts. She ordered a chicken salad sandwich and a large Coke, handed over the twenty and accepted a receipt with her change.

Small round tables were crowded into an area beside the counter. She pulled out a chair and sat down, watched shoppers go by lugging fancy bags and waited for her sandwich to be ready. The number on her receipt was called just in time to prevent her from dying of starvation. She jumped up, collected her food and sat back down. She chomped off a big bite and was chewing away when a man sat at the table next to her. Wow. Handsome. Dark hair, dark eyes, suntan, tall and lean. An actor? Maddie said most everybody out here either was or was trying to be. Should she ask his name? God, no, how gauche could she get? But wouldn't it be neat if she met a famous movie star?

Joanie would just croak with jealousy. After a big gulp of

Coke to wash down the last of the chicken salad, she wiped her hands and rummaged through her tote for her Ipod. *Then*. She didn't know how it happened, but she wanted to die. The coke got spilled all over the place. The table, her lap, the floor, the actor-looking guy at the next table.

Shit. Embarrassed. Oh my God. The guy at the table jumped up and left. She didn't blame him. Soaking it up with her napkin didn't do much. Just as she started to go after more napkins, the kid from the counter appeared with a mop and a rag and took care of her mess. As soon as he was gone, the actor guy came back and set a new Coke in front of her.

"Stuff happens." He pulled out a chair from the next table.

She nearly swooned. Deep sexy voice. On top of that, he wasn't even mad. All she could think to say was, thank you. Even that got stuck in her throat.

Taking stuff from strangers was a big no no, date rape drugs and all that, but she wasn't on a date and she had just splattered her Coke all over him. Instead of yelling at her and sending her disgusting looks, he bought her another one.

"Is that a panther on your sweatshirt?" He settled back in his chair.

"Yeah, I guess. It's actually a wildcat, but I think, you know, they're really the same thing. Large cats." Oh jerk, jerk. That was really engaging talk! Just tell him you believe in Santa Claus too, why don't you?

"Where you from?"

"Kansas," she said, and waited for a joke.

He smiled. "The Sunflower State."

"I guess."

"Excuse me." He got up to retrieve his order. When he returned, she noticed he'd gotten the very same thing that she had.

"How was the sandwich?" He cut one half into half again and picked up the small piece.

"Pretty good. As long as it isn't all wet." Like me, she thought and shrugged her backpack onto her shoulders. She gave him a smile and another thank you and picked up her tote.

"Have a good one, Dany."

She stopped. "How did you know my name?"

He pulled a sliver of chicken from the sandwich. "You told me."

No, she hadn't. She might be a hick from Kansas, but she wasn't stupid. She got all those lectures about taking candy from strangers. Which she had—kind of— just done, but that was different. He was only being nice and, anyway, why would he drug her drink? A nut might do it so he could haul her away and do unspeakable things before he slit her throat. But this was just a handsome guy eating his lunch. Wasn't he?

All of a sudden, she felt woozy. Don't be stupid. Not enough sleep last night, that was all, and she was tired. She hadn't been drugged. He could have heard her name when the kid at the counter called it to let her know her order was ready.

That was it. She kept looking over her shoulder as she walked past shops. At a book store, she ducked inside. From the nearest table, she could look up and see who walked by. She picked up a book and read the cover flap, glancing up every few seconds. After twenty minutes and five book cover flaps, she decided he hadn't followed her. She wasn't going to drop into a coma from a drug slipped in her Coke.

She left the bookstore, turned into a side aisle and spotted a movie theater. *Pirates of the Caribbean* was showing. So what that she'd seen it a zillion times before? She could sit down and watch the movie, and by the time it was over Maddie would be home from work and she could call and Maddie would come and pick her up.

Inside the theater, she stumbled a little in the dark. When her eyes adjusted, she spotted an aisle seat, stacked her tote and backpack on the empty seat beside it and settled in to watch. The movie wasn't quite as enjoyable this time. Her mind kept circling back to how the handsome guy knew her name, to what she would do if he followed her, to what she would do if Maddie still wasn't home after the movie was over.

When the last credits rolled down the screen, she gathered her belongings, left the theater and went in search of a way out to the parking lot. She decided there was no need to mention the spilled Coke and the actor guy to Maddie. She didn't want Maddie to think she was a retard who couldn't handle herself.

When she finally got outside the mall, she was surprised to discover it was dark. The movie lasted a long time. She shouldn't have watched it twice. The stores were mostly closed. Those that weren't would close soon. She only had a little over five dollars. What would she do if Maddie still wasn't home to pay the taxi driver?

It was creepy standing here in the dark. Just go. She'd worry about the fare when she got there.

Chapter Thirteen

"What do you mean you can't find him?" Jesse jabbed a finger on the desk top in the small crowded office every available space crammed with files and folders and notes.

"Can you count, Detective?" Matthew Singel, seated at the desk, looked up with irritation.

A parole officer, Singel had sparse gray hair, a long narrow jaw and eyes that were slightly bloodshot as though he wasn't getting enough sleep.

"Look around you." Singel waved a hand. "Everything you see here pertains to a client. I've lost track of the count."

Jesse yanked back on his temper and threw himself in the only chair, a straight-backed wooden with one leg shorter than the others. It tilted whenever he moved.. "How could you possibly lose the whereabouts of Thorne? The man is a sex-offender. Isn't he required to register at the place he lives?"

For a moment Singel's tired eyes held a flash of anger. "Clayton Thorne is a predator and a con artist. He's also intelligent."

A flat noise escaped Jesse's mouth before he could prevent it. "In this day of computers, it's difficult to believe that anyone could escape detection."

"The reason he has not been located is because he moved." Singel leaned back and threw down his pen.

"Moved where?"

"Florida, the last I heard."

"I see," Jesse said.

"Do you, Detective? He doesn't stay in any place for long. He keeps moving."

"How can he support that lifestyle?"

Singel shrugged. "He comes from a family that has money. He also finds seeks out vulnerable woman—especially women with a small child—and befriends them, claims to love them. And dangles the carrot of he can take care of them. She no longer has to work and struggle with her bills."

Jesse rose, so mad he was breathing fire, but had enough sense to realize yelling at Singel wouldn't help. He thanked Singel for his time and asked to be notified if Thorn was found.

You're wasting your time, Maddie. She ducked under the crime scene tape and tried the door. Locked, of course. No matter. You learned a lot about a spouse in ten years of marriage. Once she'd locked herself out and needed to call him at work to come and let her in. After that he'd hidden a key in a plastic bag under the walkway. There was no walkway at this house, only paving stones going from the driveway to the porch steps. She looked under each stone with no success.

Damn it, how could she get in? Breaking and entering would not be a good idea. Joke. Ha ha. She shined the flashlight beam at windows as she went around the house, looking for one that might open. This was simply stupid. She was exhausted, she needed to forget what Lockner said and take herself home. If she wasn't feeling so blah, she'd have no hesitation about entering the house.

Okay, that did it. She needed to find herself, her cop self, the one invested in finding answers. That self wouldn't have hesitated. That self would have leaped tall trees to get into the house. She just felt tired. Never mind. She tucked her fatigue in someone else's closet.

It was just minutely possible that her being so late in

getting here, Greg wrote something somewhere explaining his need. That vital need.

In the rear of the house, paving stones ran from the kitchen steps to a shed that housed a tricycle and a variety of lawn tools. She crawled over nearly every stone before she found it. In a hollowed-out spot beneath the stone was a plastic baggy with a key inside. She tried the key in the kitchen door.

The key wouldn't open it. Okay, you tried. Time to leave. If she got caught here, she could be fired. Just get yourself in the car and drive off. Good advice, but she couldn't. Greg had some hold on her, like he was tugging at her sleeve to tell her something. Nonsense. She knew it. California was plain stuffed with ludicrous ideas. It was rubbing off on her. Probably she'd been here too long.

She stumbled around to the front, climbed onto the porch and slipped the key in the lock. She turned it and heard a click. Okay. One quick run through and then home. She opened the door and stepped inside. The smell hit her, the slaughterhouse smell of blood. Then the hushed silence. Not even traffic sounds penetrated the stillness.

Two images of Greg came, side by side, to mind. Their wedding day, Greg, face expressionless, handsome in his tuxedo, and the day he walked out. Face eager, excited, on to a new life.

She thought of two-year-old Caitlyn in her crib. Her crying would have increased Greg's anger and his awareness of his helplessness. Whatever jealousies, whatever regrets Maddie still carried deep in her soul, were obscured by sorrow at the pain he endured. What had the baby understood when she screamed and screamed and no one came?

Did she hear noises she couldn't understand? Frightening noises that made her know something was wrong? Was she old enough to experience terror? Had she learned the dark was a scary place? Monsters were attacking her Mommy. Was she calling for Mommy? Mommy didn't answer. Mommy's blood spurted arcs over white walls.

Maddie wasn't thinking of clues. She knew she wouldn't

find any such thing. But she could find ghosts, hear what they might tell her. She put a foot on the bottom of the stairway, and looked up. Her cell phone rang, nearly sending her into cardiac arrest. For a second she thought it was the sheriff's all-seeing eye glaring down at her from some perch on high. Voice almost as shaky as her hand, she fished the phone from her bag. "Detective Martin."

"Where are you? Weren't we supposed to have lunch?"

Lunch. With Elena. Oh shit. Not again. Oh, wait a minute. "Not today. On Thursday. Are you still available?"

"Sorry, I just finished a double shift. Thursday is good. You sound very strained. What are you doing?"

Looking for signs and omens in dried blood. "I don't even know. I'll see you Thursday."

"Yes, all right. Don't over-tax that shoulder. And remind me to give you the name of a therapist you should see."

Great, just what she needed. Another therapist who would explain that all her problems were because of her crazy mother. Maddie shoved the phone in her shoulder bag. One hand lightly on the banister, she took a deep breath and climbed the stairs. At the doorway to Caitlyn's bedroom, she heard them.

Ghosts humming and whispering of terror, of pain, of promises destroyed.

They were in the books on the shelf, in the toy box with the naked Barbie, in the crib with teddy bear sheets and in the small stuffed cat with long white hair. In the cry for *Mommy,* getting more and more frantic when Mommy didn't appear.

Maddie left them all and walked down the hallway to the master bedroom. Blood. Rust colored. On the bed, soaked into the carpet, splattered in arcs on the walls. The ghosts in here shrieked and wailed. She wanted to clap her hands over her ears to shut them out.

Tears ran down her face, as she went through the house, one snarled skein of emotion at a time. She found only two items of interest. A box of business cards with Changing Biology, Inc. in raised letters at the top, a logo and a cluster of pale peach-colored cells centered below. At the bottom, *Gregory Palmer, MD. PH.D Director of Stem Cell Research.* Address and phone number.

And a gun case along with a Glock, fully loaded. What was Greg doing with a gun? As far as she knew, he'd never even held one, let alone fired one. Could it belong to wife number two? Maddie didn't know much about Clarissa, but didn't think the dainty woman was the type to keep a loaded gun in her house.

A glance at her watch made Maddie realize she'd been here twenty minutes. She should leave. Now. Before she was caught. So much for finding any hint of Lockner's big story about having the answer.

On her way through the living room, she glanced at a blood-spattered spiral notebook on the couch. Greg had scribbled notes in his tight neat hand. The last page he'd written looked like math formulas and meant nothing to her, but one phrase caught her eye.

You owe me five farthings.

Maddie relocked Greg's door, put the key back where she'd found it and got in her car. On the winding road home, whatever adrenaline she'd experienced simply dissipated without bringing back what she'd hoped for

She was halfway home before she remembered the mail. She hadn't picked it up for a couple days. As tired as she was, she didn't think she could do one more thing. Tomorrow would do. By some miracle a parking place appeared right in front of Zephyr Mailboxes. She couldn't look away from a miracle. She pulled up and went inside. Rows of numbered boxes filled the room. She unlocked hers and scooped everything out.

Ads, bills, a small flat cardboard square, the kind used to mail a CD. Her address was printed in block letters. No return address. Had she ordered some music and forgotten? If she'd done that, surely the mailer would have a return address.

She dropped the whole stack on the passenger seat and

opened the small square mailer. There was a CD inside. It had nothing on it that identified it in any way. She put it back inside the mailer and drove off. When she turned onto her street, she saw the house was dark. Hadn't she left a light on before leaving this morning? She thought she had. Apparently not.

She pulled into the garage, gathered the mail and stepped into the kitchen. She put her shoulder bag down on the cabinet top, and remembered she hadn't closed the garage door. Just as she reached for the light switch, an arm closed around her throat. She felt the sharp tip of a knife.

CHAPTER FOURTEEN

"You even twitch," he whispered, "I'll slit your throat."

Maddie froze. Where was her gun? Kitchen. In her shoulder bag.

She kicked back at him, hoping to hit a kneecap. He grunted, his arm shifted slightly. She twisted free and stumbled. Helplessly she rolled down the three steps into the living room, and sprawled across the carpet. She started to turn her head. A vicious kick to her side sent pain shooting through her ribs. She tried to scramble away.

A knee landed on her back. Hands closed around her throat. Her heart pounded. She kicked and twisted and bucked. He squeezed tight. She couldn't breathe. Her lungs burned. She fought for air.

A scream!

High-pitched and nerve-shattering. It frightened her, and angered her assailant. He mashed her face hard into the carpet. Then his knee was gone and air rushed into her lungs. She rolled to her side, pulling in great gulps. A light went on nearly blinding her.

"Oh my God, Aunt Maddie! Are you all right?" A young woman rushed down the steps and knelt beside her.

"Idana?" Maddie squinted at her sixteen-year-old niece. "What are you doing here?"

"I thought he killed you."

Maddie touched the cut on her throat and rubbed the smear of blood between her fingertips. "As soon as I call this in, I'll ask why you're here."

Idana breathed loud and hard. "I already did. You know, called about it."

"Good." Maddie swallowed, and swallowed again.

"Did you know your garage door was open?" Idana knelt by the steps to pick up the scattered mail.

Burglar? Had she come home before he could pluck up all her valuables? Of which she had none. "He had a knife—?"

Idana dropped the mail on the piano bench, bent down and grabbed the knife. She turned toward Maddie to hand it to her.

"Drop the knife!" A man stood on the steps into the living room.

Maddie looked up at Deputy Fenton

"Drop it!" He drew his gun. "Now!"

Idana, still clutching the knife, turned toward him. Fenton leveled his gun at her.

"Fenton!" Maddie yelled. "No!"

Idana stiffened, zipped both hands in the air, one still holding the knife.

"Drop it!"

"Fenton," Maddie bellowed.

Idana knelt, carefully laid the knife on the floor.

"Hands on your head!"

"Fenton!"

He glanced at Maddie. "What!"

"Put the gun away." Maddie said each word clearly. "She was the one who called you."

"This kid didn't break in?"

"No."

"Then who was it?" Fenton jammed his gun in the holster on his hip.

"I don't know, Fenton." Tired, discouraged, depressed, jazzed up on adrenalin and blitzed silly by Dany's arrival,

Maddie took herself to the couch.

"Your garage is door open. That's probably how he got in." He glared at Dany. "Where'd you get that knife?"

"Over there." Dany pointed.

"Fenton, she is not the assailant."

"If you say so," he said, sounding unconvinced. "I want to know what she's doing with a knife."

"I stepped on it. He ran. He must have dropped it. And I just—I just—" Dany took a breath. "I'm sorry. I wasn't thinking."

"Obviously," Fenton said.

Dany was nearly in tears. "Will it matter? He had on gloves."

He did have on gloves. Maddie remembered the feel of latex when his hands were around her throat.

Two paramedics in blue jumpsuits came through the kitchen and trotted down the steps to the living room. "Did you know your garage door is open?" one said. They set down their gear. The other asked Maddie if she had a headache.

Fenton said he'd go question neighbors, ask if they'd seen anyone. Maddie doubted he'd learn anything. He was more apt to get any possible information wrong.

A paramedic wrapped a blood pressure cuff around Maddie's arm and pumped it up. The other shined a light in her eyes and told her to follow it without moving her head. He cleaned the scratch on her neck, put something antiseptic over it and applied a small piece of tape. The other listened to her heart. She was certain that fear and fury had combined to produce something akin to a jack-hammer rhythm.

"Keep the wound clean and dry." They gathered up all their equipment and were going out through the kitchen just as the forensic team was coming in. "Hey," A tech jerked a thumb over his shoulder. "Did you know your garage door is open?" They went to work, looking for fingerprints, fibers, hair, anything the assailant might have brought with him.

"Wow," Dany said as she watched wide-eyed. "Just like TV."

"Special attention," Maddie said. "I'm a cop." At least she used to be. A year ago, she would have responded much more quickly and used her training to extricate herself from a creep with a knife.

"Dany, what are you doing here?" Maddie swallowed.

"Can I get you anything? You want me to make some coffee?"

Maddie dearly wanted a glass of water and an aspirin or two, but she knew a diversion when she heard one. "I want you to tell me what you're doing here. Where's your mother?"

"Home," Idana said. "Back in Kansas."

Maddie had an inkling she wasn't going to like the answer to her next question. "She know you're here?"

"Not exactly."

"Not exactly. Uh-huh. What does that mean?" She needed to call the airlines and find out when the next plane left for Kansas City. What would have happened if Dany was here?

"I left them a note," Dany said.

"A note." Maddie rubbed two fingertips up and down her forehead. "What did it say?"

"That I was at Joanie's house. I'd be back in a few days."

"I assume Joanie is a friend."

"She invited me," Dany said defensively. "She lives in Kansas City. I've visited her lots."

"What happens when your mom calls Joanie's parents and discovers you're not there?"

"She won't."

She will, Maddie thought. Her own mentally ill mother would not have. She would have been too busy listening to voices in her head telling her government agents were planning to invade the house, or she'd be too certain the numbers on the phone were poisoned and if she touched them she'd die. Then who would take care of her children? She made Maddie promise to always take care of her little sister Pamela.

"Excuse, please." A slight man with black hair stood on

the steps into the living room.

Maddie automatically slid a hand down by her side, feeling for her gun. It was still in her purse where she'd dropped it in the kitchen.

"Need money for fare."

"What?" Maddie wondered what else would occur this night.

"Need to pay."

"Oh, I forgot," Dany said. "I saw that creep choking you and everything went out of my mind."

"Door is open." He pointed over his shoulder. "Need to collect money."

"What's he collecting for?" Maddie said.

"I didn't have enough for the taxi. I thought I could borrow some from you. Just to pay him," Dany added. "I'll pay you back."

Maddie opened her mouth to ask more questions to clarify the situation, but it was just too much for her. "I think my purse is in the kitchen. See if you can find it."

Dany found the purse and Maddie gave the driver his money. He bowed, said a thank you and left.

"How did you get here?" If Idana said she hitchhiked, Maddie was not only going to yell, she was going to jump up and down while yelling and then give her niece a seriously scary-ass lecture on what could happen to young women who hitch-hiked.

"Please let me stay."

"Dany—"

"You don't want me here."

"Oh, Dany, of course, I want you here, but you saw what just happened. You could have been the one with a knife at your throat."

"You said I could come to visit."

"I did and I meant it. But right now is not a good time." Not when young women are turning up missing and I can't figure out what happened to them, and not when I don't understand why my house was broken into. And not when there have been two brutal murders. And not when I need to figure out who killed Greg and why. And if there's a connection— Maddie blinked, her frozen mind finally beginning to tick over again. Was that it? The assailant was the killer? Dany saw the man. Would he think he needed to eliminate a witness?

"I won't be any trouble," Idana said.

"You're never any trouble. It just isn't the time."

Dany's expression was so laden with angst that Maddie knew something happened at home. She remembered what it was like to be a teenager and feel nobody understood you. She also knew what it felt like to have a crazy mother. Kids said very hurtful things and behaved like assholes, pretending to be her mother and acting crazy. Her little sister always cried. Maddie got furious and whaled into them. She was constantly in trouble.

"It's just dangerous around here right now, and I can't do my job if I'm worrying about you. It just isn't the right time."

"Yeah, you said that. Three times now." Idana picked up her backpack, shoved a strap over one shoulder, swung the pack around and stuck her arm through the other strap. "Thanks anyway." She started for the door.

"Where you going?"

Dany shrugged. "I figure there's a motel somewhere around."

"Don't be ridiculous. Get back here and sit down."

Dany, mulish expression on her face, walked over to the easy chair in the corner and plopped down.

"I need to tell you something."

Dany stuck her chin out, ready to close her mind to whatever Maddie was about to say.

"Greg," Maddie said, "the man I was married to—"

"I know who Greg is."

"Yes, of course, you do. His house was broken into and—" Maddie hesitated.

"Yeah, so?"

"He was killed."

"Oh." Dany slumped off her stiff defiance. "Gosh, I'm sorry, Aunt Maddie. Do you know who did it?"

"Not yet. But I *will* find out." It's just going to be a little tricky without losing my job.

"I know you thought he was grade A neato. Are you all torn apart?"

"I am, yes."

"Even after he dumped you?"

With a helpless shrug, Maddie nodded. "As soon as the CSIs are finished, we'll go out somewhere and get something to eat. First you have to call your mother and tell her where you are."

"I know."

"Despite what you think, Pam will be frantic when she discovers you aren't with your friend."

"But—" Dany gasped.

Maddie turned to see what frightened her. Jesse stood on the steps into the living room. "Maddie, did you know your garage door is open?"

Maddie's headache was getting worse. "Idana, this is my partner, Jesse. Now you may go into the kitchen to make your phone call. And would you please close the garage door for me."

Dany murmured, "Nice to meet you," as she sidled around Jesse.

"Who's the kid?" Jesse said.

"My niece."

"What's she doing here?"

"Mother-daughter not seeing eye to eye."

"Tell me about it. That scumbag gave my daughter a birthday gift."

"What scumbag?"

"Thorne. Daughter wants to keep it, wife says absolutely not. You never heard such screeching and carrying on."

"So. Dad," Maddie said, "what did you do to settle this dilemma?"

"I said I had to go to work."

"Ah, of course. Very sensitive."

"Exactly what my wife says." He seated himself on the chair Dany had vacated. "What happened here?"

Maddie related the incident. "And Fenton nearly shot my niece."

"On purpose?"

Maddie gave him a tired smile. "Very funny."

"Did you recognize the guy?"

She shook her head. "It was dark and I never really saw him." But there had been a moment when she'd thought he was familiar. It was gone so quickly, she couldn't remember why she got that impression. She estimated height and weight, and did recall the arm at her throat was clad in blue denim. And that he was quite strong.

When Dany slouched back, Jesse asked her what she remembered.

"It happened so fast." She slid onto the other end of the couch. "I was so terrified about Maddie. In the dark, all I could tell was somebody was choking her."

"What did he look like?"

"I don't know. I screamed and he ran."

"Did you notice anything about him? How tall, clothes he was wearing, shoes? Anything?"

Dany thought a moment and shook her head. "Just that he wears Armani aftershave."

Jesse closed his eyes and took a calming breath. "Okay. Maddie, is anything missing?"

"I haven't had a chance to look," Maddie said.

"Do it now," he said.

She made a quick pass through the house, didn't notice anything missing, except the CD she'd brought in with the mail.

"What CD?" he asked

"I'm not sure. It was in my mailbox. Nothing on the packaging but my address. No return address. No label of any kind."

"You think that's what he was after?" Jesse sounded dubious enough to suggest that the incident had rattled her mind.

"It's the only thing that seems to be missing," she said a little sharply.

Jesse leaned against the side of the piano and gave her a critical look. "You okay, Maddie?"

"Fine." She shifted around on the couch, bent her knees and curled her feet up under her.

"Okay," he said. "So what happened?"

"I just told you. I came home. The bastard jumped me, put a knife at my throat."

"Right." A look of non-understanding crossed his face. "To snatch a CD with no return label and that you have no idea what was on it."

"Yes."

"That's it? That's all you're going to tell me?"

"That's all there is."

"Let me remind you what I said to you once upon a time about lying to your partner." He crossed his arms. "Don't do it."

"I'm not—"

Dany came back and held out her cell phone. "Mom wants to talk to you."

Maddie took the phone.

"You mind if I take a shower? I was on the bus for ages and ages and I've been wearing the same stuff for two days. And I just feel kind of, you know, sticky?" Dany grinned. "Besides I'll give you a little privacy to talk to your—" She waved a hand at Jesse.

Maddie managed a brief hello.

Pamela said, "You put her up to this, didn't you?"

"I'm going to book her on the first available flight home. I'll have her call and give you times."

"She said she's not coming home, she's staying."

"She can't."

"That's what I told her. She says she's going to anyway. If you won't let her stay with you, she'll find somewhere else."

"Look, Pam, she's just upset. I'll talk to her."

"Lots of luck. She takes after you. Stubborn and pigheaded and willful. Save your breath. Let her stay. At least, that way I'll know where she is."

"You don't understand. She can't—"

"Tell her I love her." Pam hung up.

Maddie clenched her teeth, and jabbed buttons to get Pam back. The call was picked up by an answering machine. With supreme restraint, Maddie didn't shout. In a calm voice, she said, "Don't be childish, Pam. Pick up the phone."

No response.

Maddie disconnected and hit redial. Pam did not pick up the phone, the answering machine did and said please leave a message. Maddie's voice was a little higher and a little louder. "Talk to me, Pam." She waited, then said, "Call me back, or I swear I'll ask Dany to leave and you won't know where she went." She hung up.

"More problems?" Jesse said.

"My sister," Maddie growled.

"Yeah? You lie to her too?"

Maddie considered throwing the phone at him.

"What's the problem?" he said.

"My head is pounding, my throat is sore, my voice is hoarse, and my niece just stuck herself in the middle of whatever it is that makes young women disappear and ex-husbands get their throats sliced. Other than that, nothing."

He grinned, sat beside her and patted her hand. "Okay. Tell me everything. You know I always have the answer."

"Ha." She turned, put her hands around her knees. "What I already told you is everything with the exception of one small omission." She confessed to going through Greg's house, but didn't mention the scribble about owing five farthings.

"Anybody see you?"

"Somebody must have. Cutter of the FBI said someone called them."

"Anything else you haven't told me?"

Fingertips against her temples, she made small circles. "What am I going to do about my niece?"

"I can help you there.

She snorted. "Really. What can you do?"

"Give her a job."

"Oh yeah? What job would that be?"

"Child care. Lara needs help. She's on the verge of stressed out. If Dany is interested, she can spend much of her time at my house."

Maddie looked at her partner. "And come here when I'm home."

"If she wants to do this, of course," he said.

"Of course." Maddie had misgivings, a strong apprehension that this would not work out like everyone hoped.

Chapter Fifteen

Dany did everything but dance up and down clapping when Jesse explained his job offer. After she was settled in the spare room—empty except for a bed—she called her friend Joanie to share in the excitement. Maddie took two aspirin and went to bed. Even though fatigue hung heavy, she had trouble getting to sleep. She worried about agreeing to Jesse's offer, she worried about Dany, she wondered how Lara would feel about Dany babysitting Cindy, she worried about the missing Francine, she worried about losing her job as she hunted for Greg's killer, she worried about little Caitlyn who was only two and had lost both parents.

Just before dawn, she finally fell asleep. She felt herself struggling against the dream, jerking her head back and forth, trying to wake, but she slid into that dark night.

Wind howled, tree branches bent and thrashed. She stumbled over uneven ground, her coat was snagged by grasping tree limbs. She yanked it free, folded it around her and played her flashlight across the dirt path. The corpse lay in a shallow grave covered with decayed vegetation. Maddie crouched. A skeletal hand emerged from the dirt, the fingers shook off dirt.

The dead lips parted. "Why—"

Heart pounding, Maddie snapped awake. Wind howled around the house and shook the windows. A moment passed before she realized she was awake, in her own bed, with an actual storm blowing outside. She lay back, pulled the blankets tighter around her chin and willed herself to go back to sleep. Lie still, concentrate, think of a quiet peaceful place. Feel yourself drifting on a cloud.

The cloud she chose had holes in the bottom. She couldn't think of a peaceful place, except the bathroom, which wasn't peaceful, only the safest she could find because it had a lock. Four years old, arms across her chest holding herself tight, squeezed in beside the toilet, hiding from her mother who was talking to someone who wasn't there. Her mother's periods of madness frightened her. Especially when her mother noticed her and yelled at her. "You'd better get out of there, Madeleine. The green zipper is coming after you."

It wasn't until she was older that she realized her mother was saying grim reaper. That wouldn't have been nearly as terrifying. At four, she had no idea what a reaper was. She turned over several times trying for a more comfortable position. No matter what she tried, thoughts pushed into her mind. Dany, Greg, Francine, Caitlyn, Jesse, Dirks, the stupid dream. A dead woman wanted to know why. Why what? Maddie sighed. Was her shrink correct? The dead woman was Maddie herself, Maddie who wanted to know why. Why what? The shrink didn't hazard a guess. Maddie would realize the answer herself when she was ready to face it. Whatever it was.

She turned over again and gave her pillow a bash. Where was Francine? Too much time had gone by. Most likely Francine was no longer alive. With a sigh, Maddie threw back the blankets, got up and grabbed her fleecy purple robe from the closet.

The dining room, empty except for a desk with her computer, desk chair, bookcase with a tuner and CD player on the top shelf. She hit the play button on the CD player and got Beethoven's Moonlight Sonata. Not one of her favorites.

She booted up her computer, hit Firefox and typed in Gregory Palmer. She got a few dozen hits and clicked on an article in the *San Francisco Chronicle*.

Kansas-born Gregory Palmer was hired to head up stem cell research at a new company in Southern California called Changing Biology, Inc.

Undergraduate degree from the University of Kansas, Medical Degree from Johns Hopkins. Married to Clarissa Ann Daniels, one child, Caitlyn. *People* magazine had his picture on the cover along with an article listing a page of accomplishments. The *Mira Vista Times* had an article with Matthew Lockner's byline. So Lockner wasn't lying about that.

"Being part of the extraordinary progress of biomedical science has given me much to work with," Greg was quoted as saying. "No branch of science has grown more rapidly or produced more dramatic results. The scientific break-through has great potential use in the treatment of many diseases. We have only hit the beginning of what can be done. We are standing on the beach looking at footsteps in the sand that are as yet unknown."

Stem cell research was intensely political, and a major issue for the President and Congress. Research depended on funds, largely supplied by the National Institute of Health to support all university researchers as well as technological and chemistry industries. The government that giveth also taketh away, in the manner of stringent rules of what could and could not be done with the resources it gave out. Committees were required to approve new experiments.

Maddie read about biomedical ethics until she was nearly cross-eyed and nodding over the key board. She typed in Changing Biology, Inc. The business was formed two years ago by a former professor from Stanford, Robert Gertz, and billionaire Justin Maylor. They acquired a building, hired a crew and brought in Gregory Palmer to head the unit on stem cell research. Now privately funded, they could ignore governmental restrictions and rules.

Something like a million hits came up for Justin Baylor. Several for Robert Gertz, including an obit. He was an avid collector of old cars, liked to rebuild engines and restore interiors. A Riley and an MG had awaited attention in his garage He had turned on a space heater to alleviate the cold and a fire broke out. Cause was speculated due to a faulty heater. Gertz suffered serious burns over thirty percent of his body and died three days later in the hospital. His family sued the maker of the heater. The lawsuit was settled out of court.

Justin Maylor said he was certain Gertz would want the work at Changing Biology, Inc. to continue and he promised to keep the company alive so the valuable research being done there would not be lost. Shortly after Getz's funeral, Maylor traveled to Switzerland for an extended stay. Whether he was still there, Maddie couldn't discover. She did learn he was generous with contributions to worthy causes.

She started to turn off the computer but decided to check email. Since she hadn't looked at it for a few days, she had two hundred and fifty-three messages. Any sender she didn't recognize, she deleted quickly, zip zip zip, one after another. Finger poised to delete a message from *cad* she hesitated. It was sent Monday with no subject line. She clicked to read it. Eight words appeared, all strung together. AlbertCorban-Charlotte MyersMasonWhiteStephanieMannington.

She assumed they were names, but she didn't know any of them no matter how she paired them. After printing the email, she checked Google. Albert Corban turned out to be Doctor Corban and she got several hits. The other three resulted in about a zillion hits each. She quickly realized the three women had two things in common. They were all rich and all deceased. Dr. Corban, as far as she could discover, was still among the living. Who sent the email and what it meant, she hadn't a clue.

Enough. Back to bed. Sleep. She managed to get an hour before her alarm clock dinged. She showered and dressed, looked in on Dany and found her niece sprawled across the bed still fast asleep. Gentle nudges on Dany's shoulder got no response. Maddie shook harder.

"Wha—?"

"Time to get up, Sunshine."

"I'm up." Dany rolled over and snuggled into the covers.

Maddie patted her rear. "Up, sweetheart. I have to leave in a few minutes."

"Uh-huh."

"Hey! You have a job. Up and at 'em!"

"Oh my gosh!" Dany shot out of bed and ran to the bathroom. A few minutes later, she dashed into the kitchen, hair dripping but dressed in jeans and a blue sweatshirt. She grabbed a handful of chocolate chip cookies and said she was ready.

Maddie backed out of the garage and noticed a black SUV on the opposite side of the street. Tinted windows kept her from clearly seeing the driver. She swung out into the street, shifted and rolled toward the vehicle. As though he'd been watching, the driver took off with a roar and careened around the corner. All she could determine was that the driver was male.

Probably somebody going to work, just like she was. She dropped Dany at Jesse's house. "I'll call you later to see how it's going."

Her partner hadn't yet gotten in to work when Maddie arrived. She took a seat at his desk.

Lara was still asleep when Jesse got ready for work. Just as well, Jesse thought. Having Maddie's niece baby-sit had seemed like a brilliant idea at the time, but he could tell Lara wasn't thrilled. It seemed she wasn't thrilled by much of anything these days.

He heard Maddie's car and opened the door to let Dany in. He took her to meet his daughter. Cindy had gotten herself all dolled up in her best party dress, pale blue with a full skirt, a ruffle around the hem and buttons from her waist to her chin. It was last year's, so it was a little tight. She'd even put on her black shiny party shoes.

All dressed up, she waited on the beanbag chair scrunched in the corner, pretending to read a book with Haley the dog in her lap. When he brought Dany in, Cindy popped up, face screwed up with doubts. After introductions, he told them to call him on his cell phone if they needed him, then he took himself to the kitchen and lingered over a cup of coffee, stretched it, stretched it, stretched it until the last drops were stone cold.

When he didn't hear any wailing, he went back to kiss his daughter goodbye. She was chattering away to Dany and barely acknowledged him. He checked on Lara, who was pretending to be asleep. He headed out for work.

He found Maddie sitting in his desk chair with the look of a cat waiting to pounce.

"What?" he said.

"The blood pattern analysis."

"What about it?"

"Still on for today?"

"Maddie—"

"I know. I know. I can't be anywhere near. I just want to be sure you'll tell me what he finds."

Jesse blew out an irritated sigh. "I told you I would. Jesus, Maddie, you're being a pain in the ass."

"Okay. Okay. You'll bring Dany to my house this afternoon?"

"Don't do it," he said.

"Do what?"

"Don't pretend you don't know what I'm talking about. I know you very well."

"You think so?" She was getting slightly pissed.

"Get out of my chair."

She didn't move. He rested a hip against his desk. "Your mind is busy spinning out—" He raised his voice an octave, *"My ex-husband, the one who loved me and left me, has got himself murdered. Why don't I scurry around my partner and figure out who dunnit? And keep it secret from my partner, the investigating detective."*

Jesse gave the chair a spin with his foot. "Grow up, Maddie." His voice went back to normal. "Be an adult. Follow the rules."

Grow up? Be an adult? Now she was seriously pissed.

"Tell me, Maddie. How much thought did you really give to this Palmer guy before he got himself offed?"

She didn't bother to reply, just stood up, turned on her heel and headed for the door.

"That's adult," he called after her. "Just walk away."

She did. She walked out to the parking lot and got in her car. So what that she hadn't thought about Greg lately? It didn't matter. She had to find his killer.

Jesse gave a vicious shove to his chair. It shot forward and clattered against the desk. Stubborn, stubborn, stubborn. Why the hell should he care? If she wanted to get herself thrown out on her rear, that was her choice. Damn it anyway. He stomped out to his car and drove to the Palmer residence to meet Agent Cutter.

Cutter, leaning against the passenger door of the black SUV, straightened when Jesse pulled up behind him.

"Jones." Cutter said flatly.

"Cutter." Jesse returned in the same flat tone with the same flat smile.

They started in the rear, outside the kitchen door. Cutter was methodical. He carefully measured and photographed blood stains and recorded all his findings on a small tape recorder.

There was no blood on the outside of the door. On the inside, a smear appeared on the knob and a splatter with a long streak ran down the door panel ending in a puddle at the bottom. Drops and splatters were prevalent on the kitchen cabinets, the counter tops and the floor. They were no longer red, but rust and brown and black. A kitten magnet pinned a painting of pink and blue blobs to the refrigerator. Jesse wondered if two year old Caitlyn had screamed while her parents were being killed. Would she have nightmares from that night?

Between the kitchen and dining room a large square of hardwood floor had been removed. It contained a footprint that was taken into the lab. So far they had no suspect to compare it with. The dining room had a large black stain on the floor near the curved window.

"This would be where Clarissa was first attacked," Cutter

said. "Blow to the head, severe enough that she fell and bled copiously." He pointed to the window pane with curved spatters. "Castoff."

A highchair was pulled up to the table. A child's pink sock lay on the tray among the smears and splotches of her mother's blood.

"There were two of them," Cutter said. "Clarissa was made to walk, or more likely half-carried into the living room."

Blood was everywhere. Cutter described each stain, shape, size, and what caused it. He explained splatter, contact smears, linear smears, and impact spatter and castoff streaks. Jesse didn't much care for Cutter, the FBI agent always moved like he had a broomstick up his ass, but he was thorough.

Blood had run along the edge of a couch cushion and collected in a corner on the underside.

"Palmer, sitting on the couch with his book, was probably threatened by a second man with a gun, and warned what would happen to Clarissa if he didn't do as he was told."

Cutter then speculated Palmer, gun at his back, was made to go upstairs into the bedroom. The first man dragged Clarissa up behind them. Cutter pointed to blood smears that showed someone was pulled up the stairs.

The master bedroom was where it ended.

Palmer was tied to the chair. With him taken care of, the two killers could relax a bit. Clarissa got tossed on the bed and tied down. They made Palmer watch while they tortured her. That got them whatever they were after, then they cut her throat, and most likely, immediately after, cut his.

Cutter thought either Palmer didn't tell them everything, or the room was tossed before they started on Clarissa.

In the middle of the afternoon, Thorne watched the young woman take Cindy's hand and set off down the street. Cindy gripped a carrying case with the puppy inside. He smiled. When they got to the park, Cindy pulled her hand free, dropped the carrier by the entrance and ran for the swings.

He walked briskly past and went all the way to the other side of the park where serious joggers were exhausting themselves running around in circles. He settled on a bench beneath a row of pine trees and opened his paper. Life was good. He was free, and he had a plan set in motion toward revenge.

He glanced over the front page. Police still had no luck finding the missing Francine Ramsey. Well now, looks like Detective Jesse Jones is not so hot as an investigator.

Chapter Sixteen

Francine had been missing since Sunday night. Still alive? Maybe. But every hour that went by reduced the odds. Maddie called Professor Osborn, who taught the art class that Paul took. Osborn was unavailable. She left a message asking him to call her and went to see Francine's best friend.

Jill Meisner, Francine's best friend according to Francine's mother, a student at UCLA, lived in the apartment with two other students. She had skipped American Lit class to meet with Maddie.

Maddie rang the bell, heard the buzzer that unlocked the door and entered the building. A young woman in baggy gray sweats bent over the railing and called down, "Up here."

Maddie trudged up a flight of stairs, and Jill led her into a room crowded with odds and ends of furniture, a kitchen table against one wall, large pillows scattered on the floor, television and CD player against another wall, and large speakers in the empty spaces everywhere. Maddie sat in the only chair, a Goodwill reject of vaguely beige color with frayed fabric on the arms.

"Have you found her?" Jill, a petite blond with an oval face, a pointed little chin and tight curls that hugged her head, crossed her ankles and folded herself effortlessly down onto a monster pillow.

"Not yet. Do you know where she is?" Maddie asked.

Jill, wide-eyed and solemn, shook her head.

"Is it possible that she and Paul went away together to some place romantic?"

Jill grinned. "If it were me, I'd jump at the chance. My idea of romance is a fireplace and a candlelit meal in a suite of some fancy hotel."

"What about Francine? What's her idea of romance?"

Jill grabbed her right ankle and folded it into her left groin, then folded her left ankle. It made Maddie wince just to watch.

"A big fancy wedding with hundreds of guests," Jill said. "A spectacular dress. Masses of flowers. Piles of food, and people talking about how wonderful it all was. Oh and tables of gifts."

"You sound very sure."

Jill nodded. "She wouldn't go away without telling me. We told each other everything."

Maddie asked questions. Did Paul and Francine have an argument, was Francine happy to be marrying him, did she resent her mother for taking over and making all the decisions about the wedding? Jill answered no to each.

"What about Paul?" Maddie said. "Was he as eager to get married as Francine was?"

"Well," Jill paused. "I think so. He never said anything like, wow, I sure wish I wasn't getting married in a few months."

"Did he ever mention any other women he was interested in?"

"Not to me."

"You never heard him mention anyone?"

Jill shook her head

"What about Francine? Any boyfriends who got dumped when she got engaged to Paul?"

"Dumped? No, not really." Another pause. "There's Charley, of course.

"Charley—?"

"Fowler." Jill twisted her mouth back and forth, deciding what to say about him. "Not a boyfriend, more just a friend. He's like in love with her, but never went with her or anything, so he never got dumped." With one fingernail, Jill scraped at something sticky on the beanbag. "He's kind of like somebody she's just, you know, friends with."

This Charley guy sounded like a lead. Maddie got his address, a condo in LA, and looked at Mapquest to figure out how to get there.

Charley lived on the first floor of a pink stucco building, parking spaces in front and a swimming pool behind. She rang the doorbell and waited. She rang again and heard stumbling around inside. A young man opened the door and squinted at her.

"Charley Fowler? Detective Martin." She showed him her ID.

"Is this about Francine?" Five ten, muscular, brown hair, brown eyes, late twenties, blue jeans, no shirt. "Jill just called me. I didn't know Francine was missing."

Maddie found that hard to believe. She'd been in the news, television and print. Charley invited her in. Unlike Jill's, his living room was nearly bare. Large plasma TV, one recliner positioned for easy viewing and a dining room chair. She passed up the recliner in favor of the dining room chair. Sunlight, streaming in through two tall narrow windows, filled the room with such brightness that she needed sunglasses.

"I don't have a lot of time," he said. "I need to get ready for work."

Maddie asked where he worked. He told her the Marvel Health Club. "That's how I know Francine. She comes in all the time and works out."

"When did you last see her?"

He dropped into the recliner. "Not for two weeks, maybe more. I've been away. My mother had surgery. I went to be with her when she got out of the hospital. That's how come I didn't hear about Francine."

"You're a close friend?"

"Yeah, I'd say we're close friends. If you mean lovers," He

shook his head. "Then no."

"You're older than she is."

"About five years. So? She was like a sister, talked to me about her problems. Occasionally we'd go out to dinner. Friends," he repeated as though the concept might be beyond Maddie's understanding.

"Did she have a problem the last time you saw her?"

"Not then, but I had a weird call from her on Sunday night."

Sunday night Francine got in a car with a stranger and disappeared. "What time?"

"About seven o'clock. The local news was just ending."

"What was weird about the call?"

"I could barely understand her. When I asked her to talk louder, she said she didn't want him to hear. I asked who and she said this friend of Paul's. That he was kind of weird."

"Weird how?"

She didn't say, she just said she'd call me when they got there."

"Got where?"

Charley shrugged. "To some hospital I think. Apparently Paul was hurt and this guy was taking her there."

"Did she mention this friend's name?"

"No. I'm not sure she knew it." Charley sucked in breath with an air of trying to remember. "Looking back I think she maybe just wanted, you know, somebody to know where she was going because she didn't completely trust this guy."

"What else did she say? Anything about him?"

"Nothing really. I got the impression he worked at the hospital."

"What gave you that impression?"

"She wasn't making a lot of sense. Something about being typed and cross-matched. For blood, I guess."

That sounded serious. Assuming it was true and not a made-up story. It was a rather elaborate story for an abduction. "Had she and Paul been getting along okay? No arguments?"

He shrugged. "As far as I know. She was happy, excited.

All she could talk about was the wedding, wedding, wedding. I doubt Paul was all that obsessive about it."

"Yes? Why?"

Charley shrugged again. "Guys just aren't. You know?"

"Paul was taking an art class. Did he talk about that?"

Charley yawned widely into his fist. "All I knew was he wanted to get into a good law school. I barely knew the guy. We weren't what you'd call close." Charley rubbed a hand vigorously across the top of his head. "I did see him once, a day or two before Francine called me."

"Where did you see him?"

"*Blakes.* He was with some girl. I don't know who."

Maddie asked him to describe her. His description, brown hair and hot, didn't give Maddie a lot to go on. She gave Charley her card and asked him to call if anything else occurred to him.

Where was Paul? Was he involved in an accident, and if so where did it occur, and where was he taken for treatment. All the hospitals and clinics Maddie checked had neither treated nor admitted anyone with that name.

What about Charley Fowler? Was he telling the truth that he was simply like a big brother to Francine? Did he want to be more? Got angry when she decided to marry another? If I can't have you, nobody can?

Maddie got in her car, and headed for the PCH. She'd just hit the on-ramp when her cell phone rang. Professor Osborn, art instructor, returning her call. He was in his office now and available to speak with her. She told him she would be right there.

With a little help from wandering students, she located Osborn's office, a small space crammed with stacks of canvasses, files heaped haphazardly on any flat surface and a pile of books in a corner. No art work on the walls. One dusty window let in a slant of sunshine.

The professor rose from behind his desk when she entered. He was tall and thin, bald with a shiny, nearly pointed dome, deep set eyes, sharp nose from which he tended to look down, giving him a supercilious look remindful of a camel. She showed him her ID and asked about the class Paul Gilford was taking. She perched on the edge of the chair that had the smallest stack of folders piled on it.

"Gilford," he said blankly. "Oh yes, the young man who's missing. Any luck finding him?"

"We're working on it. What can you tell me about him?"

Osborn rubbed his jaw. "Earnest. Wore a guilty look."

"Guilty?"

Osborn smiled. "Not that kind of guilty. He'd been pressured to feel that art was frivolous and taking this class—beginning drawing class—was a waste of time better spent studying for his law classes. He felt he was sneaking into the forbidden."

Osborn sat on a corner of his desk. "My class was a tiny step of rebellion. Mr. Gilford wanted to paint. He was stealing time away from studying for the law exam which his mother had told him to do."

Had one taste of rebellion been so good that he absconded before he got snared into marriage? "Did the tiny step lead to another?"

"That I don't know, but he seemed rather fond of one of the other art students"

"What is her name?"

Osborn had to check on the seating chart to find out. He ran his finger down a column. "Ah yes, that would be Gayle. Gayle—" He squinted. "Uh—Jasper."

Maddie asked for a phone number and address, and jotted them down. "What can you tell me about her?"

"Quite taken with your Mr. Gilford. No talent as an artist."

Maddie would think that Ms. Jasper was in the class to learn and would perhaps get better. As though he read her mind, the professor smiled. "I've been at this a long time. Some people have the fever, and some don't. Mr. Gilford might have it. Depending on how hard the young lady pushed against it."

"Ms. Jasper?"

"No, not her. The one who's also missing, the one he was about to marry."

"Francine," Maddie said.

"Yes, that one. If she convinced him art was a waste."

Maddie thanked the professor for his time, and tried Gayle's phone number when she got in her car. "Gayle Jasper?"

"Sorry. I'm Sally. I don't think Gayle is home."

"Do you know where I can find her?"

"Probably in class."

"Which class?"

"Somewhere on campus."

Right. Maddie left her phone number and told the young woman to have Gayle call.

Every friend of Francine's that Maddie tracked down and questioned all said a variation of the same thing. Francine was excited about the wedding. She didn't have a jealous ex-boyfriend, no stranger bothered her, she had no conflicts with anyone. The only thing that troubled her, she was the tiniest little bit concerned about her mom taking over the wedding entirely if she wasn't ever-watchful.

Paul had fewer friends. The ones Maddie questioned said, "Yeah, Paul was excited about the wedding," in a lukewarm manner. Happy? "Sure, happy. Why not?" Was it possible that he took off because he didn't want to get married? Possible, Maddie thought, but unlikely. Not with the complicated setup of a phone call about an accident and a friend picking Francine up. No one knew of any accident or injury that involved Paul.

Tired and discouraged, Maddie stopped at the nearest Starbuck's and bought a latte. Elbows on a small table, chin in her hands, she ignored the sneaky little thoughts that whispered in her ear. Hidden for years, disguised as brave, super-cop Maddie Martin was a fake. Under the actions of doing the job with every inch of her being, using the lights and sirens and closing in on a chase, she had fenced in, shut behind bricks walls, kept in place by denial, that fact. The one that she was not super-cop, but simply a fake.

Ridiculous thoughts. They scared her. If she wasn't a cop, who was she? What would she do? She wasn't trained for anything else. Work as a security guard? With the sun on her back, she shivered. Released like the opening of Pandora's box, self doubts were hard to stuff back.

She focused on Francine. Time was running out for her. What happened to her after she got in a car with a stranger? Maddie had no idea.

Was Francine still alive? Maddie doubted it. Maybe sometime, somewhere, some bones would be discovered. For the sake of the family, she hoped a firm identification would be possible.

She sipped the last swallow of the latte, dropped the cup in the trash and went to her car. Was Jesse any more successful in getting answers to Greg's murder? Jesse had, no doubt, gone to Changing Biology, Inc. She wondered what he'd learned. Some answers would surely be found where Greg spent most of his life.

Jesse would have been and gone by this time. She couldn't come up with an excuse to go there, but she told herself she'd think of one if she got caught.

CHAPTER SEVENTEEN

Traffic on the Pacific Coast Highway, always heavy, was even worse today. She nosed into the endless line of vehicles and the driver behind honked and gave her the finger. Californians didn't drive, they inched. With the vast Pacific Ocean on one side and the magnificent Santa Monica Mountains on the other, she had never-ending spectacular views. Hot sun shone sparkles from the water, surfers glided over gentle waves. In the distance a dark blue line separated the warm water from the cold water. Small fishing boats made dark spots on the horizon. All along the coastline were multi-million-dollar mansions.

She turned onto the exit ramp and drove winding roads over small hills up to the gated entrance to Changing Biology, Inc. A uniformed guard asked her name, if she was expected, and her reason for coming. She showed him her ID. He examined it, and told her where she could park. She angled her car into an empty slot in the visitors' lot, got out, and stood looking at what unlimited money could buy. Buildings of glass and steel in a treeless area surrounded by acres of grass.

The four-story main building had four outbuildings in a semi-circle behind it. Sunlight, reflected off the shiny metal, made her squint. Her cell phone vibrated, and she dug it from her bag. Caller ID showed her sister's number. She let the call go to voice mail and made a mental note to phone Pamela this evening.

She walked purposefully, just as though she had a right to be there, toward the main building. Greg had walked this path every day on his way to work. She walked in his footprints as she went under the canopy leading up to the entrance. The door slid open with a soft hiss and she stepped into an atrium as hushed as a church. Glass panels, on the walls that went up four stories, let in bright light. These *Changing Biology* folks must have gotten a good deal on glass.

In a corner fireplace, a cheery fire threw dancing reflections on the shiny dark granite floor with sparkly specks. Her boot heels squeaked as she walked to the security guard sitting a mile away across from the entrance. His glass-topped desk had nothing on it but a phone. Eight hours with nothing to do but answer the phone? How did he ward off boredom? Maybe he kept joke books or porn mags in his pocket. Or for all she knew, he wrote poetry. Even wearing a black suit with white shirt and tie, he looked muscular and fit and ready for a fight.

She produced her ID and requested to speak with Dr. Sherman. Holding up an index finger, he reached for a phone, mumbled a few words and hung up. "I'm sorry. Dr. Sherman is out of the building right now. Will Dr. Baker do?"

She agreed that Dr. Baker would do.

With the same index finger, he pointed at a computer sitting on a table beside a shelf full of phone books. "Please sign in and fill out the form. You'll get a visitor's pass."

At the computer, she hesitated. If she used her name, Jesse would find out she was here. He'd be furious. So furious he'd mention it to Sheriff Dirks? She wasn't sure, but she was sure she had a mortgage to pay, a niece to feed, car payments to make. She should just turn around and leave. A fictitious name wouldn't do, having shown her ID with her real one to the security guard. With no hesitation, she typed in her name. A form appeared, with a Non-Disclosure Agreement.

She didn't bother to read it. Convoluted sentences threatened the rest of her natural life in maximum-security prison if she so much as disclosed a hint of the paint color in the ladies room. At the bottom of the form, she clicked agree and typed in address, birth date, occupation, reason for visit, and social security number. The printer clattered to life and out popped a visitor's badge with her name. She peeled off the back and pasted it to her jacket. Comfortable chairs were positioned throughout the atrium. She chose the nearest and waited. The wait allowed time to worry over the wisdom of coming here.

The minute or two she was prepared to wait stretched to fifteen. Enough already. When she rose and headed toward the door, a man stepped off the elevator.

A dark-haired man in black jeans, black tee shirt, white lab coat, stalked toward her with the quiet purpose of a big cat after a baby antelope. Hairs raised on the back of her neck.

"Detective Martin?" he said.

Maddie nodded.

He had dark eyes with unwavering focus. If she needed one word to describe him, it would be dangerous.

"Jeff Baker. I understand you want to talk with me. I assume you came here to ask about Greg."

"Yes. Then I'd like to see his office."

"We'll be more comfortable in the cafeteria. Let me buy you a cup of coffee," Jeff said

She didn't want coffee, she wanted to see Greg's office. Dr. Sherman wasn't available and Dr. Baker was steering her to the cafeteria. Was she getting the run around here? Baker walked quite a distance and seemed to turn corners at random. By the time they finally reached the cafeteria, she was completely confused.

Typical cafeteria. Large rectangular room with a steam table adjacent to the kitchen. Small square tables surrounded by four chairs filled up the rest of the area. At mid-morning, many of the tables were occupied by individuals in white coats. He asked her what she'd like to go with her coffee.

"Just coffee will be fine," she said.

He filled two mugs, and pulled out a chair for her. "I'm a little surprised by your visit." He added a dollop of cream from the small pitcher on the table. "We already talked with the cops."

"And by we you mean—?"

"The staff," Jeff said. "All of us who knew him."

"Didn't everyone here know him?"

"You make that sound like a trick question." He looked amused. "Do I look guilty in your eyes?"

Oh yes, maybe not of Greg's murder, but of something. "Did you know Greg well?"

"As well as someone you rub elbows with most every day. That's not to say well. *You* obviously knew him well."

"Why do you say that?"

"You called him Greg. Not Dr. Palmer," Jeff said.

Actually no, Maddie thought, no one knew Greg well.

"I admired him. He was going to make us all rich."

If Greg was supposed to make them all rich, who killed the goose that was going to produce the golden eggs? And why? "Did you notice anything odd about him lately? Worried? Distracted? Missing work? Anything that seemed off somehow?"

"Yes."

Really? That answer surprised her. "What was it?"

Jeff slowly shook his head. "I don't know."

Ah. Evasion. Truth or lie? Her usual ability to spot a lie wasn't working with Dr. Baker.

He took a swallow of coffee, tilted the mug slightly and studied the liquid inside. "Greg was—" Jeff paused. "A little out of my league."

Maddie raised an eyebrow.

"By that I mean he was a genius and I'm just a scientist. Only a little, you understand." Jeff smiled. "I'm actually quite sharp myself, but Greg was way above everybody. Lately, he seemed—concerned."

"About?"

"I don't know. I assumed his research wasn't going the way he wanted, but he wasn't ready to discuss it."

That didn't surprise her. Greg kept his thoughts to himself. When he was thinking about a work-related tangle, it would take a tank running over him to get his attention. Until he worked out a solution, he was simply unavailable.

"How long have you known him?" she asked.

"Two years. That's how old this company is. We were hired at the same time. Myself, Greg and his friend, Eric Fuller. I wonder why you're going over all this again since we've already talked to the police," Jeff said.

"I'm a detective. I'm detecting."

"Cops have already been here detecting."

"Someone must step up and take over Greg's job as director. Will it be you?"

He laughed. "Are you setting me up as a suspect"

She smiled.

Did he know she was here under false colors or was he wary of accidentally contradicting information he'd already given to Jesse?

"Was anyone jealous of Greg? Anyone who might want Greg gone, so he or she could step in and take his place? Anything strange like that?"

"Strange? The only thing strange around here was the work we do, and it isn't so much strange as—" He hesitated, looked up for inspiration and came out with "wondrous."

Wondrous? Who used wondrous in conversation?

He focused on her, his dark eyes detached, but interested, a scientist waiting to see the results of an experiment. "He never mentioned you."

Probably because he hadn't thought about her in three years. She took a sip of coffee and rubbed her thumb over the rim of the mug. "You said Eric Fuller was a friend of Greg's. I'd like to meet him."

"Sure." Baker shrugged. He pulled out a cell phone and punched in a number. "Cop here wants to meet you." He listened a moment, then hung up.

Did he call so Fuller could make up a good story? Or to

hide something he didn't want her to see?

Baker escorted her down hallways and around corners. Dr. Fuller's office looked like every office she'd ever seen of working research, every flat surface piled with books, files, folders and papers. A wide window looked out on the parking lot. Dr. Fuller rose from his desk when they came in. Baker introduced her and then he left.

She stared at the most gorgeous man she'd ever seen. He was tall with broad shoulders that tapered to a narrow waist, like a swimmer, dark hair and dark eyes. Like Baker he was dressed in black pants and black shirt beneath a white lab coat. He should be in the movies, she thought. Los Angeles and surrounds was full of people working various jobs trying to break into show business. Probably none as striking as he was.

He made apologies for the state of his office. "I suppose you came here to talk about Greg." Soft baritone voice

Distracted by his absolute beauty, her mind searched for a question. All she came up with was, "How well did you know him?"

Fuller looked at her as though disappointed that she didn't come up with something more provocative.

"Did you respect his ability as a scientist?" There, that was a little better.

"We were all excited—Greg and Jeff and I—about the possibilities of stem cells in the treatment of debilitating disease. There's no limit to what they can do." Fuller's voice had just a hint of a television evangelist.

"And no limit to the money," she said.

He acknowledged that comment with a grin.

"I understand you were friends."

Fuller suddenly got cautious. "We were."

Maybe it was Fuller who was jealous of Greg, not Baker. Fuller who sabotaged experiments because he wanted the job.

"What can I help you with?" Fuller shoved his hands in his pockets.

"I'd like to see Greg's office."

"Sure." Eric's phone rang and he answered, listened, said yes and hung up. "Dr. Sherman has returned. He'd like to see you now. I'll take you."

On the third floor, Eric led her along a hallway to an office with Winston Sherman, MD on the door. Eric tapped and opened the door.

The man at the desk rose. "I'm Dr. Sherman." He held out his hand. "Sorry to keep you waiting. I had something going I needed to attend to.." He was five ten, short grayish hair, a long narrow face, pale blue eyes with colorless eyebrows and thin lips below a straight nose. He wore a gray suit, white shirt and a pale gray tie. She would have guessed him to be a mid-level business executive.

His office was bare, no file cabinets, no books, no papers, no journals, no book shelves, no diplomas on the walls. There was a desk with a computer and a phone, a desk chair and a straight-back wooden chair in a corner. His window looked out over the roof of a service bay.

As though he noticed her looking around, he said, "This is temporary. I'm only using it until my office has been made ready. Is this about Dr. Palmer?"

"Just a few questions," she said.

"Please have a seat." He gestured at the single chair with an open palm.

"Have you learned anything about his unfortunate death?" he asked.

"We're working on it."

"He was a good man. He might have made great strides in the research of stem cells."

Sherman missed sincerity by just a fraction. She wondered what he actually felt about Greg. Resentment? Envy?

"I already spoke with a detective a day or two ago. I'm not recalling his name."

"Jones," she suggested.

"Yes, Jones. How can I help you?"

"We always pay a second visit. Standard procedure. Often new information is gained at a subsequent time."

He looked at her like she was full of shit, which indeed she was, but he said, "I'm afraid there's nothing at all I can tell you. As I told your Detective Jones, I didn't know Dr. Palmer. I never met him, in fact."

"You have been hired to fill Dr. Palmer's position."

"Correct, my dear. And very big footprints they are to fill too."

She clamped her teeth over the *My Dear*. He had decided she was of no importance and maybe even of little intelligence and he was treating her like a pest taking up his valuable time.

"So if there's nothing else."

"One other thing," she said sweetly. "I'd like to see Dr. Palmer's office."

Dr. Sherman looked extremely annoyed. "Your colleague already went over it."

"Nevertheless, I'd like to see it."

He led her down a hallway, made a turn, and another turn, and walked another hallway. He finally stopped before an office with Gregory Palmer, PhD, MD, Director on the glass pane. With the ID card hanging from a cord around his neck, he swiped it across the key pad. The lock didn't open. He tried swiping the card again. It still wouldn't open.

"Well, obviously, this isn't going to work. Perhaps the lock has been changed. Come, I'll show you something more interesting."

She wondered if the card really wouldn't work, or if he had just put on an act. Was there something in Greg's office he didn't want her to see?

Like an obedient puppy, she trotted along behind him as he went down more hallways. He used his ID card on another door and this time it worked.

"This was Greg's special project." He stepped aside to show her a vast open room with rows of black counters, broken up by deep sinks and high curved faucets. "I'm sorry I can't let you go in any further. Contamination is always uppermost in our minds."

He pointed at a technician covered in a spacesuit. "Oocytes." He pointed to another technician similarly dressed. "Cell cultures and, of course." More pointing. "Transfections, and all the usual."

The technicians all ignored him, some didn't even bother to look up.

"Collecting oocytes," Sherman said, "is actually a simple matter of sticking the end of the pipette into the gamete and applying a little suction." His tone was patronizing, as though she couldn't possibly understand what he was talking about.

She was neither that dumb nor that ignorant. A lot got absorbed in ten years of marriage to a scientist. "Amazing," she said, the ignorant, but impressed little woman.

"The next step," Sherman said, "is adding a drop of fluid to the perivitelline space."

"I see."

His superior smile assumed she didn't see a damn thing.

"And then. A few more steps." Which he didn't bother to tell her. Another assumption that she couldn't understand all the intricacies involved. "A mysterious procedure produces fusion. After which cells begin to divide."

"And are used in stem cell research," she said.

"Some. Others for invitro fertilization."

He took her on a tour of the regeneration labs. "A special interest of our Dr. Fuller's. The idea of helping people with serious disabilities, like Parkinson's, multiple sclerosis, spinal cord injuries."

He pressed his palms together and gave her a smile, indicating, she assumed, that he had spent enough time with her. He glanced at his watch. "Well, then, that's it. The quick tour of what we do here. If you don't have any questions, then I'm afraid I really must get back to work."

"Of course," she said. "There is just one other thing."

"You have only to name it, my dear. I'll try to answer."

"I really need to see Dr. Palmer's office."

Sherman's genial expression gave way to irritation. "We did try that already. Alas, I wasn't able to open the door."

She smiled another sweet smile. "I'm terribly surprised

that you don't have the key. As director, shouldn't you have access to it? Maybe you could ask someone to bring you a card that works?" That was so smarmy she could barely stand herself.

He wanted to tell her to get lost, but after a moment of inner deliberation, he made a call on his cell phone. The request took some persuading. His face got red and he started to get short of breath. Finally whoever he was talking to must have acquiesced because he said, "Track down a card that will open that door. And do it immediately."

He walked somewhat more quickly down hallways and around corners back to the office. Jeff Baker was waiting with a card key in hand. Sherman held out his hand, slid it through the slot and the lock clicked open.

"I would like you to have my name put on this door." Sherman opened it and went inside.

Greg's office, when she finally saw it, had the messy, worked-in feel of any space of Greg's.

"Sorry about that." Jeff followed him in and Maddie followed Jeff.

"It's only been a few days," Jeff said, "since Dr. Palmer's murder. As you can imagine, there's been quite an upset around here and not every detail has been attended to."

"Please take care of it."

Dr. Sherman was obviously angry. Maddie wondered who should have seen to it that the new director's name was on the door. Had Jeff deliberately ignored this detail? It would be the sort of thing Greg might do.

"I'll have someone look into it."

"Looking won't do it. Get the name changed."

"Certainly," Jeff said in an easy unconcerned manner.

"When exactly?"

"As soon as I can find someone who can spare the time."

"I see. And all the—" Sherman waved a hand around— "personal things that are still here?"

Jeff didn't seem at all worried that the new director was losing his temper. He stuck his fingertips in his back pockets. "I'll try to find someone."

"If you'll bring me some boxes, I'll put the things inside."

Jeff nodded and said all the right things, the office is yours, it'll all be taken care of, hope we'll work well together, hope you like it here. It didn't seem like he even tried to sound sincere. Sherman walked to the window and frowned, unhappy with what he saw. Maddie thought that a view of the parking lot wouldn't be fitting his position. After a time, maybe a few months, Sherman would make a few changes. Among them, an office more fitting the man in charge, and giving Jeff Baker the axe.

As far as Maddie was concerned the office was a disappointment in that it didn't tell her anything. The small framed picture of wife Clarissa and baby Caitlyn on the desk caused a small tight pull of pain. Sherman muttered to himself as he wandered the office, yanking open drawers that were filled with various office supplies, paper clips, pens, pencils, staplers, rulers, frowning at the file folders piled on every flat surface. The window didn't please him, with the view of the parking lot. The only item that seemed acceptable was the black leather couch.

"There is no reason that all this hasn't been taken care of. They knew exactly when I would arrive. Someone should have been delegated to pack up all this junk."

He yanked open the closet door and growled. Maddie could see a white lab coat hanging inside with Greg's name stitched over the pocket. He slammed the door and looked at the bookcases, overfilled, books stuck in any which way. He plucked a book here and there at random, studied the cover, flipped threw, muttered, "Uh-huh," stuck it back and selected another.

Maddie made noises about leaving and thanked him for showing her around. Without looking up, he said, "Not at all, my dear. If there's anything else I can do, don't hesitate to call." He selected another book, flipped it open and muttered, "Uh-huh, uh-huh."

Maddie turned to see if he'd found something interesting. He slapped the book shut, shoved it back on the shelf and pulled out another. She left.

CHAPTER EIGHTEEN

The number of cars on the street suited Thorne very well. They all made his car nearly anonymous, simply another tired member of the work force on his way home. He drove slowly past the house to determine if Jones was away, leaving Lara by herself with Cindy. Just when he thought he'd better give it up before someone got suspicious and called the cops, he saw a car back out of the driveway. The car came toward him and he saw the driver was Lara and Cindy was in the passenger seat. The baby-sitter seemed to be in the rear seat. Her arrival was an irritant. She might complicate things. But maybe not. She might even make things easier.

Being a patient man, he would wait and study the situation. He'd heard little Cindy call the baby-sitter Danny. Odd name for a girl. Danny was less vigilant than Lara at keeping an eye on Cindy.

As far as he could tell, Cindy still had the birthday gift he'd given her.

A brilliant idea, if he did say so himself. Who can take a little girl's dog away from her? He relished the thought of Jones seething with fury at how close Clayton had gotten to his daughter. It was time to come up with something even better.

The unauthorized jaunt to *Changing Biology, Inc.* gave

Maddie an opportunity to see the place and meet the cast of characters, all very interesting, but it was not time well spent. Nothing helpful came of it, not a specific lead to Greg's killer. Earlier, time spent questioning Francine's friends didn't get her any closer to finding Francine. Too much time had gone by to expect to find her alive. The unproductive day left Maddie feeling tired and irritable. Just thinking of the time wasted brought on a jaw creaking yawn that made her eyes water.

As she squeezed her car into the thick traffic on the Pacific Coast Highway, a spectacular sunset stretched out over the Pacific. She cracked the window and breathed the salty tang of the sea. Southern California must have the most beautiful coast anywhere. It renewed her spirits. Her phone rang, startling her.

Something happened to Dany. Accident? Cindy hurt? Oh Lord, what? She snatched the phone and hit answer. "Jesse, what's wrong?"

"Wrong? A double homicide isn't enough for you?"

"Is Cindy okay?"

"Of course."

"Dany?"

"Fine. What's biting you?"

Maddie pulled in a long breath. "Sorry, just tired."

"Where are you?"

She didn't say just leaving Changing Biology, Inc. but she wasn't sure exactly where she was. Somewhere along PCH with its sunset and multi-million dollar mansions. "I'm on my way home."

"Good. I'll meet you there." He hung up.

Damn it, why couldn't he tell her what was going on? She thought about calling him back, but decided not to.

She flicked on flashing lights, swerved off the highway and jounced along the shoulder. She sped past the row of cars to much honking and startled looks. She pressed her foot harder and heard her father's voice. Colonel Charles Martin's disapproving tone dressing down a subordinate.

At ease, soldier. Don't assume. Gather all the facts before you come to a conclusion.

She slowed, took herself in hand and squeezed into the solid line of cars, then slowed to a crawl with the rest of them. Maybe Jesse called with good news. He could have learned something about Greg's murder. Or maybe he found out about her sneaky visit to Changing Biology, Inc. and was going to land on her with both feet. It could even be possible he had information about Francine. At the Mira Vista off-ramp, she zipped down and sped the three miles of narrow winding streets to her house. Jesse's car sat in front. She pulled up behind him.

He lowered his window. "Hop in," he called, his voice clipped, like he was mad.

She jumped out of her car and into his. "What's up?" She reached for the seat belt and clicked it snug.

"Dog found a bone. Doc said it's human."

All her anticipated panic seeped away and left her feeling like a deflating balloon. "Francine?"

"Don't know yet," Jesse said.

She relaxed her shoulders. It wasn't about Greg, or her visit to *Changing Biology*. "Where was the bone found?"

"Out by the old Chestly place."

"I have no idea where that is."

"That's why I'm driving."

As he drove along in the hills off Topanga Canyon, daylight faded. She tried to keep track of his twisting and turning. It wasn't long before she was totally confused. He hit a dirt road, followed it to a dead end and edged up to the long string of cars, and vans parked above a barbed-wire fence. Back among trees, she could see the glow of lights that had been rigged up. She flicked on her flashlight as she slid from the car and started down the steep side of the ditch. She fought for balance as she made a precarious way to the bottom, stumbled and fell. She dusted herself off and clambered up the other side.

Jesse beat her to the top and put a boot on the lowest strand of barbed-wire, then pulled up the middle strand so she could squeeze through. Even easing carefully between the rusty barbs, she managed to snag her jacket.

A uniformed officer, a rookie named Monty, strode purposefully toward them. When he recognized Jesse, he gave a nod. "Down by the creek. They're going in over there." He pointed. "Sergeant said watch where you put your feet."

Soggy grasses squelched as they tromped in the path of first responders. Halfway across the field, she felt the vibrations from the generator that fired the lights. It kicked up her heart beat. She took in a deep breath. The air smelled of rain, newly cut grass, and the menthol of eucalyptus trees.

When she got closer to the light, she saw a creek with trickling water, a soothing sound that made you sleepy when you sat in the sun on the bank and daydreamed. In the dark with a black-clad man picking through a pile of dirt, it brought to mind medieval grave robbers. She flashed her creds to a man in dark pants and dark jacket when he strode up.

"Sergeant Garrett," he said. "You got called because of the missing girls." He rubbed rain from his face. "We got a bone. Or what's left of one. Scavengers have been at it. Pretty much chewed it all to hell and gone. Doc Newel says it's human and that's all he's prepared to say at this time."

"One bone?" Maddie said.

"Yeah. I have Unies searching, but so far nothing but animal bones. Doc has us looking for everything we can find. He'd especially like the skull. Said to look down hill."

There was a shout and Sergeant Garrett turned to see who hailed him. A uniformed deputy down the slope by the creek waved his arm high in the air. Garrett started toward him. Jesse followed. Maddie came along in the rear.

"What you got?" Sergeant called. The deputy's pants legs were soaked from searching in the creek.

"Over this way."

In a shallow dip, near the edge of the water lay a small pile of bones. Not Francine, Maddie thought. The bones were too bare. Francine hadn't been missing that long. Maybe one of the other girls, Valerie Danforth or Tiffany

Kipson.

Doc Newel, in dark suit, white shirt and tie, had also been in the water. Pants legs dripped. He was a man in his forties with gray hair combed straight back, a narrow face and the intense eyes of a mad scientist. "Pack her up and get her to the morgue. I'll see if these bones can tell me anything."

"Her?" Maddie said.

"That much I can say." He pealed off his latex gloves. "The pelvic girdle is female."

"How long has she been here?" Maddie asked.

Dr. Newel pinned his dark eyes on her. "Hard to tell until I look at her more closely, but if you want a guess I'd say at least six weeks."

Six weeks. It could be either Valerie or Tiffany. Maddie turned to Sergeant Garrett. "Who found her?"

Garrett tipped his head toward the road. "A local named Alan Waterson. Sitting in a squad over there. I kept him in case you wanted to question him."

I do indeed. "Thank you, Sergeant." She left Jesse and Garrett watching the doctor pack up bones. She rubbed rain drops away from her face and hunched her shoulders as she tromped back across the field.

The back door of the squad car was door open. Waterson sat inside and held a leash attached to a large German Shepherd who sat on the ground. When the dog saw her, it leaped to its feet, and barked furiously. She froze. The trainer sat up straight and spoke one word. The dog shut up.

"I'd like to ask you some questions." Maddie did not move.

"Ask away." Alan Waterson was early thirties with longish blond hair damp from the rain, pale blue eyes, and a soft, calm voice with a pleasing hint of a southern accent.

"If I come closer, will he attack?"

"Naw. He's just kind of unpredictable."

Unpredictable didn't sound very safe to her. Slowly, an eye on the dog, Maddie approached. The dog lunged. She held her ground with her heart in her throat.

The trainer spoke softly and the dog obediently sat, tongue lolling. "It's okay," the trainer said. "He won't hurt you. He's just excitable."

Excitable, she thought.

"It's okay," he repeated.

"The dog is yours?" She took a step nearer. The dog whined and swished its tail through the wet grass.

Alan nodded. "This is Caesar."

The dog perked up his ears at his name.

Alan patted its shoulder. "He has two problems. He's smart and he's stubborn." Alan wiped his hand on his pants and held it out for her to shake. "I train dogs for search and rescue. This beast—" he tugged on the leash. "is going to be a champ. If I can figure out how to get him to believe I'm smarter than he is."

"How's it going?"

"So far, he's winning." Alan smiled. "Caesar, this is—" He looked at her. "I'm sorry, I don't know your name."

"Detective Martin. Maddie."

"This is Maddie," Alan told the dog. "She's a friend. Shake hands and behave yourself."

The dog lifted a front paw. Maddie, rather gingerly, took it. The dog sidled up against her legs.

"What are you doing here?" she asked.

"I didn't intend to come here. It was Caesar's idea. I had him in that field over there." Alan pointed to his right at a field.

"Why were you there?"

"I brought the dog to go through some basic commands and try to teach him some new ones. My plan was to keep him on the road. Give him some experience with cars. As soon as I unsnapped the leash, he took off. I followed, at a much more leisurely pace. I didn't know if that field was empty or held a raging bull or belonged to someone with a gun. And then this *dufus*—" he tapped the dog's chest— "came trotting out of the trees with the bone."

"Did you look to see where it came from?"

He shook his head. "My first inclination was to pitch it

a good long way. I didn't because he'd have chased it and brought it back. I wasn't sure what it was. It looked like some kind of animal, but—"

She jotted down Alan Waterson's address and phone number and stuck her notebook in her shoulder bag. With her head bent to avoid stepping in soggy puddles, she slogged for Jesse's car. Someone called her name. She turned. Matt Lockner strode toward her, followed by a bearded man in camo pants, video camera on his broad shoulders.

"What's going on?" Lockner said when he reached her side. "You find one of the missing girls?"

"It's too soon to tell."

"By the number of cop cars here, it's obvious something's going on."

Reporters were thick as flies anywhere they could find the rich and famous. Lockner, reporter for the *Mira Vista Times*, probably had aspirations to relocate a few miles south to LA where those rich and famous lived, amidst their scandalous behavior. Always someone was suspected of something, the murder of a girlfriend—the gorier the better, scandal guaranteed to ruin a reputation, sighting of a couple with the wrong spouses. Anything for a buck.

Maddie was glad she wasn't rich. They had no privacy and couldn't trust anyone. "Stay back," she said. "Someone will be out to give you a statement."

"Like hell," Lockner said. "Jim, this way."

Lockner and his cameraman tromped toward the lights in the trees.

"Take some shots of that." Lockner kept going toward the creek where uniforms were picking up items, examining them, putting some in bags, throwing others back.

Maddie heard the whirr of the camera and yelled, "Hey!"

Jesse, coming back from the creek, spotted Lockner and the cameraman and took off after them.

"Lockner," Jesse shouted. "Both of you, back to the road. This is a crime scene. You can't stay here."

"Of course, Detective," Lockner said. "I understand." With a wave Lockner and the cameraman retreated in the direction of the road.

Jesse stood with his feet slightly apart and his arms crossed. Maddie walked over beside him. They watched as two uniforms bumped the gurney, body bag with the bones inside, over the uneven ground.

"If Doc Newel is right," Maddie said, "and the bones have been there six weeks or more, it couldn't be Francine."

Jesse nodded. "Valerie or Tiffany."

Suddenly they were lit by a bright light. The cameraman had his camera aimed at the gurney and was filming the removal of the bones. Jesse ran. "Turn it off!" He gave Lockner a shove and pushed the cameraman aside.

"Hey! Careful, Sport! Watch the camera."

"I'll smash it over your head, *Sport,* if you don't get it out of here in one second. Lockner! Both of you! Get the hell out!"

Maddie put a hand on Jesse's arm, concerned that he'd take a swing at Lockner. "I'll need your shoes, Mr. Lockner," she said.

"What? What for?"

"This is a crime scene, Mr. Lockner." She turned to the cameraman. "I'll need yours too."

She motioned to a crime scene tech and he brought her evidence bags. She collected both pairs of shoes. "Now leave," she told the reporter and the cameraman.

"Let's go, Jim," Lockner said and the two of them set off for the road.

"You should have let me deck him," Jesse said.

She smiled wickedly. "Well, I know this is not quite as good, but the grass is damp with lots of burrs and they have no shoes on."

"Way to go!" Jesse gave her a high five and they went downhill to his car.

Valerie Danforth had disappeared six months ago. She'd fought with her mother and walked out and that was the last anyone saw of her. Two months later Tiffany Kipson stopped at a convenience store and disappeared. Just like Valerie, there had been no leads.

Hard as they tried, the cops could find no connection between the two. "Which girl is it," Maddie muttered. "When was she killed? And why? Simply in the wrong place at the wrong time? Or was it personal?"

Maddie was more or less talking to herself, but Jesse responded. "Who knows? Count on Doc Newel to give us some answers."

"What did Sergeant Garrett have to say?" Maddie asked.

Jesse shot her a look. He apparently heard the edge in her voice, but chose to ignore it while he maneuvered around parked vehicles to get his car out.

There weren't any leads to follow on either of the two missing young women. Not a one. It was like they vanished. Tiffany's parents were frantic, her boyfriend had an alibi. Cops tried everything. Talked to the people who knew them, neighbors, mail carriers, everyone they could think of. Nothing ever came of any of it. Stranger-to- stranger crime. The hardest to clear, because there was no definite direction to go in.

Jesse craned his neck to see what was coming up the PCH at him, then pulled on and threaded into traffic.

"Now I have to tell the parents of one of those girls," he said.

"Anyone in the store notice anything about Tiffany?"

Jesse snorted. "When have you ever had anybody notice anything?" He swerved into another lane. "The clerk saw her leave, got busy with the next customer and didn't see which way she went."

Jesse stopped to let Maddie out in front of her house.

Lights were on inside and good smells floated from the kitchen. A fire danced in the fireplace. The coffee table had been set with two plates, flatware and napkins.

Maddie tossed her bag on the desk in the dining room. "Dany?"

A window-rattling noise that turned out to be her niece's music blared from the bedroom. "You're finally home." Dany clicked a remote and there was blessed silence.

"What's cooking?"

"Dinner," Dany said. "I'm going to cook, clean house and wash dishes and you'll be so glad I'm here, you won't know how you got along without me.

"Just your being here is enough." Maddie gave her a quick hug and went to check phone messages. "I didn't know you could cook."

"There's lots of things you don't know about me."

Maddie thought there probably were. She played the messages. Two hang-ups, a wrong number and a call from Pam wanting to know if Maddie was ever home.

"Cooking's not all that hard," Dany said. "All you have to do is read a few cook books. Mom sure didn't teach me."

"How did it go today with Cindy?"

"Great! We did makeovers."

Maddie wondered how Lara would feel about that.

Dany slipped her iPod in her pocket. "I'm really sorry about Greg."

That hit like razor wire and tears rose in Maddie's eyes.

"I never knew what to make of him, you know? He was so— I guess he was nice and everything. I mean not mean, like you loved him so I figured he must be a good guy, you know? But I never knew what to think of him when I was a little kid." Dany opened the oven door to check what was inside. "Half the time I was scared of him, the other half I was fascinated. I know you thought he was yours forever. I always thought he belonged in outer space"

"Oh, that's kind of the way I felt about him," Maddie said lightly. She found the bottle of aspirin on a shelf, hit the tap over the sink and filled a glass with water. She shook two tablets into her hand and swallowed them with a gulp.

"Is it really bad? Him going off to be with someone else, I mean?"

"Yes," Maddie said.

"I mean, still? After all this time? Years and everything."

"I'll survive."

Dany turned off the oven. "You probably don't care what I think, but it was kind of like every time you needed him, he stepped aside and let you fall on your face."

"Hey, kiddo," Maddie smiled, "don't you know you can't just come right out and tell people what's on your mind."

"Really? Isn't that what you always told me to do?"

Did she? Probably. She probably said a lot of things that she never expected would get thrown back at her. "Sometimes people get hurt."

"Is that like saying the truth hurts?"

"All right, smarty pants, what's for dinner? It smells delicious."

"Right," Dany said tartly. "Change the subject when I want to talk about something important."

"What's important?"

"You never think about me anymore."

"I think about you all the time."

"It doesn't seem like that. It's just like Mom. When I got too big for frilly dresses with frilly socks, she didn't care about me anymore."

Dany looked bleak and sad. "I know you don't really want me here. Mom doesn't want me around either."

"Oh Dany, your mother loves you."

"Yeah. As much as she can. As long as I stay out of her way."

"No, Dany, that's not true."

"Anyway, she called. She wants you to call her." Dany served up chicken parmesan, green beans, and a salad. They ate in front of the fireplace. Maddie wondered where Dany got the ingredients for the salad. Maddie didn't recall having anything, and she assumed if there was anything it would be limp from neglect.

"Dany, I always want you here. I love you. You know that, right? It's just that now is not a good time. A lot is going on at work and I simply can't do things with you, take you places, the way I'd like to."

"It's all right. I know you're busy, and I just sort of dropped in on you. Maybe there's a gym, or exercise place I can go to."

"Sure," Maddie said, "But I won't have time to even drive

you and pick you up."

"I could take a bus."

"Unfortunately there really aren't any. People here don't take buses. They drive. There's a joke that some movie star in Malibu backed his car out of his driveway and drove to the the house next door."

"What about your bike? Do you mind if I ride it?"
"Bike?"

"Your bicycle." Dany pulled off a sliver of chicken and popped it in her mouth. "The one in the garage. It's maybe kind of a mess. I can't tell. You don't ever use it?"

Maddie finally remembered there was a bicycle in the garage. The people who previously owned her house had left it.

"I'll clean it up and everything," Dany said.

Maddie forked a lettuce leaf in her mouth and chewed. Dany grinned at her. "You want to say no, but you can't think of a good reason. Don't worry, I'll be careful."

"Yeah?" Maddie tipped her head and raised an eyebrow. "Well, that better not fall into the category of famous last words."

Ten was a little early for very many people to be at *Blake's*, but Maddie decided to stop in on the off chance that she'd find Gayle Jasper there. *Blake's* was a college hangout. A little seedy on the outside, but not so bad it looked unsafe.

Kids could play pool, drop coins in the juke box, listen to horrible music with questionable lyrics. The kind of stuff parents yelled *turn it down!* for at home. *Blake's* was named after the owner, an eighty-two year old businessman who knew everybody in town. He hired a goodlooking man by the name of Drew Kyper to manage the place. Girls swooned over Kyper and boys hated and envied him.

Maddie shoved open the massive wooden door carved with wicked snakes and dragons, and stepped inside. High ceilings, dark wooden floors, dim lighting, waitresses with short frilly red skirts and white tee shirts with red letters across the breasts. The letters spelled something racy or suggestive, changing from week to week or whenever the manager found something new that struck kids as funny and parents as horrifying.

At the bar she slid onto a stool and gazed at her hazy reflection in the mirror when a smooth voice murmured in her ear, "May I help you with something, Detective?"

Maddie turned and looked at Drew's handsome face. Compared to Eric Fuller, Drew went to the bottom of the list. Six feet, dark hair, dark eyes, devilish smile, perfect teeth, square jaw, tight-fitting black tee shirt, snug black jeans. Something about him made her think phony. She hadn't found an arrest record or an outstanding warrant. So far, she'd found out nothing. At least, under the name he was using, which made her wonder if the name was also phony.

"Gayle Jasper," Maddie said. "Is she here?"

"I haven't seen her this evening."

"Does she come in often?"

"No more than most."

"What do you know about her?"

"Sweet young thing."

Weren't they all? "Have you ever seen her with Paul Gilford?"

He hesitated a moment before he said, "I have, yes. A few times, actually."

Right. Didn't want to alienate kids by revealing their secrets to a cop. "What are the kids saying about Francine?"

"Depends on how dramatic they are. That she's run away with Paul, that she's been kidnapped, that she's in the hands of a serial killer, that she's developed amnesia and is wandering around wondering who she is."

"Which of those do you lean toward?"

He smiled, white teeth flashed in the gloom. "If I had to choose, I'd say the first. Since Paul, too, seems to be gone. Isn't the simplest answer usually correct?"

"When did you see Francine last?"

"I believe it was Thursday. She was here with Paul."

"Was that the last time you saw him?"

"No. That would have been Friday. Not with Francine, which was rare. Those two seemed joined together."

"You don't appear concerned."

"Concern is for the parents. My job is to check ID's and be sure if they ask for a beer they're over twenty-one."

Maddie wondered if he adhered as strictly as he indicated. "Paul was by himself?"

"No." Drew picked up a cloth and started to polish the bar. "He was with the young lady you were asking about."

"Gayle." Maddie's appearance hadn't gone unnoticed. Kids here and there were darting glances at her and whispering to each other. No doubt wondering why she was there and what she and Drew were talking about.

"Care for a cold beer?" he asked.

She hesitated. Technically, she was off duty. But she didn't like Drew. He was altogether too smooth and too LA for her taste. She didn't much care for beer either. "No thanks. Coffee would be nice though."

"Cream, no sugar. Right?" He stuck his finger tips in the back pockets of his black jeans and bestowed another brilliant smile on her. "Sure you don't want anything else? A sandwich? Glass of wine?"

"Just coffee."

Spine straight, shoulders back, stomach in, he strode to the kitchen, knowing he was watched. She called home to check on Dany and got no answer. Drew placed a mug of coffee in front of her.

"Gayle Jasper just came in." He indicated a dark-haired girl in jeans and a blue sweater who stood looking around, then smiled and weaved through the crowded room to join a group at a far table.

Maddie picked up the mug, slipped from her stool and ambled from table to table. At each, she asked about Francine and about Paul. Everyone she spoke with said it wasn't like Francine to just take off. Most said it wasn't like Paul either, but some said they didn't know him as well.

Only one girl, Gayle, said anything different. After her friends left her alone at the table, Maddie asked when Gayle had last seen Francine. Gayle said she couldn't remember, maybe a week ago. Where? Here. When had she last seen

Paul? "The day he disappeared. Sunday."

Maddie sat down across the table from her and took a sip of coffee. "Where did you see him?"

"At my place."

Oh ho.

"He was going to break up with Francine."

"He told you that?" Maddie wondered if this was wishful thinking on Gayle's part.

Gayle nodded. "He said he had to wait a bit. He didn't want to give her the news on her birthday."

"What else did he say?"

Gayle bit her lip.

Maddie looked at her. "Do you know where he is?"

At first, Gayle denied it, but Maddie continued to question he, and finally Gayle gave a reluctant nod.

Maddie clenched her jaw holding in the words that were wanting to yell at this young woman. Maddie took in a big breath, let it out and said quietly, "Where is he?"

"I don't know exactly."

Another stare. "Where?" This time Maddie's voice wasn't quiet.

Hesitantly, Gayle said, "Hawaii."

"Where in Hawaii?"

Gayle shook her head. "I don't know."

Maddie was getting ready to take her in for obstruction when Gayle rushed to say, "Really. Honest." She added, "I got this postcard."

A postcard. Maddie wanted to shake her. Paul's mother was in agony wondering what happened to her child. And this girl had received a postcard. Which she didn't tell anyone about. Maddie waited a moment until she was sure she could speak without shrieking. "I need to see the postcard."

"Okay," Gayle said in a very tiny voice. At least the girl wasn't an idiot. She knew she shouldn't have kept the postcard a secret.

"Where is it?"

Gayle reached down and picked up her purse. She set it on the table, opened it and pulled out the postcard. Maddie took it carefully by one corner. Not that it would matter. Gayle's prints would be all over it, as would the prints of many other people.

The picture on the front showed Waikiki beach with gorgeous people frolicking in the water. Printed on the other side: *I just couldn't handle it anymore and had to get away. I decided to come here and clear my mind. When I figure out how to tell Francine, I'll be back.*

Love,

Paul

Maddie put it in an evidence bag. "Why didn't you tell the police—or anybody— about this?"

Gayle hunched her shoulders. "I didn't know if he wanted me to. I thought maybe he wanted to keep it a secret."

Maddie asked if Gayle knew where Francine was.

"No."

"You sure?"

"Honest," Gayle said. "I really don't. Really."

Had Paul run off without telling Francine, or his mother? From what she'd learned about him, it didn't fit. So how did the postcard come about?

Maddie carried her coffee back to the bar. In front of her stool Drew had put a small plate with a large chocolate chip cookie. "To go with the coffee." He gave her a smile that hinted at secrets the two of them shared.

CHAPTER NINETEEN

Dirks tapped on the bedroom door and a sleepy voice called out, "What!" At least the kid had made it home. At what time, Dirks wondered. He was still out at one-thirty when Dirks went to bed.

Dirks opened the door, but didn't go in. The condition of the room hadn't changed. Clothes were strewn across the chair, the desk, the bed and piled in one corner. The pervading odor was of dirty socks.

Kevin, still in bed, raised on one elbow and twisted around. Irritation crossed his sleep-groggy face. He ran fingers through long blond hair and yanked it off his forehead. "What time is it?"

"Nearly six." Dirks tipped clothes and whatever else off the chair, planted it by the side of the bed and sat himself down. "Where were you last night?"

"Out."

"Out where?"

"Just out."

"I know you're pissed about being here."

"You don't know anything about me."

Progress, more than a two-word sentence. "That's true." He hadn't even known the kid existed until he found a message on his answering machine from Gloria that Kevin was on his way. The first thing Dirks did was call her back. She explained he was the father of the sixteen-year-old boy.

He tried to get a few more particulars and she told him to think back to one rainy afternoon sixteen years ago. "Well, guess what," she said. "Kevin was the result."

"Why didn't you tell me?"

"I was all set to a time or two. You weren't interested in listening."

Dirks did not yell. Quietly, he said, "Why are you sending him here?"

"Because it's time he got to know his father. And if we talk much longer, you're going to miss his plane. It's about to land." She hung up on him and she hadn't answered any of his subsequent calls.

Dirks got to the airport a few minutes after the plane landed and hurried inside. He didn't even know what the kid looked like. As it turned out, only one teenager got off the plane. A sullen-faced adolescent with jeans riding low on his hips, slouched toward the baggage area.

That was eight months ago and the sullen look hadn't changed any that Dirks had noticed. "I can't say I blame you for feeling angry, but the fact of the matter is, I am your father—"

"Yeah? Since when?" Kevin flopped back down and jerked the blankets over his head.

Dirks wanted to throw blankets aside and grab the kid by the shoulders and shake him. With an effort, he kept his voice neutral. "That also is true, but this is the situation we're in. Whether you believe it or not, I worry when you're out so late. What I want from you is a short sentence about where you're going when you leave and an estimate of when you'll be home."

Kevin grunted, which Dirks took to mean *fat chance.* "You decide what you want from me and then we'll negotiate," Dirks said.

With a quick toss of his head, blankets slid down and he looked at Dirks like he was startled, but was, at least, thinking it over.

"I have to get to work. There's food in the kitchen. I'd

appreciate it if you clean up when you were done."

Maddie got to her desk early to catch up on the never-ending paperwork. Rows of desks, separated by shoulder high dividers, filled the room. Every detective had his or her own cubicle with phone, over-filled file trays and computer terminals. Even this early almost everybody was out in the field.

Much as she stewed over it, she couldn't understand what Greg had meant by the hastily scribbled *you owe me five farthings*. If she ever figured it out, she hoped it would point her toward his killer. The dictionary was no help, and while the internet had some interesting facts about the farthing, it had nothing that could possibly be connected with Greg or murder. The thing was, she felt she did know what it meant if she could just retrieve the answer from the muck in her brain.

Three days had slipped by with no hint of who or why, and the first twelve hours of a homicide were crucial. If no promising lead or suspect was developed, the possibility of clearing the case diminished with each day.

Success depended on three elements, physical evidence, witnesses, and confession. If there was no evidence or no witnesses, a confession was highly unlikely. Her trip to Changing Biology, Inc. had gotten her nothing, except Jeff who made her nervous and Eric who was hiding something.

Her desk phone rang and she picked up the receiver. "Detective Martin."

"Rose Caudell here."

Maddie sat up straight. Rose Caudell, fifty-year-old gray-haired widow with a kind face, took in foster children. Two-year-old Caitlyn, orphaned by the horrific slaughter that had taken place at her home, was given over to Mrs. Caudell's care.

"Is there a problem?" Maddie said. "Is Caitlyn all right?"

"She's just fine, dear. Well, as fine as a little girl can be who has lost both her parents and is living with strangers."

"Yes, of course." Maddie slumped back.

"She's a very bright little girl, is Caitlyn."

"How can I help you?"

"There's something I think you should see. Is it all right if I bring the little one to your office?"

"Can you tell me what this is about?"

"She's exceedingly precocious, is Caitlyn, able to recognize and point out letters and recite numbers."

"I see." Maddie really didn't have time for this.

"No, dear, you don't understand. She's made comments I can only conclude indicate she saw something that awful night."

"What does she say?" Could Caitlyn actually know something? Was evidence locked away in her child's brain? If so, would she be able to tell anyone? Especially a stranger.

"I'd really like to show you. When would be a good time?"

"Well, Mrs. Caudell, you actually should be speaking with Detective Jones. He's the investigator on the case."

"I understand that, dear, but I fear Caitlyn would simply freeze up in his presence. Would it be possible to bring her in and if you feel she has some helpful knowledge, you can let him know."

Maddie said, "Let me check with Detective Jones to see when it would be convenient. I will let you know."

Mrs. Caudell agreed that was just fine. "Let me just say that Caitlyn knows the difference between the truth and a lie."

Maddie couldn't imagine a child that young being able to say anything useful. Especially in a courtroom. Nor could she imagine any judge allowing it. Still, if by some miracle, the little girl said anything at all, maybe it would point in a direction that might lead Jesse somewhere.

The child was only two. She could never manage a courtroom situation. However, a witness was assessed as competent at the time of testimony. Testimony, not when she witnessed the crime. A case could possibly drag on for years before it actually came to a trial. By then Caitlyn would be older.

When Jesse came in Maddie could tell by his hard face that he was in a bad mood. She weaved her way across the room anyway and plopped in the visitor's chair at his desk. He shot her a mulish look. "Whatever it is," he said. "The answer's no."

"Are you getting anywhere?"

"No. I do, however, have work to do, so if you'd just tiptoe back to where you came from, I'll get on with it."

"I want to ask you something."

He eyed her warily. "What?"

"Caitlyn."

"What about her?"

"She was there. On that night when her mother and father were killed. Is it possible she could tell us something?"

"She's two," he said with exasperation.

"I know that. You had a two-year-old not long ago. What do you think?"

"About what?"

"Questioning her. Asking her about that night."

"I think it's a bad idea."

"I do too. Mrs. Caudell has something on her mind. Okay if I see what she wants?"

Jesse shrugged. "Fine. Go ahead."

She started back toward her own desk.

"Maddie? Wait."

She returned.

"Even if Caitlyn said something useful, which I don't for a second believe, we couldn't do anything with it."

"I know."

He tapped fingers against his desk. "And God only knows what kind of damage we'd do. There sre all those abuse cases that get dismissed because of improper influence by interviewers. And if we tried bringing her in as a witness, she couldn't even get any psychological stuff—you know, counseling—help, support, whatever, until after the trial was over. So she'd be all alone with it just when she most needed help. I don't know, Maddie, it just seems fraught with complications and maybe we'd give the kid more nightmares and get nothing." He looked tired, eyes puffy, face drawn.

Worry immediately jumped to mind that there was trouble that involved Dany. "You all right?"

"Yeah." He scrubbed his hands down his face. "It's that damn rat."

"Rat?"

"Dog." He held out a cupped hand. "Fits in my hand. "Looks like a rat. That son of a bitch Thorne—that slimeball pedophile—gave my daughter a birthday present."

"We're going to find him," Maddie said. The entire sheriff's department was looking. So far, they hadn't found him. He seemed never to be at his place of residence. Sheriff Dirk's even had it staked out for two nights. Thorne never showed.

Jesse nodded. "I want to grab him by the neck and squeeze his eyeballs out."

"You still have it?"

"The rat? Yeah. Cindy loves the damn thing. Lara insists I get rid of it. Wherever he is, Thorne is probably laughing himself silly."

Jesse gave his desk chair a half-swivel. "I don't know what to do. I get rid of the damn thing and Cindy's heart broken. I don't get rid of it and Lara's going to leave me. What should I do?"

Maddie didn't venture so much as an expression.

Jesse smacked his desk. "What about Thorne? What does he have in mind? Revenge? To show me how easy it would be for him to get his hands on my daughter? I got a choice here."

"Uh—"

"The third option is to find that bastard Thorne and put a bullet in his head."

"Jesse—"

"Set it up," he said.

"What?" She thought he was telling her to set up Thorne to get shot.

"Call CPS and get the little girl in here. See what the woman has on her mind."

Maddie started back to her desk.

"And Maddie?"

She turned. "Yeah?"

"Don't expect anything."

"Right."

Maddie had chosen eleven o'clock to give herself time to check into Rose Caudell's background. Mrs. Caudell's husband had died eight years ago in a vehicular accident. She had two adult sons who lived in Oregon. She and her sister Estelle had been caring for foster children for the last five years. They currently had two-year-old Caitlyn and three toddlers ages two to four.

By eleven the day was again drizzly under gray skies and the wind had increased. Mrs. Caudell carried the little girl in. A wide-eyed Caitlyn squirmed around, turning from side to side looking everywhere. She wore pale blue corduroy pants and a white shirt with embroidered blue flowers. Blond curls framed her face, her blue eyes were wary.

Maddie led them into an interrogation room. Rose sat in a metal chair on one side of a long, scarred table with Caitlyn in her lap and her bulging tote bag on the floor. Maddie said hello and the child hid her face against Rose's chest. "Want Mommy."

"If you'll just continue to talk in a soft voice," Rose said, "she'll settle down."

Maddie talked softly, asking very basic questions of Rose: name, address, how long she had lived at her address, how long she'd been taking in foster kids.

Caitlyn pushed herself rigid and slapped her hand against Rose's arm "Where's Mommy?"

"She's not here," Rose said softly, "but this nice lady is looking for her."

Caitlyn stopped clinging so tightly and eyed Maddie.

"Is she afraid of strangers?" Maddie asked.

"She is a bit, yes. Some are and some aren't. She's a good girl." Mrs. Caudell gave Caitlyn a little squeeze. "And very brave."

Caitlyn ducked her forehead against Rose's shoulder. A

couple minutes later she pointed to the tote bag on the floor. Rose reached down, took a small sketch pad from the tote and tore off a blank sheet. She handed it to the little girl and gave her a blue crayon.

Caitlyn slapped her hand on the page and drew around it, then she colored in the tracing. Solemnly, she held it out to Maddie who exclaimed how great it was and how glad she was to get it.

Caitlyn shook her head. "For Mommy."

Mrs. Caudell provided another piece of paper and let Caitlyn choose a crayon from a full box. She chose yellow. While she was busy tracing around her fingers, Mrs. Caudell pulled a catalog from the tote. Caitlyn offered the second tracing to Maddie, scooted around until she was comfortable in Mrs. Caudell's lap and watched as catalog pages were turned.

She slapped a pudgy hand on one picture. "Hurt Mommy." She pushed the magazine away.

The model was a man wearing a red turtle-neck shirt with long sleeves. Oval face, brown or blond hair. He was posed on a stool with his forearm resting on a kitchen counter.

"A likeness," Mrs. Caudell said. "Not the actual person, of course."

"Could she be responding to the shirt?" Maddie wondered if she'd seen all the blood splashed around and the color red was what upset the little girl.

Rose turned more pages. Caitlyn slapped again. "Bad." That page had pictures of two men with long-sleeved red shirts.

Jesse came in. Caitlyn took one look at him and screamed. He immediately backed out and retreated to his desk. Caitlyn screamed and squirmed, and tried to slither off Mrs. Caudell's lap. Rose hugged her and wiped her face and promised her a treat when they got home. Finally, her cries softened and morphed into hiccups. Mrs. Caudell got out a thermos and gave her a drink of water. She bundled Caitlyn in her coat and pulled a hat over her head. The child waved goodbye to Maddie as Mrs. Caudell carried her out.

Maddie went across to Jesse's desk. "We did get some information. You look like the man who hurt Mommy. And maybe that man was wearing a red shirt. A man in a red shirt was bad. Maybe."

Jesse studied the catalog model that Caitlyn had fingered. "I don't look anything like this."

"Yeah, you do," Maddie said. The killer, or one of them, had light brown or blond hair, and was clean-shaven. Attractive, young, maybe mid-thirties to mid-forties. Little Caitlyn gave them quite a bit of information.

Amber jotted the name and number on the message slip. Whispers and rumors could be fanned into trouble for little Miss Cornfield from Kansas. And, Amber thought, I'm just the person to do it. The detective's shield belonged to her, by God. She'd been here longer, she'd worked for it, she'd earned it. Why Sheriff Dirks had to go off and hire Maddie Martin, Amber didn't know. Well, Amber Wilson did not give up without a fight.

"Plotting tangled webs?"

She turned, startled. "Hey, Fenton."

He snatched the message slip from her hand and examined it. "You're taking messages for Ms. Maddie these days?"

"So what?"

"So it's pretty clear what you're doing." He yanked on his belt, pulling it over his flat stomach.

"What are you trying to imply?"

He snorted. "I'm not implying, I'm flat out saying you're doing a wrong thing here."

"Well, maybe you ought to spend more time shining your shoes instead of accusing people. Especially when you don't know what you're talking about."

Fenton lifted a foot with exaggerated interest and peered at his scratched black shoes. "Shiny shoes are one thing. Making up lies about somebody is something else. What do you have against Maddie anyway?"

Amber shrugged. "What kind of crimes do you suppose

she investigated in Kansas?"

"Well, I've heard tipping cows was always popular."

"Tipping cows? What the heck does that mean?"

"Got me." He flicked the pink slip with a finger. "What's this?"

Amber crossed her arms. "He called. She isn't here. He asked me if I'd leave her a message."

"This guy called? You're sure he called?" Fenton rubbed a knuckle across his upper lip. "Matt Lockner, the reporter? You sure it wasn't the other way around?"

"What are you talking about?"

"I'm talking about you maybe called this reporter."

"Why would I do that?"

"I don't know, Amber. Maybe to set her up. Make it look like she's been talking to him, giving him dope for his newspaper."

"You're nuts."

Fenton pulled the slip from Amber's hand, dropped it in the trash and punched her shoulder. "Watch it, kiddo. If the Sheriff finds out what you're up to, you'll discover yourself going from the frying pan into the fire."

"I don't know what you're talking about."

"Right."

"Don't you think it's funny," Amber said. "The way he treats her?"

"How does he treat her?"

"You know, like she can't do anything right one minute and can't do anything wrong the next. I don't get it."

"Leave it alone," he said. "It's none of your business."

Oh really? Well, Amber was making it her business.

He checked the gametes thriving in their chemical stimulation medium, hit a switch, and sent a jolt through it. The electrical shock fused the enucleated cells with the added adult epithelial cells and gave each cell the necessary number of chromosomes. The adult nuclei dropped their programmed duties and embraced their embryonic roles.

These gametes had started to divide. Already they had

produced the adult cells that had been cloned three dozen times.

He reached for the phone, but before he could punch in the number to report the progress, it rang. "Yes?"

"How is your research going?" The voice was distorted by one of those electronic gadgets.

"Who is this?"

"An interested party."

"What research?" He waited, anticipating what would follow.

"Don't be coy, it only annoys me. First, let me say, I approve of what you're doing."

"Right, and second?"

"With a small token of appreciation, I can keep what I know to myself, not mention it to a soul."

There it was, not something he was equipped to handle. He was a scientist. He left the scut work to those with the skills to deal with it. "How small?"

"How does fifty thousand sound?"

"It sounds ludicrous."

"Really? I thought I was being very restrained. I can go higher if I encounter resistance."

In the background and very faint, he heard, or thought he heard, a familiar cough.

"You think it over, and we'll talk again. We'll discuss how and when the money will change hands." The caller hung up.

He punched in the number he knew well.

"Yeah?"

"There's been a development," he said.

"What development?"

He repeated the phone call.

"Huh. Some people are just plain stupid." There was a pause. "I'll have it taken care of it."

Sufficient Grounds was crowded with chattering students. Lockner was getting a mite irritated. He hated waiting. By his watch, Amber was fifteen minutes late. It wasn't like her. Usually she was here first, eager to pass along the latest. He ordered a latte from the bar, slid into the first empty booth and sipped foam. The candle in the middle of the table flickered in its little red glass globe, already giving him a headache. Amber, bless her malicious little heart, by leaking information to him thought she was being clever, but obviously she was building a pile of blame for Detective Martin.

Just when he had decided she wasn't going to appear, Amber came bustling in. She stopped to get her own latte, then scooted into the bench across from him. Without her uniform, she could pass for a student, corduroy pants and gray sweater, reddish hair pulled back in a pony tail, oval face, brown eyes alight with excitement.

"Sorry I'm late." She set the latte on the table and wriggled around getting comfortable.

"So what's new in the Sheriff's Department?" He leaned his back into the corner and slanted his legs on the bench.

"He's really got a hard on for her."

"Who?"

"Dirks. For that cop from Kansas."

"Anything for me? Besides Dirks's lack of judgment."

She sampled her latte, looked at him and smiled a this-is-good-smile.

"So, queen of cop talk, dish the dirt already."

The candle was enough light for him to notice the narrowing of her eyes. It behooved him to keep ridicule out of his comments, lest he chase away the goose who brought him the golden eggs.

He saw a brief thought cross her face. Was she going to go flouncing out? If that was in her mind, she decided against it.

"I don't get it," Amber said. "He talks about her like she's some fairy princess, and then he'll go right into yelling at her for something that even Fuck-up Fenton wouldn't get screamed at for."

"That's what you wanted to tell me? That wasn't worth the price of gas getting here."

Amber wiggled around some more. She was getting to

the good part. "I overheard them talking this morning." She used a spoon to scoop up foam from her mug.

"Who?"

"The two of them. Dirks and his pet detective."

Lockner felt like kicking her under the table. It had already been a long day and he was tired. "What did you hear?"

"He really yelled at her for disobeying orders."

"What disobedience did your Maddie do?"

"She's not mine."

"Did Detective Martin stick her nose into the investigation?"

"Yeah. How'd you know?"

It was the type of thing she would do.

"She was told in no uncertain terms, stay away from the Palmer homicides." Amber took a tiny sip from her spoon. "His face was all red. He accused her of going against orders, not doing her job, being insubordinate, and a bunch of other stuff."

"That's it? That's all you've got?" Lockner started to slide out of the booth. "Sweetie, that isn't exactly hot news."

"Maddie went out to Changing Biology."

Ah, that was the disobedience. "When?"

"Yesterday."

"How do you know?"

The candle threw glistening light on her white teeth when she smiled. "I have my sources," she said sweetly.

"Who?"

"Oh no, you don't. They're my sources, you're not getting names." Amber all but hugged herself with glee. "I could get her fired."

"I suppose I could spin some kind of story around this fact, but it's not Pulitzer material."

"Don't you want to know what else I have?"

"Is it good?"

"Oh yeah." She grinned, took a swallow of coffee, leaned forward and whispered, "She interviewed Caitlyn Palmer."

"She interviewed a baby." He didn't have the time, nor the

inclination to sit here and play Amber's games.

"She's two. And apparently very smart. But the thing is—" Amber leaned back, satisfaction all over her face. "She can identify him."

"Identify who?"

"The killer."

"What? That's ridiculous." Again, he slid to the end of the bench and rose. "She's a baby."

"That's what Maddie's report said."

"A baby."

"It said, right there on Dirks's desk, that Caitlyn Palmer could identify the man who killed her mommy." Amber leaned back and took a sip of coffee.

"You're sure about this?"

"Positive."

Lockner looked at his watch. If he hurried, there was a chance he might get this in tomorrow's newspaper. He went out to the parking lot, started up his SUV and drove off, very pleased with the information Amber had given him.

Baby Identifies Killer.

CHAPTER TWENTY

Clayton Thorne unfolded his newspaper and settled back on the couch. He'd been in this place long enough. A little later he would go to another. Headline on page one of the *Mira Vista Herald*. "Woman's Bones Found." In a smaller article, he read no progress made in the search for the missing Francine Ramsey. Thorne turned pages, didn't find much of interest and tossed the paper aside and got up. He set about changing his appearance.

Turning himself into someone else pleased him immensely and made him a little resentful that he hadn't followed his dream when he was in college. He had wanted to be an actor and he was good, but his parents were against it. Only a handful of people ever succeeded. The rest of the hopefuls had to wait tables or work at McDonald's. Thorne was coerced to drop the acting nonsense—their word—and get a business degree.

He put on a wig of long gray hair, gathered it in a clip at the back of his neck. He now had a hank of hair that reached the middle of his back. He put padding in both cheeks which made him look much fatter. Then with some makeup, very little, he aged at least ten years. Lined face, dark circles under his eyes and he was a new person.

He knew he had to be careful, especially near the park. He drove slowly past the park and watched Cindy trying to balance herself on her skateboard. She teetered and would have fallen, but the babysitter clamped a hand on her upper arm and held her steady. At the park entrance, the sitter placed the pet carrier down just inside. Thorne drove to the home he was using at the moment.

He still didn't know what he was going to do, but a plan was beginning to form. Slumped in his tired, elderly, wouldn't harm a soul persona, he perused the paper while his mind worked on what circumstances had produced for him. Nothing like working on a plan to put you in a good mood. If it wouldn't be contrary to his image, he'd hum a cheery tune.

Maddie ran her eye over Cutter's report. Nothing unexpected, but reading it brought back the slaughterhouse smell and horror of blood splashed everywhere. Most of the fingerprints in the house were those of Gregory Palmer, his wife Clarissa, or the little girl Caitlyn. Other prints turned out to belong to a postal worker, a cleaning lady who came in once a week and a gardener who also came once a week.

You owe me five farthings. Why had he jotted that in his notebook? Maybe it meant nothing. Or something to do with work. A buzz word connected with stem cells?

She tucked a printout of the email from *cad* into her purse and took off.

Far below the glossy sunshine of southern California was its diverse underbelly. Any individual of that group who got sick and didn't have health insurance shuffled off to the Medical Center. The hospital, on the fringes of poverty row, had a shine that set it off from its surrounds like a diamond in a pewter setting. The poor, the huddled masses, and the great unwashed came through its doors and left a layer of grime on the polished floors. It didn't turn anyone away. Gave one hope in the goodness of humankind.

The trauma center used up money as fast as blood gushed from its patients. Keeping it running from year to year was a gigantic struggle. It required hat-in-hand begging from whoever was in charge of any money that might be available.

Maddie drove along a cluster of old buildings that looked in danger of being shaken to rubble by the next six-point quake. At a faded pock-marked sign that read Parking, she veered right, turned into the parking garage and took the first empty slot she could find. She locked the car, took the elevator down and trotted across the street to the main entrance. Glass doors hissed open as she approached and entered the lobby.

Two volunteers waited at the desk, a spindly woman with sculpted hair who beamed a perky smile and a gentleman ready with a wheelchair in case a patient was in danger of collapse. Maddie asked where she could find Dr. Cordova. Fingers bedecked with rings handed over a folded slip of paper and pointed to the central elevators. Maddie unfolded the note and read that Elena would be waiting in the cafeteria, and she took the first set of elevators she came to. The door slid open and she squeezed in beside an orderly with a gurney and a hygienically challenged patient clothed in rags. Two residents got on at the next stop, hotly debating the necessity of the procedure they'd just witnessed. They were of the opinion the attending physician was an asshole.

She got off on the second floor and followed the row of blue tiles behind a patient wheeling an IV pole. In the cafeteria, she spotted Elena at one of the small tables by the bank of windows across one wall. A strong smell of vegetable soup hung in the air, mingled with frying hamburgers. Maddie bought a cup of coffee and went to join her friend. Elena, slender, dark hair, olive skin, big brown eyes and gorgeous smile wore green scrubs under the white lab coat with Elena Cordova, MD stitched above the pocket. She was sipping at a cup of tea.

"When was the last time you got any sleep?" Elena said.

"The last chance I had."

"You look worse than some of the patients I saw this morning."

"Thanks. You don't look all that rested yourself."

"Double shift. Takes the sparkle out. So what's up?"

"We had a date. I remembered."

"Yes? And what else? I can tell you're all atremble about something on your mind."

"Atremble? What kind of word is that?"

"It seemed apt."

"Tell me about stem cells," Maddie said.

"That's a rather involved subject," Elena said. "And I'm not an expert."

"I figured I'd start with general information and move up to expert."

"This have any thing to do with Dr. Palmer?"

"It was his field," Maddie admitted.

"What do you want to know?"

"Keep it simple. Just your basic stem cell info."

"Right." Elena thought a moment.

Probably deciding what was simple enough for her to understand, Maddie thought.

"Undifferentiated cells, meaning they aren't committed to developing into something already, like a liver or a lung. But if they go through various stages they can become specialized."

"Which means, " Maddie said, "they can be coaxed to grow into specific types of cells to replace diseased cells. Like heart muscle to replace a heart destroyed by a massive myocardial infarction."

Elena nodded. "Potentially they can be used to treat any number of debilitating or fatal diseases by creating new cells to replace those damaged or diseased."

"Like Parkinson's or spinal cord injury."

"And heart disease, diabetes, rheumatoid arthritis, osteoarthritis, stroke, serious burns, maybe others."

"Alzheimer's?" Maddie said.

Elena gave her an irritated frown. "That's the one everybody wants to treat, or eliminate. It has the public's attention. And, mind you, that research is very important. But actually, it is cardiovascular disease that's the greatest cause of death. Hypertension, stroke, congestive heart failure. With our population getting older, and things like obesity and type-two diabetes on the rise, CVD is going to grow into an even bigger problem then it is already."

Maddie took a sip of very hot coffee. "What would cause someone to kill a brilliant researcher?"

"Isn't that more your field than mine? Are you sure it relates to Dr. Palmer's research? Could it be personal and not related to his work?"

Maddie cautiously took another sip of coffee. "Maybe. The problem is I don't know anything about his personal life. And the person who would know, wife number two, was also murdered. So the only people I know to interview are his co-workers, and they don't seem to know a lot about him."

She leaned back and released a loud sigh. "Tell me more about stem cells."

Elena tilted her empty tea cup. "If this is going to go on much longer, I'm going to need more tea."

Maddie got up and obtained a fresh tea bag and a small teapot of hot water. She dropped the bag in the teapot and placed it on the table.

"Let me say again," Elena said. "I'm not an expert on stem cells."

"Okay."

"They're like master cells. They can develop into any of the more than two hundred cell types in the human body. They're originally undifferentiated. Unlike mature cells, which are permanently committed to their fate, stem cells can both renew themselves and create new cells of whatever tissue they're convinced they belong to. At some point they can divide and create cells that are highly specialized."

"Is farthing a buzz word thrown around with stem cells, or research of stem cells?" Maddie said.

"Farthing?" Elena laughed. "Not to my knowledge. A farthing, if I'm not mistaken, is something like a fourth of a penny. Why do you ask?"

"Just something I came across."

"Across where?" Elena's look pinned Maddie to the chair. "Are you getting involved in the investigation into Dr. Palmer's death?"

"Absolutely not," Maddie said emphatically, then added in a softer voice, "I'd just like to arrest the bastard who killed him."

"Isn't that your partner's job?"

"Yeah, but he's not getting anywhere. And how did you know that?"

"I heard you were told to stay away from that investigation."

Maddie lifted an eyebrow. "Who told you?"

"I hear things. In the emergency room one hears a lot of things. Cops bring in prisoners, accident victims, runaways and lost souls. They talk. I listen."

"Sometimes." Maddie sat back. "I wonder why I'm your friend."

Elena smiled. "Because I'm a font of information. You should let it go, Maddie."

Maddie sipped her coffee, which had finally gotten cool enough so it didn't remove the lining of her throat, and set the mug down with a thump. "I feel guilty."

"Why?"

Because I've lost the ability to do my job. "Greg asked for my help, and I didn't give it to him."

"You don't even know what he wanted."

"True," Maddie said. "I'm assuming it had something to do with what led to the murders."

Elena studied her, a doctor to patient not following orders look. "Is that why you aren't getting enough sleep? You fretting over not dropping everything and running to his side? Are you still having nightmares?"

"I've been busy. A lot is on my mind."

"Uh-huh. Do you think I didn't notice you didn't answer my questions? Are you still having nightmares?"

"Now and then," Maddie admitted.

"Have you considered seeing a shrink? I know some good ones. I could give you some names."

"Been there, done that."

"No." Elena strung out the one syllable. "You went to a

session or two. And didn't tell the therapist anything important. And you never went back."

"Do you know any of these people?" Maddie put the printout of the email she'd received from *cad* with the three names. She laid it on the table.

Elena lifted the tea bag from the hot water, set the bag on the edge of her saucer and tasted the tea. "Who or what is this *cad* who sent this?"

"I'm not sure, but Greg's wife is Clarissa Ann Daniels. You know these people?"

"Only one. Dr. Corban."

"What can you tell me about him?" Maddie said.

"He was one of the finest surgeons this hospital ever had."

"Was? He's no longer here?"

"Fine, fine surgeon." Elena shook her head sadly. "Until he could no longer count on his hands."

"What was the matter with his hands?"

"He had Parkinson's."

"Oh," Maddie said. "They shook?"

Elena nodded. "He managed to work a short while, but a surgeon with shaky hands is not someone a hospital can keep around."

"He was fired?"

"No. He quit on his own. He knew he could no longer perform surgery. Sad, because surgery was his life. Most physicians don't have a life outside of work, but he was especially dedicated."

Before Maddie could ask another question, the PA system went off. "Dr. Cordova. Needed in the emergency room. Dr. Cordova. Needed in the emergency room."

"We'll have to continue this another time." Elena stood up and pushed her chair back to the table. "Just a word of caution. Not that I expect you to listen, but I feel I'd be remiss if I did not point out that somebody is going around slicing throats. You'd do well to watch your back."

The sun had slipped into the Pacific by the time Maddie left the Medical Center and a brisk wind brushed her face as she crossed the street to the parking garage. There was a big difference in temperature between day and night. Ocean breezes could drop the temperature until it was nearly cold. She redeemed her car and started home. Why had Clarissa, or whoever *cad* was, sent those four names to her?

Half-way home, she had a thought, an uncertain thought, but she turned around and went back to the hospital. Outside lights lit up the walkway to the entrance, shining down on huge green vases with some sort of vegetation. She went inside and asked the same white-haired volunteer at the desk where she would find the billing department. Dr. Coban had worked here, they would have his address.

"That would be sixth floor, but I don't imagine anyone's there this time of night."

The clock on the wall showed eight-thirty. No doubt the volunteer was correct. How had it gotten so late? Billing personnel probably didn't work past five.

"Do you happen to have Dr. Corban's address on your computer?"

The volunteer pecked at the keyboard and squinted at the monitor. "Room 412. That would be the fourth floor. The elevator is that way." She pointed.

Dr. Corban was a patient? Elena didn't mention that. Maddie went up to the fourth floor and down the hall to room 412. The first bed was empty. She peered around the curtain between beds and the window bed was also empty. At the nurse's station she asked the nurse writing on a chart where Dr. Corban was.

"He left."

"Where did he go?"

"His family checked him out"

"I need his address."

The nurse, her name tag read Blanche, looked up from the chart she was working on. "Are you a relative?"

Maddie pulled out her ID.

"What do you want with Dr. Corban?"

"I need to ask him a few questions."

"What about?"

"It has to do with a current investigation. I can't really go into it."

"Well, I'm sorry, but I can't really give out information about a patient."

A little pressure, a little bullying didn't get Blanche to change her mind. The nurse wouldn't even tell her why the man had been a patient.

Maddie got back on the elevator, rode down to the first floor, went back across the street for her car. As she pulled out of the garage, she kept an eye on the rearview mirror for an SUV. She headed for home with no tail until she reached the freeway. An SUV entered directly behind her.

Dr. Sherman had just finished stuffing his briefcase with what he needed to take home when the painters showed up to put his name on the office door. About time. His name should have been on the door the minute he accepted the offer.

He snatched a pamphlet from the bookshelf, sat at his desk and studied it to look busy while the painters worked. He dare not leave until they finished. The way things were done around here, he needed to make sure they did it right. They were fast about it, that much he could say. A few brush strokes and they were done. One packed up the gear while the other tapped on his door.

"Yes?" Sherman looked up.

The painter opened the door and stuck his head in. "We're finished now, sir, if you'd like to take a look."

Sherman went out into the hallway, stepped back and eyed his name on the door in gold letters. Winston Sherman, MD, Director. Ha. Director. He took a white handkerchief from his back pocket and covered his mouth as he made a soft cough.

Okay, now he could get to work in earnest. He'd spent the day looking at on-going projects and glancing his eye over proposals for new ones. He felt quite satisfied he had a feel for the company. He'd walked through every foot of the physical plant. He remembered with pleasure when that *underling* Jeff Baker told him he couldn't go into a research lab because of the danger of contamination. Well, by God, he let Jeff know who was in charge. He was the director and he'd go anywhere he wanted.

He jotted some new notes about changes he'd make. Not right away, of course. It was better to take these things slowly. He stuck the pamphlet into his briefcase, locked the office and made his way along corridors to the elevator. From behind doorways, he felt eyes tracking him all the way. It made his skin crawl. He knew he wasn't liked by the staff. It was the old thing of the new guy having to prove himself.

Well, he'd do that, all right. He'd do more than that. Their beloved genius Palmer had left some scribbles that might prove interesting. Sherman just might give that a try tonight and see what happened.

Baker was still in his office. What was he working on so late? Sherman decided to find out. He made one soft rap on the door and opened it without waiting for an invitation.

Baker looked up. "Sherman? Something I can do for you?"

Something about Baker gave Sherman the willies. Nothing he could put his finger on, but Sherman made a promise to himself that he'd keep a sharp eye on Baker. No disrespect in Baker's voice, it was just flat. And so was his expression. No telling what he was thinking. Not that Sherman was afraid of Baker, but it paid to be prudent.

"No, no. I just noticed you were still here." Sherman wanted to know what Baker was working on, but couldn't bring himself to ask. And of course, Baker didn't volunteer the information.

"Well I'd best be on my way." Sherman hesitated.

"Good night," Baker said.

With a soft cough into his fist, Sherman left. Instead of going straight down to the exit, he made a detour that took him past Fuller's office. Fuller was also still at his desk. What were the two of them doing? Scheming behind his back?

He rapped a knuckle against the door and grasped the knob, intending to go right in. The door was locked. By

God, Fuller made him wait until he finished typing something before he got up and opened the door.

"Sherman." Fuller looked at his watch. "I thought you went home long ago."

"I'm on my way. Just checking in to see if you need anything before I go." Sherman moved closer to the desk so he could see what was on the computer monitor. Screen saver with bears doing hands stands. All right, Sherman wasn't stupid. Fuller was doing something he didn't want Sherman to see.

Eric Fuller had everything. Privileged background. Handsome. Prominent family. The best school. He was accustomed to getting whatever he wanted.

"Well," Sherman coughed once softly. "Don't work too hard."

"Not a chance," Fuller closed the door after Sherman stepped out and then locked it. These two clowns might think they were funny, but it was Sherman who would have the last laugh.

On the way home, he stopped to pick up Chinese and let his mind anticipate the enjoyment of firing Jeff Baker. And probably even Eric Fuller, the man who had everything. Little snots, both of them. That would let the rest of the staff sit up and take notice.

The house he'd rented temporarily had a driveway that seemed to go straight up. As soon as he had the time, he intended to look around for something better suited and buy it. He gunned the motor and roared up the drive and into the garage. Then he remembered the mail. Damn it, he'd driven right past again.

Inside the house, he turned on lights to dispel the gloom and stuck the food in the microwave for a few seconds to warm it. With a beer to wash it down, he ate straight from the cartons while he jotted notes to work out what he'd say. It was nearly ten when he picked up the phone.

When the call was answered, he said, "How is the research going?"

"Who is this?"

"This is my second call."

"You got the wrong number."

A click and then the dial tone.

Sherman called back. "You don't want to hang up," he said hurriedly. "All I need is a little incentive to keep this information to myself." He didn't bother to cover his mouth when he coughed softly.

"Yeah?"

"Yes. Not a lot. A one-time-only request." This time Sherman hung up.

After throwing away the empty cartons, and plastic utensils, he settled in his recliner and clicked on the television. Only halfway paying attention to whatever came on, he ran the phone call through his mind. Now all he needed was to decide how much he wanted, and figure out a way to collect safely. That was always the difficulty. Getting the money and getting away with it.

It had been a good day. He was satisfied. Things were accomplished. This was the beginning of his new position. This day was the most promising he'd experienced in a long time. Tomorrow would be even better. He thought of the good things coming his way. Appearances were important. He tried on his blue suit. Ha. It still fit perfectly. He added a white shirt and selected a discrete tie, blue with cheery dabs of red.

With a critical eye, he examined his image in the mirror. Appearances were important and his was perfect. Yes, he would wear this tomorrow on his first day of implementing his own programs and eliminating Palmer's influence. He'd get rid of certain people, hire a few who would be loyal to him, and he had that unexpected bonus coming his way as soon as he made decisions about how much and how to get it safely. He hung up everything ready for morning.

After an hour of trying to watch television, he gave it up and spooned grounds in the coffee pot, poured in the correct amount of water and pushed the button to set it for morning motion and went out to collect the mail sixteen steps on the curb below.

Carefully he started down. The steps were slick with wet moss. What he really needed was a railing. Never mind, he'd soon be finding another place to live.

Just as he descended another step, he sensed someone behind him. Before he could turn, hands closed around his throat.

A vicious twist and a shove and Dr. Winston Sherman's body ended up at the bottom of sixteen stone steps. He died of a broken neck.

Dany must be wondering where she was. Maddie thought she should have called. She wasn't used to checking in and explaining her whereabouts. A light was on in Dany's window when she got home. As soon as she got inside, Maddie kicked off her shoes, then she tapped on Dany's door and stuck her head in. Her niece was sprawled across the bed, phone glued to her ear.

Dany said a hasty goodbye, hung up, and twisted around. "You're really late. I was beginning to worry."

"Sorry. I should have called. I got busy and didn't realize how late it was."

Dany grinned. "That excuse never worked for me."

"All right, smartass." Maddie swatted her across the rear. "Who were you talking to?"

"Just Lara. Wanted to let me know she's going to be out tomorrow getting her hair cut."

"She thought you needed to know this at—" Maddie checked her watch. "Almost nine-thirty?"

"Yeah. She gets a little uptight. Tells me all the time not to let anyone talk to Cindy, and not let the kid talk to any strange men. Duh. What does she think I am? A ditz? Mom called, by the way. She wants you to call her."

Dany rolled off the bed. "I fixed pasta for dinner. Want me to heat it up for you?"

"I think I can manage." Maddie found fettuccini with Alfredo sauce in the refrigerator, scooped some into a bowl and stuck it in the microwave. While she waited for it to heat, a little worry scooted across her mind that Dany was up to something. Hey, when did she turn into a parent?

And speaking of parents, she really should call Pam. Did she have the strength to talk with her sister tonight? She was too tired and it was too late to call anyway. It was after eleven-thirty in Kansas. A little ding told her the pasta was ready. She got a fork and sat at the table.

As tired as she was, the damn dream was sure to screw up her sleep tonight. She'd gone to a therapist, damn it, to rid herself of the thing. The shrink didn't say do this, do that, you'll be fine. Instead, the shrink prattled on about connections within family, with the sister, jealousy, loss of mother's attention. Okay, Maddie could go with that. One day her crazy mother plunked a baby in Maddie's arms and announced, "This is Pamela. She's your sister." Maddie had been four years old and very quickly knew that Pamela was her responsibility.

At the time baby Pamela arrived, Maddie had just accepted it. Later she'd started wondering. Four-year-old kids can notice quite a lot. Her friend Timmy had a baby sister and Timmy's mom had been fat before the baby sister arrived. Maddie should have some memory of her mother with a large stomach, maybe having morning sickness, seeing a doctor, buying baby clothes, talking about a new brother or sister for Maddie, picking out names.

She remembered none of that. Her mother never saw a doctor, bought a crib, went into a hospital. Maddie told herself, let it go. Pam was content with her life and Dany and her little sister Molly. Just drop it for now.

Maddie brushed her teeth, peeled off her clothes and managed to pull on pajamas before she toppled into bed and fell asleep. She dreamt.

The night was dark, clouds covered a sliver of moon. The wind tugged and tore at her clothes as she stumbled over uneven ground. She found the body, partially covered with leaves, in a shallow ditch. She crouched and shined her flashlight at the dead face.

The eyes opened, blinked. The mouth tightened. The lips

parted. Maddie leaned closer to hear what the dead woman would say.

Her alarm clock went off.

Maddie shot up from sleep, her heart pounding along her ribs. She silenced the clock, yawned, and shuffled to the bathroom. After she showered and dressed, she started a pot of coffee and tapped on Dany's door. She filled an insulated cup with coffee, checked her gun, gathered her gear and let Dany know she'd be home at seven, or she'd call.

Chapter Twenty-one

The extra edge to the buzz of talk hit Maddie as soon as she entered the crowded room. She sidled past a half dozen officers in the last row, careful to avoid stepping on feet, and squeezed in beside Jesse.

"What's going on?" she asked him.

Before he could answer, Dirks rapped on the podium. "All right, people, let's get started."

The drone of voices faded to quiet. Amber, across the room, spoke to the FBI agent beside her. When she side-stepped to create space for a late-comer, her glance swept over Maddie. A look flashed over her face and though quickly gone, Maddie caught it. Amber was smugly pleased with herself. Maddie knew Amber resented her, that Amber expected the detective spot to be hers. Maddie dropped her thoughts when Dirks started to speak.

"Let's don't dawdle," Dirks said. "We need to get on, as I'm sure you'd all like to get to the job. Jones, you want to let us all know what you have on the bones found near the old Cleary place?"

"Doc Newel's got the bones at the morgue." Jesse said "We're waiting on a positive ID from him. He said the bones were that of a female, age twenties to thirties. His estimate as to how long she'd been dead six months. He couldn't get any better than that. This suggests they were the bones of Valerie

Danforth who disappeared six months ago. She was twenty-two, kindergarten teacher. Dedicated teacher according to the parents. Went to church on Sundays. Got along with everybody. We gave it everything we could, but there just wasn't anywhere to go."

"Boyfriend?" Dirks said.

"We looked at him real hard. Some kind of computer expert. Works at Lloyd's Electronics. Has an alibi for the pertinent times. He was demonstrating new products at a convention in Texas. He called her twice. Left messages. Was somewhat concerned, but assumed she was at a school function that came up."

"You questioned friends?" Dirks said. "Neighbors, co-workers?"

Jesse looked irritated, but simply said, "Yes, sir. We talked with all the teachers at the school, every friend we know of, and tracked down every name we came across."

"Right," Dirks said.

"She was killed somewhere else and her body left where the dog found it. We found soft drink cans, gum wrapper, one used needle that could possibly mean something. A short piece of plastic tubing."

"Needle have anything on it?"

"Nothing."

"Did you connect it to her?"

"No, sir. No evidence of drug use. Boyfriend said she never used drugs. Mother said the same."

"What kind of plastic tubing?"

"Uh—the kind that are used in hospitals for IVs. Use was undetermined. Nothing was found in it."

"Manner of death?"

Jesse shrugged. "With nothing but a few bones, Doc didn't have much to work with. He did say he'd give them another closer look, but he wasn't going to promise anything."

Dirks moved on to the Palmer homicides. He asked Jesse where he was.

"Neighbors were questioned, all the nearest ones, didn't get us anything. Nobody saw anything, nobody heard anything. Colleagues, interviews ongoing," Jesse said. "With special attention to Jeffrey Baker and Eric Fuller who, worked closely with Palmer, and Dr. Sherman who is temporarily in charge. None of the three have an alibi for the pertinent times. Home alone, nothing to corroborate."

"Any indication they were involved in homicides??"

"No, sir," Jesse said. "Nor to indicate they weren't."

Dirks asked FBI agent Cutter if he had anything new to add and he replied that he didn't. Maddie got a sense that he lied. Not surprising. Interagency sharing of information was a great theory, but while promises were made, they were often not kept.

Dirks leaned his forearms on the podium and curled his fingers over the front edge. "I need to, once again, mention Matt Lockner. Most of you probably saw his article in the *Mira Vista Times* this morning. Somebody is leaking this guy information. Potentially dangerous information. I want to know who. And I want it to stop. I don't know how much credence will be placed on little more than a baby being a witness, but this killer just might not want to take any chances on the toddler fingering him."

Fuck-up Fenton said, "There's probably a hundred or more people working on those homicides. It could be anybody. And they have wives and girlfriends and friends."

"We have a leak and I want it stopped." Dirks looked around the room. "That clear?"

He waited a beat and then he said, "And I want to reiterate that Clayton Thorne is still to be found. Try harder people." Dirks tapped the podium once. "Anybody have anything else to add?"

Nobody did. "Okay, people, let's get to work." Dirks tapped the podium twice and everybody started for the door.

Maddie followed her partner and was out the door when Dirks said, "Detective Martin."

Maddie turned back. Oh-oh. She didn't like the tone of his voice. Was he about to drop the axe?

"I got a message," Dirks said.

"Message, sir?"

He nodded. "Message said you were the one passing information to Lockner."

"What?" Maddie was so startled that she took a second or two to shift from about to be fired to accusation of passing info to a reporter.

"Who said that?" She didn't sound quite as indignant as she'd have liked.

"Anonymous. Said you were seen in a cozy situation chatting with the guy."

"I did have lunch with him. Lunch," Maddie repeated, although she had walked out before she actually got to the lunch part. "There was nothing cozy about it. I met him at the restaurant Rosarita's. He suggested he could make it worth my while if I would collaborate with him on a book about Greg. I don't know what he considered worth my while. I didn't ask. I walked out before I told him what I thought of him."

"According to this source, you told him you'd think about it."

To keep from yelling, Maddie spoke very softly with a space between each word. "Your anonymous source is mistaken or a liar." She was spitting mad that someone she worked with would deliberately lie about her.

"Do I understand that's a denial?"

Damn right. She started to tell him to go to hell. Instead she pulled in a deep breath and let it out slowly.

"It wasn't Martin."

She looked up and saw Jesse in the doorway. His jumping in on her side meant a lot to her.

Dirks crossed his arms. "You know that for a fact?"

"She wouldn't do anything that might put a kid in jeopardy, sir. We've been partners for two years now and I know her pretty well. She said she turned Lockner down. Then that's what she did."

"Uh-huh," Dirks said.

Maddie didn't know what that meant, but Dirks said they were through for now and Jesse touched her arm when he left.

She tried to concentrate on paperwork, but the accusation kept tiptoeing to mind. Who accused her of leaking information? Did that person actually believe she'd do such a thing? Or was it meant to cause trouble?

Stewing over who had accused her of leaking information to Lockner, she didn't pay attention to the time and would be late for Dr. Newel's examination of the bones Caesar the dog had found.

"Too bad you didn't find any teeth." Dr. Newel said when Maddie walked in.

Valerie Danforth, with very even, very white teeth, smiled from her high school graduation picture tacked to the bulletin board. He sighed. "It happens. They got scattered by animals, by rain and wind."

Lucky they found the skull, Maddie thought. Dr. Ed Newel, the forensic anthropologist for Mira Vista, bent over the stainless steel table where he laid the bones in anatomical order. Newel looked like a creepy undertaker in a slasher movie. With long thin fingers, he picked up a small bone, held it up and inspected it. Maddie stood by the wall out of the way. As he worked, Newel kept up a constant stream of conversation, occasionally to her, mostly to the bones.

"See what they did to you, those scavengers with their sharp little teeth?" A clicking of his tongue. "Metacarpal." He held it out for Maddie to see. "Mouse snacked on it." He turned it around several times, then replaced it at the end of a string of small lumps.

"The environment has a profound effect on the body," he said. "Above ground, it's subjected to weather. Sunlight, rainfall, heat, cold." His fingers isolated another bone and he peered closely. "Ah." He looked at Maddie over the tops of his glasses. "Her medical records state that she fell while skateboarding and broke her right tibia." He ran a finger across a section of bone. "I'll compare with the X-rays for certainty, but this is Valerie Danforth."

Maddie had the heartbreaking responsibility of telling Valerie's family. The worse part of the job.

"Knowing for sure, I'm told," Newel said, "even if the loved one is dead, is better than not knowing." He placed the bone on the table. "Sometimes I wonder."

He selected another bone to examine. "The human body is a much-wanted food source. Size plays a part in the process, of course, and whether the body is clothed or unclothed, above ground or underground, and how deep. Insects get to work almost immediately."

Maddie thought if she slipped quietly away, Dr. Newel would continue to talk to the bones. Maybe the sound of his own voice was like listening to his favorite music."

"There was a study done back in—" He paused for thought. "I don't remember the year. Recent. They determined a body could be reduced to a skeleton in twenty-eight days."

He straightened the row of vertebrae. "Of course, any number of things—winds, running water, wild life. Dogs, bears, squirrels, mice, rats scatter the bones. Birds and small animals like mice take the hair for their nests. Unless it's something like a skull, bones lying under a clump of decaying leaves are often not recognizable as human."

When he finished studying each bone, he muttered that he'd send her a report. She thanked him and left.

Caitlyn occupied Maddie's mind as she drove back to the Sheriff's Department. Lockner was a dirtbag, no question. How could he write that story for the newspaper with no concern for the two-year-old he was putting in danger? As if the little girl didn't already have enough tragedy in her life. Mother and father both viciously killed. Caitlyn present when—

Jesse leaned back in his chair. "Where you been?"

"Bones."

"What about them?"

"Valerie Danforth." Maddie snagged a chair from a cubicle whose owner was out and plopped it next to his desk. "A written report is forthcoming."

"Okay. So what are you dithering about?"

"I don't dither," she said.

"Right. Hanging on my every word."

"I got an email." She stopped.

He looked at her. "I understand they're very popular these days."

"It was from *cad*."

"Who's cad?"

"That what I'm trying to explain. I'm not sure."

"Maddie, I don't have time to play games. Just tell me."

She clamped down on her back teeth. "I started to delete it without looking at it, then decided to read it first. The text was just a string of names. I didn't know any of them."

"Are these names of any interest to me?"

"I'm getting to that" she said. "Greg's wife's name is Clarissa Ann Daniels."

He rested his chin in a hand. "You still have the email?"

"No, but I did print it." She handed him the list of names. "You think it's from her? The wife?"

"I don't know. Maybe Sammy can retrieve the email and tell us where it came from."

Sammy was their computer whiz. Sammy could perform miracles.

The sky, a uniform gray, meant more rain on the way.

Californians got real excited about rain. It was given first spot on the news, and tracked by radar. Weather forecasters, dressed in L.L. Bean gear, stopped pedestrians on the street and asked, "So how're you handling this storm?" Inches were reported and compared with inches in previous years. The possibility of thunder and lightning, a rare occasion, had forecasters ecstatic, and Maddie nearly homesick.

Just after eleven, she arrived at the Medical Center. Since Dr. Corban had been a patient, she was certain they'd have his address. The billing department was one large room divided by cubicles, each with a government issue desk and a computer. Overhead fluorescent lights made everyone look slightly anemic. This had to be the most depressing place in the hospital, except for the basement where the dead awaited attention.

All the problems facing health care ended up in billing. They were so many and they were so complicated and so seemingly unsolvable that even the air felt thick and difficult to breathe. Problems kept accumulating and gathering bulk like a huge snowball that rolled and bounced, faster and faster down hill gaining on our heels.

The top half of the double door was open, and a bell rested on the level shelf of the bottom half. She tapped the bell. A man with a long face who looked like he'd been in this section too long, asked in a lugubrious voice what he could do for her. Mid-morning and he already seemed tired, on the edge of misery, with nothing to look forward to but another day dealing with insurers, including Medicare—oh my God, Medicare—and sending collection agencies dogging some poor bastard with a stack of medical bills a foot high.

She showed him her ID and explained she wanted to take a look at the billing record of a patient who had been discharged. She fully expected him to say she needed a warrant to look at a single word of anything, even the yellowed cartoons tacked to the bulletin board. To her great surprise, he told her he'd find someone who could help her. He unlatched the lower door and led her through a maze of desks with people busy on phones, typing at computers and reading lists of charges.

He introduced her to Mrs. Waverly, a round woman in her fifties with wispy gray hair and a white blouse tucked into brown pants. "Would this have anything to do with those awful murders that happened?"

Maddie smiled back, albeit a smaller variety. "I'm not at liberty to talk about an ongoing investigation."

"Oh, of course. Patient's name?"

"Albert Corban."

"Oh yes, Dr. Corban. Worked here for some years, then he came down with that awful Parkinson's and had the tremors so bad he couldn't even hold the instruments when he tried to operate."

Mrs. Waverly shook her head. "Poor soul. Yes, here it is."

She turned the screen so Maddie could see it. Admitted for observation, hospital stay one day. Discharged. Bottom line. Amount owed. $68,482.29.

"Goodness," Mrs. Waverly said.

"Something wrong?"

"Well no, but it is odd. This was already paid." She pointed at yesterday's date. "Paid by check." She made a genteel little humph. "Good for the hospital, I guess, but it's the first time I've seen this. Usually we send bills. Sometimes several bills before anything gets paid."

"What's Dr. Corban's address?"

Maddie again expected to be told that they don't give out that information, but Mrs. Waverly read it off the screen. Maddie scribbled a note, thanked the woman and left. As soon as she got in her car, she used her cell phone to get on the internet for directions. The promised rain was just getting started, large drops splattered on her windshield. She felt a brief stab of homesickness for a spectacular midwest storm with thunder and lightning.

Be careful what you wish for. Before she could find the right street on her map, her cell phone vibrated. Caller ID showed Jesse. A storm descended on her. He yelled. He wanted to know what the hell she was playing at. With a number of colorful words, he demanded to know if she understood the meaning of the word *no.* That was spelled N O and it meant she was to keep her sticky little guilt feelings off the Palmer homicides.

Okay so he was angry that she went to Changing Biology. "I just wanted to—"

"I don't care what you *just wanted.* Stay out of it!"

"It was just—"

"With you it's always *just* something." He hung up.

She thought about calling him back and apologizing, but right now she needed to read street names. Not familiar with the area, she pulled over to consult GPS. With only two wrong turns, she found the address she was looking for. Stucco, pinkish, with a two-foot stone wall-facing across the front, lawn soggy with water from recent rains, two large pink flamingos. Large window across the front with curtains closed.

She hesitated. She really had no reason to question Dr. Corban, but she needed to find out who sent the email with his name included in the text? Was it Clarissa who sent it? If so, why? And what was her connection with Dr. Corban? Was there a connection to the murders? She got out of the car and walked up to the house. Her thumb against the doorbell brought immediate opening. A little girl, maybe nine or ten, in jeans and a long-sleeved yellow tee shirt, reddish hair pulled back in a pony tail, peered out suspiciously through round glasses.

"My name's Detective Martin. I'm a police officer," Maddie said. "What's your name?"

"I'm not supposed to talk to strangers."

"That's very smart. Is your mom home?"

"Yeah."

"I need to talk with her. Is it all right if I come in?"

"I'm not supposed—"

A woman in her mid-thirties with blurry eyes, grabbed the child and pulled her aside. Her beige trousers were rumpled as though she'd just yanked them on after being awakened. "Who the hell are you?"

"Detective Martin." Maddie held out her creds.

The woman didn't even look at them. "I got nothing to say to you."

"I need to speak with Dr. Corban."

"No."

"Are you Mrs. Corban?"

"Just go away." She started to close the door.

So far today had not gone well. "Ma'am, I really need to talk to Dr. Corban." Maddie stepped forward.

"You can't."

The little girl watched owlishly from across the room.

"Just a few questions," Maddie said. "It's important. I promise it won't take long."

The woman sighed heavily, then moved aside to allow Maddie to come in. "What is it you want?"

Maddie hesitated. The woman nearly gave off sparks, she was so angry, maybe also confused, certainly dealing with grief. "What's your relationship to Dr. Corban?"

"I'm his sister, Sybil Shearing." The defiance went out of her and she was simply a middle-aged woman very upset about something. "You're too late."

"Too late?"

"He's dead!" Sybil Shearing's words were quick with exasperation.

"I'm so sorry," Maddie said. "When did he die?"

"Sometime last night. The damn fool!"

Maddie raised an eyebrow.

"I'm just so mad at him. He said it would help. The shaking. They wanted to cut into his brain."

"He had surgery." Maddie wanted to be sure she knew what Sybil was saying. "For his Parkinson's Disease, to alleviate tremors."

"I thought it was too dangerous."

"Was the surgery done in the Medical Center?"

"No. I told him this surgery was a bad idea. What if something went wrong? Things go wrong all the time with surgery that isn't even brain surgery."

"Where was the surgery done?"

"I don't know anything." Sybil angrily rubbed tears from her face. "Some clinic somewhere."

"What was the name of the clinic?"

"I just told you, I don't know."

"Where is this clinic?"

"I have no idea. He got this into his head and there was no changing his mind. It was all done before he called me."

"He was a patient at the Medical Center," Maddie said.

"That was later. After he came home from the clinic. Then he called me and told me what he'd done. Said he needed my help. The damn fool!"

"So you came to look after him."

Sybil nodded. "I no sooner got here than he got real bad. I couldn't wake him up. He was breathing funny."

She shot a defiant look at Maddie. "I called 911. I thought

he was going to die before they got here. They took him to the Medical Center. In a few hours, he got some better and he was furious at me. I almost grabbed my airline ticket and walked out right there. He was only at the Medical Center overnight, next evening he insisted on coming right back here."

"Your brother was a doctor, he must have know there were risks."

She sniffed and softened her voice. "Al was so crazy with the shaking he didn't care. When he called me and told me what he was planning, I knew I couldn't stop him. Either the surgery would cure him, or he'd die from it." Her words were thick. "He didn't much care which."

She gave Maddie a watery smile. "He told me he knew what he was doing. That's the last time I listen to him, right?" Tears rolled down her cheeks and she rubbed at them.

"Who was the doctor who performed the surgery?" Maddie said.

"Some quack. Promising he'd be cured. Shaking would stop. Life would be positively rosy."

"What did he look like?"

"How would I know I never met him."

"Did he happen to mention a name?"

"A quack named Gregory Palmer."

Chapter Twenty-two

The garage door rattled down and the noise woke Dany. Her room was dark as night. The clock showed six minutes to five. She groaned. Why was Maddie going to work so early? An hour before Dany needed to get up. Raindrops splattered at the window. She stretched and rolled over, tucked up her knees and snugged the blankets tighter over her shoulder. Jesse must be picking her up since Maddie'd left already.

The house phone rang, yanking her out of sleep. She yawned and plopped a pillow over her head. A minute later, her cell phone rang. She propped her chin on one elbow and took a glance around the room for her backpack. Ah. Chair by the window. She unzipped the backpack and plowed through the contents for her phone. Caller ID showed Lara's number.

"Hi," Dany said.

"It's Lara. I'm sorry to call so early. But I wanted to let you know Jesse can't pick you up. He already went in to work. Take a cab. And I'll pay for it, of course. Okay?"

"Uh-huh." Dany flopped back on the pillow. She wanted some way to get around without having to wait for Maddie or Jesse. Both of them worked all the time, at least long long days. Dany wanted the ability to go at her own schedule. She'd asked Maddie about taking a bus, Maddie said that wasn't done here. Why not? Buses just weren't available. Maddie took her everywhere she needed to go.

Not only to Jesse's, but the mall if she needed nail polish

or the convenience store for whatever. If she was headed for someplace she didn't want Maddie to know about, it got really awkward. That meant lies. Lying was really really not good. For one thing, it meant remembering whatever had been said. For another thing, it made her feel really icky.

The bicycle. Was that a possibility?

Dany tossed the covers back and switched on the lamp by the bed. Top priority, transportation.

Just as her feet hit the floor, the light went out. Damn it. Shuffling in the dark, she made for the doorway, stubbed her toe on a chair leg, stumbled over her sneakers and groped for the switch to the ceiling light. Nothing. Power out.

Where did Maddie keep a flashlight? Hands against the wall, Dany felt her way along to the hallway and into the living room. Her toe, the same one, bashed into the wooden rocker. Ouch ouch ouch ouch. Damn. She massaged the toe. Now, just watch where you're going. Though she couldn't exactly watch, since she couldn't see, but she moved with more care to the fireplace, mindful of the hearth coming up. Her reaching fingers touched rough stone and she felt along the mantle until she found the matches. She struck one and lit one of the tall candles that sat there.

Candle in hand, she searched the linen closet, the drawers in her bathroom, the drawers in the other bathroom, drawers and cabinets in the kitchen. All right, where's a flashlight? She crept into Maddie's bedroom and hesitated. This was way beyond accepted behavior. A guest did not go rifling though the hostess's private things. Just a peek in the bedside table? Dany stood, hesitating. Would she like it if Maddie went through her stuff? No. Maddie was good to her. She deserved better. Okay. No flashlight.

Maybe Maddie's office, though. Good place for a flashlight. Dany made her way to the office, which was really the dining room, set the candle on the desk and opened the top right-hand drawer. She pawed through a bunch of papers and stuff, spilling some on the floor. She scooped them up, dumped them back, and tried the center drawer. Yes! Success! She grabbed the flashlight and switched it on. All right! Let there be light! She blew out the candle and shoved the drawer shut. An envelope fluttered to the floor. She bent down and picked it up.

A snapshot was inside. She held the flash beam closer. Picture of a baby. Looked very young. Face scrunched, eyes squinched. She'd never seen the picture before. She wondered who it was. Oh, a thought came to mind. Could Maddie have had a baby? A strong feeling of trespass came over Dany. This was a secret, or Maddie would have mentioned it.

In the kitchen, Dany filched a small candy bar from Maddie's leftover Halloween stash. Suddenly the refrigerator hummed, nearly scaring her to death. Power was back. All right! Rain pattered intermittently against the garage roof. Her bare feet curled away from the cold cement floor. She should have put on shoes.

Whole bunch of stuff out here. Garden tools leaning in corners, hanging from walls, stacked in the rafters, boxes piled under the window. Why didn't Maddie get rid of some of this junk? Maybe Dany could do it while she was here. Just a thoughtful thing to let Maddie how useful she was, and another reason to let her stay.

Dany used the flash for more light and aimed at the rafters, moving it slowly. Lots of stuff up there too. She couldn't really make out—

Footsteps?

She spun around, listened. All she could hear was rain. Okay, no getting creeped out. As hard as she tried to shake it off, she felt someone was out there in the dark, watching her. Stupid. Why would anyone watch her? Well now, maybe contemplating rape. Or murder. Or kidnapping.

Stop! Get a grip. Nobody can see into the garage. Unless the creep is in the rafters, you're safe from prying eyes. She located the bicycle—inaccessible. Natch. Way toward the center with stuff piled on top. She needed a ladder. Yes. Behind garden tools and bags of potting soil. She set to work moving stuff so she could get it out. It was an aluminum step ladder and had two drawbacks. It didn't look very sturdy and it didn't look tall enough.

She dragged it to a spot under the bike. Yep, not tall enough. Okay, she'd just have to see if she could reach the beam and pull herself up. She climbed up and hesitated on the last rung. If she stood on the top, she'd have nothing to brace herself against. Besides which, you're never supposed to do that. If she didn't, she was out of luck.

Okay, here goes nothing. Tentatively, she put one foot on the very top step and then the other. She teetered a bit and waited until she got her balance.

She climbed up. A little precariously, she grabbed hold of a rafter and pulled at the bicycle wheel. Stuck. She yanked. The bike slid about two inches. Aha. The hang-up, she realized was that the bike was tied to a cross beam.

Down off the ladder. Among all the garden tools, she found a pair of shears. Back on the ladder, she realized she had another problem. Even if she got it loose, it was too heavy to hold. If she just let it fall, she might mess the shit out of it. Okay, think.

Climb up beside the bike and then like pitch it down. Good idea, except the beam wasn't wide enough to climb onto. How about if she opened the garage door and crawled onto it? Then she could get close enough to cut the rope and hurl the damn bike to the floor. So what if it got smashed to a tin can? Better than just leaving it where it was. She got down off the ladder, hit the button that opened the door and climbed back up.

With her arm stretched out, shears in hand, she could almost—

A hand grasped her ankle.

"You look like you could use some help."

Chapter Twenty-three

Clayton Thorne looked out the motel window at a gray sky that looked strongly like rain. He considered staying another day where he was. LA was, after all, a big place. No, he decided. Not sticking to his schedule might get him caught. A move every two or three days kept him safe. He had the time and the money and his friendship with a man he'd met in prison gave him a driver's license, ID for every occasion. Giving little Cindy the puppy had been a stroke of brilliance. The frustration it must cause Detective Jones brought sweet pleasure. It also established Clayton as a man of exciting surprises.

Pretty little thing, Cindy. He pictured her lovely face. In his fantasy, he called her Cinderella. When she was in his hands, he'd be very gentle, move very slowly, with a soft voice and reassuring words,

How satisfying. Revenge for Jones and exquisite pleasure for himself. Be vigilant. Be patient. The opportunity would present itself. He swallowed the last of his breakfast tea and rinsed the cup. Who would he be today? He could be anything. One of the many homeless? No. That required a bit of grime and smell that he didn't want to take on. A traveling salesman? Ah, he got it. An insurance salesman. He dressed in a dark suit, white shirt and discreet tie, paused while he considered his raincoat. He decided to bring it, just in case, and stuck a hat in his pocket.

Don't, he told himself, let impatience cause imprudence. You mustn't be lead astray, or create a complication. He collected a paper from a corner stand, took the PCH to Mira Vista and exited the freeway. He drove passed the Jones house. No little girl in the bedroom window. He didn't really expect it, but how challenging that would be. The little one snatched from right under the detective's nose.

He made another circle around the block and saw mother and daughter, hand in hand, walking toward the park. In her free hand, the mother had the pet carrier with the puppy inside. He watched Lara set the pet carrier down just inside the entrance to the park. Well, well, would this be a good day for him?

With a wary eye out for cops and the *Mira Vista Times* under his arm, he strolled to a bench beneath the pine trees. He sat down and glanced over the front page. Still no progress in locating the missing Francine Ramsey. What a shame. The business section reminded him too much of his parents disappointment in their only child. He turned to the crossword puzzle.

Cindy knelt by the carrier and whispered to Haley inside. The puppy yipped. Cindy raced to the swings. She shrieked at Lara to push her. Lara pushed. And pushed, and pushed. Cindy leaned back, legs straight out in front, and cried, "Higher! Higher!"

Thorne very quietly folded his newspaper and got back in his car. He drove around to the main entrance to the park and, keeping alert for anyone watching, parked, strolled to the gate and reached over to pick up the pet carrier. Just as leisurely, he strolled back to his car.

After twenty minutes Lara had enough. She was bored, cold and needed to go home and do something about her hair and makeup. "Ready to leave?"

"Not yet."

"Aren't you cold? I'll make us some hot chocolate to warm

us up. What do you think?"

"Yeah! I love hot chocolate. It's my most favorite thing to drink"

"Okay then, let's go."

"In a minute."

Lara sighed. More like fifteen went by before Cindy would agree to leave. Lara grabbed the chains to stop the swing. Cindy slid out and scampered off.

"Cindy! Wait!"

"The slide," Cindy yelled. "Before we go." She raced passed the merry-go-round, clambered up the steps of the slide and zoomed down, landed in a puddle, picked herself up, ran around to the steps, and climbed up again.

"You're getting all wet," Lara said. "If you want hot chocolate, we need to go home now."

Cindy thought it over and nodded. She skipped ahead, then suddenly stopped and gasped.

"Mommy!" She raced back full tilt and grabbed her mother's hand. "We forgot Haley!"

Cindy ran back to the swings and looked around. "Where's Haley?"

"By the gate."

Cindy sped off that way, skidded to a stop and peered left and right and over on the other side. "He's not here! He's gone!" Cindy tugged on her mother's arm. "What happened to Haley?"

"I don't know."

They walked around the park, stopping to ask the few people they saw if anyone had seen the dog. There weren't many to ask. The dreary weather kept people home. Nobody had seen Haley.

"He'll get scared!" Cindy cried. "We have to find him!"

Lara didn't know where else to look. "Come on." She squeezed Cindy's hand. "He has a tag. Somebody will find him and let us know."

"Nooo!" Cindy threw herself on the ground. "We can't leave without Haley!"

Cindy landed in a muddy spot. Lara lost patience and

picked her up. Cindy stiffened and kicked.

"Stop it! We need to go home."

"We can't. We have to—"

"I'll tell you what we'll do." Lara set Cindy on her feet and took her hand. "We'll wait for Daddy and we'll tell him."

"He'll find Haley!"

Thankful that Cindy agreed to leave, they went home. Lara was irritated to discover Dany still hadn't arrived. She was hoping to turn Cindy over to her and change clothes.

"Hot chocolate!" Cindy said.

"Right." Lara took off Cindy's wet clothes and muddy shoes and put them on the washer. In the bedroom she took out dry pants and a clean shirt for Cindy to change into, then went into the kitchen and called Jesse.

CHAPTER TWENTY-FOUR

He inspected the operating room for readiness, hoping his anesthesiologist would be on time. Every day he performed surgery was a day he blessed Henry's arrival in his life. Henry was perfect. A skilled anesthesiologist, he showed up when needed, did his job and didn't ask questions. What more could a surgeon want?

Henry arrived at fifteen minutes to eleven and went over his equipment. Hospital privileges had been taken away, due to Medicare billing. Henry claimed it was a stupid misunderstanding. Maybe he'd added some extras with bills, but nothing extravagant. It certainly wasn't anything to get heated about, nothing his colleagues weren't doing. The government hadn't seen it that way, and the topper was the accusation of Henry being drunk while in the OR. He came near to losing his medical license.

That's when he had packed up and come to California. It was no surprise that he had trouble finding work. He answered the ad on the internet, desperate and eager to take the job. Of course, the money helped. It was more than he could ever expect, given his circumstances.

He never asked questions or pried into patient care, or mentioned it was odd that some procedures were performed that were not what he expected. He administered the anesthetic, collected his money and went home until the next time he got a phone call.

The patient was wheeled in on a gurney. She'd been given some pre-op sedatives to relieve the anxiety and appeared sleepy. Henry didn't even know the patient's names and that was fine with him. He went about the business of getting her ready.

When the patient was on the table, Henry put the electrodes on her chest, then attached the EKG leads, checked the IV, and placed the oximeter on the patient's finger. He kept close watch on his monitors and then nodded that the patient was ready for surgery.

Francine lay on the narrow bed looking up at the track lighting in the ceiling of this pseudo-perating room. Anxiety clamored at her mind. Would it be the last thing she ever saw? She should run. Jump off the gurney and run as fast as she could.

"This may sting a little." Henry injected something into the IV tubing.

She watched his eyes. They were focused on what he was doing. He had not once made eye contact with her.

The anxiety stopped its stabbing chatter and she drifted to sleep.

When Henry nodded at him that she was ready, he looked at her and felt regret that she had to be disposed of. It was too bad, but he couldn't take a chance that she might talk to someone and cause trouble. His research was too important to allow interference. With complaints, authorities could obtain a search warrant and that would be the end. Being of small minds, they would not understand the importance of his work. After everything he'd gone through he couldn't let that happen.

As usual the surgery went quickly and without a problem. When he finished, he took her back to the holding cell and gently slid her onto the bed.

She opened her eyes and stared at the track lighting in the ceiling.

"Ah, you're awake."

She shifted her gaze from the ceiling to his face. "You told me you were going to—do something—"

He pumped up the blood pressure cuff, put the stethoscope earpieces in his ears and the end thingy against the inside of her elbow. "Correct."

Correct. What did that mean? She had no sense of any time having gone by.

"Blood pressure's fine. You feel okay?"

She felt confused. She fully expected to wake up dead and here he was saying her blood pressure was fine. Had he really done something? Or was this part of his research? "What time is it?"

One corner of his mouth lifted in a knowing smile. "About an hour has passed."

An hour? How strange. It didn't seem like more than two minutes.

"I want you to sit up."

She cringed from his gloved hand as he took her elbow and put his arm around her shoulder to help her into a sitting position. He propped her up while she moved her legs over the side of the bed.

"Do you feel dizzy? Light-headed?"

"No."

"Pain?"

No physical pain, but the anxiety came whispering back, and building up to screaming panic. He stepped back, made scratchy notes on his clipboard.

"Lie back down."

He continued to scribble as she drew her legs up and stretched out on the bed. "I'll be back later to check on you."

"What did you do to me?"

He smiled, that movement of his mouth that wasn't really a smile. He unlocked the door, and just as he stepped out, he said. "You're all done."

She waited, wondering if this was some subterfuge and he'd come storming back. When she judged two minutes had passed, she threw back the sheets and pulled up her flimsy hospital gown.

Bending her chin, she peered at her bared abdomen. Three small squares of gauze bandages were taped in the lower area. One below her navel, one lower down on the right side and the third on the same spot on the left side. What had he done? She felt fine, no pain, no queasy stomach from a drug.

All done? What did he mean *all done?*

He checked the gametes thriving in their chemical stimulation medium, hit a switch, and sent a jolt through it. The electrical shock fused the enucleated cells with the added adult epithelial cells and gave each cell the necessary number of chromosomes. The adult nuclei dropped their programmed duties and embraced their embryonic roles.

These gametes started to divide and had been cloned three dozen times.

CHAPTER TWENTY-FIVE

Jesse sped home, not sure what the emergency was. When he sprinted into the house, he heard Cindy wailing in her room and Lara making soothing murmurs. He hurried to his daughter's bedroom and took a breath when he saw both his females on their feet and neither was bleeding.

"Daddy! Daddy!" Cindy launched herself at him and clung to his knees.

A look of relief crossed Lara's face.

"Hey." He bent to detach Cindy, and picked her up.

"Find him, Daddy? Please please, will you?"

He hugged her close. It squeezed something inside to see her so upset. Gently, he rubbed small circles on her back, and looked over at Lara. "What's going on?"

"Haley," Cindy said. "He's gone."

"Where'd he go?"

Another burst of tears. "I don't know, Daddy."

Lara pulled a tissue from the box on the chest and handed it to him. He used it to pat at his daughter's face. "What happened to Haley?" He wondered if Lara had been instrumental in whatever happened to the dog. When it chewed up her new shoes, he had a feeling its days of being a family member were numbered.

"He was at the park, Daddy, and then he was gone. Somebody stole him. Will you find him? Please, Daddy? Please?"

Lara explained.

"Did you look for him?"

Cindy scrubbed at her face with her fists. "Mommy and me did. We went all the way through the park. That's really far for Haley, isn't it?"

"You looked?" he asked Lara.

"Yes." She crossed her arms.

"You can find him. Right, Daddy?"

"We can get another dog," Lara said.

Cindy pounded her fist on Jesse's shoulder. "I don't want another dog! I want Haley! Please, Daddy."

"I'll see what I can do," he said.

"You promise? You promise you'll find Haley?"

"I promise I'll try really hard. Right now I want you to lie down on your bed and rest very quietly while I talk with your Mommy. Okay?"

Cindy stared at him rebelliously, then gave a nod. He set her down and she climbed onto the bed. "Please, Daddy," she said in a small voice.

In the kitchen, he leaned against a cabinet, hands behind him on the counter top. "Did you do something with that dog?"

With a glare, she started to walk away.

"Okay, okay. I apologize. Tell me again what happened."

She rubbed her forehead with a thumb and forefinger. "We went to the park. Cindy insists on taking that—*rat* with her wherever she goes. He was in the pet carrier. I set it down inside the entrance. Cindy ran to the swings and I went after her."

"Why didn't you take the carrier with you?"

Lara pulled in a breath and let it out on a huff. "Have you ever taken her anywhere with that stupid animal?"

"Yes."

"No." Lara shook her head. "You haven't. Or you'd know that thing yips and yelps if it's in the cage and it can see her."

"So?"

"Barking," Lara said. "High-pitched noise. Drives you nuts and irritates everybody else around."

It suddenly occurred to him that he hadn't seen the teen-ager he'd hired to do the things like take Cindy to the park. "Where's Dany?"

"She's not here."

"Did you call her?"

Lara shot him a look. "You think I'm an idiot? Of course, I called her. She said she's on the way."

"Why is she late?"

"I don't know," Lara said impatiently. "I told her to take a cab. She said she was on the way. We both hung up."

"Did you notice anyone near you? Hanging around, watching."

She shrugged. "Not really."

"Not really! What the hell! Weren't you paying attention?"

"It's a park. Yeah, there were a few other people there. I didn't see anyone take the dog." Lara's tone was clipped.

"Did you keep an eye on the carrier?"

"Yes." Her voice had risen. "But I wasn't watching it all the time."

"Did you see a man in his fifties around anywhere?"

"No."

"You didn't see a white-haired man, looked kind of like a seedy Santa Claus? Not anywhere?" he said. "Not at the park, not when you walked there, not when you walked home?"

"Oh my God! You think it was him?"

"I've told you, you need to pay attention to your surroundings. You have to stay aware." He had a bad feeling about this. First the dog was given to Cindy, and now it was taken away. He couldn't see what was accomplished. Unless maybe just Thorne pointing out he could get to Cindy as easily as he got the dog.

"For now, stay away from the park and—" His cell phone rang and he checked caller ID. Dispatch. He answered, listened, then said, "I'm on my way."

He put the phone back in his pocket. The address he was given belonged to the new director of Changing Biology, Inc. "I have to go. We'll talk when I get back."

"Sure," she muttered. "Whenever that might be."

Rain started to fall steadily as Jesse left home. Great, just what he needed.

Winston Sherman, new director of Changing Biology lived in a two story stucco perched on top of a hill. The driveway went up, detoured around a tree and up again. Stone steps zig-zagged from the street to the porch. A squad car sat across the foot of the drive. Jesse parked across the street.

The responding uniform who'd arrived first had secured the scene and left his squad car to squelch his way around. When Jesse exited his car he got a faceful of rain. This day just kept getting better.

"What've we got?" Jesse looked up the steps and rapidly blinked rain out of his eyes.

"Looks like an accident, sir."

Maybe so, but these Changing Biology people sure seemed to have extraordinary bad luck. Jesse squinted at the officer's nametag. "Greene, what have you done so far?"

"Secured the scene, sir, and waited for you."

Jesse hunched his shoulders against the wind and crouched for a closer look at the body. With the head twisted at the wrong angle, it appeared Winston Sherman MD had a broken neck. The clothing was soaked. He'd obviously been here awhile.

"Who found him?"

"A neighbor, sir. On his way to work."

"Get the crime scene techs here," Jesse said. "Then help me put up a shelter around him before any more evidence gets washed away."

Jesse got a tarp from the trunk of his car. Just as he and Greene got the tarp positioned over the body—better late than never—the techies arrived. Jesse told them to treat this like a crime scene, and yes he knew it was raining, and yes he knew that compromised the scene, but he told them to do the best they could. Outside first, then inside.

When dispatch mentioned Changing Biology, Maddie paid attention. Possible homicide. Jesse was sent to the home of the new director. She stopped at Starbuck's on the way and bought two lattés. The coroner's van was just arriving. To be out of the way, she pulled in down the block, yanked up the hood of her raincoat and slid from the car.

When Jesse spotted her, he growled, "What are you doing here?"

She handed him a coffee. "What's going on?"

"Thanks." He raised the paper cup and took a sip. "You don't belong here."

"I know. At least tell me what happened."

"Apparently an accident."

"Apparently?"

"Steps." He pointed up the flight of stairs.. " Wet, covered with moss. Slick. Looks like he slipped, tumbled all the way down, ended on the bottom step and broke his neck."

"You treating it like a crime scene?"

"What do you think?"

"It has to be connected to Greg's murder?"

"Maddie—" Jesse took in a breath, got his irritation under control and said quietly, "None of your business. Get out of here."

"Okay. But I want to tell you—"

"And this is important now?"

Annoyed at his attitude, she clamped her mouth shut and turned on her heel.

"Hey," he said. "Since I'm waiting for the crime scene techs to finish their thing, tell me what's so important. Let's at least get out of the rain."

He opened the passenger door of his car for Maddie, went around and got in on the other side. She reminded him of the email from *cad* with the string of names, and told him what she'd learned about Albert Corban.

"What does this have to do with Sherman or Palmer?"

"I don't know exactly."

He took a gulp of coffee and called Lara again. "Has Dany

arrived?"

"Not yet. She called again and said something came up. She'll be a little late."

"What came up?" Jesse didn't like the sound of that.

"I don't know."

He said to Maddie, "Didn't you tell me Dany didn't know anyone here?"

"You're changing the subject. And yes, I did say that. Why?"

"Something came up."

"What?"

"That was my next question," Jesse said.

Maddie shook her head. "Ask Lara to have Dany call me when she gets there. I don't like her being late." Maddie opened her car door to leave. "Maybe I can think of something fun we can do tomorrow since I'm off."

Jesse's eyebrows shot up with exaggerated surprise. "*You* have a day off?"

She smirked. "I do. You should look very closely at this."

"At your day off?"

She gave him a pained look.

"I intend to," he said, "if you mean the unfortunate demise of Winston Sherman. What's this theory you got about emails from your ex?"

"I think he knew about the unauthorized surgery."

"What unauthorized surgery?"

"Illegal experimenting with stem cells."

"Yeah?" he said sarcastically. "Isn't that what the business out there is all about?"

"Animals," she said. "Not people."

Chapter Twenty-six

"Let go of me!" Dany screamed. She yanked her foot free and started kicking.

"Hey, take it easy. You're going to fall."

"Let go!"

"All right, all right." He held up his hands and stepped back. "It's okay. I just thought you needed a little help. And if you don't stop wobbling, you're going to fall."

Heart pounding, breath coming in short gulps, Dany clamped a hand around the rear wheel of the bicycle. She wondered if she could pull it down on his head. "If you don't leave right this minute, I'm going to call the cops."

He grinned. "Actually, that's what I came for."

"What?"

"A cop. I thought Detective Martin lived here."

"Why do you want to see her?"

"You don't really want to pull that bicycle down. I'd have plenty of time to jump out of the way and you'd fall and hurt yourself."

"Who are you?"

"Kevin McGuire—uh—Dirks. I guess."

"You don't seem to know your own name."

"You want to stay up there while we talk? Or do you think you might come down on solid ground, so you're not in danger of falling."

While she was no longer panicked, she was still smart enough to be wary. She didn't know him, she was all by herself and she didn't think any of the neighbors would hear her if she yelled for help. "You want to tell me why you can't decide on your last name?"

He shoved his fingertips in his back pockets. "Long story."

"Just give me the highlights." He was kind of cute. Looked about the same age as she was. Dark hair, probably brown eyes, although she wasn't close enough to tell for sure. Jeans and a dark blue shirt, black leather jacket, black boots. Tall, looked in good shape.

"McGuire," he said. "My mom went off on a honeymoon, didn't want me around so she sent me to Al Dirks. He's supposed to be my father."

"Supposed to be?"

"Yeah, well, that's what I was told. He doesn't want me around either."

She unclamped her hand from the bike wheel. "That sucks. But at least you have one. Some of us don't even have a father."

"Uh, hey, yeah, sorry. You want me to help you get that thing down?"

"Depends. You're talking about Sheriff Dirks, Aunt Maddie's boss?"

"If Aunt Maddie is Detective Martin, then, yes, that's who I'm talking about."

"Why do you want to talk to her?"

"Could you just get down off that stupid ladder? I feel like I'm talking to Juliet or somebody."

Dany climbed down and stood by to help while he pulled and maneuvered the bicycle from the rafters to the floor.

"You really going to ride this thing? It doesn't look in great shape. Hold on a minute." He got a can of compressed air out of the SUV he was driving and inflated the tires. "That'll help a little. You do know it's raining out there?"

"Yeah, I do." She decided it was worth getting wet to have her own transportation.

"Come on, I'll give you a ride." He started wheeling the

bike to the SUV.

At Jesse's house, Kevin took the bike from the vehicle and set it on the ground. Dany took the handle bars and thanked him for the ride. She waved goodbye as the vehicle took off. She wheeled the bicycle toward the house.

Lara answered her knock. "There you are. Uh—I guess you better put it in the garage."

Cindy came running out. "Wow. Can I ride it?"

"It might be a little big for you," Dany said, "but if you open the garage door, you can help me bring it in."

Cindy scurried back inside and moments later the garage door opened. She ducked under it and ran out to help. She took one handle bar, Dany took the other and they rolled the bike in.

"Where shall we put it?"

"If you move your skateboard out of the way, right here is good."

Cindy snatched up the skateboard. "What shall I do with it?"

"Just set it in the basket."

Cindy popped the skateboard in the bicycle basket and held onto the seat to help Dany push the bike in next to Lara's Camry.

In the kitchen, Lara turned down the burner on the stove. "You need to change, Cindy. You're all wet."

Cindy dashed off to her room and Lara told Dany. "A friend is picking me up in a minute. Maybe you can take over this project."

"Sure." Dany took the spoon and stirred the pot of hot chocolate.

"I won't be long. Probably only a couple of hours."

By the time Lara had thrown on her rain coat, a car had pulled into the driveway and she dashed out. From the window, Dany saw her get in the car, but couldn't see the driver.

"Don't be scared, Haley," Cindy said as she yanked off her wet shirt. "It'll be all right. Daddy will find you. He can find anybody." She pulled on the dry pants and shirt her mom had set out, then dug through a drawer for her red sweater. Her favorite. A noise at the window sounded like somebody threw a rock. She went to look.

Daddy's friend was outside by the street. He put a finger against his lips to tell her to be quiet and held up the dog.

Haley! He found Haley!

With his finger over his mouth again, he motioned for her to come outside.

Careful that Dany wouldn't see her, Cindy tiptoed down the hall and across the living room to the front door. Silently, she turned the knob and slipped out.

CHAPTER TWENTY-SEVEN

Dany stirred the hot chocolate, and banged the spoon on the side of the pot. "It's ready."

She poured the hot sweet liquid into two mugs. "Cindy?"

The kid didn't answer. "Hey, come and get it before it gets cold."

Dany put the mugs on the table and went down the hallway. "Hey, you. I thought you wanted hot chocolate. You better get out here before I drink it all." She pushed open the bedroom door.

The room was empty.

"Cindy?" She loved to hide and then jump out with a giggle and a shout of boo! Dany knelt and peered under the bed. "Not there. In the closet." She yanked open the door. Usually Cindy was either under the bed or in the closet. Unless she managed to sneak past Dany and get to her mother's room without being seen.

Dany glanced out the window just in time to see Cindy running toward a white van. *No-oo-o!*

She whirled and ran flat-out to the garage, looked around frantically, then grabbed the skateboard. She jumped on and took off, pushing furiously with her right foot.

The van was approaching the corner. The stop sign slowed it down and it waited for cross traffic to pass, giving Dany a chance to catch up. Heart pounding, Dany rolled up behind the vehicle. *Stupid thing she was intending to do. Probably get her killed. Cell phone in her pocket. She should just call 911.*

But how long would it take her to convince them that a cop's daughter had been kidnapped? And how long would it take for someone to get here? Meantime the kidnapper could zip away to who knows where? He could do terrible things to Cindy before he was found. She couldn't let that happen.

Pushing as hard as she could, she inched up to the van. Scared that she would fall and get herself killed, or even worse, scared that she would miss and he'd get away, Dany kept a sharp eye on the traffic. Before she could chicken out, she stuck out her arm and grabbed the bumper.

She tensed as she caught up with the van going north. Arm out and stretching, she managed to clamp a hand on the bumper. It nearly got her arm wrenched out. Did he know she was back here? The van pulled ahead as the driver goosed it. One hand on the bumper, the other held out a few inches from her leg for balance, she sailed along at twenty-five miles an hour. When he braked for a red light, the skateboard wobbled. She dropped a foot to the ground.

Cindy popped up in the rear window of the van and waved at her.

The driver took off, dragging her and the skateboard along. As long as he was moving, she just needed to hang on. When he stopped, she planted one foot on the ground to keep from falling over. Sooner or later this creep was going to get somewhere deserted with the idea of getting rid of her. Then what?

Cars behind honked and swerved around the van. Dany's heart kicked into double time. Drivers used hand signals to alert the creep that she was back here. Ha! As if he didn't already know.

A freeway on-ramp was coming up. He'd probably stomp the accelerator and shake her loose, moving at sixty-five or more. Then he'd disappear to who knows where with Cindy.

Think! Do something before that happened! Hurry! The

on-ramp was just ahead. A thought popped into mind.
Dread mixed with fear. Would she have the courage? Yes.
Even if she ended up road kill.

A giggle caught in her throat. *Dany pancakes!*

She eyed the oncoming traffic. Okay. It was now or never.
The string of cars going south came toward her. She gauged
the speed of the silver Honda in the lead.

Oh God, oh God!

At the last possible moment, she let go of the van and
turned directly in front of the Honda coming at her.

Horns blared, brakes squealed. Heart in her throat, Dany
weaved back and forth, trying to keep herself from falling.
If she fell, she'd be flattened by a car behind. She struggled.
Cars came at her, swerved around. The skateboard shud-
dered over uneven ground. Dany bit her tongue and tasted
blood.

The Honda's driver landed on the brakes. The car skidded
into a half circle and slid into a head-on collision with the
van. Metal scrapped against metal, glass shards scattered
into the road.

Both drivers leaped from the vehicles and yelled at the
other. All lanes of traffic were blocked and cars piled up
behind the accident. Dany jumped off the skateboard and
ran to the van. She yanked open the rear door and scooped
up Cindy.

Six people pulled out cell phones and punched in numbers.

"No," Cindy cried. "We can't leave Haley."

Dany ran with the squirming child. Cindy pounded on
her shoulder. "Put me down! Put me down!" She stiffened
and nearly slid from Dany's arms. "I want Haley."

"Shhh," Dany said. "It's all right. We'll get him."

"No! Now! I want him now!" Cindy sobbed.

Sirens screamed toward them and two squad cars pulled
up. Uniformed officers got out and started asking questions.
Fingers got pointed at Dany. One of the cops swaggered in
her direction.

"We'll tell them," Cindy gasped on the air she sucked in. "Tell them we need Haley."

"You caused this mess?" The cop had his notebook out and started writing in it.

"This child was kidnapped!"

"Let me go! Let me go!" Cindy banged clenched fists against Dany's shoulder.

"Kidnapped," the cop said. His name tag said Steward. "You want to explain that."

Dany explained.

"I have to get Haley!" Cindy insisted.

Dany tightened her arms around Cindy to hold onto her.

The cop eyed Cindy struggling to get down. "This is Jesse's kid?" He got on his radio.

"I want to get Haley!" Cindy wailed.

Officer Steward requested dispatch to send an urgent message to Detective Jones. He rattled off the destination, then he turned his attention on Dany. "Who's this Haley she keeps trying to get?"

"Haley is a dog. It's in a pet carrier in that van."

"Is it hers?"

"Yes," Cindy said. "Haley's mine! He said so!"

"Hey, Ron," the cop called.

"Yeah?" The officer with the sun glasses was talking to the guy driving the Honda that swerved to miss Dany and bashed into the van.

"See if there's a dog in a cage in that van."

"Right on it." Ron made his way around the Honda and looked in the windows of the van. He slid open a door and reached in.

"This it?" He held up the pet carrier. "Looks more like a rat."

"It's Haley! It's Haley! Give him to me!"

"You know the driver of that van?"

"No," Dany said.

In a few minutes, Jesse arrived and swooped Cindy up in his arms. He gave her a kiss on the forehead. "You all right?"

She nodded. "Put me down. I have to watch Haley."

"Okay. We'll get him." Jesse stashed Cindy and the pet carrier in his car. One hand of the open car door, He bent over and said. "Don't move. I'll be back in a few." He talked with the cops on the scene, then he leaned against a car fender and questioned Dany. The more he heard, the madder he got.

"You keep an eye on Cindy. Don't lose her."

Dany got into the back seat with Cindy and Jesse talked with the cops again. "When can we go home?" Cindy said. "Haley's hot."

Jesse returned, asked if everybody was all right. "Can we go home now?" Cindy said.

"Yeah. Everybody fasten seatbelts." When Lara returned she wanted to know why Jesse was home in the late afternoon. He explained. She promptly had hysterics.

When he got Lara calmed down and Cindy had a bowl of snack crackers she happily shared them with Haley, Jesse took Dany into the family room. She held herself rigid, expecting to be chewed out and told not to come back.

"Have a seat," he said.

She lowered her butt to the edge of an over-stufffed chair and clasped her hands together between her knees.

"Do you know what you are?" Jesse said. "Do you realize—"
Dany stared at the floor.

"Look at me!"

She raised her eyes and glared at him. It wasn't as though she had a whole lot of options. What did he think she should have done?

"Do you know what you are?" he said again.

She held steady looking him straight in the face. "A lousy baby sitter?"

He shook his head. "No. You, Idana Martin, are a hero! I shudder to think what might have happened to Cindy if you hadn't caused a serious accident that tied up traffic for six hours." He took her hand and kissed the back of it. "*You* are a hero. For heroic action you deserve a reward. For your bravery, in lieu of a gold medal, you get tomorrow off. Get your things, I'll drive you home."

She felt a silly grin on her face. "Really?"

"Absolutely. Get your stuff and we'll go."

"No, I mean the hero part."

"*You* are a hero! And don't you forget it!"

"Thanks for a ride, but I'd rather take my bike. I'd like to go to the bookstore."

She said goodbye to Cindy and Haley, told them she'd see them in two days and got on her bike. "Don't worry I'll be fine."

Chapter Twenty-eight

A kid, for God's sake. That wasn't in the job description. What if he just flat out refused? Huh. He'd have to get on the first plane out of town, or start planning his funeral. But a little kid? Maybe the kid wasn't anything to worry about. I mean, come on. Who'd believe a two-year-old?

Didn't matter what he thought, he wasn't the decision maker. He just did as he was told. He pictured a cute tyke standing up in the witness chair, pointing at him and shrieking in a high-pitched voice, "He did it!"

All of this was Palmer's fault, damn it. None of it would have happened if Palmer hadn't been such a self-righteous prick. Who knows how he figured it out. Walk the straight and narrow, follow the rules Palmer, probably just smelled it in the air. *It was against the law. Human subjects were a long time in the future. Much had to be done before people were used in research. Shut it down! Immediately.*

Palmer didn't stop there. He not only meant to pull the plug, he was fiery with righteousness and headed for the cops. Even with all the persuading to find out what Palmer had already done, he didn't give out everything. The terrible things they'd done to Palmer turned his stomach. And, by God if the bastard didn't hold out, even when his wife's pretty face was getting attention. The sneaky bastard kept quiet about the CD he'd mailed to his wife. Make that ex-wife.

How weird was that? Maddie—the cop! She turned out to be Palmer's ex.

Seeing her pick up her mail was a piece of good luck, and he managed to intercept it. Not without some damage to himself, he might add. Too bad about Maddie, he sort of liked her, but if she didn't stop sticking her nose in where it didn't belong, something would have to be done.

In the beginning, it had seemed so easy. He was getting some real money and it was welcome. Now the situation was way out of hand, nothing but a big mess. He wasn't sure it wouldn't get worse either. With the FBI snooping around, who knows.

In his opinion, this current assignment was a mistake. Pick up Maddie's niece so she could enjoy the hospitality of the holding cell. He'd tried to convince the damn genius to keep everything low key for a bit. As usual, he wasn't listened to.

Free free free. With the wind in her face, Dany pedaled through the green light. She felt all warm and happy inside, like bubbles were running through her veins.

Now that she had the bike, she could go places. It was a dorky bike, the old-fashioned kind without gears, and had big fat tires that had to be pumped up. She probably looked like a dork too, she felt like one when she was riding it. Never mind. She was a hero. Jesse had said so. She wanted to tell somebody. Maybe Maddie would be home, or she could call her best friend Joanie back in Kansas. She was a hero! And she had transportation, and she could go wherever she wanted. Yeah!

And tomorrow she had the day off. Jesse hadn't explained why and Dany didn't ask. Lara was secretive about something. Dany guessed she had appointments with an attorney. Lara was unhappy and maybe exploring the possibilities of divorce. Jesse hadn't a clue.

Dany wondered if she should mention something to him. No. None of her business. Stuff didn't turn out so well when you got involved in other people's shit.

It was exhilarating to be on her own. Traffic was a little hairy. Drivers seemed to resent giving up an inch of space. They swooped up behind, then gunned the motor and swung past with an irritated glare at her. The dark car behind her was making her a little nervous. She could stay as long as she wanted in the bookstore, because she had her own transportation to get home.

She took a right into the strip mall. Drugstore, grocery store, restaurant, antique store, and her very favorite, the bookstore. She chained the bike to the rack by the door and went inside.

When she left on her bicycle, he followed. It was damn near impossible to follow anyone on a bicycle. At the bookstore, he parked where he could watch the door and opened *The Mira Vista Times*. If anyone noticed, he was just a bored male waiting for someone to finish shopping.

If they only knew.

He'd made himself inconspicuous. A ball cap, glasses with heavy frames, clothes a little past their prime—worn jeans, a dark blue shirt with frayed cuffs—but nothing so bad that he looked like a bum. His shoes were black lace-ups, not new, not old. His appearance was ordinary, nothing memorable, not even the car. It was a six-year-old Ford, a nondescript gray. He didn't spend any time keeping it shiny, but neither did he let it get so filthy it got noticed. He was just a guy reading the *Mira Vista Times*. He glanced up as a couple went by.

"...yellow, I think would be the best, you know, like daffodils, because..." She was explaining the virtues of some curtains she wanted to show the guy with her. He was acting like he was listening, even gave a nod, but his eyes were on the Jag they just passed.

How the hell long was the kid going to stay in there anyway?

The door to the bookstore opened and Maddie's niece came out. She glowed with health and vitality. Five-three, blond hair cut in points around a pixie face, blue eyes, and teenage insincerity. Pampered and spoiled, believing nothing bad would ever happen. She wore blue jeans and a blue sweatshirt, and white jogging shoes. She flipped through a book she'd bought as she went toward the bicycle.

She might not have any worries now. But her life was about to change. He folded the paper, stepped out and left the door open a couple inches. "Hi." He turned his back toward the sun.

She blinked and put up a hand to shade her eyes. "Oh, hi." She unchained the bike and tossed her books in the basket.

"What are you doing here?" he said.

"Just getting some books. It's a place I like. I can look at every book I want to, and if I'm careful, I don't even need to buy one."

"Looks like you're about done." He nodded at the package in the bicycle basket. "You need a ride?" He looked around the parking lot.

She gave him a smile. "No thanks."

"Just toss the bike in the vehicle and I'll get you home in no time."

"Thanks, but I kind of like to ride it, you know?" She got on and started to pedal toward the street.

He pulled the taser from his pocket and fired it. A crackling buzz. Her eyes rolled back in her head and the bike wobbled. He grabbed her shoulders and pulled her from the bike as it fell.

He sent another quick glance around the lot. Nobody paying attention. If anybody questioned him, he had a story ready. His daughter had epilepsy. She'd be fine in a few minutes. He cradled her in his arms and kicked the door open wider. He gently placed her on the passenger seat and brushed hair from her face.

The sedative was already prepared. He swabbed her arm with alcohol and injected the liquid in the hypodermic. That would keep her quiet until he got her to the clinic. He straightened the bike and wheeled it out of the way, then trotted to his car, slid in under the wheel, started it up and pulled out of the lot.

Dany shivered. *Cold.* Headache. Hurt everywhere. Mind full of pain. Jostling. Bumping bumping. Where was she?

Moments later, the fog in her mind cleared enough for her to realize she was lying on her back. Moving. Being moved. Strapped down. The back of a pickup.

She remembered looking at books. Did she look at books? Or was that what she set out to do? Wind in her face. Riding through streets. Traffic. Going to the bookstore with her own transportation

She dreamed about freedom. About books.

A sting in her arm. She drifted, thoughts swirled around and down into a dark place.

She didn't know how long she was out, so she couldn't guess how many miles she'd gone. The engine strained. Going up hill. She felt the pull of gravity. Reached the top. Leveled off. Going downhill. Picked up speed. Bumpy road. Unpaved.

Motor noise, gears shifted. Truck slowed. More turns and the vehicle rolled onto a smooth surface and came to a stop.

Whatever the destination was, it had been reached.

Dany tried to keep her head up as he dragged her toward a large, sinister building with no light. Both her wrists clamped in one hand, he yanked her over the uneven ground. Her arms ached, her legs were scraped over grit and dirt. Pain shot through her head with each jolt.

With effort she managed to pull her eyelids halfway open. Eyes blurry. Hard to focus. Trees, everywhere. Turning her head a tiny bit right, she saw more trees. Where was he taking her? Getting dark.

She tipped her head, straining to see him, and saw only his back. Looking up, he seemed tall. Couldn't determine anything more. Dressed in a sweater, maybe black or dark blue, jeans. Boots. Small feet for a man. She knew him. Didn't she? Yes, she was almost positive. If she could just see clearer. If she could just clear the fog from her mind.

Mostly what she saw was the darkening sky. Clouds piled together. Rain whispered through the leaves.

Whatever he'd done to her was wearing off. Keeping her head off the ground was a tiny bit easier. She could move her ankles slightly. Where was he taking her? Oh God, he was going to kill her. And probably do worse things before he did. Her heart beat faster.

The dark building loomed close. He pulled her along a walkway to a large double door. When he dropped her hands, her arms flopped to the ground. She wiggled her fingers.

He stuck a hand in his pocket and fished out keys. They jingled as he held them up to isolate one. She got one finger under her watch band, peeled off the watch, and let it drop. He jammed a key in the lock, tried to open it. Fiddled. He swore, yanked out the key and tried another one. After banging and swearing, he got the door open.

He grabbed her hands again and dragged her inside. Subdued light in the ceiling, brighter light in a hallway. He slammed the door shut and snapped home two dead bolts. Why two? Something very bad going on here. Something very bad was about to happen to her.

He pulled her along a hallway, made a turn, went past an office with a lighted desk lamp. A telephone. Could she get away from him? She could call for help.

He made another turn into a dark hallway and she quickly got disoriented. Do something! Don't just give up!

She pulled her hands free and spun on her rear. He turned around and reached for her. She bent her knees and shot her feet into his face. He grunted, staggered back and grabbed his nose. She crawled to the wall, pushed herself up and tried to run.

She wobbled, her knees buckled. With one hand against the wall, she guided herself along the hallway. At a dead end, she was confused. Which way? The office, the office. Which way? She had to find it before he caught her.

He called her name. Sing-songy voice telling her what he'd do to her when he got her. She came to an empty space and nearly tumbled. Stairway. Should she go down? Might be a place to hide. No. Find the office!

Had to be close. Yes! A glow of light ahead. She tried to hurry, stumbled and fell, scrambled herself up and moved as quickly as she could without falling.

Light. There. Desk lamp on beside the telephone. Moving at a staggering run, she bumped the desk. Reached for the phone and dropped it.

Kneeling, she groped. Found it and put the receiver to her ear. Dial tone! She punched in a number

A hand clamped around her arm. "Gotcha."

She felt the prick of a needle.

Dany swallowed. Bad taste. What had she been eating? She turned on her side and brought up her knees. Headache. Bad headache. Must be sick. Home in bed, middle of the day. Flu or something.

She drifted into a fog. Dreaming, but the dream was slipping away. Pain. Awful pain and— Someone moaned. Another moan. She realized she was the one moaning. She blinked, blinked again. She opened her eyes halfway. Blackness.

She couldn't see. Her mind felt slow. Slow as molasses. Some kind of— what was it called? She almost had it. It slithered away. The fog returned and she floated out with it. When she returned, she thought simile. Right. Big sense of relief. Wait. Metaphor?

Her hands explored along the edge of the bed. Narrow. She plowed through sludge in her mind and found no answers. Where was she?

Flashes of memory. Man. She knew him. Did she? He said he'd give her a ride. Then pain. He hit her with something that squeezed like a gigantic vice. She tried to call for help. No words. Only a squeak.

Breath coming in noisy gasps, heart banging at her ribs,

she closed her eyes tight. Don't panic. Opened them again. Only the same blackness.

Blind. He'd done something terrible to her and she was blind.

He stood by the mirror and watched Dany come awake. It had taken so long, he'd begun to worry the fool had given her too much of the drug. Maybe Dany should have been omitted as a subject. But she was so available, he just couldn't resist. His lack of restraint would have Maddie looking for her niece, but the risk that Maddie's search would lead to him was minimal.

Dany stirred. Her fingers twitched. Relief came over him as he gauged her degree of consciousness. What was done was done and couldn't be undone. If Maddie got too close, he'd simply have to give instructions for taking care of her.

Maybe do something so that she'd never be found. Or was that a mistake? Cops might then put in more man power and effort. Best put her out where she'd be found quickly. For another two minutes, he continued to watch Dany. When he felt she was waking up, he went to check on the embryos.

All his study, all his work, all his research, all his hopes were right there just past his fingertips. Small muscles in his jaw rippled as he thought of the father who'd never spoken any words to him that weren't criticism. Whatever he strived to do, didn't warrant his father's attention. His father was always busy, working, reading, studying. A closed-in man who never showed emotion, or any interest in his only son. His mother was less stiff and rigid, but she always deferred to his father in any dealings with him.

They hadn't expected a child, and when he came along, his father was resentful, barely tolerated him, actually ignored him and left it for him to fit himself into their busy lives. He had managed to live with emotional emptiness in his life, had learned to find satisfaction in study, in science. No matter the outcome of experiments, or the number of articles in journals, none of it impressed his father.

His father felt the goals of his only son were trivial, that they'd never be reached anyway. His father's voice rang in his head. "You'll never amount to anything. You don't know how to apply yourself. Your goals are way beyond your abilities, you'll never attain them. And what did it matter anyway." His goals were unimportant, so far from anything that he could achieve that he might as well give up before he embarrassed himself.

Nothing he did was good enough to elicit any interest, let alone praise from his father. Not grades, not jobs, not the hoped-for results of his current research.

"Give it up. You aren't cut out for greatness. You're only wasting your time. Get some job where nothing much is expected of you. That way you won't be so frustrated all the time."

Well, Dad, what do you think of me now? Think I'll make a name for myself?

His mother wasn't cold and cruel like his father. She was just weak, and reduced to quivering jelly by his father's scathing words. His mother, the person who should have loved him unconditionally, who should have taken care of him, protected him, was unable to rescue him.

She wasn't even able to take care of herself. A timid, quivering creature, there was no way she could stand up to his father. One look from his father and she withered, fully aware that she'd done it again, disappointed him in some way. She never knew what would set him off. She tiptoed around him and let him continue to emotionally abuse her only child.

The cold critical father, the weak pathetic mother. Classic. Forget them. They didn't matter anymore. He went back to the mirror and looked in on Dany. "Hello, Dany. I see you're back with us."

She froze.

The voice was calm, soothing. She knew that voice. Didn't she?

She opened her eyes. Light seared her retinas. Immediately, she squeezed her eyes shut, opened them again slowly. Blurry. Can't focus.

A ceiling light, inside a wire cage. Hospital? She struggled to sit up. White walls, machinery above the bed, IV stand with a hanging bag of clear liquid. Accident? Hit by a car? She seemed to recall cars zipping toward her as she rode the bike.

"It's okay. Just take it easy, Dany."

Did she know that voice? She tried to search her mind.

"I'm doing some important research," he said. "You're going to help me with it."

Research?

Chapter Twenty-nine

The house was dark when Maddie drove home. Why hadn't Dany turned on some lights? A glance at her watch told her it was after seven. She went inside. "Dany?" No answer. "Hey, I don't smell any food cooking. Resigning from that job?" She checked Dany's room on the off chance that Dany decided to take a nap. The room was empty, and no sign that Dany had gotten home. Oh, Lord, was she supposed to pick Dany up? Maddie punched speed dial for Jesse's cell.

"Jones."

"With all the excitement, did I fail to register I was supposed to pick up my niece?"

"She's not there?"

Anxiety crept along the edge of Maddie's mind. "What do you mean?"

"She left on that bike. Over two hours ago."

Maddie immediately thought, accident. "Why'd you let her do that?"

"Hey, I wanted to bring her home. She insisted on riding the bike."

"Something happened. I better call hospitals."

"Hold on a minute," he said. "She mentioned stopping at the bookstore in the mall. Maybe she's still there. Let me check."

"Okay." Maddie called local hospitals. None had seen Dany Martin, or a young female injured while riding a bicycle. Jesse called back to say the bookstore had closed at six. "I talked to the owner, who happened to still be there. Dany had been in earlier and bought a couple of books."

Maddie grabbed her shoulder bag, fished out the key and drove to the strip mall. The parking lot was nearly empty and she pulled in close to the bookstore. When she got out of the car, that creepy itchy feeling came over her. Someone was watching. She scanned the lot, ran her eye over the few parked cars still there, and threw a quick glance at the rear of the building. Not only was no one watching, no one was even around. She hustled to the door and pounded.

A voice called from inside. "We're closed."

"Sheriff's Department." She pressed her badge against the window and waited. Her fist was raised to pound again when she heard the tip-tap of heels. Locks were turned and Peg O'Connell opened the door a couple inches to peer out.

"Detective? What's wrong? What can I do for you?"

Peg was the owner. Thirties, small at five-two, slender, with auburn hair. She wore a brown ankle-length flowered skirt and a peach-colored sweater. Maddie knew her slightly from dropping in when she got the chance.

"Was there a teenage girl here around four or so?" Maddie said. "Dany Martin."

Peg nodded. "She was here? Why? Something happen to her?"

"That's what I'm trying to find out.."

Maddie tried to tell herself not to panic. It didn't do any good. A psycho was snatching young women and Maddie was terribly afraid he had Dany. "Was Dany by herself?"

"Seemed to be. I didn't notice anyone with her."

"Was anyone else in the store when she was here?"

Peg leaned back against the check-out counter and folded her arms. "There might have been. What is it? What's wrong?"

"She's late getting home." Like about an hour and a half.

"Who was here when she was?"

"Well, I can look." Peg went to the register and opened it. "Let me check to see what she bought, and who bought something around the same time."

"Dany bought a book? What did she buy?"

"She bought two. One nonfiction about Chihuahua dogs. The other was a kid's book. Also about a dog."

Peg looked through receipts. "Let's see. Mrs. Smith was in. One of my best customers. And Helen Albright. And that's about it."

Maddie said she needed to talk with them, but Peg wouldn't give out their phone numbers or addresses.

At this point Maddie didn't feel she could waste any more time in arguing. She gave Peg a business card and said to give the phone number to the customers and ask them to call.

"Did Dany seem anxious?" Maddie said. "Worried about anything? Seem like she was trying to avoid someone?"

"Just the opposite. She seemed higher than a kite. Asked me about dog books. Was pleased with the ones she found, picked out two to buy, and she left."

"Did you notice anyone hanging around, or watching her, or following her?"

"No. But I wasn't watching for anything like that. You think something's happened to her?"

Maddie made a noncommittal shrug. She thanked Peg. In the car Maddie checked her cell phone for messages. There were none. On the way back home she prayed that Dany would be there. As soon as she got inside she checked the land line for messages, hoping Dany had called while she was out. No messages. Maddie called hospitals again to ask if a Dany Martin was brought in. No one by that name was seen, no young female involved in an accident with a bicycle. She called Jesse again to see if he'd learned anything. He had not.

All right, she'd screwed around long enough. Something happened to Dany between the bookstore and home. Little pinpricks of dread ran across Maddie's scalp. She drove to the Sheriff's Department and hurried inside.

The dispatcher looked up in surprise. "Maddie, girl, what are you doing here?"

"Is Sheriff Dirks in?"

"You came to talk to the boss? He's here, but he's in a bad mood. You might want to think twice before talking to him right now."

"This can't wait."

"Ooo-kay. Don't say, I didn't warn you."

Maddie nodded that she'd heard the warning. His office door was shut. She knocked.

Dirks, slumped in his desk chair, admitted the situation with Kevin hadn't improved any. If anything, it had gotten worse. The boy hated him, and Dirks didn't blame him. Gloria simply packed him up, told him from now on he was living with his father and shipped him off. Got rid of him, the boy insisted, because she didn't want him around any more. Another problem was that the boy thought Dirks didn't want him around either.

That wasn't actually true. Dirks didn't have a clue about what to do. He'd tried talking with Kevin. Kevin listened with a barely concealed contempt. Trying to get the boy to open up about anything was impossible. He conversed in one word answers to questions. Dirks thought he had something with the negotiation idea. Thing was, the boy didn't like it here, he was homesick and missed his buddies. Dirks didn't know what to do with him.

The soft knock on the door made him pull in an irritated breath. He figured one more problem had come his way. He growled, "Yeah."

Maddie opened the door, then hesitated. While not exactly pitch black, the room was decidedly dim. The ceiling light was off, and even though the desk lamp was on it was bent way down and lit up the lower part of Dirks's face with a sinister result. He did not look good. Oh please let him be okay. She needed him.

Before she could say anything, he barked out, "What!"

"Uh—is everything all right? Uh—sir?"

"Fine." Dirks snapped. "Couldn't be better." He pushed away from his desk, got up, and stood behind the chair with both hands gripping the back. Now the lamp shone on his belt buckle. "I assume you came for a reason." His tone was definitely uninviting.

If she weren't so worried about Dany, she'd apologize for disturbing him and quietly close the door. "It's my niece, sir."

"I've known several people who have one."

He was often abrupt or preoccupied, even moody, but she'd never known him to be surly.

"She's missing."

"Missing," Dirks repeated. "By that I assume you don't know her whereabouts."

That's usually what missing meant. Maddie calmly and succinctly explained the situation.

"And this niece hasn't come home from where?"

"She's working as a nanny, taking care of Jesse's little girl. After the six-car pileup—" Maddie explained the abduction and skateboard incident. "Dany rode a bicycle to a bookstore, she left the bookstore, but she never arrived home."

"Probably with a friend."

"She has no friends here."

"She's a teenager. Of course she has friends. They meet people, make instant friends, take off without thinking."

"I'm worried, sir."

"She has a habit of running away." Dirks sat back in his chair and adjusted the angle of the desk lamp. Now it shined in her direction.

Maddie squinted. "Not really a habit. She left home without telling her mother. She came to see me."

"Boyfriend?"

"No, sir." Maddie had no idea if Dany had a boyfriend at home, or not.

"What do you want to do?"

"I want to fill out a missing person's."

Dirks grunted, waited a few seconds, then nodded and

sent her to the Missing Persons Unit and she answered their questions. Age, height, weight, hair color, eye color, last seen wearing, description of bicycle.

Dany was missing. Kevin had mentioned he'd met the kid. Dirks felt the tingling in his chest again, the one that was a precursor of pain. He re-angled the light and searched through his center desk drawer for the pills. Kevin had arrived on an airplane. After that the Danforth girl and then the Kipson girl went missing, and then Francine. Kevin met Dany Martin and now she was missing.

He placed the small white pill beneath his tongue and told himself to relax, that he was creating nightmares for himself. Kevin was just a troubled kid. No way could he have anything to do with the missing girls.

Dirks sighed. No doubt about it, he was too old for fatherhood.

Saturday morning there was still no word from Dany. Maddie delayed calling her sister until there was something to say. Telling Pam that Dany was missing would send her into guilt-biting despair, and she'd likely leap on a plane for California.

She thought about calling Jesse, but knew she'd more likely be successful if she just showed up. She stopped at a drive through-window for a large coffee and went to his house.

Lara answered the door and on seeing Maddie greeted her with a frosty, "What is it?"

"Is Jesse home?"

"Why?"

"It's about Dany. Please tell Jesse I'm here."

With an exaggerated sigh, Lara left her standing at the door. Maddie waited. A minute later, Jesse appeared and nodded an invitation for her to come in.

"What's up?" he said.

She could think of no elegant way to say it, so she just blurted it. "I need to speak with Cindy."

Jesse's eyebrows went up, but Maddie could tell that he wasn't exactly surprised. "What do you expect to get from her?"

"I don't *expect* anything. I'm just desperate."

"She cannot talk to my daughter," Lara stated. "I will not have Cindy upset. Why she thinks she can waltz in here and question my little girl like a criminal is beyond understanding. There's no reason for it and I won't have it."

"Lara—" Maddie wondered how best to reduce Lara's anger. Jesse shook his head at her.

"It'll be all right," he said. Maddie didn't know if he were telling her or Lara. "I will be present."

This was meant to reassure Lara and to let Maddie know he would be in control of the questions. She nodded.

"No." Lara crossed her arms.

Jesse took her elbow and gently edged her into the kitchen. Maddie could hear them arguing, but just when she thought her request would be denied, he came back without Lara.

"I'm sorry." Maddie hated to cause friction between him and Lara, but she intended to ask Cindy a couple of questions.

"I have to be present when you talk to her," he said.

She promised she wouldn't upset Cindy and hoped it was true. They went down the hall to Cindy's room.

"Hey, kiddo, look who I found," Jesse said.

"Maddie!" Cindy was curled in a nest of blankets on the bed. "Have you seen Haley?" She dug through the blankets and emerged with a tiny dog. "Isn't he neat?"

Maddie smiled. "He certainly is."

"You can pet him if you like." Cindy held up her hand, dog in a boneless slump with feet dangling. "He's my best friend."

Maddie traced one finger over Haley's head. "He certainly is neat."

"Dany likes him, but Mommy doesn't." Cindy shot a glance at Jesse. He looked back expressionless. Cindy tucked Haley under her chin.

Maddie sat on the edge of the bed. "And do you like Dany?"

"Yeah. She's neat. We have lots of fun."

Maddie asked innocuous questions. What kind of fun did they have? What did they have for lunch, did they read books, what else did they do? Then Maddie got to what she came to ask. "Do you have lots of friends?"

Cindy nodded and mentioned a number of kids in the play school she went to, and a name of two kids who weren't friends.

"How about Dany? Does she have friends?"

Cindy thought about that. "Well, she has me, a'course."

Maddie nodded. "Who else?"

Cindy twisted her mouth to one side. "There's the friend who brought the bicycle."

Maddie nodded again. "Did you like him?"

Cindy shrugged.

"What's his name?"

Mouth twisted the other way in another moment of thought. "I think it's Kevin. There's a Kevin at school and I don't like him so much."

Maddie asked more questions about Dany's friend Kevin, but she didn't get any information, and Jesse said enough. Maddie apologized for interrupting his Saturday and upsetting Lara. Should she apologize also to Lara?

He said probably better that she just leave.

Maddie wondered about Kevin. She tried the cell phone number the sheriff had given her and the call went to voice mail. "Leave a message if you think it's important, otherwise don't take up my time."

Maddie had a long restless night. *She dreamed of Greg. In the dream he described his new wife. She's different, he said. Different than what, Maddie wanted to know. Different than you, he said. Clarissa is—she's different.*

She dreamed of Dany, lost and calling for rescue, tortured and crying for help. She dreamed of the wind whipping around her causing her to stumble. Clouds scudded across the sliver of moon and her flashlight bobbed over the dirt path as she searched for the grave.

Howling wind bent tree branches nearly to the ground, tore at her clothing, scratched her face. Just as clouds covered the moon, she spotted a small mound at one side of the path. She knelt, brushed away dead leaves, twigs, decaying vegetation and clots of mud.

The clouds rolled on. She shined her flash on the grave and gasped in horror. The dead gray face was Dany's. Maddie shot up from sleep, heart pounding, gasping for air. It was her greatest fear, that she'd find Dany dead, thrown like trash in a ditch.

She had to call her sister. Pam must be told her daughter was missing. She would blame Maddie. And why not? It was Maddie's fault. If she hadn't let Dany stay in the first place, if she had only bundled her in the car and driven her to the airport, put her on the next plane home, Dany wouldn't be missing. Even when she knew a psychopath was snatching, torturing and killing young women, she hadn't sent Dany back to her mother. Now she was afraid it was too late.

She hadn't found even the barest hint of what had happened to Francine. After all this time there wasn't a hope that the girl was still alive. At some time a body might surface, like the small pile of bones by the side of a dirt path. And she feared she wouldn't find Dany either. This very morning she had to call Pam. She dreaded that call but it couldn't wait any longer.

She hadn't done right by Francine. She hadn't found even a trace of where she was, and no wonder. Maddie's passion for the job, her eagerness to work a case to the end, and her ability to was missing.

She hadn't done right by Greg either. She hadn't figured out what he was telling her by scribbling about farthings in his notebook. He had counted on her to know what he meant and she didn't. As far as she could tell Jesse wasn't making any progress identifying his killer. Not for a moment did she believe that Cutter, hotshot FBI agent, was doing any better. He was floundering just as much as Jesse was.

Maddie opened her eyes at five minutes past six on Sunday morning, with a crippling headache and a paralyzing fear that she was useless, she'd never find Dany. And much as she hated to, she really had to get hold of Pam today. It was only four am in Kansas. Too early. She would call later. If she couldn't even find Dany, her own niece, she wasn't much of a cop. Suddenly, she felt cold. If she wasn't a cop, who was she?

Rain battered the roof and slashed at the windows. A faraway sound edged into her half-sleeping mind. More and more it pushed at the remnants of sleep. Though she tried to hang on, sleep slipped away like a satin sheet she tried to clutch.

She rolled onto her back and stared at the dark ceiling. What woke her? She heard only rain peppering against the window like hail. Forget it, go back to sleep.

Then she heard something. In the distance. Church bells. Sunday morning. Calling all the faithful to service.

Bells. Yes, bells.

Oh my God, of course.

You owe me five farthings.

CHAPTER THIRTY

"Bells," Maddie muttered to herself.

> *Oranges and lemons,*
> *Say the bells of St. Clement's.*
> *You owe me five farthings,*
> *Say the bells of St. Martin's.*
> *When will you pay me?*
> *Say the bells of Old Bailey.*
> *When I grow rich,*
> *Say the bells of Shoreditch.*

She grabbed the phone book, propped it on one corner of her desk and looked up churches. She ran her finger down the list searching for Saint Martins. *The bells of St. Martin's.* Two were nearby, one in Malibu and one in Los Angeles. She jotted down the addresses, started a pot of coffee, and hit the shower.

The phone rang just as she scooped a large dollop of shampoo on her hair. Dany? She cracked open the shower door hoping to hear her niece's voice. It was Dirks. He growled like an angry bear.

"Maddie! Pick up the Goddamn phone!"

"Maybe he had some news about Dany. She turned off

the water, grabbed a towel and sprinted to the kitchen. "Yes, sir," she said into the phone, patting at her face with one end of the towel to keep soapy water from running into her eyes.

"How are you on the Francine Ramsey case?"

Her hope sank. Not about Dany. "Working on it." Absolutely nowhere.

"Yeah yeah. Are you getting anywhere?"

She took a breath. "No progress."

A grunt, a pause, then, "Have I been hearing rumors that you're interfering with Jones in the Palmer homicide?"

She should have expected it, but her mind was occupied with bells. She stammered, "No, sir. I wouldn't interfere." Okay, sort of a lie, but she didn't interfere, she just did a little investigating on the side. "I'm as anxious as Detective Jones to have that one cleared."

"Uh-huh." Dirks asked her what she was doing on the Ramsey case.

What she was doing was essentially starting over. She told him so.

"Have you interviewed Kevin?"

Kevin? The one Cindy mentioned? "No, sir. Not yet, sir. Does Kevin have a last name?"

"McQuire. He has a cell phone." Dirks rattled off the number. "Or try my home number."

Kevin McQuire? "Your number, sir?"

"Yeah." Dirks glared at her. "He's my son."

"Excuse me?"

"You heard."

"Right. What should I ask him?" Silence. "Sir?"

"What have we been talking about?" He growled at her to wake up and pay attention. "The Ramsey case."

"Right," she said again. "Anything on my niece, sir?"

"Nothing yet," he said and hung up.

The sheriff had a son? When did that happen? Was there a reason to question this Kevin about Francine? What Maddie really should do was call Pam. She kept putting it off hoping to have something concrete to tell her. Maddie punched in Kevin's number. The call went to voice mail. She

explained who she was and left a message with her name
and numbers asking him to call, then turned on the shower
and rubbed the shampoo from her hair.

Her going-to-church clothes had been packed away when
she left Kansas and hadn't been unpacked. What to wear
required some thought. Custom was a lot more casual in
California. A skirt with panty hose and high heels would
label her as a tourist. Finally, she decided on tailored wool
pants in a dark brown with a beige long-sleeved silk blouse.
No jewelry. Brown belted raincoat. If the church in Malibu
didn't turn out to be the right one, she'd try the church in
Los Angeles. If that wasn't it, she'd check the phone book
and go down a list until she did get the right one.

With coffee in a travel mug, she went to her car, started
the motor and backed down the driveway. No black SUV
with tinted windows popped up in her rear view mirror.
Maybe the driver had a Sunday off.

She eased onto the freeway, cruised the short distance to
Malibu and zipped down the off-ramp. She checked street
signs, consulted her map, turned right and drove up in front
of St. Martin's Lutheran Church.

The sign read services at eight and ten. Reverend Fleming
officiating. The parking lot was three-quarters full. A vacant
slot near the walkway had a large mud puddle in the center.
She pulled her car in, cut the motor and sat back. Suddenly
she had doubts.

Oranges and lemons,

Maybe Greg didn't scribble the phrase about farthings as
a message to her. Maybe it was simply something that came
to his mind. What might she sound like when she explained
that her last name was Martin and she thought her ex-husband wanted her to come here? Whoever she spoke with
might dash off for butterfly nets to catch her and haul her off
to the loony bin.

The church was imposing. Gothic in style with a tall
bell tower and narrow arched windows of beautiful stained
glass. When she exited the car, she accidentally stepped in

the puddle. She closed her eyes, sighed, and headed for the church. Two tall carved wooden doors, heavy and intimidating, covered the entrance. She tugged on one and it opened easily.

She slipped into an entryway. Several rows of pews in the nave were occupied, but the place was by no means crowded. A well-modulated male voice read from a gospel passage. She intended to wait where she was until the service was over. A man rose from the last pew, came out to her and whispered, "This way."

It seemed less disruptive to follow than to explain. He led her to a pew and handed her a folded bulletin which listed the order of the service. When the congregation rose to sing the hymn, she glanced through the bulletin. The man with the pleasant voice was apparently Reverend Leland Fleming. Doubts about her conclusions for being here made her feel defensive, and that made her think, irreverently, that he looked like he was straight from central casting. He was dressed the part in a long black robe with a white clerical collar and a gold cross.

After the last hymn, the organist played a Handel postlude. The worshipers rose and filed out. Maddie waited until they had all shaken hands with the Reverend Fleming before she made her way down the aisle.

"Welcome." Reverend Fleming offered his hand. "We're very pleased you joined us."

His voice was just as smooth when he spoke softly as when he was reading from the gospels. He was an inch or two over six feet with thick wavy brown hair touched with gray, trimmed close on the sides. Intelligent blue eyes, a narrow face with a high forehead, a straight nose, and a strong jaw. "We have coffee in the library. You're more than welcome to join us."

"I'd like to ask you a few questions." She showed him her ID.

"Detective Martin." In two seconds flat, he snapped from gentle pastor to hard alertness that said ex-military. He stood on the balls of his feet, in a ready-to-act stance that was like her father's. Everything about him was no-nonsense, from his short haircut to his vivid blue eyes that probed into secret thoughts. "Is something wrong?"

Many things. "Not that I know of."

He took in her face and clothing and came to some conclusion. "Let's go into my office." His manner, attitude, everything about him changed. He even seemed taller as he walked down the hallway. He had the bearing of a superior officer looking into the misconduct of a private.

With the skirt of his robe swinging, he led her to an office crowded with a desk, two straight-backed chairs, a couch, a coffee table, and a file cabinet. He indicated the couch. Maddie chose a chair and immediately he noted her disobedience. He sat on the couch, long legs angled out to one side, feet crossed at the ankles.

"How can I help you?" he said.

"Do you know Greg Palmer? Dr. Gregory Palmer?"

"Why are you asking?"

Again that sharp focus on her. It told her he knew the name. His reactions were fast. He waited for her to answer his question.

"You do know him."

He nodded. "I met him."

Met him, not knew him. Greg wasn't religious. Maybe his new wife took him to church with her. "Was Greg a member of your congregation?"

"May I ask what your interest is?"

She decided the best way was to tell it straight, no matter how ridiculous she sounded. Fleming would probably spot evasive action and not give her what she needed. "Gregory Palmer was killed," she began.

Fleming nodded. "I read that in the paper."

"I think he left me a message—" Maddie hesitated. Reciting the rhyme about the bells and the farthings would not improve her image.

"Message?" he prompted.

Again that sharp focus. Well, as ridiculous as she might seem, he couldn't send her to hell. He could only explain that he didn't have any idea what she was talking about and ask her to leave.

To her surprise, Fleming suddenly relaxed. "You're Maddie Martin." He went from sharp-eyed colonel to pastor pleased to meet her.

"You did know Greg?" she said.

"Not really. He came here and asked if I would keep something for him. He didn't say anything about a detective. He said a Maddie Martin would come and pick it up. He appeared to be under some strain, and I got the impression he was greatly worried about something."

"Had you met him previously?"

"No. He came to me just before Evensong, desperate and in a hurry. I was not inclined to grant his request." Fleming's mouth twitched in a rueful smile. "I asked questions. Are you in some kind of trouble? What is the problem? What can I do to help? Let's just explore possibilities. Are you in any danger? I wondered about his mental state. He was agitated, in a hurry, and he was giving something to someone. I was concerned about possible suicide."

Fleming paused a moment. "I believe your Dr. Palmer knew exactly what I was thinking. He said he was leaving an explanation for you in the event that something happened."

"Something such as what, I asked him. He just said you never know when something might happen. He just wanted to be prepared." Fleming rested one hand on top of the other. "I didn't believe him for a moment. I thought, he's in trouble of some kind or he's paranoid. Either way, I wasn't inclined to keep anything until he explained his position."

"What changed your mind?"

"He said he understood that I was trying to help, and if he had more time he'd be glad to discuss it all with me. He needed to leave something for Maddie Martin. He didn't have a lot of time, if I wasn't willing to help he had to quickly find someone who would."

"You agreed to keep whatever it was?"

"I asked if it was an illegal substance. He assured me it wasn't."

No, Greg wouldn't have an illegal substance, and if he did, he wouldn't just hand it over to someone.

"He said Maddie Martin would be here sometime to collect it. I wanted to know specifically when, but he said he didn't have any idea. Whenever you understood what he meant." Fleming raised an eyebrow. "Does this make any sense to you?"

She nodded.

"I also wanted to know who Maddie Martin was and why he wanted her to have this item. He said you were smart and you would know what to do with it."

"What is it?" she asked Fleming.

"I'm not doubting in the slightest that you are who you say you are, but may I see your identification again? I didn't pay close attention the first time and I'd hate to turn it over to the wrong person."

Maddie dug out her ID and handed it to him. He examined it carefully and gave it back.

"Excuse me one moment." He left the office, was gone about two moments and when he returned he handed Maddie a cardboard CD mailer. She took it gingerly by one corner and dropped it into a plastic bag.

"I assume there's a CD inside," she said. "Did you touch it?"

"No," he said. "I considered it. I thought if it was filled with nude pictures of small children, maybe I should know that. But I simply opened the mailer and saw it was a CD."

"You don't know what's on it?"

He smiled. "I'll admit I was worried, and I am curious, but I did not yield to temptation and put it in my computer."

Maddie thanked him and stood up to leave.

He walked with her to a side door and opened it for her. "I'd like to extract a promise," he said.

She did not like to make promises.

"When you can," he said, "I'd like to know what is on the CD and what this is all about."

If she ever knew the answers, that was a promise she might be able to keep. Optimism was the only way to go. She smiled. "I promise," she said.

She wanted to dash home and stick the CD into her computer. Whatever was on it might lead to Greg's killer, or explain why he was killed, or hint at a direction to look for the answers. She called Jesse and got his voice mail. She hung up without leaving a message and drove to the Sheriff's Department. Probably there was nothing on the surface or the packing of an evidentiary nature, but she couldn't take a chance that she might contaminate it.

Since Greg went to some lengths to hide the CD, whatever was on it had to be important. He expected her to find it. She wouldn't have even looked she hadn't had lunch with the obnoxious reporter. What if she hadn't figured out what Greg was trying to tell her? Her throat got tight and she blinked away tears. He knew he was in danger.

At the Sheriff's Department, she pulled into the parking lot, got out of her car and locked it. As she turned, she felt a tingling sensation high on her spine, a creepy feeling that someone was watching. A careful look around didn't reveal anyone anywhere.

Inside the building, deputies worked at computers, spoke on the phones, or read through reports. She went in search of Sammy Winter, the best in electronics, and wasn't surprised to find him in his office at his desk. The small room was crowded with electronic equipment, pieces of things she couldn't even identify. Stacks teetered on the file cabinets, lined the floor, climbed up the corners, and covered the desk. She knocked softly.

Sammy looked up, leaned back in his chair and waved her in. He wore his usual jeans and denim shirt, unbuttoned at the throat with the sleeves rolled up, black boots that looked like they hadn't been polished since he bought them. His narrow unlined face made him seem ten years younger than he was. Black eyes, black hair hanging over his forehead that he was forever brushing back. "I hope you don't want me to do something. I'm way behind with what I've already got."

She handed him the evidence bag with the CD inside the mailer.

"Ha. You'll have to get in line," he said.

"You might want to put this at the head of your line. It has something to do with the Palmer homicides. You know how much pressure Dirks is getting on this one. Give him something that helps and just think of the strokes you'll get."

"Yeah, yeah. You all try tricks like that."

With a sweet smile, she handed it over. "When can I come back?"

He narrowed his eyes. "I'll give you a call."

She thanked him and left him to it. Given that she had to wait, she went to her desk to make some headway on paperwork. First she tried Kevin again and the call went to voice mail. She left the same message and got to work. She wasn't aware of time going by until the shift change. With double the number of cops in the room, the noise level rose.

Sammy didn't call until nearly five o'clock. She went racing back to his office.

He handed her a written report. "Numerous fingerprints on the mailer. Dr Palmer's as well as God knows who. Prints overlapping prints, partials, smudged and one lovely clear thumb all by itself." He dropped the mailer in her hand.

"What's on it?"

"Stick it in your computer, and find out."

His demeanor didn't say whether he thought the CD was useful or not. "Thanks, Sammy. I owe you one."

"Huh. You owe me a lot more than one."

She scurried back to her cubicle and stuck the CD in her computer. Let there be something that would explain the murders. Otherwise, why would Greg hide it?

My dear Maddie,

If you're reading this it means I am no longer among the living. What a weird surreal sensation it is to talk about yourself as dead. Dear dear Maddie, I know I hurt you very badly, and for that I'm deeply sorry. Please find it in your heart to forgive me. Under the circumstances, it's presumptuous of me, but I know you so well I know, too, that I can count on you.

Some things I speculate, some things I'm sure of. Here's what I want you to know...

CHAPTER THIRTY-ONE

When she went around the corner and saw the same laundromat, Maddie should not have been surprised. Greg with his brilliant mind had been notoriously bad at giving directions, often leaving out an important step. The windshield wipers worked frantically, gusts of wind periodically blew small tree leaves and debris across the road. Locating street signs was a struggle. They appeared only sporadically. She was beginning to re-think her decision. She seemed to be totally lost.

She was way out of her jurisdiction and she had no back-up in case of trouble. She pulled to the side of the road and punched in Jesse's cell number. The call went to voice mail. Irritated, she hung up.

When another small shopping area appeared she drove slowly past until lights of a café sign popped up in the gloom. Zoë's Place. Someone there might be able to give her directions. She pulled in close to the entrance and got out of the car. Rain blew in her face, plastered her hair to her head and whipped her pants legs. Dodging puddles, she hurried toward the door.

Inside, out of the shriek of the wind and the pounding rain, she took in a breath of silence. Booths ran across the large window in front and down one side. A row of stools sat along the counter with two swinging doors at the far end that must lead to the kitchen regions. The place was empty, except for lingering smells of past grilled burgers and frying onions.

A bell sat beside a cash register on the counter. She gave it a tap. The resulting ding rang loud. Seconds later, the swinging doors parted and a tall attractive woman appeared. Brown hair, flecked with gray and pulled into a tight bun at her neck. Oval face with clean features, a nose just slightly too long and brown eyes, intelligent and curious. She wore navy blue trousers, a blue and white striped blouse with a blue scarf around her neck.

"May I help you?"

"I'm trying to find the LB Clinic." Maddie loosened the collar of her raincoat.

"Yep. I figured you were lost. You just have that look. You're headed in the right direction though, the old Beal hospital? Mental hospital. Closed some years ago."

"Beal," Maddie said.

"Lawrence Beal. Used to be a town around here named Beal ages and ages ago. Railroad stopped coming through, then the post office up and closed, and after that the place slowly dried up. The Beal family either died out or moved on. I'm not sure which."

"Can you give me directions?"

"Sure." She seemed curious, but didn't ask why Maddie wanted to know. "Just keep going that way." The woman pointed. "Until you come to a traffic signal. Make a right and keep on going until you come to Edith Street. Make another right and stay on Edith until you come to this big old place. Brick building, if you can believe it. Around here? In earthquake country? You can't miss it."

Maddie hated that phrase. Any mention of you can't miss it usually meant she was certain to miss it.

"Got a reputation for being haunted." She went behind the counter and picked up a pair of tongs. "My name's Zoë, by the way."

"The hospital's no longer in use?"

"It sort of is. Couple years back, it was renovated and

gussied up for business. Infertility. You know, invitro stuff, and like that." A sharp glance took in Maddie's clothes, including shoes and hair style.

Trying to figure out if Maddie was looking for infertility treatments? She seemed to decide in the negative. Maybe Maddie didn't look rich enough for anything that expensive. Zoë pulled out a paper bag, unfolded it and set it on the counter. Using the tongs, Zoë selected three items and dropped each into the paper bag. She offered it to Maddie. "Scones. Just made. They're very popular."

"Oh, well—" Maddie started to dig out her wallet.

Zoë waved a hand. "No charge. Stop on your way back if you're hungry and try my soup. Clam chowder today. I make really good soup."

Maddie said maybe she'd do that, thanked her for the scones and the directions and left. The rain had slackened somewhat. She made the right turns at the appropriate places and ended up on a two-lane road, deserted except for trees on both sides. Headlights appeared, coming toward her. It made her less anxious. At least she wasn't the only individual traveling this way. After a mile she came to a fork in the road and a sign, LB Clinic, with an arrow pointed to the left. The road narrowed to one lane that became even more narrow with pockets of standing water.

Around a bend, her headlights shined on a chain-link gate across the road. She rolled up to it, and looked around for a button to push, or a box to speak into. How was she supposed to get in? There must be cameras or buzzers or something to alert the staff. Patients had to get in somehow. She waited. And waited.

Enough. She maneuvered her car around until she was headed the opposite direction. Just as she was leaving, a pickup jounced to the gate at a fast speed, braked to a stop, and the door popped open. One long leg ending in a western style boot extended out, and then the other, followed by a tall, muscular man with the stiff posture. Cowboy hat, denim pants, leather jacket and boots. He looked perfectly capable of defending the gate against marauders.

"Something I can do for you?" he said.

"I'd like to speak with someone at the clinic."

No change in expression on the bland face, but the eyes focused, like a hawk that just spotted a mouse. "Anyone in particular?"

"The man who owns this place."

One side of his mouth lifted the merest fraction of an inch, the most unfriendly smile she'd ever seen. "If you don't have a name, I got to figure you don't really have an appointment."

"You own this place?" Obviously he was hired help and since he wasn't the rightful owner he couldn't keep her out.

He looked back at the multi-million dollar property with its decaying clinic and made a sound of derision. A man not impressed by wealth. He should have been. The kind of wealth represented here could flatten him with a smack of the fly swatter and brush him off the table.

"Do I look like I could own something like this?"

She dug out her ID and held it out where he could see it.

"A lady cop. What do you want here?'

"To speak with the owner. Or the manager."

"Send a letter asking for an appointment."

"I will do that. But since I'm here, please ask whoever's available if I could have a moment of his time."

"I got to tell you, lady, they don't like people to just drop in. I will ask if somebody's free. That suit you?"

"Admirably," she said.

Another chilling smile and he strutted back to his pickup and spoke into a cell phone. When he snapped the phone shut, he opened the gate, came up to her car and leaned down at her window. She lowered it.

"Stay on the road until you come to the house." He touched the brim of his hat and returned to his truck. With a roar, he backed, and with a screech, he made a U-turn and pealed off.

She rolled to the gate and waited. And waited. Just as she had about decided the Doberman guarding the gate had played her for a fool, the gate slowly swung in. Wind buffeted the car, rain splattered the windshield, thunder rumbled, lightning cracked and forked across the night sky. The road was long and winding. She felt like the next victim in a slasher movie.

When she came around a turn, she saw the clinic in the distance. A large brooding building dark against the horizon. It brought to mind sinister experiments, lobotomies, mental patients chained in attics, insurgents with bloody knives roaming the halls.

As she got closer, she saw lights glowing in two or three windows, most were dark. She was glad of the few lights she could see. They suggested people somewhere in an otherwise menacing environment. A circular drive curved in at the front of the building. Broad stone steps with pillars on each side. She grabbed her flashlight from the glove box and hurried through the rain toward the shelter of an overhang.

Once out of the rain, she rubbed her hand over her face and wiped it down her trousers at her thighs. A poke at the doorbell resulted in chimes somewhere deep inside. A sonorous sound that raised the hairs on her arms.

Suddenly aware that she was standing in the dark, in the rain, out of her jurisdiction, with no backup, not a soul knew where she was, and she was about to enter a former mental hospital.

Could she have been any more foolish? As she turned to head back to her car, the flash beam caught on something shiny for just an instant and then she lost it. She moved the light back and forth, searching. Damn, where was it?

Never mind. Probably nothing more interesting than a discarded candy wrapper. She took a step and suddenly the light picked out a glint of something shiny in the mud beside the walkway. She reached down and picked it up. A watch. Just like Dany's. With the flashlight beam close, she turned it over and examined the back. It was Dany's. To D.M. from M.M. was etched on the back cover. Maddie had given it to Dany for her thirteenth birthday.

Maddie stuck it in her pocket and tried the doorknob. It turned easily in her hand. A gentle nudge with her toe and the door eased silently inward another inch.

A gush of wind blew the door wide open. It banged against the wall. Heart fluttering in her throat, she went inside. Lobby. Empty. Two couches at angles to each other. A scattering of easy chairs with lamp tables beside them. The lamps were lit, and the tables held a selection of magazines. No one stood behind the check-in counter to her right. Wasn't she expected? Someone should be here to meet her. Although the cowboy had only told her to follow the road. She had no idea who he spoke with. For all she knew, he called his girlfriend.

Leave, she told herself. Call for backup. Call Jesse again. Get out of here. Except Dany was here somewhere.

Both hands on her gun, she moved across the lobby, alert for any movement. She reached a hallway. Dim light. Nobody around. Doors on both sides. All closed. Against the wall, she sidled up to the first door, tried to open it. Locked. She kicked it hard, it swung in, she entered moving quickly to the left. There was a desk with a computer and a phone. Bookcase, bare except for the television on the top shelf.

She backed out, crossed the hallway and tried the knob. Locked. She kicked it open. It was empty. At this rate, she'd end up forever kicking doors open. It could not be a secret that she was here. With all the noise she was making, someone should come to investigate. Where was Dany?

She was somewhere in this building. The watch couldn't have fallen off. It had an expansion band that fit snugly around her wrist. It wasn't broken. Dany deliberately took it off and left it in the mud alongside of the walkway. Why was she here?

Back in the hallway, overhead lights in the ceiling were dim. She kept her back to the wall. At the end of the hallway there was a room lined with file cabinets, desk in one corner with a computer and telephone.

She heard someone behind her. Before she could turn, an electrical jolt shot pain jagging through her body, ripping away her breath.

Chapter Thirty-two

Most of this day, this miserable day, Jesse labored at the scene of Sherman's death. Homicide, he felt in his gut, but for all the time and effort he put in, nothing surfaced that he could take to the D.A. Rain fell in various degrees throughout the day, back and forth from drizzle to downpour. When the hell would this rain stop? The moment he headed to the office, it came down in sheets, and the wind blew with fury. He stopped at a Starbuck's drive-thru and bought their largest cup of coffee. Umbrella in one hand, paper cup of hot coffee in the other, he jogged toward the entrance. Within a foot, the wind snatched the umbrella. In trying to save it, he spilled hot coffee all over his pants.

He chased the runaway umbrella and managed to retrieve it. Inside, he shoved the thing under his desk and went to get office coffee. Not as good as Starbuck's maybe, but better than none at all. He filled a cup, dumped in sugar and stirred with a wooden stick. Maddie wasn't at her desk. Where the hell was she? She'd left him a convoluted message that made no sense about being somewhere and needing help. Twice he had called and got no answer.

Just as he sat down at his desk, his phone rang. About time. He assumed Maddie had all kinds of reasons and explanations.

It wasn't Maddie on the phone, it was the sheriff. He sounded wound tight, like he was working on building up a big mad. "In here." The command was followed by a sarcastic," Whenever you can spare the time."

Jesse took one sip of coffee and headed for Dirks's office. He paused at Dispatch and asked, "What's bothering the boss?"

"I don't know. But if you're going in there, I hope you have you life insurance paid up."

"That bad, huh?"

"Yeah, and you better not keep him waiting."

Jesse tapped on Dirks's door, heard a curt, "Come in." Dirks, reports spread across his desk, glared at Jesse and pointed to the chair in front. "Sit."

Jesse sat.

"Where's your partner?" Dirks said.

"Out in the field." He didn't want to admit it but in truth he had no idea where she was. He only knew she was concerned about her own safety—which wasn't like her—and that she wanted some backup. The next time she called, he was going to yell even louder than Dirks.

"Uh-huh." Dirks's expression suggested he knew Jesse was lying.

Jesse waited. A long pause, so long that Jesse was beginning to get an itchy feeling on the back of his neck.

Dirks said, "What have you got on the death of the second director at Changing Biolody.

"Not a whole lot. On the surface, it looks like he fell down a flight of stone steps and broke his neck."

"On the surface? You have something that suggests otherwise? Dirks patted the stacks of reports on his desk as though searching for something. "Why don't I have information here?"

"I have nothing new."

"Get something. When I get questions, it looks better if I have answers."

"Yes, sir," Jesse said. "I believe that's what it was supposed to look like."

"What does that mean? Just say it plain out."

"The steps are covered with moss and there's no question that they're slippery. But there's nothing to show his neck wasn't broken first and then he fell down the steps."

Dirks grunted. He picked up a pen and rolled it through his fingers. "Seems like working in that biology place doesn't lead to a long career."

"No, sir." Jesse waited. Dirks's obviously had something more on his mind.

Three or four seconds went by before Dirks said, "How old is your little one?"

Jesse was so surprised, it took him a moment to figure out what Dirks was asking. "My daughter? She's almost five."

"You like being a parent?"

"Yes." What the hell? Dirks didn't make chit-chat, and he didn't ask idle questions. "It's quite demanding." Jesse attempted a small bit of humor. "And a hedge against ending up in the old folks home when I get senile."

Dirks didn't find the comment amusing. "Wait till she starts driving," he muttered. "See how rewarding that is."

Not knowing how to respond to that, Jesse cleverly kept his mouth shut.

"Don't just sit there," Dirks said. "Get to work."

"Right." Maybe the autopsy had shown something. He'd jack up Dr. Newel to get the report.

"Tell your partner to get in here." Dirks leaned forward over his desk with a squeal of the chair. "We're not paying her to take off and lollygag around."

"Yes, sir." Jesse left Dirks's office and asked the dispatcher where Maddie was.

She eyed him up and down. "You don't look too bad for having bearded the lion in his den. What does that mean, anyway? How do you beard a lion?"

"Where's Maddie?" Jesse asked again.

"You don't know? Now I'm really worried. I left two messages that she was to call in. She never replied. Something is wrong."

Yeah, he got that. Did this lead, whatever it was, connected with Dany get her into trouble? Or was she poking her pointed little nose into the Palmer murders and got her throat cut?

"Something's been not settled with her lately. Dealing with her demons, I think."

"What demons?" Jesse said.

"I'm ashamed of you, that you haven't looked after her. You get yourself out there right this minute and find her."

"Yes, ma'am."

"She's in trouble."

Dreaming. Dreaming.

Lost.

Headache.

Dreaming

Maddie struggled to open her eyes.

Dark.

Must be still dreaming.

Hands under her stomach. Numb. Couldn't pull them free.

She raised her head.

Pain. Nausea.

Dream was different. Hadn't found the dead woman. But she smelled it. Breath in. Smell of decay. Death. Never before had she smelled the corpse.

Maddie rolled on her side to ease the weight on her hands. Lying on something hard. Fingers felt like sausages. She tried flexing them. Scratched at surface beneath. Dirt?

She listened. Rain. Wind. Storm. Always storming in the dream.

She tried to move one hand. Both moved. Handcuffed?

She bent her knees. Ankle bones rubbed painfully together. Tied.

Think.

Where was she? Buried? Odor of mildew over the smell of decay. Why was she buried? Was she dead? She could inhale and exhale. Must be alive. Then why did she smell death?

A frantic search for memory. Nothing.

Cold. She shivered. The dead don't feel cold. How did she know? Nobody knew what the dead felt.

Wait. She had a memory. Almost. She was throwing stuff in boxes. Why? Moving. Yes. She was packing. Going to California. Two years ago?

Greg. An argument? She had a vague memory of him walking out the door. And confusion. Anger? She was mad at him? He was mad at her? The harder she tried, the more broken the memory became.

In frustration, she rolled onto her back, yanked at her

wrists. Brought her knees up and slammed them straight.
Pain shot up her arms.

Red color danced across behind her closed eyelids.
Blood. Swirls and splattered arcs of blood.

Then nothing.

When she again opened her eyes, she felt some time had
elapsed. How much? No way to tell. Glasses of water came
to mind. Tall glasses of orange juice. She tried to swallow.
Her throat was dry.

What was wrong with her? Head injury. Head throbbed
with pain. How had she hurt her head? Drugged?

The darkness felt oppressive. Dense. Thick. Where was
she? How did she get here?

Abducted. The word circled her mind. A memory sur-
faced. Francine abducted. Detective Maddie Martin of the
Sheriff's Department was searching for her. Dany missing.
Maddie was looking for her niece also. Detective Maddie
Martin hadn't found either of them.

Had she been attacked by him? The person who took
Francine? Why? Did he think she was making progress?
Had an inkling of where Francine was? He was way off base.
She didn't have an inkling. All she had was a bladder that
was beginning to feel uncomfortably full.

She tried to get to a sitting position. Writhed around to
get her knees flexed, but then she couldn't get her hands
down to lever herself upright.

"Help! Somebody help!"

She kept up the futile yelling until her throat burned.
Nothing came of it. Of course not. If someone grabbed her,
he wouldn't stash her anyplace where she could attract attention by noise.

Tears collected in her eyes. She jerked her head to rid
herself of them. A lightning crack of pain sizzled through
her mind.

No. No. No.

Shaking from cold and fear, she took a breath and turned
onto her back. Knees bent, she reached her hands up. Fin-

gers stretched out, she felt for a surface. Nothing.

Digging with her heels, she scooted her hips along and tried again. Nothing.

She inched further and felt out again. Nothing, but black emptiness.

Disoriented, with no cues to go by, she could not tell if she was moving in a straight direction. She scooted, moved more inches. A short rest, then she scooted.

Exhausted. No more. She couldn't do any more. She promised herself she could close her eyes after one more time.

Bend knees, dig heels, scoot.

She rolled onto one side, flexed her knees, and struggled with her heels to shift her weight onto her legs, and using the solid surface as leverage, she managed to kneel. With the wrists handcuffed together, she felt the surface in front of her.

As she reached up, she over-balanced and toppled to one side. Her head smacked against the hard dirt. Waves of pain rushed over her.

Blackness crept in.

When awareness returned, she was so cold her teeth chattered. She would die in here. Even if somebody were looking for her nobody knew where she was

She'd be entombed here until she was nothing but bones. Who would miss her? Dany? Jesse? Her sister Pamela?

On a huge intake of breath, the sobs built, then spilled out in great heaving bursts. Flattened, defeated, she crumbled, face resting against the dirt.

Eyes closed, she rode with the pain.

At his desk, Jesse again tried to call her cell phone and was surprised to get an answer, then it went immediately to voicemail. He sent a message back and it was a message that suggested she get back to him immediately, if not sooner. He disconnected and called her home number and left the same message. Then he got back to typing a report on the Sherman investigation. He didn't get far. His mind kept sliding into worry about Maddie. It was making him irritable and moving toward anger. Finally, he gave it up, shrugged into his wet raincoat and went to his car.

At Maddie's house, he rang the doorbell. No response. No surprise. He had a key. For emergencies. He hesitated.

Screw it. At the rear of the house, he dug out his bunch of keys and isolated the right one. He unlocked the door and stepped into the kitchen. It was neat, no dirty dishes in the sink or food left on the table. The only thing he learned was that she needed orange juice, tomatoes and milk. He cleverly detected that from the pad by the phone that had her grocery list. A quick look through the house showed no signs of struggle, no puddles or splatter of blood.

In the dining room, he glanced at her desk and didn't see a thing of any use. Like a note saying Help, I've been kidnapped by human traffickers. He yanked open a drawer and found the usual crap, pens, pencils, paper clips. Second drawer, more of the same. Third drawer, hospital records for Helen Martin. Maddie's mother was schizophrenic and had been hospitalized several times. He closed the drawer without going through it.

Down the hallway, Dany's bedroom was a typical teenager's room. Neater than most. Maybe Maddie's influence. In a spiral notebook, he found pages of doodles with hearts and birds. Maybe meant something, but he had no idea what. He wondered if Dany had turned up at his house.

He dug out his phone and punched in the number. Lara answered on the first ring.

"Hi," he said. "Everything all right there?"

"Why?" she blurted. "Something wrong?"

"No, no. I'm just trying to find Maddie."

"Oh." Lara's voice went flat.

"Has Maddie called?" he asked.

"No."

"What about Dany? Did she turn up?"

"Not yet."

"How's Cindy? Haley doing all right?"

Lara laughed. "They're both doing fine. Much as I dislike

that rat, I must admit, it keeps Cindy entertained."

"Does that mean you're changing your stand about getting rid of it?"

"I wouldn't go that far."

He told her to give him a call if she heard anything from Maddie or if Dany showed up.

Then there was Maddie's bedroom. All he did was pull open the drapes, stand in the doorway and glance around. Since he'd never seen the bedroom before, he didn't know if anything was different, like missing.

It was only a fluke that he spotted the bug. It was behind the mirror on the back of the bedroom door. Who put it there? Obviously somebody who wanted to spy on Maddie. Why? That ratcheted up the worry. Where the hell was Maddie? He hesitated about two seconds, then called dispatch and told her to send a tech out.

He took another glance around the room and was about to leave when a muffled crash came from the closet. He reached for his gun and yanked open the closet door. "Hold it right there!" He aimed the gun at whoever was hiding in the corner behind the hanging clothes.

Chapter Thirty-three

"Hands on your head!" Jesse yelled.

The guy's hands flew up. "Don't shoot."

"Lace your fingers tight and come out of there!"

Jesse kept the gun on him as he stumbled over shoes and boxes and whatever the crap was on the closet floor. He tripped and made it out. A kid, teenage, maybe sixteen or so.

"Hands on the wall!" Jesse kicked the kids feet wider apart. "You got any weapons or needles that I should know about?"

"Of course not." He started to turn around.

"Stay right where you are." Jesse patted him down and the kid was clean. "What the hell were you doing? Looking for money? Anything you could steal? What drugs are you on, kid?"

"I don't do drugs." The kid was six three, looked fit, wore blue jeans, navy blue shirt, black leather jacket. Dark brown hair in need of a trim. Thin face, high forehead, intelligent brown eyes, full lips, determined chin. And from the kid's expression, he had a temper. "Now can I turn around?"

"Keep your fingers laced over your head and go slow."

When he turned, Jesse got a better look at him. "Empty house. Thought you could just come in and take whatever you wanted." The kid didn't look like a druggie. His skin was clear, although pale, and his eyes were focused. Designer jeans. Clean.

"No!" Explosive and exasperated.

There was that temper coming through. "No? You just stroll in to watch the occupant take a shower? Most voyeurs look through the window."

"I'm not a damn voyeur."

"I see. Petty burglar."

The kid clenched his hands and clamped his jaw. Along with his temper, Jesse suspected he had a bit of a problem dealing with authority. "What's your name, kid?"

"Kevin. Kevin McQuire. Uh, actually it's—uh—"

"So? Is it Kevin McQuire or Kevin Uh?"

"Would you just listen a minute?"

"Sure." Jesse looked at his watch. "Okay, I'm listening. Go."

"I came to see her."

"Her who?"

"The woman who lives here. Martin. Ms. Detective. Detective Martin. Okay if I put my hands down?"

"Slow and easy." Jesse kept his gun ready, partly to push the kid's buttons, partly for his own satisfaction. He didn't yet know what was going on. "You may not be aware of this, but most people when they came to visit, knock on the door, maybe ring the doorbell. Sometimes, depending on the circumstances, even call out a yoo-hoo."

"Very funny."

"They don't hide in the closet."

"If you didn't keep interrupting me with what you think is clever repartee."

"You don't think I'm clever?" Jesse waited. Kevin just glared.

Jesse nodded. "Okay, just the facts?" He waited, then put a little menace in his voice. "What were you doing in the closet?"

The kid started to say something like "Fuck you," thought better of it and substituted a sigh. "I'm staying with Al."

"In the closet?"

The kid gritted his teeth. He started toward Jesse, but caught himself. Pushed just a little further, the kid would lose his temper. That wouldn't be good. Jesse didn't want to hurt the kid, nor run him in for assaulting a police office. "Who's Al?"

"Your boss," said with a sneer. "The big man."

"Careful, kid. I have a gun. That means I am the big man. Stop with all the lies before I get tired of you and book you."

"Al Dirks. Is that clear enough?"

"Sheriff Dirks?" Jesse tacked the words together with skepticism.

"Yeah, Sheriff Dirks." Kevin grinned. "Feel free to use handcuffs."

"What do you know about Sheriff Dirks?"

"I'm staying with him."

"Staying with him," Jesse repeated. "And why would that be?"

"It's a long story."

"Okay, moving right along. Why'd you break in here? I doubt *Al* would approve."

"No," Kevin said. "Nothing like that. I came to see Maddie. Ms Martin. Detective Martin."

"Right. We've already been there. You came to see Detective Martin. And why did you do that?

"Is it all right if I put my hands down?"

"Not yet."

"I don't think you should shoot me. Al is my father." Cocky smile. "That would be Al Dirks. You know, the guy who's your boss?"

"Good try, kid, but *Al* doesn't have any children."

"He does now. Like it or not. Mostly, he doesn't. Like it, that is."

What? What a day this has been, Maddie disappears and some kid he's never seen before thinks he's dumb enough to buy his story. Jesse used his cell phone to call the Sheriff's Department. He asked the dispatcher if she knew a Kevin McQuire.

"How'd you hear about him?"

"Never mind. Do you know him?"

"Not personally. Apparently Dirks's son. Unknown by Dirks until recently."

Jesse disconnected. The phone rang immediately and, expecting Maddie, he answered before it got to a second ring. "Jones."

"Detective Jones. I was hoping for Detective Martin. I've noticed a lot of activity going on at her place. Have you found another of the missing women?"

Lockner, the pushy reporter for the *Mira Vista Herald*, was not one of Jesse's favorite people. Jesse didn't care for reporters in general, and he especially didn't care for reporters who found a leak in the department.

Without saying a word, Jesse hung up and cursed himself for an idiot. GPS. Maddie's cell phone would tell him where she was. He holstered his gun and told the kid he could put his hands down. Another call to the Department got someone finding out Maddie's provider and a tech crew coming out to check the house for anything they could find.

Jesse shoved the phone back in his pocket and studied the kid. "Why doesn't Dirks like you?"

Kevin shrugged. "Who knows?"

Jesse nodded. "How could anybody not like a charmer like you?"

"Exactly," the kid grinned.

Jesse, aware of time going by, felt something was very wrong or Maddie would have responded to all the calls. A glance at his watch showed almost seven. "Why did you want to talk with Detective Martin?"

Kevin hesitated and took in a chestful of air.

Jesse went on alert. Kevin was debating whether he should answer the question with the truth or a lie. Before the kid made a decision, the crime scene guys arrived and went to work looking for listening devices, signs of a struggle, blood drops, anything that might give a hint at what happened to Maddie.

"You were explaining why you wanted to see Detective

Martin."

"I was looking for her niece."

"You know Dany?"

"Sort of."

"Sort of won't do it, kid. You want to elaborate on that a little?"

Kevin took in another breath and blew it out on a long exhale.

"*Elaborate* means say a little more."

"I know what elaborate means."

"Good," Jesse said. "Then get started."

"The girl," he said and stopped.

"What girl?"

"The one who's missing. Francine."

"You know Francine?"

"No." Kevin said. "Sort of."

"Sort of again? You want to tell me what you sort of know about her?"

"Her picture was in the paper. On the news. Everything like that. And Al talked about her."

"So?"

"So." Kevin hesitated. Whatever was on his conscience was sticking like guilty glue. "I saw her. The girl. Francine."

That got Jesse's attention. "Where?"

Kevin looked around the room, looked back at Jesse. "I was the one who picked her up at that place she works."

If Francine was dead when she might have been rescued... Jesse felt rage gathering, but he kept his voice low and neutral. "That's been almost a week. Why didn't you mention it?"

Kevin shrugged.

Jesse was close to smacking him. "Since you read about her in the paper and saw her on TV and heard the sheriff talk about her, why *the hell* didn't you tell him? Or Maddie, or anybody?"

The kid cringed. Good. At least he had some awareness that Jesse was displeased. "Okay." Jesse's voice was still carefully neutral. "Why did you pick her up?"

"I got this message. Like, you know, on my phone. Text message."

"Right. And what did it say?"

"Get her boyfriend's car, go to that place she worked. You know, Home Cookin', and get her and take her to see her boyfriend."

"And where was the boyfriend?"

"At some hospital. He'd been hurt somehow."

"What hospital?"

Kevin shrugged. "I don't know. It didn't say. I figured I'd get another text that would let me know."

"And did you?"

"No."

"So you just took off without a destination in mind."

"It was something to do besides sit in Al's living room and stare at his TV. Which isn't a very good TV in the first place."

"Where did you get the boyfriend's car?"

"Just where the text said it'd be. Right in front of Maddie's—that is, Ms Martin's house."

"And you walked all the way from Al's couch?"

"Yeah. That's what I did."

Jesse wondered if that was the truth or a lie.

"That's all I know," Kevin said. "How did I know the girl was going to get herself kidnapped?"

"You a pretty smart kid? Get good grades in school, know right from wrong, red from green?"

"Yeah." The word was tentative like Kevin didn't know where this was going.

"Then why didn't a smart kid like you, one who reads the newspaper, and watches the news on television—why didn't you say anything?" Anger leaked through in every word.

"Because."

"Because won't do it, kid. You're going to have to come up with something better than that."

"Because," Kevin said again. "The text was from Big Al."

"Big Al. You talking about Sheriff Dirks?"

"Who else? Big Al. The sheriff himself."

Jesse took in so much air he practically choked on it. "And did Big Al tell you in a text to come to Detective Martin's house and hide in the closet?"

Kevin started to breathe rapid and loud. "No," he said drawing it out into three syllables. "I knew Dany, sort of. We had a date. Okay? And then she disappeared. And I came to see if I could find anything like why. Okay? And I was just looking in Dany's room. And I heard you come in and go through the place. And I didn't know who you were, and I didn't know what you were looking for. And I thought it was just better to not be visible. Okay!"

"How did you get in?" Jesse said through gritted teeth.

"The window was open!" Kevin almost yelled.

"What window?"

"The one at that end." Kevin tipped his head.

Dany's room. Mental note, Jesse thought. Suggest to Maddie a talk with Dany about keeping windows closed.

"Satisfied?"

Grin substituted with smirk. Jesse was within an inch of strangling the kid when he was saved by a crime scene tech who'd found two more bugs. Jesse's first inclination was to yank them. But on second thought, if they were removed whoever put them there would know they'd been found. Leave them. Find out who installed them.

He talked to Kevin in the kitchen while the tech crew went through the house. "Francine. Where did you take her?"

"Some café in some rinky-dink little place."

"Why there?"

"I was supposed to take her to this hospital, but she said she had to use a bathroom and she couldn't wait."

"So what's the name of this rinky-dink place?"

" Zoë's Café."

"Where did you take her after that?"

Kevin shrugged, realized that added fuel to Jesse's anger and said, "I didn't take her anywhere. That was the last I saw of her. There was this little rinky-dink café in this rinky-dink little town and I stopped there and she got out and went inside and that's the last I saw of her."

"What happened to her?"

Kevin started to shrug, thought better of it and said, "I waited for a long time, man. When she never came out, I went looking. I talked to the woman who owns the place and she said the girl—Francine had changed her mind and decided not to get back in the car with me."

"And you just let that go?"

Kevin ducked his head, looking very sheepish. Jesse wanted to shake the kid, loosen the oatmeal he had for brains. Had he just told someone, he might have saved Francine's life.

"Come on, kid. We're going for a ride."

CHAPTER THIRTY-FOUR

Jesse started his car. Kevin, slumped in the passenger seat, kicked his heels on the floor. "Seatbelt," Jesse said.

He drove off, hit the on-ramp and slid onto the PCH. He rolled along with all the traffic. "What exactly did the Sheriff say when he talked to you?"

When Kevin didn't respond, Jesse glanced at him. "Hey!"

"What!"

"I asked you a question."

"We didn't talk. Okay?"

"Didn't you say that Sheriff Dirks asked you to pick up Francine Ramsey?"

"Yeah." That one sullen word was all he said.

"So," Jesse said slowly, "what did he say?"

"I told you, he didn't *say* anything. He hates me."

"I'm beginning to get a little impatient here. You don't want that to happen. So just answer my question."

"We never talked. We got nothing to say to each other. In all the time I've been here, we haven't said more than ten words. And those were mostly telling me he was going to work."

"If you didn't talk, then how did you get all this stuff about where to go and who to get and where to take her.

Loud sigh. "He texted me."

"Texted you?"

"Yeah. And he said to get this girl from this place where she worked, and to tell her that this Paul guy got hurt and I was supposed to take her to see him."

"What?' Jesse couldn't believe what the kid was saying. "And the text was from Dirks."

"That's what I just said."

"Why did you think the sheriff sent it?"

"Because. Duh. It came from Big Al's cell phone."

"Anybody could have used his phone," Jesse said. "Has he ever texted you to do something before this? Didn't it occur to you to check with him and ask what it was all about?"

Kevin shrugged.

"With something that odd, why didn't you call him and ask what the hell it was all about?"

Kevin kicked his heels, one after the other, against the floor.

"I am very close to stopping this car and wrapping my hands around your throat."

"I thought it might be a test, you know? Like he was kind of getting used to me and he was asking me to do something for him and was going to see if I'd do it or kind of do it right. Dumb, huh?"

Oh yeah. Dumb as only an unhappy kid can be.

Kevin hadn't lied about one thing. It was a rinky-dink little town. Jesse followed the kid's direction to the café. It was open and empty except for Zoë, who owned the place.

Jesse introduced himself and showed her his ID.

"Another one?"

"Another?" Jesse repeated.

"Police officer. Now there's been three."

There was something hypnotic about the young woman and Jesse almost echoed *Three?* He cleared his throat. "Other two?"

She smiled as though she liked to deliberately cause confusion.

"Tell me about the other two," he said.

"Detective Martin. The first. I thought she was lost, but

she was looking for the Beal clinic. She seemed—" Zoë searched for a word "tense. Worried but trying to hide it."

Why the hell was Maddie here? What did she want with a clinic? More important, where was she? In trouble, otherwise she'd return his calls. "What kind of clinic?"

"Well, used to be a mental institution. Closed some years back."

"Did she say why she wanted this place?"

Zoë shook her head. "Only wanted to know how to get there."

"Where is this Beal clinic?"

Zoë gave him directions along with a brief rundown of the town of Beal and the clinic that used to be a mental hospital. He interrupted the narrative to ask who the other officer was.

"Well—" She hesitated. "Jesse Jones." She eyed him to see how he was taking that information.

"You sure that's what he said?"

"Positive."

"Describe him for me."

"Well, I can try." She sounded uncertain. "He was maybe five-ten, brown-hair, wore a suit and tie."

Probably no more than several million people fit that description. "Anything else about him? A scar, an accent, walked with a limp?"

She shook her head. "Nothing like that. He isn't you, is he?"

"No, ma'am. I can assure you, he isn't. Did he show you a badge?"

"Yes, but to be perfectly honest, I didn't pay close attention to it."

Right. Most people didn't. They saw a silver badge. With all the places around that supplied costumes for making movies, a badge wouldn't be hard to come by. Hell, maybe it came from a crackerjack box. "Anything else you can tell me about him?"

"He had a gun."

"You saw it?"

"No," Zoë said. "I could tell by the way his suit jacket fit. I've had enough film- makers in here to spot a shoulder holster."

"What did he want?"

"He said he was looking for Kevin. He said that Kevin was connected with a kidnapping."

"You remember seeing this kid?" Jesse nodded at the kid. Zoë shook her head. "Never."

"Hey!" Kevin said.

Kevin had lied to him? So why the surprise? Everybody lied. Jesse had swallowed the kid's story.

Kevin opened his mouth to say, "Remember the night—"

"Shut up!" Jesse came down hard on each word.

Kevin gave him a mutinous look, but closed his mouth. Wasn't hard to decide which one was lying. Kevin, claiming he was here Sunday night? Or Zoë claiming he wasn't?

"Sunday evening," Jesse asked Zoë. "Tell me about that evening."

"I was very busy that night." Zoë had an expression almost as mutinous as Kevin's. "My waitress couldn't make it so I was trying to take care of everything."

"Ask her about the girl," Kevin muttered.

Jesse gave him a look that said, "if you don't shut up I'll stuff a sock in it."

Kevin slumped onto a stool at the counter. The kid seemed to be boneless. "Francine would have come in by herself," Jesse said. "Around six-thirty or seven that evening."

"Oh," Zoë said stretching out the word. "Yes. She just went to the ladies room."

"It didn't occur to you to call the police?"

"To use the ladies room?"

Kevin made a sound of disgust. Jesse said, "You didn't recognize her?"

"No," Zoë said, "but I can see you're about to tell me who she was."

"Francine Ramsey. The girl who appeared on the news and in the paper."

"Oh." Zoë thought a moment. "I'm not sure."

Another sound from Kevin. Jesse thought he might have to strangle the kid. "What was she wearing?"

Zoë's description fit Kevin's. "She wanted directions to the Beal clinic."

"Did you give them to her?"

"Why wouldn't I? She kept looking around like she was afraid of someone and asked about a back door I assumed she had an abusive boyfriend she was avoiding."

"And you let her go?"

Zoë crossed her arms and cupped her hands over her elbows. "I asked her if she needed anything or wanted me to call someone. If there was anything I could do? She said don't tell anyone that she was there and she dashed out when a car drove up."

Jesse thanked her, handed her a card and asked her to call if she remembered anything else.

Cold seeped through her thin silk blouse, even her wool pants and into her bones. Teeth chattering, Maddie thought this place must be endless. Room after room, tunnel after tunnel. She would die in here.

Suddenly, claustrophobia grabbed her tight. She couldn't breath. All the air had been used up.

No. Don't panic. Relax. Breathe in slowly, breathe out. Breathe in, breathe out. Right. See? There was air, it just smelled bad. As she concentrated on breathing in and out, she thought of rats. The smell might come from dead rodents.

Her shoulder bag with her gun was gone, but what about her cell phone? She remembered trying to make a call, discovered no service was available and she'd— stuck it in her pocket. What an idiot. A simple call would get her out of here.

Okay, check pockets. She rolled to one side, the metal of the handcuff cutting into her thigh. She squirmed around until she could feel the pocket on the right side. No phone.

She rolled to get to the left pocket. Ignoring the pain and the progressing numbness of her hands, she felt the pocket.

Empty. A turn onto her back had the cuffs pressed painfully against her wrists. With great effort, she raised her rear, touched the pocket on the right and then the one on the left. No cell phone.

And a more urgent problem, awareness of an increasing fullness in her bladder.

Her throat was dry and sore. She needed water! No, don't think about water, think about food! In a luxury hotel, what would she order? In a comfortable warm room with room service. And a phone. She could order a steak, maybe, rare. A salad?

I'll die in here. Nobody will know where I am, or what happened to me. I don't even know where I am. The thought reduced her to tears. They trickled down her face. Her nose ran. Snot collected in her mouth. That did it! She was getting out of here, wherever here was. She tried to wipe her face with her wrists.

With the minimum of movement that she was allowed, she rubbed her numb fingers against her wool pants. It was awkward and slow, but she kept moving them, rubbing. Finally, her fingers started to feel less like sausages as sensation began to return.

In dark so total she couldn't see anything, she eased onto her side and reached out. Hard-packed dirt. She made the agonizing turn to the other side and felt the same dirt. The space about three yards wide, a basement or crawl space. How far did it go? Above she felt wooden jousts. With agonizing slowness, she inched along, digging with her elbows, pushing with her toes. Periodically, she reached out to one side, then the other. Nothing but hard dirt

Dig with elbows, push with toes. Progress in inches.

The tunnel must go on forever. She was cold, with a bone-shaking, teeth- chattering cold. She considered yelling for help again, but dropped the thought. Nobody had responded the first time and someone might be tracking her movement. She didn't want to give away her position. As she inched along, she kept bumping into debris, damp sagging cardboard, slithery stacks of what she guessed were old magazines, rotting boards. She squinted trying to see through the blackness.

Her arm caught on something hard. She went sprawling, landed on one shoulder and her chin. Her teeth clacked together on her tongue. Blood flooded her mouth, a warm trickle ran down her cheek. She pushed herself to keep moving, ignored the little voice back in her mind that pointed out she wasn't getting anywhere. Fatigue and thirst nagged at her. That same little voice suggested she should lie down, rest. Only a little while. Think how much quicker she could move, once she had rested. Just lie down. For a little while.

She was about to do that very thing when she wondered if she'd ever get up. The thought of becoming rat food kept her moving.

Scoot with her elbows, push with her toes. She moved. Scoot, push. She gave a hard push and went a little further. Satisfying. Then her head banged into something and blackness crept around the edges of her mind. She lay still and breathed deeply. When she felt like she could move without sliding into an abyss, she moved her hands to determine what she had run into. Splintery wood. She ran her hands up and down and across. She had bashed into a door, about two feet wide by two feet high.

She traced the outlines. Cold air seeped in around the edges. Honest to God, real air.

It had to be coming from somewhere. Her fingers felt no latch or knob. The wood was rippled and splintery. Like it was old and damaged by dampness. She struggled to her knees, clasped her hands together and swung at the door as hard as she could. Pain shot up her arm. The door remained closed.

"Help!" She yelled over and over, hoping that someone might be close enough to hear. Walking a dog, hiking, heading for the market.

Throat stinging, she flopped back down on frigid ground. She shivered. Her teeth chattered. Down comforters, she thought, wool blankets.

The misery of her full bladder, the fatigue and the cold, made her determined to figure a way out. Right. Good plan. Now what? One step at a time. First, get through that door. Flailing away at it didn't work.

She scooted around like an upsidedown turtle. Lying flat on her back, she drew her knees up to her chest and took a deep breath. She kicked straight out against the door.

Repeat five times.

She relaxed, legs quivering, head buzzing as darkness circled. Breathe in, breathe out.

Rest, relax.

She brought up her knees and shot them out against the door. Five times. Rest. Relax. Listen for sounds of humanity, a voice, footsteps, rescue party, murderers. All she heard was her own heavy breathing and her heart laboring.

Five kicks against the door.

Rest. Relax.

Five kicks.

She kept alternating rest and kicks until she could no longer raise her legs. Exhausted, she rolled onto one side. Her mind dozed.

How long? Minutes? Hours?

She started again. Her legs felt like lead. The rest periods got longer, the kicks got feebler.

Rest. Kick.

Rest. Kick.

Finally, she heard a small crack. She spun around and felt the door. Was it loose?

Yes! She pressed her fingers against the wood. Barely perceptible move in.

On her back, muscles trembling with fatigue, she flexed her legs and battered away at it.

Again.

Again.

Again.

At last, she felt a give. The door wiggled slightly. She spun around and forced her leg muscles to kick. She kicked and kicked.

Crack!

Yes! One more kick.

Nothing happened.

Right. Just one more.

When she could not raise her legs one more time, when she felt that she would absolutely loose consciousness if she tried, she managed one last kick

She felt the wood give. So tired she couldn't move, she just sat. Okay, it will take more that sitting to get out of here. With her sore knees protesting, she knelt and felt the door. A crack had developed in the center. A dim light showed through.

With renewed vigor, she kicked and kicked. Finally, with a shriek of nails pulling free one side of the door caved in. She waited for shouts, running footsteps.

Nothing happened. She stuck her head through the opening

Eerie blue light showed a stairway going down. She slipped her cuffed hands though and felt a concrete floor. Trying to squeeze though the small space would be tricky. Or impossible. The space was too small.

Tears popped up in her eyes.

No, none of that. Since the opening is too small, make it bigger.

She struggled around, flopped on her back and resumed the attack on the door.

Five kicks. Rest.

Five kicks. Rest.

Five kicks. Rest.

It didn't take as long to bash in the remaining half. Panting, she lay back for a short time. Then she sat up, bent over, and pulled at the ropes binding her feet together.

Along one edge of the broken piece of wood, she found a hinge with a nail in it. She pulled and twisted until it came free. Curved over, she picked at the knotted cords until a strand came loose. Then another. Then another.

Her back ached. She picked and pulled until she felt the

rope give way. She jerked her legs apart, the ropes fell loosely around her ankles. She slipped one foot free, then the other. If only the cuffs could be removed from her chaffed wrists.

Even with both sides of the door removed, the opening was tight. She twisted to one side and wedged her shoulders through. Frantically, she dug with her elbows and shoved with her heels. She wiggled and squirmed, and finally she slid through. Slowly, one step at a time, she went down the stairway and wanted to scream when she came to a door. This one had a knob. She grabbed it and turned, and stumbled, almost fell, when the door swung inward.

Breath caught in her throat, heart thundering in her ears, she couldn't make sense of what she saw. A few moments, realization came that she was in a store room. Broken chairs, bed rails, old-fashioned wooden wheel chairs, even bed pans. She heard the skittering of tiny creatures. Rats!

She sidled along one side to get past the piles of junk, keeping an eye out for rats, and came to another door. It opened easily, and she saw a curved corridor with doors set at intervals. The same eerie blue gave her a small amount of light. The first door along the curve was recessed metal. It opened with a hiss. Instead of broken junk, she found lab equipment. And electricity. A ceiling light was on and there was a switch just inside the door.

The room was excessively hot and filled with incubators. Probably, she thought, the heat was to preserve the contents of the incubators. Each one had a label stating the number ova and date obtained. Maddie backed out and shuffled on to the next room. It was just as hot and also contained incubators. The labels read "embryos."

The last door led to a tunnel with very dim strip lighting. She hesitated. If she followed this tunnel would it get her to a way out? There had to be an exit somewhere. She started down the tunnel.

The sides seemed to close in. Beads of anxiety quickly set up her claustrophobia. Would she ever reach the end?

Her breathing began to get heavy. Should she go back?

Finally she came to another room, this one very large

with rows and rows of what looked like large aquariums filled with fluid. Maddie had no idea what they were for. She moved in closer and peered into one of the tanks. Small round items, walnut sized- with a pocked surface floated in the fluid. Tiny wires were attached at various points.

With a hand clamped around Kevin's arm, Jesse escorted him to the car, trotted around and slid under the wheel.

After a few miles of silence, Jesse said, "Why did Francine run away from you?"

Kevin's shrug indicated it wasn't up to him to figure out why people did what they did. "Hey, it wasn't me. She was all crying and ape-shit about this Paul guy and she got spooked."

"Spooked how?'

Kevin dragged in air and blew it out in a heavy sigh of one who couldn't be understood. "I don't know, she just was."

He refused to say anything else. Jesse continued throwing questions at him that he wouldn't respond to. Either Kevin didn't know the answers or they incriminated him. Jesse gave it up and they rode in silence. Kevin stared out the windshield, Jesse concentrated on the road.

The directions had been clear. Even in the dark with rain starting again and few landmarks to guide him, he had no problem until he ran into trouble. The paved section abruptly ended and he jounced along a dirt road. He kept one eye on the road as he searched for the locked gate Zoë had describe.

When it didn't appear after some miles, he said, "Are we going the right way?"

"Some detective," Kevin muttered from the depths of his boneless slump.

Rain splattered against the windshield, the wipers clacked back and forth. Lightning split the night sky and thunder boomed. Thunder happened so seldom in Southern California that it was an omen to be listened to. He pulled over and shined a flashlight on the directions Zoë had given him.

Okay. He figured he'd missed a turn at the last crossroad. He should have gone right. "Take Main Street through town." He made a three-point turn and back-tracked until he came to Beal. It was a wide street with rows of one-story buildings.

"This place looks familiar." Kevin said.

"You've probably seen it in a dozen movies. This is your stock mining town from old westerns."

Two blocks later, they were through town and he spotted a wooden sign with "Cemetery" burned into it. "Follow signs to the cemetery," Jesse muttered to himself. The road curved up and led to a bridge. Lightning strikes illuminated tombstones below surrounded by a wrought-iron fence.

Glancing at directions, he read, "When you come to a huge boulder with a thick rope around it, continue until you have counted five large rocks and then turn right."

Kevin snickered. "Haven't you people ever heard of street signs? Count rocks. This is some sophisticated high-tech place. Wait till I tell my friends."

Jesse's cell phone rang. He fished it from his pocket and answered. "Jones."

"We got it."

"Fenton? You know where Maddie is?"

"Negative. The car. We think we located the car. It's about five miles out..." His phone faded out.

"Five miles from where?"

"Not positive yet...trying to check the license plate but..."

"What?"

"Uh— it's dark and with the rain..."

"Just tell me where it is," Jesse said.

More static. "Where?" Jesse yelled.

"...trees on the...registration in the glove compartment and..."

"Fenton! Don't touch the car."

"...popped the trunk, to see..."

Too late. Jesse hoped Fenton hadn't contaminated evidence or destroyed leads to Maddie's whereabouts. The urge to hit somebody shifted from Kevin to Fenton.

Cursing softly, Jesse bumped along the unpaved road outside of Beal and splashed through potholes of puddles until the road came to an end at a grove of trees. If Fenton was correct—and he often wasn't—Maddie's car was somewhere under them.

"Do you think we should be out here?" Kevin looked around nervously. "Couldn't we get hit by lightning?"

"Probably." Jesse said.

If Fenton was wrong and he'd directed them to the middle of nowhere in the midst of a monsoon, Jesse would wring his neck. Lightning forked the sky, and thunder crashed. He turned up the collar of his raincoat and exited the car. Pitch black. No lights anywhere.

"Stay there," Jesse told Kevin and slammed the car door.

Some seconds after Jesse disappeared into the rain and the gloom, Kevin leaned forward to open the passenger door and jumped out. He pulled up the hood of his sweatshirt and tromped off.

CHAPTER THIRTY-FIVE

Maddie backed out of the large lab room and continued along the tunnel. The quality of the air got worse the further she went and the darker it got. Everything in her wanted to go back where there was heat and light. She was ready to give in when she stumbled and fell. Her cuffed hands touched something when she went down. Fingers stretched she searched around and found— a small handle near the ground. When she pulled up she heard a screech. Feeling around carefully she discovered she'd found an opening that slanted down, like a laundry shute only larger.

Without allowing herself to think, she slithered. Down she went, fast, and hit the end so hard her knees buckled. She'd landed on a dirt floor. The air smelled strongly of decay. Twisting around, she crawled on knees and elbows. She bumped into something and suddenly knew she'd found the source of the smell. Fingers lightly moving over the body, she touched little pointed hard things, one by one. Buttons. A row of heart-shaped buttons down the front of a shirt. Or blouse. Ruffled lace ran along beside the buttons. She sucked in a breath, afraid she'd found Francine. Or what was left of her.

Either Maddie was delusional or the darkness was less dense. She still couldn't see anything, but instead of oppressive blackness everywhere, she observed gray in some areas.

Crouched, cuffed hands outstretched, she duck-walked around the body and sprawled over a solid object. Touching gingerly, she felt pants legs that ended in a cuff, and then a sock and a leather lace-up shoe. Francine's fiancée, she thought.

If the two bodies she'd just found weren't Francine Ramsey and Paul Gilford, she'd found two other dead people. Were there more? Would she find Dany here somewhere if she kept searching?

God-damn it, she needed a flashlight.

She inched away, groped blindly in what she hoped was a straight line. With no visual cues to guide by, she had no idea whether she was successful or not. She stumbled and fell over Francine again.

"Goddamn it, no!" Shouting was useless, absorbed by the dirt all around. If there was danger of her being heard, her captor would have taped her mouth shut. Or killed her. Since he didn't, she could only assume he had plans for her before he dispatched her.

Would anyone come looking for her? Eventually, yes. When she didn't turn up for work, she'd be missed. Jesse would wonder before that. He'd worry. Would he come looking?

Yes. But how soon?

While she was still alive? Was Dany alive? Was her body also down here?

Maddie's teeth chattered. Would she succumb to hypothermia? Her flesh would rot. Her bones would give up secrets if they were ever found. Would they provide any clues to her jailor? Or would he dump her decaying corpse in an empty field for the natural predators to dine on?

She got mad, and less cold.

She would get out of here. She would find the bastard. She would wrap him in duct tape and toss him in a field for the coyotes and the foxes and the insects to eat. Slowly she stood. With one hand on the dirt wall, she took small steps.

She stumbled and jammed her nose into a pile of bricks before she could catch herself. The pain caused tears to pop up. Angrily, she rubbed her eyes with the back of one hand and was surprised that the darkness actually had thinned. Somewhat, she hedged. Or was it just wishful thinking?

Cuffed hands made picking up a brick difficult. Once picked up. holding onto it was awkward and heavy. A weapon! Okay, not much of one, but beggars and choosers and all that.

The further she inched herself, the less black the darkness. Still too dark to see, but the air was definitely dark gray. Maybe vision simply adjusted?

Don't be ridiculous. She'd been here for hours. Adjustment would have occurred long ago. That meant there had to be a reason why it was less dark.

Don't get your hopes up.

Panic seized her when she stumbled and couldn't feel the wall. Floundering around, she finally found it again. Fingertips pressed against it, she shuffled on. Panic still hovered, whispered at the edges of her mind. No. Had she, in her confusion, started going back? No.

A fit of shivering seized her. She could barely wiggle her fingers. She flexed them and rubbed them against her leg.

There is a way out, she chanted to herself, like a mantra. *There is a way out..*

With awkward steps, she resumed inching forward (backward?). After many minutes, hours? Years? Maybe only seconds.

The air smelled different. Fresher? Was she approaching a way out? Or just an air vent? Or just wanting so bad, she was convincing herself.

She rested, breathing hard, testing the air with her mouth open. Gritting her teeth, she started out again, moving carefully. Her sense of direction had never been her greatest asset. The dense blackness that had eased to gray and so elated her with hope, hadn't gotten any lighter.

Sets of ten. Ten steps. Rest. Ten more. Rest. Ten times. A hundred steps.

When she didn't run out of space, she had grave (ha) doubts that she'd moved in the right direction. Could any structure be this large? She must have gone the wrong way. She had to go back to the laundry chute.

Back?

That thought was so overwhelming, she sank to her knees. No. She couldn't. She was done. No more. She should just lie down and rest.

But what about Dany? Just let her end up here too? And what if that damn newspaper story worried the sick bastard who killed Greg? Would he believe a two-year-old could identify him and think he had to kill Caitlyn too?

If she let anything happen to his baby, he'd haunt her in the afterlife.

Get up!

She groaned.

Up!

She struggled to her feet. It took some doing with her hands cuffed. Okay, I'm moving. Should I sing Hi Ho, Hi Ho, like the seven dwarves?

Maybe not.

She hadn't gone very far when her outstretched finger jammed into something hard. Solid. Smooth. Cold. She touched it again, moved her fingertips across and up and down. Metal. How was she going to get through metal?

She rubbed the back of one cuffed hand, hard, up and down her thigh in an attempt to bring some feeling into it. Then she rubbed the back of the other. She alternated back and forth, one to the other. She flexed her fingers. There had to be a way to get through the metal door.

God wouldn't be so cruel as to give her a door, but not give her a way to get through it.

She put her ear against the door and listened. All she heard was her heart pounding in her ears. She flexed her fingers, rubbed them against her thigh and took a breath. She stood. Dizziness threatened her balance. She stiffened, willing herself not to fall. She touched the door, went across it, then up and down.

She could not find a doorknob.

Goddamn it! She swung her arms back and, in fury,

swung them hard against metal.

A loud clang. The door opened.

Spring action.

Clutching her brick, she clambered from her prison. No sound. She looked at her watch. Ten o'clock. AM or PM? She had no idea. She felt like days had gone by, but she was almost positive the time elapsed was in hours.

She set down the corridor and followed it to the right. The light was getting a softer gray. Surely, a way out lay just ahead. She had to be going the right direction. No feel of dampness on this floor.

She passed shadowy rooms. As nearly as she could tell, all empty, no rustle of bed linens, no sounds of breathing. No sounds of any kind. Could the place be abandoned? Somewhere there had to be a way out. Which way?

Light shone though a window down the hall on her right. She crept up, ducked beneath the frame and inched upward until she could look through the glass. She pulled in a breath. Not a window, a one-way mirror.

On the other side of the mirror was a hospital room. Monitors were mounted on the wall, IV stand with a bag of clear liquid dripping into her arm. Dany lay in the narrow bed, unmoving, covered to her chin with a white sheet.

Injured? Dead?

Maddie tried to open the door. The knob wouldn't turn. She looked around for wires that ran to an alarm and didn't see any. The place was silent and creepy.

Would an attempt to enter the room set off an alarm? Heavy beveled glass would make it difficult to break without a sledge hammer. Using a corner of the brick, she tapped the glass.

Dany looked up at the noise. Fear washed across her face.

With a tight grip on the brick, Maddie stiffened her arms, spun herself in a half-circle and smashed the brick against the glass. The horrendous noise echoed through the silence.

Nerves skittered up her spine.

The glass remained intact.

Any second someone might come to investigate. She smashed again. No break. With all the force she could manage, she brought the brick down on the door knob. Again. Again and again, she smashed the knob.

It bent.

She battered until it fell. She pushed the door open.

"Maddie!" A naked Dany burst into tears and rushed to throw arms around her.

"Are you all right?" Maddie couldn't even remove her raincoat and wrap it around Dany. "Get the sheet."

Dany yanked a sheet from the bed and wound it around herself. Maddie increased the pace. At the end of the hall, Dany opened a door to the lobby. Straight ahead was the heavy wooden door to the outside.

"Open it," Maddie said.

Dany pulled back the locks and tugged the door open.

Maddie gave her a small push. "Run like hell. Don't stop for anything."

"But—"

Rain splashed from the overhang. Shadows got tossed in the wind. Trees limbs thrashed.

"Run! Dany, run!"

Dany hesitated.

"Run!"

A gun jabbed Maddie's temple.

Chapter Thirty-Six

Dany ran.

Faster. Outrun the monster behind, concentrate on running, running faster. Stay ahead.

She clutched the sheet in one hand and sprinted for the trees. Branches smacked her face. She tried to fend them off with her other hand. She stumbled across slick rotting vegetation. The sheet snagged on brush that reached out with thorns like pointed fingers. The further she got, the harder it was to see. Rain soaked through the sheet. Her bare feet landed on sharp rocks.

She heard him thrashing behind her. His flashlight beam swept back and forth. Where was a road? There had to be one. He had brought her in on one. If she could find it— Which way? The sheet tangled on a low-hanging branch. She tugged hard. It wouldn't come free. She heard him closing in behind. She ran on without the sheet.

"Dany!" he yelled. "I'm freezing. You must be even colder. Stop trying to hide. You know I'm going to find you."

Why not give up? She was so cold.

"You can get warm and dry. Then you can leave if you want."

Oh yes, warm and dry. Why not give up? It was only a matter of time before he caught her. Save herself from the misery of cold and wet and scared. She could get warm, do something about her feet.

"Dany? I'll forget all about this little rebellion."

Yes, okay.

Wait a minute! He's lying! And what about Maddie? Dany had to get help. She scooted behind a tree, huddled down, shivering, heart pounding, feet so cold she could barely feel them.

"Dany? I'll build a fire and make something hot to drink. What would you like? Tea? Hot chocolate? Whatever you want."

He was close! Oh my God! Lightning lit up the sky. She saw him, only a tree branch away. Thunder boomed like a cannon shot. She yelped and pressed her hands against her ears.

Lightning forked through the dark. Jesse thought he saw someone, or something, moving through the trees. As thunder rumbled away, he heard someone—or something—crashing its way toward him. He drew his gun, trying to locate the noise. Rain splashed and splattered all around him. The flashlight beam picked out sodden brush, fallen leaves, pine twigs and small branches. Rain dripped on the back of his neck.

He heard shouts. Coming from the right. He aimed the light where tree limbs swayed wildly.

Lightning sizzled overhead. Kevin ducked. Stupid, really, ducking wouldn't stop his getting fried by a bolt from above. He clicked on the flashlight he'd found in the glove box and went in the general direction that Jesse had taken. Kevin didn't intend to do anything but observe. Maybe he'd have something to tell Sheriff Al that would be of interest to the old man. Something that would have Big Al, important sheriff, looking at him with more than irritation.

Though Kevin tried to be stealthy, he made noise tromping after the cop. Wind blew. Tree branches smacked him in the face. In the drizzle, he was getting soaked. Maybe he should have stayed in the car like Jones said. Naw. He didn't want to miss whatever was going on.

Wow! A huge building rose up on the other side of the road. It creeped him out. Talk about your Bates Hotel. Before he could decide whether to go in or not, a naked girl came racing from the trees behind him and sped by.

From the dubious shelter of the trees, Jesse eyed the building across the circular driveway. Before he could decide whether to go in or not, a naked girl streaked toward him from the trees. She barreled right into him and nearly knocked him down when she flung herself at him. He grabbed her. She screamed and hammered him with her fists.

"Hey, Dany. Take it easy."

She wrapped her arms around his waist.

"Thank God!" She clung to him and rubbed tears and snot on his wet shirt.

"You gotta help. He's gonna hurt her."

Dany was sobbing and talking so fast, he couldn't make sense of what she was saying. "Slow down. I can't understand you." He peeled her away from his chest.

"Maddie," Dany gasped.

"You all right?" Jesse said.

She shook her head, teeth chattering. "This is the most not all right I've ever been. I don't know where she is. I think he already hurt her. He did something to me. I don't know what, but I suspect it wasn't good. I conked out."

Jesse looked at Kevin to see if he understood any of this. Kevin simply shrugged. Dany was shivering. Jesse tore off his raincoat and held it out for her to slip her arms into.

She wrapped it tight and hugged it across her chest. With teeth chattering, she babbled. "You gotta do something. You gotta help her."

Jesse spoke slowly and calmly. "Take a breath."

She huffed in air. He nodded when she complied. "Good. Take another"

She opened her mouth and drew in a long breath.

"Okay. Now slowly—slowly," he repeated with emphasis.

"Tell me what happened."

"I don't know what happened. I shouldn't have left her. She told me to run. I should have stayed. I just ran and I left her there. All by herself. And he's crazy. I know he is. He's crazy! You got to do something."

"Who?"

"Maddie," she said as though he were dense. "We have to save her. I told you. He has her. Somewhere in that—that—that—" She waved back toward the building.

Jesse looked at Kevin. "Do you know where Detective Martin is?"

"No." Kevin shook his head. "I have no idea."

Dany was shaking. Cold and shock. He needed to get her someplace warm and dry. He could use the same. No doubt Kevin also.

He looked directly in her eyes. "Dany—"

"You have to hurry. No telling what he's doing."

"Yes. Dan—"

"You don't understand. He—"

"Listen," he said quietly. "Listen to me. Okay?"

She nodded.

"I want you to tell me—very slowly—I can't help her unless I know what the situation is. Who has Maddie?"

"I'm not sure."

"What is his name?"

"I don't actually know." She gulped air. "He said—he said—he said—"

"Slowly, Dany. Slowly. Tell me his name."

"He told me it was Shane, but I don't believe it. Jason Shane. No, he just made it up."

"Why do you think so?"

"I'm not sure really. Who has a name like that? And he kept changing things he was telling me. Like he couldn't remember what he'd already said and—"

"What does he look like?"

"Uh…He's kind of tall, kind of like you, maybe taller. Brown hair, kind of sandy. Hazel eyes. Looks like a movie star. Then I went to the bookstore and I felt this awful pain—" Words tumbled out faster and faster.

She took another breath. "And then I woke up in this hospital room and I didn't know how I got there or what I was doing there and I thought I must have been sick or in an accident or something and then I couldn't get out. The door was locked."

Dany shook his arm. "You have to find Maddie. You have to find her!"

"I will, I promise." Jesse dug out his cell phone, requested backup and gave dispatch his location.

Chapter Thirty-seven

"You couldn't stay out of it, could you?" He gripped a flashlight in one hand, gun in the other. "You had to interfere, just like Greg with his righteous morality."

"You killed him." Maddie watched his face, barely discernible in dark shadows. Could she get the gun away from him before he shot her? "You cut his throat."

"If he'd just kept out of it, he wouldn't have died."

"And the young women you abducted?" Maddie held out a hand. "It's over. Give me the gun. It'll go better for you if I take you in."

"Nice try. However, a tragic accident happened. You broke into my clinic. I thought you were after drugs. You had a gun and I believed you were going to kill me. I had to shoot you to protect myself. Only then was I aware of who you were. Such a tragedy."

"You won't get away with it. Just like you won't get away with Greg's murder."

"He should have stuck with being a genius."

"And you, not being a genius," Maddie said, "couldn't keep him from finding out what you were doing."

"I was just as smart as Greg."

"No, you weren't."

"No vision! He had no vision. He wouldn't even consider the number of people I could help. Hundreds were suffering from debilitating diseases and I could help them. Your precious Greg wasn't a scientist." He sneered. "Just a technician."

"Greg had integrity."

He stepped closer and slapped her.

Maddie put her shoulder into it and swung at him. Metal cuffs clipped his nose. She followed through with a backward bash against his jaw. He dropped the flashlight and grabbed his nose. Blood ran between his fingers.

Gasping for air, he moved quick as a snake and got an arm around her throat. Unable to breathe, she clawed at his arm, and sagged down letting him support her. To maintain his balance, he shifted his weight to his right leg. She hooked her left foot around his calf. Without giving him time to change position, she jerked hard and smashed her right foot at an angle against his kneecap.

He screamed, the eerie noise of a wounded animal, and crumpled to the ground. She kicked the gun, picked up the flashlight and shined it at his face. Nose broken, kneecap dislodged, face twisted in pain. Dr. Eric Fuller was not beautiful.

Nor was he as smart as he thought he was. Greg, director of Changing Biology, who spent more time in his mind than noticing what went on around him, wasn't blind to what Eric Fuller was doing. Fuller tried to cover unauthorized surgeries with the charitable goodness of helping the suffering.

She needed to get crime scene techs to go over that horror of a mental institution. She needed to call Jesse. She needed to find Dany. She needed to get out of the rain. And, last but also least, Eric Fuller needed medical help. He groaned and tried to stand, but collapsed under his ruined kneecap.

He screamed at her. "You idiot! Do you know how many people you deprived of much needed help?"

"Who helped Greg? You tortured his wife and made him watch."

"He didn't understand the concept of the greater good."

Maddie heard noise. Voices? She listened. Only the rain. Then she saw the flicker of a flashlight weaving through the trees.

A man's voice called out, "Detective Martin?"

Help had come. She felt a big relief. "Fenton?" She was surprised, but glad to see another officer, even Fenton.

"Put some cuffs on this man," she shined the flashlight on Fuller. "Get on your radio. Get an ambulance. Get crime scene techs here."

"I don't think so." Fenton pulled his gun from the shoulder holster and pointed it at her.

CHAPTER THIRTY-EIGHT

Maddie squinted, blinking rain from her eyes. "For heaven's sake, Fenton, put the gun away before somebody gets hurt."

"Shoot her," Fuller ordered. "She's an intruder. She attacked me. Shoot her!"

Oh my God. Surprise, even shock, finally dawned on her. Fenton, fellow officer, hadn't come to her aid. He was aligned with Fuller.

"Shoot!" Fuller yelled.

"Did it ever occur to you that I got tired of it?" Fenton's hand steady on the gun pointed at her head, curled his finger around the trigger.

"Think about what you're doing," she said. "You'll go down if you do this."

"I am thinking. I'm thinking about years of being the butt of all your jokes."

Maddie shook her head. "Fenton. You don't want to be connected with this—this—scum." She waved at Fuller.

Fenton, a sour smile of satisfaction, said, "You never suspected me. Not one of you. Did you? Fenton, the bumbler. Somebody you all could feel superior to. Laugh at."

"Killing me will only make it worse." She edged a small step in his direction and felt a broken branch under her foot. Maybe two inches thick. How long? Long enough to be of any use?

"Maybe it can't get any worse," Fenton said. "Maybe it can give me a certain pleasure. All of you constantly making fun of me. Carrying on about what I'll do next with a big laugh. Thinking I was stupid."

"I never thought you were stupid."

"Don't lie. I'm calling all the shots now." His smile widened. "So to speak. I think I have the upper hand here."

"Stop talking and shoot her!" Fuller demanded.

Fenton's focus shifted to Fuller. Maddie took another step, concentrating on what was under foot and guessed the branch was maybe a foot long.

"I want to enjoy this moment," Fenton said. "Maybe I'll even have a little fun with the Detective here."

"Stop playing around," Fuller said. "I need to get to a hospital."

"She thinks I don't know that she's taken two steps toward me. I think that means she doesn't have any respect for me. I think I should teach her a lesson. What do you think?"

"I need medical attention!"

"I think I'm in charge," Fenton said. "I think I have captured a killer." Gun still pointed at Maddie, he spoke over his shoulder. "The bastard we've been looking for. The monster who abducted young women and did God knows what to them before he killed them. Alas, before I could arrest him, he killed Detective Martin, one of our own." Fenton shook his head. "Gunned her down in cold blood."

"You try that," Fuller said, voice cold with menace, "and I'll be forced to reveal who actually did the killing."

"Come come now. Surely you don't think you're going to be around to tell anybody anything." Fenton laughed.

Maddie moved fast. Her foot stomped on Fenton's instep, her knee slammed into his crotch. He doubled over. She brought her cuffed hands up fast and clipped his nose. His knees slowly gave way. She smashed hard on the back of his neck. He fell forward. She stomped on his hand and kicked away the gun.

A flashlight blinded her.

"Maddie?" Jesse said. "What—?" He shined the light on Fuller, then on Fenton.

"Do you know where Dany is?" Maddie asked.

"Here!" Dany came running up. "Are you all right?" She threw her arms around Maddie. "I shouldn't have run off and left you. I know—" She noticed Fuller on the ground. "Oh," she said.

"Thank God you're here, Detective Jones," Dr. Fuller said. "I need medical attention."

Dany marched over and kicked him in the rear.

Chapter Thirty-nine

Fenton, escorted to the smallest interview room by a uniformed officer, sat in one of the two chairs. Leaning back, he crossed his ankles and tried to look confident as he waited, but his eyes kept glancing at the mirror, aware he was watched.

And indeed he was. Maddie and Jesse stood on the other side. After a few seconds, Fenton held up a middle finger with a gesture toward the mirror.

"What do you think?" Jesse said. "Trying to tell us something?"

"I doubt it," Maddie said.

"Let's see what he has to say." Jesse opened the door and Fenton looked gratified, as though he'd just won a bet with himself. For a long moment Jesse stared at Fenton. Maddie knew that stare. It had been known to draw out confessions without a question being asked. While Fenton sat straight, back rigid, he didn't rush into a confession. Jesse turned on a recorder, repeated the Miranda warning, gave the time and date, and identified himself and Fenton. Fenton hadn't yet asked for a lawyer and Maddie wondered why. Did he think he didn't need one?

"You're in a lot of trouble, Fenton." Jesse sat in the vacant chair, scooted it back a bit and rested one ankle on the opposite knee.

Fenton threw away any attempt to appear relaxed. He kept his eyes on Jesse like a mouse watching a big cat.

"Three counts of homicide—"

"I didn't kill anybody."

Jesse raised an eyebrow in disbelief. "Dr. Fuller says you did."

Fenton shook his head. "It was the Boy Scientist. He killed them."

"Boy Scientist?"

"Fuller. Always talking about his important research. The greater good. He did it. I didn't do anything."

"Fenton, that's not going to wash. You're going to be tried and found guilty. Probably spend life in prison."

"No," Fenton blurted.

"Fenton," Jesse said, "You killed them. There's no way you're going to get away with it."

Fenton shook his head. "All I did was bring females to the Boy Scientist. He told me who to bring. He said he only wanted to talk to them. So I picked them up and brought them to him. That's all I did. Bring them to that place so he could talk to them."

Maddie heard the thin note of fear in Fenton's voice and thought he was beginning to understand he was in serious trouble he couldn't get out by saying he didn't do anything but drive around.

"Why'd you do it, Fenton?"

Fenton shook his head. "No."

"For the money?"

Maddie thought that was only part of it. A strong part, she felt, was the frustration and anger at the way he was treated by his co-workers in the Sheriff's Department. Fuck-up Fenton.

With a hard stare at Jesse, Fenton requested a lawyer. Jesse noted the time for the benefit of the recorder and stopped the questions.

Dr. Eric Fuller asked for an attorney immediately and didn't say one further word.

Even early on Wednesday morning, the sun blazed hot. Maddie felt sweat prickle her back as she stood with Jesse and Cutter on the sidelines as bodies were removed from the tunnels beneath the fertility clinic. Two were immediately identified, Francine Ramsey and her boyfriend Paul Gifford. They had not been dead long.

"What do I tell the families?" Jesse said softly.

Maddie shook her head. Since he worked on the disappearance of the first two women, he would tell the families. Although, Maddie thought, they were probably watching the live news program and had already guessed. She didn't envy him.

Clayton Thorne watched the live television coverage of cops swarming all over Dr. Eric Fuller's clinic. According to the newspaper, the clinic was doing a good business. If the idiotic man had just stuck with infertility, he wouldn't be on his way to jail in the near future. Ah well, none of it mattered.

Suddenly he sat straight. A reporter was asking questions of Detective Jones, who talked around answers that said nothing. Thorne turned up one corner of his mouth. Jones was going to be very busy for days to come. He'd work long late hours. That meant he wouldn't be home much. An opportunity would arise. Little Cindy would be happy to see him again. All he had to do was wait patiently, not rush into anything. He also had to be extra careful with police looking for him. That's all right. He could be careful and patient. He was good at both.

The day had been long and exhausting. As soon as Maddie got herself out of her car and into the house, she kicked off her shoes off

"Hey." Dany, sprawled on the living room floor, turned to look at her. "You're famous. You're all over the news." She pointed to the television set that ran a repeat of earlier footage. "What was this perv doing, anyway?"

Maddie dropped onto the couch, grabbed a pillow

and tucked it behind her head. She sighed. "Fuller, the hard-working Dr. Fuller collected ova—egg cells."

"I know what ova are," Dany said. "Tell me what he did with them."

"He removed their nuclei. You know what that is?"

"Yes. Go on."

"Now what he had were oocytes. He immersed them in a culture media to keep them alive. Later he added a drop of fluid that contained one adult cell obtained by scraping the inside of a mouth. The Oocytes were now gametes. They were suspended in some kind of fluid between electrodes, and *zap*."

"Yeah," Dany said. "So this shock sends the cells back to the beginning. Right?"

"Right. They reverted to embryonic possibilities."

Dany sat up. "That means they could turn into all different sorts of cells."

"Sort of like that, yes."

"Aren't there women who sell their ova? Why didn't Fuller simply buy them? Why did he kill them?"

"He wasn't just collecting eggs, he removed the ovaries. He stored them in a fluid similar to their natural environment to keep them alive. If he could keep them alive, and if he could manage to get them to produce ova, he could develop embryos and then he'd have an unlimited supply of stem cells."

"Ugh," Dany said. "What a creep."

"So? You want to go out for dinner?"

"Okay. But what about—what's his name? The new director? How did he know who to blackmail?"

"Greg had a habit of scribbling down a thought on anything handy. He scribbled something in one of the books that got left in his office."

"Really? What?"

"*Callidus scelestus fullo.*"

"Cunning criminal fuller," Dany said with a smug smile. "And how do you know that?"

"Hey, Kansas high schools teach Latin."

Dirks, very carefully, didn't say anything when Kevin, sprawled across the couch in the boneless way of teenagers, clicked the television remote every few seconds. The evening news had repeats of film showing the removal of bodies from the former mental institution. Kevin clicked to a reporter who mentioned the site had been used for several different businesses in its lifetime. At one time it had been a cheese factory, following that overalls and then jeans were made for farmers. Most people remembered it for being a mental institution. When the mental institution closed, the building remained empty for a number of years.

"And more recently it was a clinic for invitro fertilization as well as some specific surgeries." The camera pulled back to show the thick stand of trees. "Sheriff Dirks," the reporter was saying, "walked these big birch trees and discovered the real reason—"

Kevin clicked the remote. "Okay if I call you the big birch?"

"Sure, kid. As long as I can call you a son of a birch." Dirks saw the small smile that came and went in an instant. Nevertheless, he thought, there was hope.

"You know," Kevin said. "I could show you how to put a password on your cell phone that would lock it so nobody but you can use it." He shrugged. "If you like."

Roy Wightman of the FBI watched the television set in his office as another body was brought out. A spokesman for the Sheriff's Department announced that both Dr. Eric Fuller and Officer Fenton had been arrested and taken into custody.

Nothing lasts forever, Roy thought. Except his wife's iron-fingered hold on her money.

It had worked very well for quite a while. A lot of sick people out there. Some of them wealthy. Willing to pay great amounts of cash for the surgery that had potential to alleviate, even cure, whatever ailed them, devastating illness such as cancer, spinal cord injury, Lou Gehrig's disease, Perkinson's, diabetes, heart disease.

Using stem cells with the patient's own DNA eliminated the ever worrisome possibility of rejection. No worry about the patient's body rejecting transplanted cells. Not having to take mounds of drugs just to stay alive.

Patience, Roy told himself. He'd find someone to take Fuller's place. There was money to be had.

CPSIA information can be obtained
at www.ICGtesting.com
Printed in the USA
LVHW080129021020
667693LV00011B/1398